Gabrielle

"Cade Montana, I won't allow you to harass me or to intimidate me or to frighten me!"

"Frighten you?" he asked. "By offering you your fan?" A mocking smile played about his mouth. "I would think a hellion like you wouldn't be afraid of anybody. But just to prove to you that I'm a gentleman, would you like me to put it down on the flagstones and back away so you can safely retrieve it?"

Humiliation burned through her. "No, I would *not!*"

He opened his hand and she grabbed for the fan. Her fingers had just curled around it when his hand closed over hers. The warm pressure made her gasp.

"Why, Gabrielle St. Claire," he said, grinning at her, "I do believe you *are* afraid of me." He tugged gently on her hand and pulled her so close that she could feel his warm breath on her face. Almost casually he bent his head and kissed her. His lips seemed to ignite a leaping flame inside her . . .

Other Books in
THE AVON ROMANCE Series

BLACK-EYED SUSAN *by Deborah Camp*
DESTINY'S DREAM *by Joanna Jordan*
DREAMSPINNER *by Barbara Dawson Smith*
EDEN'S ANGEL *by Katherine Compton*
A HINT OF RAPTURE *by Miriam Minger*
SILVER CARESS *by Charlotte Simms*
WINTER'S FLAME *by Maria Greene*

Coming Soon

CHERISH THE DREAM *by Kathleen Harrington*
HEART OF THE FALCON *by Diane Wicker Davis*

Gabrielle

LETA TEGLER

AVON BOOKS ◈ NEW YORK

AVON BOOKS
A division of
The Hearst Corporation
105 Madison Avenue
New York, New York 10016

Copyright © 1990 by Leta Tegler
Inside cover author photograph by Bradley Photographics
Published by arrangement with the author
Library of Congress Catalog Card Number: 90-92984
ISBN: 0-380-75616-1

First Avon Books Printing: August 1990

AVON TRADEMARK REG. U.S. PAT. OFF. AND IN THE OTHER COUNTRIES, MARCA REGISTRADA, HECHO EN U.S.A.

Printed in the U.S.A.

RA 10 9 8 7 6 5 4 3 2 1

Chapter 1

New Orleans, 1861

Gabrielle St. Claire stood on the balcony outside her bedroom and breathed deeply of the heady scent of jasmine and roses. The night had turned humid and close, and heavy dark rain clouds hung over the city. Thunder rolled threateningly in the distance. She looked beyond the courtyard, across an expanse of manicured lawn toward the century-old oak trees that hid the gazebo. Ruben Guillotte should be there waiting for her by now. He didn't dare come any closer to the house.

The family quarters of Camden Hill Plantation ran in parallel wings to each other. She and her sister, Celeste, occupied the entire upstairs of the east wing, while her uncle's chambers lay directly across the courtyard. Their proximity increased the possibility of being caught, but once she was out of the courtyard the large, carefully tended garden would hide her clandestine activities.

Tucking her sister's letter inside a pocket, Gabrielle gathered up her skirts and prepared to make the risky climb down the trellis. The ornate white ironwork that looked so much like French lace made an effective ladder, but her voluminous skirts and petticoats were difficult to manage. As she climbed over, she held on to the ivy-covered trellis with one hand and adjusted the flowing length of her clothing with the other. She found a foothold and started down, step by step. The decent was dangerous, but it was the best way she could think of to keep from running into nosy servants. She had scrambled up and down this trellis a thousand times as a child and knew just how to do it.

The thunder that had been rumbling overhead intensified suddenly, sounding quite close. To her dismay she felt a sprinkle touch her cheek, then another and another. Within seconds rain had started to fall in a steady patter. Her thick auburn hair, arranged so carefully less than an hour before, began to slip from its pins and fall down her neck and shoulders. Her dress grew heavy with the weight of the rain.

Her soft mouth clamped tight with frustration, Gabrielle stopped, shivering as water ran down her back. Since Tyler had forbidden Celeste and Ruben from seeing each other, he kept such a tight watch on her that the only possible means of communication they had was the letters that Gabrielle smuggled back and forth for them. She had agreed to act as their courier because she thought that the idea of forbidden lovers sending secret letters was romantic, and even though Ruben was Celeste's boyfriend, she always felt a thrill of excitement in his presence. But now the message would have to wait. She would not face Ruben looking like a drowned rat.

Gabrielle started to climb up again, but her sodden clothes hampered her ascent. By the time she reached the second-floor railing she was breathing hard from exertion. She dragged herself over onto the balcony and took a moment to catch her breath before going inside, deciding she would not try climbing down the trellis in skirts again.

Unfastening the back of her dress without her maid's help was a twisting, squirming struggle. Because it was dripping wet, the bodice stuck to her like a second skin, and she shivered as she peeled it off. She then carried the dress out to the balcony and lifted it over the railing to wring it out. Just as it hung free she remembered what was in the pocket.

"The letter!" she cried.

Too late, she saw a white blur as the envelope fell to the flagstones below. She leaned over and stared down at it. She would have to go after the letter or one of the servants would surely find it in the morning, and Celeste would kill her if it was discovered. Gabrielle stomped into her bedchamber, grabbed her silk robe from the foot of her bed, and slipped it on. Belting it around her slim waist, she padded back onto the balcony.

Without the weight of heavy skirts, she was as agile as a young animal. She climbed over the railing once again and started down. Almost immediately she felt a tug at her waist, and after another step downward she heard a tear. She looked to see what the problem was and found the tail of her robe caught on one of the fancy iron curlicues. She tugged, trying to wrench it free, but her efforts only tore it more. She dropped her head against the wrought iron and drew in a sharp breath of annoyance. Then, gazing across the silent and empty courtyard, she made a sudden decision. She slipped out of her wrapper and left it hanging on the ivy-covered wall. No one would see her, and she would retrieve the robe on her way back up.

She climbed the rest of the way down wearing only her camisole and pantaloons. A few feet above the ground she paused, remembering from the past that this was the tricky part. Beneath the trellis was a bed of roses covered with prickly thorns. At eight years old she had found a way to avoid the thorns, and she still remembered it. Holding on to the trellis tightly, she stretched sideways with her foot extended, toes pointed, feeling for the flat cold surface of the railing that separated the courtyard from the patio of the guest quarters. At the touch of the cold iron she shifted her weight to the railing and steadied herself by holding the trellis with her left hand.

"Need some help?"

The man's low voice sent Gabrielle's heart catapulting in her chest. She peered into the darkness and saw the blur of a white shirt and an untied black cravat.

"You scared me," she accused.

The man chuckled. "Sorry."

Horrified, Gabrielle couldn't believe her Uncle Tyler had invited a guest without informing her. Now she'd been caught in her underclothes! For a moment she felt almost faint, then her mind started working again. Maybe it was too dark for him to see that she wasn't dressed.

Badly unnerved, yet hoping to get the corner of the wall between them, Gabrielle began to edge back along the railing for the trellis. But she was so shaken that she lost her balance, tottered awkwardly for a moment, then lunged for a handhold just as her feet slipped off the railing. She swung heavily against the side of the wall.

The man stepped closer to the railing. "Are you all right?"

She thought she heard amusement in his voice, and her cheeks burned with embarrassment. "Yes," she snapped, a little more sharply than she should have.

She found a foothold and looked up just in time

to see a glowing arc as he flipped the last of his cheroot into the wet shrubbery. Then she heard the fall of his footsteps as he walked toward the door of his room.

She closed her eyes with relief until she realized he was walking back toward her. She stared toward the corner, her heart thumping.

"I didn't get your name," he said. "I believe Celeste has blond hair, so I suppose you're Gabrielle."

She panicked. Her reputation would be ruined if anyone ever learned of this escapade. She crossed her fingers and squeezed her eyes shut. "No, I'm the governess."

Suddenly Uncle Tyler's voice broke the quiet, falling across the rainswept courtyard like the voice of doom. "Gabrielle? Is that you down there?"

"Oh, merciful heaven!" she whispered as she pressed her forehead against the cold iron and waited in paralyzed silence. Would Uncle Tyler go back inside or come looking for her?

"Arron, go down there and see what the hell is going on," Tyler ordered at the top of his voice. "I could swear I heard Gabrielle's voice."

"Is it possible, miss," the man asked, "that you are the young woman St. Claire is looking for? His niece, I believe?"

"Oh, do be quiet," she snapped impatiently, "or we'll both be found."

He laughed softly, "No. *You'll* be found. I'm going back inside."

Gabrielle gritted her teeth and poked her head around the corner. "Sir," she rasped beneath her breath, "the truth of the matter is that if you hadn't delayed me with your questions, I would be in my room by now, safe and sound."

His teeth flashed in a grin. "I don't think so."

Oh, he was so smug, she thought irritably. In moments Arron would be coming down the south stairs. She would be in trouble, and if Uncle Tyler found the letter, Celeste would be in even *more* trouble. Gabrielle could only hope that Arron wouldn't see the soggy white blur in the darkness.

"Let me hide in your room," she whispered suddenly, edging onto the railing again. "Just for a minute," she pleaded. "Arron will check the courtyard and then they'll go back inside."

The stranger shook his head. "You're not coming into my room—not looking like that."

Gabrielle glanced down and felt her ears burn. Her wet clothes clung to her skin and revealed the shape of her body in a very unladylike manner. For a stricken moment she tottered on the railing, hopelessly off balance. Then she gave a smothered cry and fell headlong into the stranger, landing with solid impact against his broad, hard chest. His arms came about her waist as he stumbled backward, trying to keep them both from falling.

"Holy Christ!" he exclaimed.

"Please help me," she begged.

"No."

Fear and frustration made Gabrielle bold. "If you don't let me hide in your room, I'll tell my uncle you were trying to take advantage of me," she said furiously. "I'll scream and you'll be in as much trouble as me. I swear it."

His tall form went rigid. Stunned by her own words, she stared at him, so close they were eye to eye. Then he grinned, an absolutely wicked, evil grin.

"Well, aren't you a piece of work?" he drawled, putting his arms around her and pulling her closer.

Gabrielle suddenly felt frightened of him. "Let me go," she pleaded, making sure to keep her voice low. Pressing her hands against his shoulders, she struggled, her legs brushing against the muscled length of him. "Let me go," she whispered, conscious of his masculine body next to hers.

The man released her so suddenly that she stumbled backward, then he seized her wrist and jerked her out into the falling rain.

"What . . . what are you doing?" she said as he dragged her down the path."

"I'm turning you over to your uncle."

Gabrielle pulled against his hold. "Why?" she demanded frantically.

He wheeled about. "Because you're a brat who needs to be taught a lesson." His long strides carried them quickly down the flagstone path. He didn't stop until he reached the chinaberry tree underneath her uncle's balcony.

"Tyler," he called out, his deep voice lifting in the night, "I believe I've found the cause of your disturbance. This young woman claims to be your governess. I found her climbing down the trellis outside my room."

Gabrielle prayed she would die; die and never wake again. It would be quicker than the slow death to which her uncle would condemn her.

"Governess!" came his explosive reaction. "Why the hell would I need a governess? The girls are grown."

Shoved unceremoniously forward, Gabrielle stared up at the balcony, fully aware that Uncle Tyler's wrath was about to descend on her head.

He peered down through the mist. "Governess, my royal backside!" he thundered. "Gabrielle, what have you been up to?"

The state of her undress must have been apparent even in the rain, for he shrugged quickly out of his robe, wadded it into a ball, and threw it to her. "Put that on," he commanded.

She caught the garment and slipped into it quickly. Tyler leaned over the railing and yelled in the general direction his servant had taken. "Arron, I found Gabrielle. I want you to bring her to my study right away."

"Yes, sir, Mista Tyla," came the distant reply.

Tyler straightened. "I'm sorry your evening has been disrupted, Cade. If it's all right with you, we'll talk over breakfast in the morning."

"Of course."

Gabrielle waited for Tyler to disappear from view, then she pivoted and glared at the man. "You certainly are no gentleman. I cannot imagine what you're doing in our home!"

He laughed. "I see I ruffled some feathers."

"Don't patronize me! You have certainly done more than ruffle my feathers!"

He grinned and bowed sardonically. "Excuse me, ma'am."

To make the situation even more awkward, her maid, Hetty, chose that precise moment to slip through the double doors of the downstairs parlor and wail out like a banty rooster at the sight of her mistress.

"Miss Gabrielle! Yo' clothes is all over up there on the balcony. I near broke my neck just now, a-trippin' over 'em. When you wasn't in bed, I came a-lookin' for you. Did you fall or somethin'?" She must have seen the figure of a strange man standing close by her mistress, for her voice took on a note of horror. "Oh, Miss Gabrielle, what happened to you? Mista," she screamed out, waving her hands as if to ward him off, "you leave Miss Gabrielle alone! You hear me! Mista Tyla will beat you within an inch of yo' life if you even touch her!"

Tyler reappeared on the balcony. "Hetty, hush your mouth!" he ordered, his voice seeming to vibrate the walls of Camden Hill. Without another word he stalked back inside.

Hetty straightened. "Yes, sir, Mista Tyla," she answered, disappearing into the house.

The man cleared his throat. "Well, I don't wish to detain you, Miss St. Claire."

Face flaming, she watched him walk away, his footsteps echoing hollowly in the night. He had all the manners of a field hand, she thought. Suddenly her green eyes widened. Just as she heard Arron's approach down the path, she remembered the letter. Without stopping to think she darted back through the garden. Just under her own balcony she stopped, her hand pressed against her pounding heart while she searched the darkness. Then, just beneath the edge of the roses, she saw a glimpse of white.

"Miss Gabrielle, where are you?"

"I'm coming, Arron." Gabrielle scooped up the soggy envelope and stuffed it in the pocket of her uncle's robe. "I'll be right there!"

Gabrielle followed Arron, dread lying heavy in her heart. What would she tell Uncle Tyler? How could she explain her bizarre behavior without revealing the truth? As innocent as she had been, the situation certainly looked bad. Apparently Tyler thought so, too. He was waiting for her outside his study, his black hair rumpled, his gray eyes angry. From the set, furious expression on his aquiline features, Gabrielle knew she faced dire consequences. He had already donned another robe, and he snapped at her impatiently when her steps lagged.

"Come on in, Gabrielle, I'm very interested in knowing what the hell you were doing out there in the middle of the night without your clothes."

Gabrielle looked desperately at Arron's departing back. "Uncle Tyler . . ."

"Come in here, dammit!" he exploded. "I don't want to discuss it in the foyer for everyone to over-hear." Despite his protest, he kept talking. "I'm scandalized by your behavior. Mortified! I want to know why you climbed down the trellis and why you told Cade Montana you were a governess."

Gabrielle's face whitened and her footsteps faltered. "Cade Montana?"

"Yes, ma'am. You just embarrassed me in front of a good friend, a man all of New Orleans is calling a war hero. I'm furious with you!"

Gabrielle's heart seemed to stop beating. Of course she had heard of Cade Montana. Everybody had heard of him.

"Are you listening to me?"

"Yes, sir."

"Then tell me what went on tonight."

Gabrielle opened her mouth, then shut it again. What could she say? Certainly not the truth—not that she had been taking a letter to Ruben Guillotte for her sister. Tyler had forbidden their courtship and there was no telling what he would do if he found out Celeste had gone against his wishes.

To Gabrielle's enormous relief, Celeste called out from the gallery above. "Uncle Tyler, wait!"

Both Tyler and Gabrielle stared at her as she leaned over the railing, her long blond hair swinging forward.

"Listen to me, please," she pleaded. Turning, she ran along the banister, then flew down the stairs, her long robe with its edging of white ruffles floating out behind her. "It's not Gabrielle's fault. It's mine!"

Tyler reacted before her bare feet touched the marble foyer. "Please explain to me," he de-manded, his furor suppressed into a minor roar, "how you can be at fault when it was Gabrielle I found in the courtyard dressed like a shipyard doxy. Damnation!'' he exploded, his temper boiling over again at the very thought.

He turned angrily to Gabrielle, observing her wet head and slim figure swallowed by his outsized robe. Just the sight of her incited his rage again. ''I want to know who you were going to meet.'' His finger stabbed the air in front of her face. ''I swear I'll challenge him.''

Gabrielle could only stare at her uncle, her eyes wide with fright. His temper had always rendered her speechless.

''By God, I'll settle this.'' Tyler pivoted and started off down the corridor. ''Arron, where are you? I want you to find whatever son-of-a-bitch is out there and shoot him.''

Celeste chased after him, her face ashen. ''No, no, no! Uncle, don't say these things. It's my fault,'' she cried, placing her body in front of him. ''It truly is. And nothing is as bad as it seems. Gabrielle and I were in her room talking about our childhood. I dared her to climb down the trellis, Uncle Tyler.''

''The hell you did,'' he said, disbelief ringing in every word.

''No, no. It's the truth! She used to do it when she was a little girl, and I was teasing her about it. But, honestly, Uncle Tyler, I didn't think she'd do such a crazy thing now that's she grown up.''

Even in the grip of panic, Gabrielle shifted uncomfortably, wishing Celeste wouldn't make her sound so young and stupid.

''You know how headstrong Gabrielle is,'' Celeste continued, ''She wanted to prove she could still do it.'' Celeste clasped both hands against her chest, out of breath. ''Uncle Tyler, I swear she wasn't going to meet anybody. We didn't know Mr.

Montana was in the guest room below. We had no idea we would cause such a scene!''

Tyler's fury seemed to lessen as Celeste continued to explain, but he looked from one to the other, still very suspicious. ''No matter what the reason, she shouldn't have climbed down the trellis.'' He turned to Gabrielle. ''Why did you tell Mr. Montana you were the governess? Don't you have any qualms about lying?''

''Because . . .'' She drew in a shuddering breath. ''Because I didn't want him to know who I was.''

Celeste quickly stepped between them. ''It happened so fast she said the first thing that popped into her head.''

''That sounds like Gabrielle.'' Tyler's anger was now directed at Celeste. ''What on earth were you thinking to let her do such a thing?'' He waved a hand in Gabrielle's direction. ''And in her underclothes!'' He turned to enter the study, then swung back. ''Your sister could have fallen and broken her neck. Do you realize that?'' After heatedly glaring at the two of them, he pivoted and stalked inside. They followed meekly, not looking at each other.

''And you, Gabrielle,'' he said. ''How can you be such a sophisticated, charming young woman one minute and behave like a street vendor's monkey the next? If you had fallen on those flagstones you would have killed yourself! Now, dammit, I don't want any more trouble. I want you to act like a lady, look like a lady, and think like a lady!''

Gabrielle's eyes filled with tears, and Tyler felt some remorse about being so hard on her. But he couldn't count the times she had gotten herself in trouble since he had taken the girls into his home seventeen years ago, when Gabrielle was a baby and Celeste only four, after his brother and his brother's wife had been killed in a carriage accident. Even as a little girl Gabrielle had been in one scrape after another, her zest for excitement always overcoming any sense of caution.

With a muttered oath Tyler stalked over to his desk, his arms crossed over his chest, and scowled down at the paperwork. He had to admit she'd been a sweet child despite her mischief: quick to laugh, quick to cry, easy to love. As a matter of fact, he found it hard not to favor her. Feeling frustrated, he ran his hand through his thick black hair. He'd been wrong to jump to conclusions, but hell, considering the circumstances, it seemed logical to assume she'd intended to meet a young man. What else could he think?

He picked up a stack of the plantation's crop reports, then threw them back down. Despite Celeste's explanation, he still felt too upset to dismiss the incident altogether. "Gabrielle," he said, abruptly making a decision, "I want you to come down here tomorrow morning and apologize to Mr. Montana."

"Oh, Uncle," Gabrielle burst out, "please don't make me do that!"

Celeste gave her a painful pinch to silence her, but Gabrielle couldn't let the matter rest. "Uncle Tyler," she pleaded, "don't make me apologize. I just can't face him."

Tyler turned. "And why not?"

"It would be so embarrassing!" Just thinking of facing Cade Montana made Gabrielle press her hands against her cheeks in distress. "I just can't do it. He would never believe me!"

"I don't see why not," Tyler returned flatly. "I do."

"But you're a gentleman," she wailed.

Her uncle's tone held a warning. "He is also a gentleman, Gabrielle. And you, young lady, must be accountable for your behavior. After you explain, Mr. Montana may think you don't have the sense God gave a goose, but at least he'll know you're a good girl. That's important to me."

"But he'll be going back to wherever he came from," Gabrielle protested, "and it won't make any difference! What do we care what he thinks of me?"

"You will apologize!" Tyler exploded, all patience gone. "That's final. Cade and I will be in this study all morning." He rapped his knuckles against the desk top for emphasis. "You will be here."

Without another word the two sisters fled from the room. They knew that Tyler followed them into the main hall and watched with a black scowl as they hurried up the curving stairway. When safely out of his hearing, Celeste muttered beneath her breath. "Only you could create such a mess of things, Gabrielle!"

Gabrielle's response came instantaneously. "If it weren't for your stupid romance with Ruben, I wouldn't even be in trouble!"

"That's beside the point. What were you doing in the courtyard without your clothes?" Veering down the second-floor hallway and out of sight of Tyler, Celeste caught Gabrielle's hand. "You knew Cade Montana had been invited."

"I did not!" Gabrielle cried. Tears blurred her eyes. "What am I going to do? I would rather be shot dead than face him tomorrow."

Celeste gave her a scathing look. "I think Uncle Tyler is about ready to oblige you." She sighed when she saw her sister's stricken face. "It's very simple. In the morning just go down and apologize." She shook her head in exasperation, then continued down the corridor. "Thank heavens I overheard Uncle Tyler. I knew I had to come up with a story to help you out. I didn't want you to get all flustered and tell the truth. That would have been a fine mess.''

Gabrielle stared at Celeste in hurt astonishment. ''I wouldn't have done that,'' she bristled. ''I would never have told your secret, no matter how much trouble I got into.'' She pulled the soggy letter from her pocket and thrust it angrily at her sister.

Celeste glanced down, and her expression softened. ''I'm sorry.'' She hugged Gabrielle briefly. ''Go to bed and get some sleep. We'll talk in the morning. Don't worry, everything's going to be all right.''

Celeste appeared in Gabrielle's chamber just before lunch the following day to find her sister still in bed, pale as a ghost and refusing to get up.

''Gabrielle,'' Celeste began impatiently, ''I feel responsible for the trouble you're in. I want you to go down, apologize, and get it over with. Don't make Uncle Tyler angrier than he already is. The gala at the St. Charles is only two weeks away. Do you want to miss it just because of your stubbornness?''

Gabrielle didn't answer. She continued to lie on her side, eyes closed, covers pulled to her chin.

Celeste paced back and forth at the foot of her sister's bed, the yellow ruffles of her summer frock rustling softly with her movements. She had slept poorly because she had been worried sick that Tyler would find out about Ruben. Coming to a stop she glanced impatiently at her sister's still form. ''I can't understand why you're being so spineless. Of course it's humiliating to be caught as you were, but it's not the end of the world. Just tell the story about the dare. Uncle Tyler believed it and so will Mr. Montana. He'll think you're charmingly young, nothing more.''

Gabrielle turned her head into the pillow with a moan.

"In two days this whole matter will be forgotten," Celeste said, walking closer to the bed, "unless you continue to stay under the covers feeling sorry for yourself!" Frustration and bewilderment sounded in her voice. "Why are you so distraught?"

Gabrielle clenched her eyes shut. Celeste would be distraught, too, if she'd been the one to leap on Cade Montana in her underclothes, and if she had threatened him with a silly line from a book. Just thinking of it caused her to turn on her side and curl into a ball of misery. She had taken the line from a book hidden away in the bottom of her crochet box. The heroine had made the same threat with stunning results to the evil Monsieur de Baroque. "Sir, I shall tell them you have tried to compromise me!" Well, it certainly hadn't worked for Gabrielle! Cade Montana had yanked her out in the courtyard and turned her over to Tyler like a nasty-natured child in need of discipline.

"Gabrielle, you can't offend a man of Cade Montana's stature!"

Gabrielle's head popped up, and she supported herself on her elbows, her tangled auburn hair making her look like a rebellious child. "Stature!" she cried, provoked out of her mute misery. "Do you know what Dominique dePaul told me about him?"

"No, I don't, and I don't want to hear! She is a mindless gossip."

Undaunted, Gabrielle proceeded to tell Celeste the rumor with vicious relish. "She told me that Cade Montana has a harem of Indian women in Texas. He keeps them as slaves for his twisted desires!"

"Gabrielle, hush your mouth!"

"It's true. He's rich and powerful and he lives like a feudal lord and I believe it! He is definitely not a gentleman. I don't see why I have to apologize to the likes of him!''

Celeste was horrified. "Gabrielle, all of New Orleans is celebrating because of this man. He ran the Yankee blockade, risking his life to bring in weapons and medical supplies.''

"He's rough and uncouth.''

"He is not. He's handsome, he's accomplished, and he's a gentleman. The Confederacy wouldn't have sent him on a diplomatic mission if he weren't an extraordinary man of courage and intelligence.''

"Oh, pooh.'' Gabrielle dropped back on her pillow, ignoring her sister's outrage.

Celeste settled her hands on her hips, her blue eyes flashing fire. "I can't abide you when you get stubborn and unreasonable, Gabrielle. Go ahead and do what you want. I don't care!'' The door slammed resoundingly shut behind her.

After an hour of tossing and turning Gabrielle flopped over on her back, kicked off the covers, and stared up at the ceiling. "I might as well get it over with.''

Jumping out of bed, she jerked the bellpull and paced impatiently as she waited for Hetty to arrive. Finally, too restless to wait, she opened the wardrobe and rifled through the array of brightly colored dresses until she found her plain dark blue linen. She had always hated it for its severity, but it seemed appropriate for what lay ahead.

Moments later the door opened and a black face peered in, the picture of innocence. "You want me, Miss Gabrielle?''

"Yes, I do. I only have a few minutes to get ready. You must do my hair quickly. I want to look exactly like Mamie Artson.''

"But she's an old maid and she wears her hair in a bun at the back of her head.''

"Hetty, please."

"Yes, ma'am." Hetty hesitated, then walked in with a saucy swagger. "I figured you'd come to yo' senses. If you didn't, Mr. Tyla would be plenty mad."

"Hetty!" Gabrielle cried out in exasperation. "Just help me, please. I'm late."

Chapter 2

Cade sat in one of the big wing-back chairs in Tyler's comfortable, book-lined study and stretched his long legs out in front of him. The double doors to the outside gallery had been opened, and even though the afternoon had turned unseasonably warm, a breeze wafted through, cooling the room. He glanced again at the portrait of Gabrielle and her sister that hung over Tyler's desk. He had noticed it earlier, but he had been too preoccupied to pay it much attention then. Now, while Tyler selected a brandy from the array of crystal decanters atop a cherrywood cabinet, Cade idly examined Gabrielle's face. Her green eyes danced with mischief under delicately arching brows. She had finely boned features including a small, straight nose. Her mouth was full and generous. The artist had captured a beautiful young woman who looked fragile and appealing. Cade had not seen Gabrielle's face clearly that night, but he wondered if the artist had been a bit too flattering. He grinned. He'd probably never find out. Celeste had joined him and Tyler for breakfast, but he had seen neither hide nor hair of Gabrielle.

Shifting his broad shoulders to a more comfortable position, he watched as Tyler poured each of them a brandy. He had arrived late the night before and had not had a chance to speak privately to Tyler until now. The morning meeting had been preempted by the appearance of John Freemont, an agent representing Jefferson Davis and the War Department. After apologizing for being too rushed to observe the proper amenities, Mr. Freemont had requested a meeting with Cade. Tyler had offered his study for their use. On behalf of the Confederacy, John Freemont had asked Cade to accept another diplomatic assignment, this one in Texas. Somewhat relieved at the location, Cade had accepted.

"To winning the war," Tyler said, handing Cade a snifter, "and to the cargo you brought back."

Cade lifted his glass in acknowledgment and waited until Tyler sat down across from him. "And to a quick victory, before many more die."

Tyler nodded and glanced thoughtfully at the younger man. He had known Cade for several years now, ever since Cade had graduated from West Point. Not only was he a handsome man, tall and broad of shoulder, but he had character that showed in his steady gaze and resolute chin. "I'm glad you're back in one piece," Tyler said solemnly. "I sure as hell wouldn't have wanted to be aboard that steamer when she sailed in last week."

Cade grimaced wryly as he remembered. The fog had been heavy that night, and the captain of the *Warhawk* had ghosted past the Yankee gunboats without incident. It had appeared they would dock in New Orleans unscathed, until the fog lifted and they were sighted by enemy lookouts. By the time the ship had run the blockade, the rigging had almost all been blown away and three men were dead. "I'm not anxious to try it again," Cade assured him quietly.

Tyler observed Cade over the rim of his glass.

"I'm glad the War Department decided to send you instead of Brubaker. For a while there it was a toss-up." He shook his head. "Brubaker is an old hand at bargaining, but he's too plodding and careful. He would never have braved that blockade on a ship loaded with ammunition. He'd have waited the war out down in the Caribbean somewhere."

Cade's blue eyes darkened. "It was a hellish few hours, no doubt about it." When he had left for Europe, the North had not yet sealed off the Southern ports. His return trip had been extremely dangerous—although necessary to get supplies in. Had one of the Yankee shells struck dead center, the ship would have exploded out of the water.

"I understand your negotiations in Europe were successful."

"Yes, they were." Cade sat his brandy on a small table nearby. "The Austrian manufacturers pledged one year's output of small arms to the Confederacy with the option to continue as long as the war."

Tyler nodded, obviously pleased. "Can we trust them to keep their promise? Or will they sell to the North if it offers more money later on?"

A hint of ruthlessness slanted Cade's mouth. "There's no worry there. We have a contract."

"Good." Relieved, Tyler leaned back in his chair. "And the cargo you brought with you?"

"I closed a contract for one hundred thousand rifles and ten batteries of field artillery ready for service—including ammunition. Soldiers have been unloading it all this week."

Tyler laughed. "My God, that's splendid. I bet Mr. Freemont was happy to hear it."

Cade nodded and rubbed his hand along his cheek, his expression thoughtful. "I'm sure you know why he was here," he said, looking up. "I have a feeling you recommended me for this new assignment negotiating the cotton sales with the Mexican government.''

Tyler grinned. ''I figured you wouldn't mind getting back to Texas for a while.''

''Thank you,'' Cade said sincerely. ''I've been gone for a long time.''

''Well, you're the man for the job. You've spent a long time in Texas and you understand the border situation there. The War Department took that into account. You've worked with officials in Matamoros, and you know who in the Mexican capital will cooperate with the Confederacy.'' Concern darkened his features. ''If we don't get cotton out to European markets, there won't be any money to buy the munitions you've contracted for.''

Cade agreed. With the Southern ports blockaded, a fortune in cotton had been left sitting in warehouses while Europe clamored for it. Then a few planters had started hauling it across East Texas and ferrying the valuable cargo down the Rio Grande. Millions of dollars' worth of cotton had been sold to the Europeans before the North caught on and the Union navy closed the port.

''I think I can easily convince the Mexican government to buy our cotton and sell it to the Europeans themselves. The North won't risk alienating Mexico, England, or France by interfering. We'll get the money we need, Mexico will make a profit, and the Yankees will have their hands tied.'' Cade grinned.

Tyler nodded. ''When do you leave?''

''As soon as we clear up this problem in New Orleans.''

A knock sounded at the door, and a flicker of annoyance crossed Tyler's face. ''Who is it?''

''Gabrielle.''

At the sound of her voice, Tyler glanced at Cade.

He had forgotten all about the episode the night before, but he saw that Cade had not. "Come in."

Gabrielle opened the door, glancing uncertainly at her uncle. "Have I interrupted?"

Tyler's face softened, and after putting down his brandy he rose and went over to her. "No, no, it's all right. Come in, my dear."

Amusement sparkled in his gray eyes. Extravagant Gabrielle, who normally preferred ribbons and bows and bright-colored finery, was dressed quite severely. Her pride didn't take kindly to apologies, and he guessed she was feeling quite humbled. It would be good for her to be brought down a peg or two, he thought. She had a tendency to be too full of herself.

Dropping his hand lightly onto her slim shoulder, Tyler turned. "Cade, I'd like you to meet this young woman under more appropriate circumstances. I want to introduce my niece, Gabrielle St. Claire."

Gabrielle watched as Cade crossed to her with a lazy, lithe stride. Reluctantly she extended her hand, glancing at him only briefly.

"It's a pleasure to meet you, Miss St. Claire."

"Thank you," she said stiffly, flushing at the shiver his deep voice caused along her spine. She looked up, and when her eyes met his she unknowingly held her breath. He was handsome, just as Celeste had said. Not with the casual elegance of Ruben Guillotte, but with the rugged, biting edge of the sun and windswept prairie. He had hair the rich color of tobacco, steely blue eyes, and a lean, tan face. She had no doubt that in a room full of men, this man would stand out. Something about him commanded attention.

"Gabrielle has asked if she might offer you an apology and explain what happened last night," Tyler went on, unaware of the current between the two. "She felt some concern that you might have gotten the wrong impression."

When she saw the satiric smile on Cade's mouth, Gabrielle jerked her hand free.

"Oh, she needn't worry about that," Cade answered smoothly. "I don't think I got the wrong impression."

Gabrielle felt her face flame with embarrassment.

"That's what I told her," Tyler said. "Go ahead, my dear, say what's on your mind."

Gabrielle tilted her chin. "Mr. Montana, last night I had absolutely no idea we had a guest. I realize my actions could be, ah, misconstrued, and I wouldn't want you to think . . ." Her voice trailed off as one of his dark brows lifted with a hint of mockery. Clearing her throat, she continued, determined to ignore him. "The circumstances made it look as if I was slipping out of the house . . . to meet someone. But that was not the case. My sister and I—" Seeing him shake his head, she stopped, distracted.

"No, ma'am," he insisted. "I never thought for a moment that a lady like you might be slipping out to meet someone."

Gabrielle bit her lower lip. "Well, I only mention that because my uncle thought that at first . . ."

Cade shugged. "Well, I'm sure he knows you better than I do," he returned politely.

Gabrielle stared at him. This vile man was making her look like a fool. She drew a deep breath, her eyes flashing fire.

"Last night I . . . Climbing down the trellis was a silly prank, a dare. Celeste and I were reliving the past. We never thought that anybody would be— disturbed." Her voice faltered. How could she go on? How could she pretend to be an empty-headed, silly child after the way she had threatened him last night? Just remembering made her ache with embarrassment.

Tyler frowned, displeased by Gabrielle's awkwardness. "Celeste dared you to climb down the trellis, I believe."

"Yes, sir."

The clock on the mantel ticked loudly in the silence. "Just repeat what you told me last night," Tyler prompted.

Gabrielle shifted uneasily. "But I didn't tell you what happened last night," she hedged. "Celeste did."

Tyler scowled, he voice lowering menacingly. "Gabrielle, have you apologized or not? You've been talking, but I'm not sure you've said anything yet."

"Yes, sir."

"Yes, sir, what?"

"Yes, sir, I will apologize," she whispered.

"Then, by God, apologize!"

Gabrielle took a deep breath. "My sister dared me to climb down the trellis and I did," she said sullenly, without one whit of sincerity. "I apologize for disturbing you and for telling you I was the governess."

Tyler's face flushed a deep red and his body stiffened with anger. Gabrielle knew he wanted to throttle her. Cade's expression remained carefully bland, but there was a liveliness in his midnight-blue eyes that suggested he was enjoying her discomfort.

Tyler caught Gabrielle's elbow and led her toward the door. "Are you finished?" he demanded. At her nod, he pushed her through the doorway. "Then you may go."

Gabrielle needed no more urging. She fled down the hall as if the hounds of hell were after her. As he watched her hurry away, Tyler's face settled in unpleasant lines. "Please excuse me," he said to Cade. "I'll be back in a minute."

Gabrielle was halfway down the hall when Tyler caught up with her and grabbed her arm. He swung her around and saw that tears streamed down her cheeks. "What in the devil is the matter with you?"

"I'm sorry, Uncle Tyler," she whispered, catching his hand in both of hers and holding tightly as if she feared he might pull away. "Please don't make me talk to Mr. Montana again. I'm making a horrible mess of everything!" Her face began to crumple, and tears choked her voice. "What happened last night embarrassed me so. He saw me undressed and acting foolish." She pressed her hand against her flushed cheeks, her emerald eyes tragic. "Just think how it makes me feel to see him again. Please, Uncle Tyler," she pleaded.

Seeing her torment brought an instant change in Tyler. Compassion replaced his anger. "You little goose," he said, touching her chin and lifting her head. "To hell with it. Everybody makes a mistake now and then. You go upstairs and rest for a while. I'll check on you later."

Gabrielle drew in a tremulous breath. "Oh, Uncle Tyler, I love you."

He kissed her forehead and gave her a push. "I love you, too. Now go on. I have business to attend to."

Cade stood at the door for a long moment, chuckling over the scene in the study. Gabrielle had nearly choked on her apology, and he still didn't regret revealing her presence to Tyler last night. He'd caught her little tail in a gate, and he'd enjoyed watching her try to pull free. He couldn't believe that she had been sassy enough to threaten him last night.

He crossed to the window, his thoughts drifting to the night before and how provocatively her rain-soaked clothes had molded against her sleek, long-legged body. No, he conceded wryly, glancing at her portrait, the artist hadn't exaggerated her beauty. She might be a little hellion, but she was put together just fine. Amusement crinkled the corners of his eyes. Gabrielle had waltzed into the study armed with a rehearsed apology and an expression of guileless purity on her pretty face. What a wonderful act for Tyler's benefit.

As he leaned against the windowsill, his amused gaze followed the double row of giant moss-covered oaks that shaded both sides of the lane. Whoever Gabrielle had been going to meet last night must have been terribly disappointed when she failed to appear. His mouth crimped wryly. How unfortunate that the girl was the niece of his good friend, because he couldn't deny the strong physical attraction he felt toward her. His first thought this morning had been the image of her slim, curving body outlined against the night. He shook his head, knowing his thoughts of Gabrielle St. Claire could only get him into trouble.

An expression of annoyance crossed his features, and he glanced at the clock, hoping Tyler wouldn't waste too much time with his spoiled niece. Feeling restless, he lit one of the thin dark cheroots he favored and exhaled, his thoughts turning again to the security problem he had discussed with Tyler earlier. A few months before, a Yankee courier had been captured, and during his questioning, he'd revealed the identity of a Southerner who was selling information to the North. The traitor was Ruben Guillotte. A grimace hardened the line of Cade's mouth. The disclosure hadn't been a surprise to anyone, especially Cade. The son-of-a-bitch would do just about anything for money. Before Ruben could be brought into custody, however, they had to find out who had given *him* the secret documents. It had to be someone connected with the secret Committee, because only Committee members could have obtained the documents Guillotte had given the courier.

Cade frowned, thinking of the powerful men who made up the Committee—a select group that served as a liaison between the military, elected officials, and influential civilians. They had all been chosen by Jefferson Davis and reported directly to the War Department. Their purpose was to handle important problems that demanded secrecy and immediate decisions, and they were empowered with the authority to act on those decisions. The thought of a traitor in that group was disquieting. Hearing the door to the study swing open, Cade turned as Tyler reentered.

"I'm sorry for the delay, Cade. I hope there will be no further interruptions."

"Don't worry about it. It gave me a chance to do some thinking."

Tyler sat at his desk, obviously intending to get to work. Drawing up a chair, Cade pulled a plain white envelope out of an inside vest pocket. "I believe this is just the enticement we need to coax our man into the open." Spreading the official-looking papers on the desk, he explained briefly, "These documents detail Confederate plans to place underwater explosives in certain harbors."

Tyler looked up in surprise and Cade smiled grimly. "This information seems close enough to the truth to ring authentic and encourage whomever we're dealing with to act rashly."

Leaning over his desk, Tyler studied the details of

an underwater detonating device. "Rash enough to get caught?" he asked.

"We hope so. We'll have to wait and see how our man reacts." Cade remained silent while Tyler read the information. When he finished, Tyler whistled appreciatively.

"My God," he burst out. "I wish to hell these bombs would work. I'd love to string them out across our harbors and then let those Yankee bastards come sailing in."

Cade shook his head. "Sorry, Tyler, but they don't work. Our informant, however, won't know that."

Tyler nodded. "All right. I'll put this document in my safe until the Committee convenes, just as I always do. At that time, all the members will have a chance to look it over."

"And I'll have my men keep an eye on Guillotte. If one of the Committee members tries to contact him, he'll be caught."

Tyler shook his head sorrowfully. "I've known these gentlemen for years. I hate to think that any one of them has turned traitor."

"Perhaps they haven't," Cade reassured him. "We may be losing the information elsewhere."

"I don't know how we could be." Agitated, Tyler paced over to the window, his thoughts on Ruben Guillotte. "I'll be glad when this is over." His brows came together in thought, and for a moment he forgot Cade's presence. Months before he had ended a courtship between Celeste and Ruben. All along he had had doubts about Guillotte, but when the Creole had killed Charles Girard, a young man from a good family, in a duel under very questionable circumstances, his doubts had grown into an active dislike. Thank God Celeste was a levelheaded young woman and had agreed to stop seeing him.

Suddenly remembering his guest, Tyler turned. "You've known Guillotte for some time, haven't you?"

"I don't know him well. I met him in Texas a few years back. I didn't like him then any better than I do now."

Tyler nodded. "Who's watching him?"

"Two good men," Cade answered. "Billy Williams and his older brother, John. I've known them both for years. They worked for me in Texas."

Tyler nodded. "Good. Okay, let's get to work."

Over the course of the next few hours, Cade and Tyler refined the plan, considering all possibilities, determined to make sure nothing would go wrong. By the time they left the study, they had a plan they figured would entice the culprit. They had to find out who was passing the information to Ruben Guillotte.

During the two weeks before the St. Charles gala, Gabrielle put the unsavory incident involving Cade Montana firmly out of her mind. She had seen him only once, on a Sunday afternoon as she sat beside her uncle watching all the local militia go through their maneuvers. Turning to call out to a friend, she had seen him, and her cheeks had flamed with embarrassment when he touched the brim of his hat in sardonic salute. Nodding curtly, she had tilted her umbrella to shield her face and wondered what on earth had kept him in New Orleans.

At breakfast the next morning she had learned the reason for his extended stay. Cade had bought Metairie Place, a graceful plantation outside the city, and had hired Gillam Bertram as his overseer. She had sniffed indignantly when Tyler mentioned the news, causing him to look at her curiously. So the rascal Texan had infiltrated the gentry. That's what happened, she thought viciously, when the lowborn came into money.

Gabrielle closed her eyes and listened for just an instant to the sounds of the ball being held in the St. Charles Exchange Hotel, a hint of a smile on her mouth. A string orchestra played a lilting waltz, and the scent of roses filled the air. Gabrielle loved the excitement and gaiety of these occasions.

She opened her sparkling eyes and looked about the ballroom. She thought it had to be the most beautiful hotel in the world, with its magnificent gilded dome which soared above the dance floor. With possessive pride, she gazed up the wide stairway as it curled to the gallery above. The decorating committee had adorned the banisters and the mezzanine railing with flowers and greenery and huge white satin bows. It looked splendid.

So far it had been a magical night. The war had added a dash of desperation to the gaiety of recent parties. It seemed to make the colors brighter and the music sweeter. Gabrielle knew that during the evening she had skirted the edge of what her uncle deemed acceptable behavior. She had smiled and flirted and had allowed herself to be twirled about the dance floor until her ruffled skirts flared out to show off trim ankles. Finally, her cheeks flushed with good spirits and exertion, Gabrielle pleaded that she could dance no more until she caught her breath. She retreated to the fringes to stand beside her best friends, two beautiful Creole sisters she had met at St. Teresa's Ladies' Academy.

"I see someone coming for you, Gabrielle," Rachel Lecroix warned her teasingly. "I'm afraid he's not going to let you out of his sight."

Gabrielle glanced to her left and saw Phillip Bienville heading toward her. "Oh, no," she gasped dramatically.

Desiree Lecroix leaned close. "I saw your uncle watching the two of you when you were dancing. He looked very displeased."

"I know," Gabrielle whispered. "Phillip held me too close on the dance floor." Still, she turned to smile engagingly at the young man she had known all her life.

"Please dance with me again, Gabrielle," he pleaded. Confident of his charm and good looks, Phillip smiled at her winningly, and Gabrielle had to acknowledge that she thought him quite handsome with his straight black hair falling rakishly over his forehead. Her thoughts did not show in the imperious arch of her brow, however.

"I certainly will not. The evening has scarcely begun and you have been most forward."

"What did I do?" he asked, sounding boyishly young.

"First you insisted I dance with you, and then you held me too close," she admonished. "Uncle Tyler has been glaring at me ever since. Just look at him."

Phillip followed her glance to Tyler, and upon observing the older man's scowl he smiled and inclined his head in greeting. Turning back to Gabrielle, he exhaled softly. "Maybe you're right." He winked and squeezed her hand. "I'll be back later, when he's not paying attention." His glance settled on Rachel and Desiree. "Good evening, ladies. You're looking mighty pretty."

"Oh, that one's a charmer," Rachel whispered under her breath as Phillip swaggered away.

"Yes," Gabrielle agreed. "I wonder why all the 'nice' young bachelors that Uncle Tyler approves of are so boring, and all the rash ones like Phillip are so entertaining. It really makes one wonder . . ."

Suddenly she went still, her fan held motionless in midair.

"What's the matter?"

"It's Cade Montana," Gabrielle whispered. She glanced curiously at the woman on his arm. "Do you know the lady he's with?"

Desiree shook her head. "I've never seen her before." She drew her shawl closer about her body. "My goodness, he's handsome, isn't he? Just from the look of him I imagine he's a bit of a ladies' man, too. Don't you think?"

Oh, yes, Gabrielle thought with a kind of venomous despair, he was handsome, and big, and tall, and sun-bronzed. But if she could have one wish, it would be that he were as ugly as a toad. She watched as Cade inclined his head to hear something the woman said, and when he laughed in response, his teeth gleamed whitely against his dark skin. Something about their intimacy caused an unfamiliar tightening in Gabrielle's middle. He moved fluidly, and when he smiled down at the woman, there was something so possessive and thoroughly male about him that Gabrielle shuddered. She turned away, her heart thudding in her chest.

All at once, she realized that both Rachel and Desiree were looking at her as if they were awaiting for a response. "I'm sorry, were you speaking to me?" she asked, a trifle breathlessly.

"I asked if you are going to be spending the summer in the country."

"We'll be in New Orleans, I think," Gabrielle answered, attempting to sound calmer than she felt. "But Uncle Tyler has yet to make up his mind."

Again she looked back at the couple, noticing that Cade wore his black formal clothes with elegance and careless unconcern, as if he were accustomed to such fine attire. He shifted sideways, leaning back slightly to allow someone to pass in the crowded room. When he did, he looked up, and his eyes met hers.

Gabrielle whirled around, breathing rapidly, her cheeks burning. For a moment she couldn't think at all, she just felt heat surge through her like a fever. Why on earth did this Texan cause her wits to scatter like birds in a storm?

She forced herself to listen to her friends and their discussion of the Women's Guild. Desiree suggested knitting woolen socks for the soldiers, and Gabrielle, her mood gone sour, could not help thinking that because every women in the South occupied her time at that task, each man would have at least fifty pair. The notion had no more than formed in her head when Desiree smiled at her.

"Would you like to help us a few mornings each week?"

"Of course. I would love to," Gabrielle replied flatly. With relief she heard Phillip's voice, silky soft and a bit slurred with drink, over her shoulder.

"Well, well, who have I found here?" he drawled, his mouth near her ear. "I do believe it is the fair maid, Gabrielle, and her wicked uncle is nowhere in sight. What a lucky moment for the prince."

Gabrielle turned. "You make a very convincing libertine, Phillip, but a prince?"

"I'll settle for libertine. I wanted to grow up to be a prince, but my second choice is libertine. May I have this dance, fairest one?"

"Yes."

A roguish grin transformed Phillip's features. "Gabrielle, I've been chasing you for three years now, and I do believe that's the first time you've ever said yes to anything I ever asked."

"That's not true," she objected. "I've danced with you many times."

He laughed as he guided her toward the dance floor. "But you never said yes. You always said, 'But if I do, Phillip, you must not hold me too close.' 'Phillip, you must not talk like that.' 'Phillip, you're being terrible.' You have always scolded me like a little banty hen."

The sparkle in his eyes took the edge from his words, but still Gabrielle recoiled. "I don't think that sounds very flattering."

He gave her a lopsided grin. "Well, hell, Gabrielle, you're so pretty I never cared what you said. I think you could speak gibberish and still be the most sought-after female here."

"I see."

Gabrielle turned her head away, deliberately taking a moment to gaze over the crowd while she decided how to deal with him. He had had too much alcohol and he was being too familiar. She knew she should distance herself from him entirely, but she did not feel inclined to do so. Basking in his admiration had restored her good spirits. She looked at him, pursed her soft mouth for an instant, then gave him a dazzling smile.

Within a short time they were whirling around the dance floor. To Phillip's dismay, she also danced with other men. For Gabrielle, the evening became a kaleidoscope of waltzes and quadrilles, smiling friends, and outrageous compliments from Phillip each time she was near him. Although she outwardly ignored Cade, his presence added to the excitement of the evening.

The merriment of the ball was at its height when Rachel sought her out with a message that Celeste was waiting for her upstairs in the Napoleon room, another ballroom that wasn't being used tonight. Gabrielle sighed and threaded her way through the crowded ballroom.

Crystal chandeliers cast sparkling lights and shadows over the hotel's guests, and she thought the colorful ballgowns of the ladies made the hotel look like an early spring garden. Gabrielle saw no widow's black tonight to remind her that a war was in progress.

She made her way to the less congested east corridor. Lifting shimmering silk skirts, she hurried down the darkened hallway, her expression thoughtful. No doubt this summons had something to do with Ruben Guillotte and those blasted letters. That's all Celeste ever wanted to talk about these days.

Preoccupied, Gabrielle didn't notice the masculine form waiting in the shadowed corridor until he stepped out suddenly to block her way. Startled by his abrupt appearance, she cried out softly before recognizing Phillip.

"My goodness," she chided, clasping her closed fan against her breast. "I thought you were a Yankee."

"I want to talk to you."

His voice sounded belligerent and accusing, and Gabrielle's slim brows arched in disapproval. Phillip had had too much to drink. During the course of the evening he had grown sullen, and his charm had been replaced by an unattractive possessiveness. If he didn't watch his step, one of the men would throw him out soon. She half turned, purposely dismissing him, and didn't see the scowl that darkened his face.

"I'm in a hurry, Phillip," she said cooly, brushing past him. "Celeste is waiting for me upstairs."

"Damn Celeste," he growled, lunging forward to seize her wrist. He jerked her around by the arm and pulled her through the French doors onto the veranda.

"Phillip Bienville!" she whispered in surprised protest. "What do you think you're doing?"

Without answering he pulled her across the terrace to a dimly lit flagstone path. Gabrielle panicked at the thought that he might cause a scene. "You're hurting me," she protested, keeping her voice low so they wouldn't be overheard. "Turn me loose right now."

Phillip didn't stop until he reached a secluded spot hidden behind climbing roses and wisteria. The hotel lights were faint here, and the laughter and music muted. He whirled about to face her, his mouth open to speak, but Gabrielle cut him off.

"Have you lost your mind?" she burst out, regarding him with incredulity and outrage. "I can't stay here for even a minute. You know that!" She tugged at his hand, her voice growing angrier when his fingers tightened. "How can you be so irresponsible with my reputation? If Uncle Tyler finds out that I'm in the garden alone with you, I'll be in terrible trouble and so will you."

"Oh, Gabrielle, for once shut up!" Phillip said blackly. "I'm tired of listening to you! You bat your lashes and smile at me, then puff up like an adder if I respond."

Indignation flushed Gabrielle's cheeks pink. "Phillip, I have tried to be courteous to you all evening. I have not batted my lashes, and I have not puffed up like an adder. You are drunk, that's all!"

"Just be quiet." With a groan, he clasped her in his arms and, eyes closed, pressed his body insistently against her slim form.

"Let me go!" Gabrielle gasped, going rigid with shock. She tried to wedge an arm between them, but he held her too tightly. "Uncle Tyler will try to find us, and if he does . . ." Her growing distress rivaled her anger. "Oh, please, Phillip, stop this!"

But he didn't seem to hear as he bent his head against hers, inhaling her fragrance. Her struggles only seemed to excite him more.

"Phillip!"

His mouth descended, and her words were muffled into inarticulate whimpers. Only her toes touched the flagstones as he lifted Gabrielle, limp with shock, against him. But her paralysis lasted only a moment, and Phillip had to use all his strength to hold her as she struggled madly. Gabrielle's earlier indignation had turned into a towering rage, and she kicked his shins hard.

"You cad!" she cried, tearing her mouth from his. "How dare you!" Her fists pounded against his chest. "How dare you manhandle me. Now turn me loose or I'll scream, and the whole place will know!"

"Gabrielle," he muttered, dodging a blow that came close to his face. Suddenly he went still as they heard footsteps on the flagstones.

"See," she whispered furiously, her hand tightening to a fist in the linen of his white shirtfront. "Now look what you've done!"

"I'm afraid Miss St. Claire's right," a lazy Texas voice drawled, and a moment later Cade Montana sauntered into sight.

At the sound of his voice, Gabrielle whirled about. Without thinking, she edged closer to Phillip, absurdly feeling that they were now both on the same side against Cade.

"What the hell do you want?" Phillip growled.

Gabrielle's head snapped around, and she stared at Phillip in disbelief. His hands were clenched into fists, and his face was flushed with fury. Surely he wouldn't be crazy enough to start a fight with Cade Montana! She turned then to look at Cade's silhouette against the lamplight, and her eyes widened in anger at his response to Phillip.

"You can't drag Miss St. Claire into the garden as if she were a house wench." Cade moved slightly and light illuminated his face. "She's a flirt, and she might deserve it, but you can't do it. You play the hound with her, and Tyler St. Claire will skin you alive. Now I suggest, Bienville, that you go back inside and leave the girl alone."

"What I do with Gabrielle isn't any of your business," Phillip bit out, his voice thick with fury. "And I don't like your implication about Gabrielle deserving anything. She's a lady."

Cade was unmoved by this display of gallantry. "I'm not implying anything. I saw her behavior tonight, and to call her a flirt is an act of courtesy on my part. And right now Gabrielle *is* my business. I'm here at Tyler's request."

"Why didn't he come himself?" Phillip demanded.

"Because I interceded on your behalf. I believe Miss St. Claire misled you into thinking your attentions would be welcome."

Gabrielle sucked in a shocked breath. "That's not true! I'm not responsible for Phillip's behavior tonight. He's had too much to drink, and that's his fault, not mine!"

Cade ignored her. "You take too many unnecessary chances, Bienville. One of these days you're going to be challenged, and reckless flirtation is hardly worth fighting a duel over." He let silence punctuate his words, and when he went on, his voice held a rough authority. "*You* know the boundaries whether or not she does. As a gentleman you should observe them. If you want to see Gabrielle again, I suggest you handle the courtship properly."

Montana's last statement seemed to strike a note

with Phillip and mollified his anger. He straightened and smoothed his jacket, standing militarily rigid.

"I *am* a gentleman, sir, and I thank you for reminding me." His voice slurred, and he was hard put to keep his balance despite his efforts to stand up straight. "Gabrielle is a bit of a coquette, but I was wrong to bring her into the garden. I have behaved poorly. I didn't mean to frighten her," he said solemnly.

Gabrielle clamped her teeth together in rage. "You didn't frighten me, Phillip," she said tightly, her hands clenched into fists. "You made me angry!"

Giving her only a brief distracted look, Phillip focused his attention on Cade. "I won't make any excuses for my conduct, except to say that I normally don't drink so much. I enlisted just last week and I guess I was . . ." He paused, then smiled grimly. "I was either celebrating or mourning, I'm not sure which."

Gabrielle whirled to look at him, a sudden pang of fear in her chest. "Phillip, for goodness sake, why didn't you tell me?"

"I don't know." Phillip again addressed Cade. "Thank you, sir. I wouldn't want to embarrass my family just before I leave, and I wouldn't want to dishonor Gabrielle."

"I know about your enlistment," Cade said quietly.

Gabrielle glanced from one man to the other in astonishment. Moments before they had been ready to fight. Where had this sudden camaraderie come from? She regarded Cade with loathing. How did he always manage to influence people who should be loyal to her? Her anger was so intense that their images blurred and for a moment she felt sick with rage. Closing her eyes, she drew in a calming breath, determined to tell them both exactly what she thought of them. When she opened her eyes again, Phillip had disappeared and only Cade remained.

"I hope, Mr. Montana," she said, unleashing the force of her temper on him, "that you do not expect a thank-you from me. Is this how they rescue ladies in Texas? By blaming them for the intemperate conduct of men?"

He shrugged his wide shoulders. "I can't say I expect you to thank me."

Bitter words crowded her throat, and it took all her control to keep quiet. She would not engage in an argument with a low-down, arrogant man. Giving him a last scathing glance, she turned abruptly and started to walk away from him. She had taken scarcely two steps when she heard Cade's sardonic voice behind her. The sound jerked her to a stop.

"I believe you have forgotten something."

Holding her back rigidly straight, Gabrielle turned in time to see Cade stoop, pick up the fan that she had dropped during her struggle with Phillip, and rise slowly to his full height. She stepped forward, prepared to snatch it from him.

She stopped just short of her goal, his stillness suddenly making her uneasy. Silence crackled as she stared at the pink tasseled fan, thinking how small and frivolous it looked against his open palm. After an uncertain upward glance at his shadowed face, Gabrielle drew back, a flush staining her cheeks.

For a moment she couldn't speak, then indignation surged through her. "Cade Montana, what you said about me just now to Phillip is untrue. I think you are a bully and I think you are trying to get even with me because I threatened you that night. I have apologized. What more do you want?" She drew in a ragged breath. "I won't allow you to harass me or to intimidate me or—or to frighten me!"

His dark brows swooped upward. "Frighten

you?'' he asked. ''By offering you your fan?'' A mocking smile played about his mouth. ''I would think a hellion like you wouldn't be afraid of anybody.'' He looked thoughtfully down at the fan. ''But just to prove to you that I'm a gentleman, would you like me to put it down on the flagstones and back away so you can safely retrieve it?''

Humiliation burned through her. ''No, I would *not!*'' she hissed. ''Now give me my fan!''

He opened his hand and she grabbed for the fan. Her fingers had just curled around it when his hand closed over hers. The warm pressure made her gasp.

''Why, Gabrielle St. Claire,'' he said grinning at her, ''I do believe you *are* afraid of me.''

''I most certainly am not.''

He laughed softly, and Gabrielle went still when his gaze dropped to her mouth. Suddenly he tugged gently on her hand, and she stumbled forward like a puppet. He pulled her so close that she could feel his warm breath on her face. Slowly he slipped his hand around her waist and tightened his arm until their bodies touched. Almost casually he bent his head and kissed her. His lips were warm and soft, and his breath seemed to ignite a leaping flame inside her. When he lifted his lips from hers, she drew in a shuddering breath, shaken clear through to her bones.

She barely felt his hands slide up her back and settle on her shoulders, holding her away from him. Gabrielle regarded him dazedly, still lost in the wonder of their kiss, feeling like warm honey inside. Then she saw his silent, watchful face, and her expression changed to one of angry confusion.

''Why did you do that?'' she demanded, shrugging away from him. Tears brightened her eyes. ''Why did you do that?'' she repeated, but this time her outrage muffled her question. Gabrielle retreated until she reached the obscurity of darkness, where she stood for an instant, hands clenched. Then she whirled about without another word, skirts billowing, and disappeared down the path, heading for the safety of the hotel.

Chapter 3

After speaking with Celeste, Gabrielle slipped through the massive iron gate of the hotel's back entrance and pushed it shut behind her. Camouflaged in the inky-black shadow of the trees, she bent her head against the cold metal spikes and breathed deeply, staring for a moment at the fat marble cupid on the other side. Her conversation with Celeste had left her feeling numb and resentful.

After running away from Cade, she had flown up the back stairs to the salon and poured her heart out to Celeste. She had expected full sympathy, or even outrage, from her sister, but Celeste hadn't been upset at all. Maybe she had overreacted a trifle, Gabrielle thought. A kiss wasn't the end of the world, after all, but Celeste was her sister, and Gabrielle felt she had a right to expect at least indignation from her.

Gabrielle gritted her teeth. How frustrating it was to be patronized by Celeste. "Were his attentions unwelcome?" Celeste had asked. "I don't understand why you are so upset if it was only a kiss. Did you not resist? Is that why you're overwrought?'

Gabrielle stared at her, feeling there was something wrong with her sister's reaction. She repeated

44

the question slowly. "Did I resist?" Their passionate embrace flashed into her mind, and her gaze faltered. Remembering the warm, melting sensation that his kiss had caused, she felt tricked. She *hadn't* resisted. But how could she explain that to Celeste? How could she tell her that she hadn't been able to move as Cade's lips met hers? That she had stood there, her body as still as the stone cupid nestled in the flower patch, and let a man she hated walk up, take her into his arms, and kiss her? She had been furious when Phillip had tried the same thing three minutes earlier.

Celeste's voice then became ingratiating. "Did he do something to frighten you?" she asked, suspense hanging on every word. "Did he . . . touch you?"

Gabrielle's expression had turned sullen. She knew what Celeste was hinting at, and that her answer would make her look like an innocent schoolgirl. "No. He just kissed me, that's all."

Celeste appeared relieved and laughed softly. "Oh, Gabrielle!" She crossed the room swiftly, her skirts rustling, and swept Gabrielle into an embrace. "Oh, honey, you are such a baby!" she cooed. "You're not scared of *him*. You're just scared of your own feelings."

Yes, Gabrielle thought viciously. She *was* scared of her feelings—she was scared that she would kill Cade Montana if she ever saw him again.

Celeste pulled away, regarding her with uncharacteristic big-sister tenderness. "I can certainly see why a man like him would seek you out. You have a good family, connections, and you're beautiful. Wouldn't he make a wonderful match for you," she breathed, pushing Gabrielle away abruptly. "He's handsome, wealthy, responsible, personable. He doesn't have any vices"—here she reconsidered, and added—"that any other man doesn't have."

She pressed her palms together, and her counte-
nance took on a calculated look. "Goodness! We
must arrange a small dinner party."

After noticing Gabrielle's stormy expression, Celeste warned impatiently, "Don't be a ninny, Gabrielle. You always make a mountain out of a
molehill. Now settle down and think about this.
There's a war going on and men will soon be in
short supply." Restlessly she smoothed the lace
gloves over her fingers. "Believe me, Cade Montana
is a man who's worth considering seriously. But he's
not going to put up with any foolishness. He's
courting you, you silly thing, that's why he kissed
you."

Gabrielle just stared at her. Cade wasn't courting
her, she thought. He was harassing her. He was toy-
ing with her like a cat with a mouse!

Finally she was unable to listen to any more of
Celeste's nonsense and she interrupted her. "What
did you want me for, Celeste? Did you summon me
here to drill me on the subtleties of romance or did
you have a purpose?" That had seemed to bring her
sister back to earth. And the reason had been exactly
what Gabrielle had expected. Celeste wanted her to
deliver a letter to Ruben.

With a sigh, Gabrielle now looked up at the star-
sprinkled night. Their secret courtship had seemed
so romantic only a few weeks ago. Now it seemed
unnecessarily complicated and appeared to offer few
rewards for either of them. But why should she care?

She had grudgingly agreed to deliver the slim
leather packet containing a letter and poetry to
Ruben at the old Craddock mansion on Rampart
Street. Gabrielle had considered refusing to go, out
of pure spite, but she wanted to get away from the
hotel to clear her head. The errand would take only
fifteen minutes, and she wouldn't be missed at the

ball. A carriage rumbled around the corner and Gabrielle stood motionless until it passed, then she started walking fast down the dark path. At the corner she turned left onto a roughly paved street lined with trees and looming old mansions. An occasional stir of air rustled the leaves overhead, making restless shadow patterns on the ground. Feeling a bit uneasy, Gabrielle increased her pace.

She walked block after block in heavy silence, hearing only her muffled footsteps, and she gradually felt a prickly feeling between her shoulder blades. She was sure somebody was walking behind her. Unable to stand it, she finally whirled about. She carefully scanned both sides of the street, but there were only a few lights, dim beacons that cast little illumination, coming from seedy and rundown buildings. It was no small wonder she thought acidly, that Celeste hadn't wanted to deliver the letter herself.

Unnerved, she increased her pace. Why on earth had Ruben chosen the old mansion for the meeting place? The back gate at the St. Charles would have done fine. Hearing a woman's coarse laugh, she glanced up at an upstairs window and saw the naked figures of a man and woman silhouetted against a thin curtain.

Cheeks burning, Gabrielle clutched the packet to her chest and looked ahead, searching for the landmarks Celeste had mentioned while a shiver of fear edged its way up her spine.

Suddenly her spirits rose as she saw the two stone lions that marked the entrance to the sleeping old mansion. Lifting her skirts, Gabrielle ran to the gate, but she hesitated at the entrance, her will failing. The courtyard was pitch-black and looked forbidding. Steeling herself against her growing fear, she slipped through the heavy stone arch. She surveyed the inky tangle of undergrowth, her heart pounding.

"Ruben," she called softly.

A shadow moved in the darkness, and she gasped.

"Gabrielle, it's me," Ruben whispered. "Do you have the letter?"

She nodded, feeling so relieved that tears stung her eyes. She held the slim packet out in front of her and felt it being taken from her hand.

"Is Celeste all right?"

An indignant spark ignited in Gabrielle's chest. Why shouldn't she be, she thought angrily; she was safe and sound at the St. Charles. "She's fine," Gabrielle said, still trying to catch her breath.

Ruben braced a hand against the side of one of the stone lions and peered into the street. He listened intently before turning back to her. "Thank you, Gabrielle," he whispered hurriedly. "Tell Celeste I'll get in touch with her in a couple of days."

To her disbelief, Ruben turned to leave. "Wait a minute," she demanded, grabbing his sleeve. "I want you to escort me back to the hotel. I'm not going back there alone."

"Shhh . . . keep your voice down."

"Ruben," she cried, her voice edged with panic, "you surely don't expect me to go back alone! I was really scared a while ago."

He hesitated and frowned, then he shook his head. "I can't do it, Gabrielle. It's too risky."

"Risky!" she exploded, her patience gone. "If it's risky for you, then what do you think it is for me?"

"Keep your voice down!"

"I'm not returning alone!" she cried, stamping her foot. Feeling increasingly helpless, she felt tears fill her eyes. "You must walk me back, Ruben," she pleaded. "Please. I've been doing favors for you!"

He studied her intently before reluctantly nodding. "All right, Gabrielle, I'll do it. But I have an errand to run first. It's not far." He gripped her chin and looked into her face. "Now listen to me carefully," he warned. "We must move quickly and quietly, without saying one word. No one must see or hear us. It'll take a quarter of an hour at most, then, on my way out of town, I'll drop you by the St. Charles. Do you think you can be gone that long without anyone missing you?"

She nodded, willing to agree to anything to avoid returning alone.

"All right. No talking. Promise?"

"I promise."

He caught her hand and dragged her along an overgrown path which led onto the street through a crumbling section of the wall. Gabrielle followed Ruben along a terrifying maze of alleys and backstreets, gradually noticing that they were heading toward the docks. They moved at a breathless pace, and Ruben refused to slow down, even when she complained in a choked whisper that her side ached. When they emerged from a jumble of warehouses, Gabrielle saw the bulky outline of riverboats lined up along the docks. Their giant smokestacks seemed to nod with the water's lapping movement.

Gabrielle and Ruben silently threaded their way between stacked bales of cotton, lumber, and crates that were piled to mountainous heights. It was so dark between the towers of freight that Gabrielle could only see the moving shadow of Ruben's body ahead of her. He stopped suddenly and she bumped against him, but he was too preoccupied even to notice.

"Johnson, you about?" he called softly.

"Yes, sir," a large man answered, seemingly to appear out of nowhere. He stood so close to them that Gabrielle could hear him breathing.

"I'm going aboard to get my things. Seen anybody around?" Ruben asked.

"A cleaning crew was on earlier, gettin' her ready for the trip upriver," the man answered in a gravelly voice. "Dock is quiet tonight."

"Let's hope it stays that way."

"Yes, sir."

Gabrielle followed Ruben up the walkway and stepped gingerly onto the deck. "Is this your boat?" she asked, sensing that the situation was less tense now that they were on board.

"It *was*."

Gabrielle didn't ask any more questions. She knew his family had suffered financial losses during the last few years, and she didn't want to embarrass him.

Neither one of them had noticed the two stealthy shadows that had trailed them all the way from the old mansion. Billy and John Williams had been following Ruben for days and they knew his habits almost as well as their own. They knew he had been spending his nights aboard the *Jordan B. Mason* riverboat and that a Goliath-sized man stood guard at the gangplank. After making sure Ruben and the woman had gone aboard, they moved a short distance away to talk without being overheard.

"This is it," John whispered. "You go get Cade. He'll be real interested to find out the informant is a woman." Pressing his wide shoulders against the wall of cotton bales behind him, John Williams crossed his arms over his chest. "I'll wait here."

"What are you going to do if they start to leave?" Billy asked, glancing doubtfully toward the riverboat.

"What the hell do you think I'll do, little brother?"

John patted his holster and chuckled. "I'll politely ask 'em to stay awhile."

"Well, don't shoot the woman," Billy cautioned, his white teeth gleaming, "She has a fine figure,"

John punched his brother's arm playfully. "Go on, and keep your mind on business. The St. Charles is about five minutes away. Be back in fifteen, no more, even if you have to return alone."

Ruben led Gabrielle through the darkness with surefooted certainty. He stopped, opened a door, and pulled her inside. "Stand here," he ordered, "while I light a lamp."

A moment later a pinpoint of light grew stronger and illuminated the entire room. Gabrielle's eyes widened. "How beautiful," she whispered, admiring the spacious salon with its soft carpeting and rich draperies. They were a delicate shade of yellow and cream which nicely complemented the brighter floral pattern of the chairs. The polished dark wood paneling and gleaming brass fixtures were accented by crystal chandeliers.

"This is so exquisite!" she said softly and turned to Ruben. Something in his manner caught her attention, and she watched him for a moment as he flipped intently through the pages of the letter she'd given him. It hardly seemed like the behavior of a man reading endearments. Gabrielle shrugged and thought meanly that any man would shuffle quickly through her sister's bad poetry.

Ruben looked up, suddenly aware Gabrielle was watching him. "Yes, it is beautiful," he agreed absently, folding the letter and returning it to his pocket. "And I don't intend to part with it easily." He didn't explain his comment. "I'll get my valise and be back in a few minutes. Then I'll return you to the St. Charles, safe and sound."

"And breathless and bedraggled," Gabrielle added. Frowning at the door that closed behind him, she touched a hand to her hair, smoothing its auburn wisps back into place. What on earth could be so important that Ruben *had* to stop here before walking her back to the ball? Her illusions about him were certainly wearing thin. He wasn't particularly gallant, or chivalrous, or genteel, and he was preoccupied to the point of being rude. No wonder Uncle Tyler didn't like him.

Ruben was gone so long that Gabrielle started pacing the floor, racking her brain for good excuses for her long absence from the ball. She couldn't let her uncle find out she'd been roaming the docks with Ruben Guillotte, and it had been a half hour or more since she'd left the St. Charles.

Hearing footsteps, she turned to see Ruben reenter carrying a valise. "Are you going on a trip?" she asked, surprised.

"Just for a few days. Would you tell Celeste—" Suddenly he broke off, turning toward the door and listening intently.

"I don't hear anything—"

His scowl and raised hand stopped Gabrielle in mid-sentence. Ruben cocked his head to one side, listening again. Gabrielle moved impatiently. Then she heard an almost inaudible scuffling, followed by the distant rumble of masculine voices. There was a sudden explosion of gunfire, and Gabrielle looked quickly at Ruben, whose face had grown pale.

"Ruben," she whispered frantically. "We must hide. I can't be found here alone with you!"

"No!" He caught her shoulders in a hurtful grasp. "They already know we're here. They'll only think that we are . . ." He clamped his mouth shut, biting off the last word.

Ruben quickly grabbed the packet of poems out of

his pocket and looked around the salon. Booted footsteps clammered up the gangplank as more shots shattered the quiet night. When Ruben's eyes rested on her, Gabrielle knew instinctively what he wanted, and her heart flip-flopped. The shouting voices and running footsteps sounded louder, pounding along the promenade.

"Hide the packet," he whispered.

"Where?"

"They'll never search you."

She stared at him dumbly.

"Do it," he whispered urgently. "Hurry! Inside the waistband of your petticoats."

Without considering the consequences or wondering why love poems needed to be hidden, Gabrielle accepted the packet he thrust into her hands. She turned, pulled up her silk dress, and tucked the packet inside the waistband of her skirt. Just as she released her voluminous skirts, the door swung violently open.

An animal sense of danger radiated through Gabrielle, raising the hair on the back of her neck. Two men with savage expressions burst into the room, and leveled their rifles on Ruben and Gabrielle. Seeing that Ruben was unarmed, the intruders slowly straightened. Petrified with fear, Gabrielle could only stare at them.

"Well, well," one man said, pushing his wide-brimmed hat back off his forehead. "Looks like Mr. Guillotte and his pretty lady have gotten themselves caught."

A stocky man appeared behind them, dressed in evening clothes. Gabrielle recognized him as James Maffitt, an acquaintance of Tyler's. Then the tall, black-garbed figure of a fourth man stepped into the soft light of the salon. Gabrielle looked up slowly, past the revolver in his hand, past the white shirt-

front, to the sculpted features of Cade Montana. The
tawny streaks of gold lacing his thick brown hair
glistened in the lamplight, and his mouth curled into
a grimace.

"Gabrielle."

Hearing him say her name so grimly chilled her
to the bone, and pure terror shot through her. Cade
glanced at one of the rifle-wielding cowboys. "Billy,
you find the documents?"

"The girl just dropped her skirts," the man answered. "I'd be willing to bet she's got them hidden
on her."

When Cade turned back to Gabrielle, his eyes
were as cold and unfeeling as a hawk. "Let's have
them, Gabrielle."

Her heart catapulted in her chest as he began
moving slowly toward her. Dear God, she thought
with growing hysteria, did he intend to look for the
letters here, in front of the men?

She glanced at Ruben. "Stop him," she cried, her
voice low and ragged. "Do something!"

Cade's face remained impassive as he walked toward her. Consumed with fear, Gabrielle failed to
recognize that the poetry and letter weren't worth
such effort. She realized now only that something
was terribly, terribly wrong, and that she and Ruben
were in grave danger. Then pandemonium broke
loose as one of the men and Ruben began to fight,
their hard-muscled bodies falling heavily on the floor
in front of Cade, blocking his approach. Without
thinking further, Gabrielle fled through the side door
Ruben had taken earlier.

A long, dark hallway stretched before her. Lifting
her skirts, she ran for the light at the far end. Just
as she heard footsteps pounding behind her, her
heel caught in her petticoat and she fell sprawling
on the floor. While she lay gasping for air, Cade

knelt beside her and ran his hand over her bodice, searching for the letter. Gabrielle was so stunned that she couldn't react at first, but when his hand slid beneath her petticoats, she gasped in shock and, rolling over on her back, fought him off fiercely. Nevertheless Cade found the packet seconds later and rose to his feet.

He lifted her up like a rag doll and shoved her back against the wall. "Don't move," he ordered, then glanced briefly at the contents of the packet. When he looked at her again, his face showed so much disgust that she couldn't help shrinking away. "You stupid little fool," he said.

Yanking her from the wall, he pushed her down the hallway ahead of him. "Move." He shoved her all the way along the corridor and back into the salon. There she stopped, her mouth opening in surprise at the changed scene. Ruben lay sprawled on the floor, blood trickling from the side of his mouth. Broken furniture testified to the violence of his struggle. Gabrielle, horror-stricken, looked at James Maffitt.

"What are you doing?" She whirled on Cade. "Have you lost your mind? What are you doing?"

Without thinking she rushed to Ruben's side and knelt beside him, her skirts billowing in a shimmering pink cloud. "Dear God, have you killed him?"

"He'll be fine in a few minutes," Maffitt answered coldly.

Gabrielle saw the slight rise and fall of Ruben's satin vest and knew he was still alive. In a rush of feeling, she grabbed his outstretched hand and pressed it against her cheek. He did not deserve such treatment! Turning, she confronted Maffitt in baffled rage. "I know you, you've been at Camden Hill many times. How could you allow these . . . *jackals* to beat him unconscious?"

The lawyer lowered his heavy black brows, and stared at her. His mouth twisted contemptuously as he watched how tenderly she attended Ruben. "Mr. Montana," he said abruptly, "what did you find in the packet?"

Cade handed him the papers without comment, his expression grim. Maffitt glanced through each page before turning back to Gabrielle.

"I am shocked to find you here, Miss St. Claire," he said icily. "Please explain your relationship with Mr. Guillotte."

Gabrielle's mind whirled. "He's a friend," she answered slowly. Her slim brows came together in bewilderment. "Why did you do this to him?" She pulled Ruben's handkerchief from his pocket and pressed it against his lips, shuddering at the sight of the blood on the white linen. "I don't understand—"

Maffitt tapped the papers in his hand. "Tell me how you obtained these documents."

"Documents?" Gabrielle looked at him blankly. Something in the posture of the men and the intensity of their expressions caused her to rise unsteadily to her feet. "What are you talking about? Celeste gave me the packet." Slowly the disparity between the small transgression of receiving clandestine love letters and the men's brutality struck her. "But I don't see that it's any of your business, or that . . ." She looked down at Ruben and felt her throat choke with desperate tears. "It's no reason to beat a man senseless!"

"You say your sister gave this to you?"

"Yes."

"Did you know what it contained?"

"Of course."

"Would you please tell me?"

Although her face was pale, a glint of imperious

anger darkened her eyes. "You know very well what's inside. You just looked at it."

Maffitt's gaze held hers, and Gabrielle found something threatening in his demeanor. "The packet contains a love letter . . . and some poetry for Ruben," she said softly. "But I don't believe my uncle sent you! He would never sanction your conduct tonight." She looked uncertainly at the circle of grim faces. Feeling a panicky surge of fear, Gabrielle edged to the side. "I'm leaving now. Uncle Tyler will be—"

Maffitt blocked her path. "Sit down, young woman."

"No."

"Sit down or I'll have you bound and placed in a chair."

Gabrielle stared at him in disbelief. "Celeste knows I'm with Ruben, and she'll send someone for me soon. Maffitt started to move toward her, and Gabrielle dropped into a delicate brocade-covered chair, her heart thumping in her chest.

"If the packet is your sister's, what are you doing with it?"

Gabrielle forced herself not to shrink away from him. "I don't have to explain to you."

Maffitt shoved the papers in front of her face. "Are these what she gave you?"

Indignation overcoming fear, Gabrielle met his gaze squarely, her eyes shooting sparks of green fire. "Mr. Maffitt, my uncle will have you horsewhipped for insulting and threatening me!"

"Look at them," he ordered.

Gabrielle waited a long, belligerent moment before she obeyed. She was surprised to see that the papers contained unfamiliar and very official-looking drawings and diagrams. Puzzled, she reached out and took them, scanning quickly through the five pages.

"No, this must be something else," she declared, handing them back. "Celeste gave me a letter and some poetry."

"The packet contained these documents."

"No, it didn't" she said. "Why would Celeste send Ruben something like that?"

"That's what we want to know." He shifted his weight and leaned toward her. "I suggest you stop being evasive and tell us how you got involved."

"Involved?" Gabrielle's delicate brow lifted.

"Yes, young woman. Involved," Maffitt echoed.

Gabrielle stared at him. "I don't know why you are using words like *involved* and *evasive*, or why all of you are acting so strangely. I carried a letter to Ruben from Celeste. That's all. It's certainly no reason for you to be rude or to wave guns around like hooligans."

Maffitt turned to Cade. "Since she has implicated Celeste, we'll have to talk to her, too."

"Implicated!" Gabrielle exclaimed. "What are you talking about? Implicated in what?"

"Spying," Maffitt rasped. "Selling military secrets to the Yankees."

Incredulous, Gabrielle stared at him. "Spying," she repeated softly. She pressed trembling fingers against her mouth to prevent herself from laughing. "You can't be serious! I was hardly spying! Uncle Tyler wouldn't let Celeste and Ruben see each other anymore and I carried notes from one to the other. Maybe that was wrong, but it's not spying, and it's also none of your business!"

Maffitt snorted derisively. "We have known for some time that Guillotte is a traitor, but we had to find out who was helping him." His mouth curled up as if he were tasting something bitter. "Apparently it was you."

"That's preposterous!" Gabrielle objected, jumping to her feet.

"Gabrielle," Cade said calmly, entering the discussion for the first time, "the papers we found on you were falsified drawings of bomb components. Tyler and I put them in his safe two weeks ago, as bait for Guillotte's informant."

"Well, that's not me—"

"We found them hidden on you," Maffitt interrupted. "After the way you've behaved tonight, it's damned hard to believe you're innocent."

"I certainly haven't behaved like a spy!"

Maffitt spoke patiently. "You're asking us to believe you didn't know what was in the packet, yet you were sneaking through alleys with Guillotte, and when you apprehended, you hid the documents on your person, hoping you wouldn't be searched. And then you tried to escape. You're asking us to believe that you did all this to hide something as innocent as love letters?"

"It's true." When she saw his look of disbelief, a frustrated anger rose in her. "Why on earth would I ever want to help the Yankees?" Seeing Maffitt's face harden with skepticism, she cut off her denial and demanded stubbornly, "I want to see my uncle."

Maffitt stared at her for a moment, then slapped the papers against his open palm. "I think that's a very good idea." Dismissing Gabrielle, he crossed to the coat rack and put on his cape. "We will need to get in contact with the rest of the Committee." He pulled on his gloves in quick, jerky movements. "I'll go after Tyler myself. Mr. Montana, you stay with the girl." He glanced at Ruben's still figure. "Someone should tie him up before he comes to."

When John started toward Ruben, Gabrielle stood up and tried to block his way. "There's no need to tie him up. He isn't even conscious!"

"Move aside, young woman," Maffitt thundered, "or we'll be forced to restrain you as well."

Cade lifted Gabrielle up by the shoulders and drew her away from Ruben. "Don't say anything else," he whispered harshly in her ear.

"I will say what I please," she cried, jerking from his hold. Her throat constricted when she saw how defenseless Ruben looked with his hands bound behind his back.

Maffitt clamped his derby on his head and tugged down the brim, and he and the other two men exited into the night without another word.

Thunder rumbled menacingly over the riverboat, and Gabrielle shivered. She threw an acid glance at Cade. "You have made a terrible blunder. You'll be lucky if Uncle Tyler doesn't shoot you on sight for treating me so badly."

"Sit down, Gabrielle," Cade said wearily. "Save you indignation for Tyler."

Gabrielle crossed her arms over her chest. "I'll have you know I plan to tell Uncle Tyler everything—how rude Mr. Maffitt has been to me and how you searched me like a common criminal!"

Cade took a swift step forward and gripped her wrist. "Don't you realize what you've done? You've provided secret documents and information to a traitor who sold them to the North! You've gotten yourself into a lot of trouble, but more importantly you've hurt the South's chances in the war!"

Gabrielle tried to pull away from his hurtful fingers. "I haven't gotten myself into anything!"

He stared at her for a moment. "That night when you climbed down the trellis, you were slipping out to meet Ruben, weren't you?"

Gabrielle finally jerked her wrist free. "Yes, I was," she cried. "But it had nothing to do with spying!" Her emerald eyes sparkled with tears. "But you don't want to believe that, do you?" Squaring her shoulders, she lifted her chin. "It doesn't make any difference. Uncle Tyler will clear up this whole matter as soon as he gets here, and then you'll be sorry!"

Cade stared at her in disbelief. She honestly believed that her privileged world would still protect her. She had no idea that it lay shattered at her feet and could never be restored. Shaking his head, he sat down on one of the chairs and stretched his long legs out in front of him. "Just have a seat."

Ruben moaned softly. Gabrielle saw him move and shot Cade a scathing glance. "At least help me get him on the sofa," she ordered.

"Leave him alone. He's fine where he is."

"Only a true cad would refuse help to a defenseless man," Gabrielle snapped accusingly. Fighting to control her temper, she knelt at Ruben's side and smoothed a lock of ebony hair from his forehead. "Are you all right, Ruben?" she asked softly.

"I think so," he said weakly, grimacing at the light.

"They tied your hands, Ruben, but I'll help you stand up. Together we'll get you on the sofa. Do you think you can manage?'

Nodding slightly, Ruben rolled onto his knees and stood unsteadily. With Gabrielle's support he crossed to the sofa and sank down, trembling from the exertion.

"I can't believe they've done this to you," she whispered, sitting beside him.

Ruben, pale and disoriented, flinched when she touched his bruised shoulder. "I'm sorry you got caught, Gabrielle," he said wearily. "Did they hurt you?"

"No, no, I wasn't hurt . . ." Her voice broke at the thought of their unfair treatment. To cover her lack of composure, she pressed the linen handkerchief against the cut on his lip, then took a deep breath. "But don't you worry. They've gone for Uncle Tyler." Keeping her voice low, she explained what had happened.

"They think we're spies, Ruben! Someone put documents in that packet. I saw them; they were drawings of some sort of explosive devices. They said you were going to sell them to the Yankees!" Her green eyes darkened with puzzlement. "I saw you glance through the pages when we came in. They were poems from Celeste, weren't they?"

Ruben, looking deathly pale, closed his eyes and dropped his head against the back of the sofa.

"Are you all right?"

"My head feels like they hit me with a crowbar."

"Did you see the poetry, Ruben?" Gabrielle asked anxiously.

He didn't open his eyes. "Yes, I saw it."

"Then how did the documents get in there?"

"I don't know, Gabrielle," He sighed heavily. "Maybe they switched them somehow."

"But who would do that? Who would try to frame you?"

Suddenly a key rattled in the lock, and Gabrielle's heart soared with hope. The door flew open and rain was blown in by the storm. An instant later Tyler stepped through the entrance. Gabrielle thought she might sob out loud like a child at the sight of him. She rushed across the room and threw her arms around him. "I'm so glad to see you," she whispered, pressing her face against his chest and feeling reassured by the warmth of his big body.

Tyler hugged her tight, then held her away, looking at her as though he were trying to assure himself
that she was, indeed, Gabrielle. "Some very serious
charges have been leveled against you, young lady,"
he said quietly.

"I know," she answered, her voice trembling.
"These men have frightened me half to death!" Off
to the side, Gabrielle saw Celeste, looking pale and
frightened. Gabrielle reached out and caught her
hand, squeezing it tightly. James Maffitt stood close
by, his face impassive. Behind him, one of the men
who had been there before, rifle in hand, pulled the
door shut.

Gabrielle looked up at Tyler. "Uncle Tyler, the
men think I'm a Yankee spy! And they beat poor
Ruben half to death!"

Tyler put his arm around her shoulders and led
her to a chair. "Sit down and tell me what happened tonight, Gabrielle." He sat down near her.
"Start when you were still at the St. Charles."

Gabrielle looked at all the somber faces surrounding her and felt a chill crawl up her spine. "I want
to go home now," she whispered, slipping her hand
into Tyler's. "Please."

For a moment Tyler stared at her face. "I'm sorry,
but we can't do that," he said quietly.

Gabrielle saw the grim line of his mouth, and her
heart fell. Maybe the situation was more serious than
she had thought.

"Start at the beginning."

"I was dancing," she began slowly, "and Rachel
told me that Celeste wanted to talk to me." Suddenly unsure, she glanced at her sister and saw Celeste nod ever so slightly. It made her feel better
knowing she had her sister's permission to speak.
"I knew what she wanted because I have carried a
few letters to Ruben for her before." Her face crum-

pled. "Oh, Uncle Tyler, I know you didn't want them to see each other, but I didn't think it would do any harm if they corresponded."

Tyler waved aside her explanation, his expression grave. "Go on. What happened after that?"

Gabrielle was unnerved by his lack of concern. Normally he would have been furious at such a breach of his orders. "I met Ruben at that old mansion on Rampart Street. I was scared to walk back alone and asked him if he'd escort me. He said he had to come here first and that afterward he would see me back to the St. Charles. A few minutes after we came on board, we heard a scuffling noise outside, and then that man"—she pointed at him—"and another man broke in. They had guns aimed at us, and I swear if we had moved one inch they would have shot us dead, that's how dangerous they were! I could only think they were robbers or Yankees." Her expression turned angry and accusing. "Then Mr. Montana and Mr. Maffitt came in."

"Go on."

She drew in a ragged breath. "They beat Ruben, and then they accused us of being spies!" She looked at Tyler and kept her voice low. "Uncle Tyler, I think they're trying to frame Ruben. Mr. Maffitt said the packet contained war documents, but it's not true. Ruben looked at the packet when we first came in and it was a love letter from Celeste. He told me so."

Tyler stared intently at Gabrielle, then turned to Celeste. "Did you ask your sister to deliver a letter to Ruben?"

Celeste shook her head "No," she said wearily.

Gabrielle stared at her sister in astonishment. "Celeste, I know you didn't want anyone to find out, but this is important. It's better for them to learn about your relationship with Ruben than to think we're traitors!"

Gabrielle's words seemed to hang in the silent room. Celeste looked grief-stricken and pale, almost spiritual in her white ballgown with its blue satin bow. Her eyes darkened with sadness as she looked from Gabrielle to Tyler. "I knew Gabrielle was infatuated with Ruben, but I didn't know it had gone so far."

Gabrielle's fine-boned face turned white as porcelain. "That's not true!" she cried, leaping to her feet. "Celeste, please!" Getting no response from her sister, Gabrielle turned to Tyler. "Celeste and Ruben were in love. Uncle Tyler, you yourself forbade their courtship!"

Tyler looked questioningly at Celeste, and she shook her head. "I would not go behind your back to see Ruben," she said simply. "It was over a long time ago."

"That's a lie!" Gabrielle cried. "Why are you doing this?"

Tyler stood up. "Hush, Gabrielle." He turned to Ruben, making no effort to hide his contempt or his cold, deadly rage. "Guillotte, listen closely to me. You have been under surveillance for more than two months. We know all about your activities, whom you sell to, and how much you make. You are a traitor. Don't bother to deny it. I need to know only one thing. Who was helping you? Celeste or Gabrielle?"

Ruben lifted his head, his mouth twisting with cynicism. "I asked Gabrielle to help me and she did. Mr. St. Clair, you were worried about me ruining one of your nieces, but"—he grinned slowly—"you were watching the wrong one. While you were busy protecting Celeste from my attentions, I was meeting with Gabrielle."

"You bastard!" Tyler swiftly stepped forward, hand lifted, but caught himself before striking Ruben. Breathing hard, he clenched his hand into a fist and brought it back down to his side. "Did Gabrielle know what was in the packet?"

"Yes."

"Was Celeste involved?"

"I had no access to Celeste." Ruben's mouth twisted. "I did have access to Gabrielle. She had more freedom, and I knew I'd have better luck with her. She fancied herself in love with me."

"That's not true!" Gabrielle cried.

Ruben looked at her, resignation stamped on his face. "We've been caught red-handed, *ma petite.* They're going to find out the truth anyway, and there's no point in lying now."

Tyler's next question sounded hollow. "Has Gabrielle brought you information before?"

"Yes."

In a daze of horror, Gabrielle saw the look that passed between Cade and her uncle and knew that they were both thinking about the night she had been caught climbing down the trellis. She sank into her chair in a paralysis of shock as she realized the magnitude of the situation.

As they proceeded to interrogate Ruben, Gabrielle pressed both hands against her face and slumped back in exhaustion. They asked him endless questions about people, places, names, and it slowly became evident that Ruben was indeed a spy. Handsome, debonair Ruben, who loved good times, racing, and gambling, was a spy for the Yankees! The questioning went on and on, and through it all, Ruben provided answers that absolved Celeste and buried Gabrielle in lies.

Numbed, Gabrielle had lost all track of time when a knock sounded at the door. A moment later, a man

Gabrielle had seen earlier pushed it open. "The Committee members are assembled in the casino," he announced.

For breathless seconds no one moved. Finally Cade picked up his black frock coat. "Thank you, Billy."

Tyler rose to his feet with a sigh. Gabrielle had never seen him look so weary. She felt sad for him. After all, they had both been tricked.

"Billy, lock Guillotte in one of the staterooms," Maffitt ordered. He pursed his mouth, then turned. "Tyler, we'll have to leave a guard with Gabrielle during the meeting. One of Cade's men can escort Celeste home."

Celeste reacted instantly. "No! Please let me stay with my sister," she pleaded, tears running down her cheeks. "Please."

Gabrielle followed John Williams meekly, devastated by Celeste's deceit. When he opened the door to one of the staterooms and lit the lamp, she entered behind him without a word. Gabrielle sat on the bed after he left, and Celeste sat opposite her in the only chair. Gabrielle stared at her clasped hands, then finally lifted her head and asked, "Why?"

"I'm sorry, Gabrielle," Celeste said tiredly. "I'm truly sorry."

"Did you put those documents in the packet?"

"Yes."

Gabrielle felt tears swell again in her chest, and this time she allowed herself to cry. She cried so hard her racking sobs hurt. Celeste did not try to comfort her; she only handed her a handkerchief. Celeste didn't speak until Gabrielle finally stopped crying.

"Gabrielle, I'll tell you what happened, and I can only hope you'll understand. Ruben *was* selling information to the Yankees, but it was worthless. It didn't hurt the South. He only gave away tidbits the North would have gotten hold of anyway. He simply *used* the Yankees to get what he wanted.''

"Oh, dear God," Gabrielle said wearily, "you make it sound so innocent."

"It *was* innocent," Celeste insisted. "He wanted to buy back the steamboat business. We couldn't marry until he had reestablished himself and made some money."

"He's a *spy!*"

"Don't say that!" Celeste whispered furiously. "He's no worse than the blockade runners who do business with both sides! Everybody is happy enough to see them when they bring bonnets from Paris. Every woman in New Orleans thinks they're heroes."

Gabrielle stared at her sister. "It's different, Celeste. No one will think Ruben is a hero." She crossed her arms over her chest. "And what about me?" she demanded bitterly. "You're going to sacrifice me because something went wrong in this crazy scheme?"

"We never dreamed this would happen to you." Celeste stood up, walked restlessly over to the window and then turned back, her voice low and urgent. "Gabrielle, do you know what's going to happen to Ruben?"

She shook her head.

"He will probably be hanged, and he doesn't deserve that. If I'm free, I know people to get in touch with who will help him escape."

"But, Celeste," Gabrielle interrupted, her voice breaking, "what if they put me in jail—or hang *me?*"

"Don't be so melodramatic! Nothing will happen to you because you're a woman. As soon as Ruben escapes, I'll tell Uncle Tyler the truth." She sat down

beside Gabrielle and caught her hand. "It'll take a
week, two weeks at the most. Uncle Tyler will probably just lock you in your room. That's all the punishment you'll get."

Gabrielle pulled her hand away as fresh hot tears
brimmed in her eyes. "I don't want him to think
I'm a spy. I don't want anyone to think I'm a traitor
to the South!"

"Do you want Ruben to die?"

"No, but I don't think what he did was right, and
I don't think you should help him!"

Celeste pressed both hands against her face and
drew in a ragged breath. "I love Ruben, and I will
not see him hanged. You will simply have to manage until he is safe. When it's over, I promise I'll tell
Uncle Tyler the truth."

Tyler stopped just outside the doors to the casino
and stepped back so the other men could pass
through. "Cade, could I talk to you a few minutes
before you go in?"

"Of course." Cade glanced at James Maffitt.
"We'll be in shortly."

The lawyer nodded, stepped inside the casino,
and closed the door behind him. Once they were
alone, Tyler turned to Cade. "There's not much
time, so forgive me for being blunt. You asked me
for a favor ten years ago when your father lost everything, and I loaned you the money to rebuild.
You have repaid the loan with interest, but now I'm
asking you to repay the favor.

Cade nodded. "What can I do?"

"The Committee is going to deal harshly with
Ruben. There's no doubt about that. What I'm afraid
of is that they might decide to deal harshly with Gabrielle as well. I've been racking my brain trying to
think of a way to protect her. I want to have an

acceptable punishment to offer them before I go into that casino. I don't want them to come up with a punishment of their own."

Cade frowned, feeling uneasy suddenly. "What do you have in mind?"

Tyler held his gaze. "I want you to take Gabrielle to Texas."

Cade straightened, his astonishment obvious. "You can't be serious."

"I am. Montana, listen to me," Tyler rushed on. "You have a remote and isolated ranch there."

"It's not that isolated," Cade hedged, stepping backward.

"It will be for my niece," Tyler said. "The Committee might accept exile as a suitable punishment for her . . . if I tell them you have agreed to become responsible for her . . ."

"Hold on a minute—"

"They respect you, Cade, and they just might go along with it if you agree."

"Tyler, I can't take on responsibility for Gabrielle. My God, it's crazy."

"I can't let them incarcerate her—"

"They won't do that."

"What if they do? Cade, maybe I'm grasping at straws, but I don't have time to come up with anything else. I'm trying to protect her. Please help me."

Cade paced the length of the corridor, then turned back. Tyler could be right. Maffitt considered this a serious situation or he wouldn't have convened the Committee in the middle of the night.

"Do you think Gabrielle is innocent?" Tyler pressed.

Cade shook his head. "I don't know."

Tyler nodded, his point made. "See? That's how they're going to feel. They won't turn her over to me with a slap on the wrist and a lecture to behave herself." He sighed raggedly. "I'm afraid they might take serious measures."

Cade ran long fingers through his thick hair. "Jesus, Tyler, I owe you a lot, but this is more than just a favor. My ranch is isolated, but it's not so remote that Gabrielle couldn't run away. I'd have to have someone watch her all the time."

Tyler met his look squarely. "I know I'm asking too much, but I'm asking anyway."

"What about sending her to a relative somewhere?"

Tyler's mouth twisted. "To Georgia, to South Carolina? My relatives all live in the heart of the South, and the Committee would never agree to it."

Cade rubbed his fingers against his forehead and grimaced. It would be a son-of-a-bitch living with Gabrielle in his home. His way of life was different in Texas, and he didn't want to give up his freedom for a bullheaded, strong-willed Southern belle who didn't have an ounce of sense and whose curves tantalized him despite his contempt for what she'd done. Hell, the truth of the matter was that he wanted to bed her, not be entrusted with her care and well-being by one of his best friends.

"Tyler, I'm a man, for God's sake, and I'll be blunt. How can you ask me to take Gabrielle into my home? You know I'm not married."

"Cade, you are an honorable man. I trust you. I am faced with extraordinary circumstances and I am doing the best I can. Please."

"I know." Cade sighed. He looked at Tyler and saw the anguish on the man's face. "I'll do it, Tyler, but I have strong reservations."

"And be appointed her guardian? That's what they'll want to know."

Cade looked angrily at him. "Tyler, don't you realize this is a lot to ask? Your niece has been caught spying. It won't be like having a guest in my home."

Tyler's face hardened. "Yes, I know it's a lot to ask, but I love Gabrielle, and I believe she's innocent of deliberately trying to hurt the South. I'm sure Guillotte duped her into it. And I *am* asking."

Cade shook his head and walked away a few feet. It was a long moment before he turned back. "Okay. I'll do it."

Tyler had been right, Cade thought. The Committee remained in session for the rest of the night. Ruben's fate was decided quickly. He was sentenced to be hanged as a spy. But Gabrielle posed different problems.

Judge Dahlman, chairman of the Committee, regarded Cade thoughtfully, his elegant old features composed in stern lines as he considered Tyler's proposal. His fingers tapped the table top for an agonizingly long period before he finally spoke.

"I realize Tyler is a friend of yours, but are you willing to turn your ranch into a prison and yourself into a guard for the sake of that friendship? It is a serious responsibility, Cade, and Gabrielle is a headstrong young woman. She may not resign herself to exile easily. You may be condemning yourself to a great deal of misery."

"I realize that and I am still willing to do it." After a quick glance at Tyler's haggard features, Cade eyed Judge Dahlman. "I don't believe I'll have much difficulty. My ranch is a two-day ride from the nearest town. I have a crew of men I can depend on, and I'm willing to guarantee that if you entrust Gabrielle to me, there will be no problems. You have my word on it."

"I don't like this," Maffitt interrupted, slamming

his fist down on the table. "The girl is a traitor and must be punished!"

Dahlman raised a hand, stopping him from saying more. "I have made my decision."

Cade walked out of the meeting just before dawn, solely responsible for Gabrielle St. Claire. He would take her away straight from the boat. She would not be allowed to visit her family or return to Camden Hill for any purpose, not even for her clothes. The orders were to keep her whereabouts secret, even from Celeste. Tyler would explain Gabrielle's absence by saying she was visiting his sister in Georgia. Both Tyler and Cade swore to follow the restrictions set down by the Committee. Judge Dahlman assured them both that if any problems arose, the Committee would deal harshly with Gabrielle.

Gabrielle listened to her uncle in total disbelief. "I don't want to go to Texas. I don't deserve punishment! I didn't do anything!"

"It's better than prison."

She stared at him, then dropped down on the bed. Celeste had promised that nothing would happen to her. She pressed a hand to her forehead, feeling ill. Exile to Texas! Celeste wouldn't even know where she was. She wouldn't be able to help her.

Tyler was impervious to her pleas. Looking up, she tried again. "Can't I please go home with you tonight? Just one more time. Who will know but us?"

"Gabrielle, do you realize the serious trouble you are in?"

"No! I don't!" she cried, jumping to her feet. "I don't understand anything about this night. I expected to be kept home from parties as punishment for helping Celeste and Ruben. I never dreamed that

some secret committee would think I was a spy!
I didn't think when I left the St. Charles tonight
that I would lose you, my home, my friends—
everything!''

She threw herself against him and wrapped her
arms around his waist. "Uncle Tyler, don't send me
to Texas," she pleaded. "I don't even like Cade
Montana. I don't want him to be my guardian. I
don't want to go away. I don't want to leave you.
Please, please, please," she cried, pressing her head
against his chest, "don't send me away.''

Tyler smoothed her hair back from her forehead.
"Gabrielle, I love you, but I can do nothing to help
you or change anything now. Nothing. The minute
you helped Guillotte you were lost to me.''

"I didn't help him!''

Tyler just hugged her tight against his chest, and
then kissed her forehead. "Goodbye, sweetheart.''
Disengaging himself from her arms, he left the room
without looking back. He nodded to Judge Dahlman, who stood waiting for him farther down the
hallway, then he stopped next to Cade, who also
was waiting for him.

"Cade, I'm not supposed to be in touch with you
or Gabrielle for several months. For some reason that
doesn't make any sense to me.''

Cade shrugged. "I suppose they want her to feel
deprived of family.''

"I suppose so.'' Tyler inhaled sharply, then extended his hand. "Thank you.''

Cade nodded. He watched as Tyler walked away,
joined Judge Dahlman, and turned the corridor out
of sight. Dreading the scene before him, Cade
opened the door of the stateroom.

At the sight of Gabrielle sitting on her bed, her
delicate features as white as marble, he felt a twist
of pity. Tyler's departure had been a final, brutal

blow. Her ruffled pink ballgown served as a forlorn reminder of where she had started the night.

"Let's go, Gabrielle. My carriage is waiting outside."

Without replying, she rose and allowed herself to be led to the door. Cade wrapped a cape around her to protect her from the blowing rain, and they stepped into the storm.

Chapter 4

A gust of rain swept the carriage, causing the heavy coach to sway as it traveled along the gravel road in the early morning hours. Gabrielle sat across from Cade, mute with misery as she huddled in the many-layered cape he had settled around her shoulders. The entire night seemed like a nightmare, including this unchaperoned ride alone with Cade. Hours ago it would have been an unspeakable impropriety. Uncle Tyler would never have permitted it, much less arranged it, but now it did not matter.

Gabrielle bowed her head as hot burning tears rolled down her cheeks. She had always been Tyler's favorite—he had never said so, but she knew it just the same. She had never been so hurt, or so terrified, as when the door had shut behind him tonight. Did he actually think she had stolen Southern secrets to help the North? Remembering the sad resignation on Tyler's face, Gabrielle squeezed her eyes shut and pressed trembling fingers against her mouth.

She imagined her room at Camden Hill as it would look this morning, with her bed turned down but unslept in, and her nightgown lying across the foot of it. Cut with fresh grief, she sobbed out loud. She

76

might as well be dead. Celeste had torn her life apart with her lies and deceit. Warm tears slipped over her fingers. Even if Celeste decided to tell the truth, it would be too late because she would already be in Texas.

"Here's a handkerchief."

Gabrielle looked down and saw the white blur in Cade's outstretched hand. "I don't want it," she whispered raggedly. "Not from you."

Cade's tone remained patient. "Gabrielle, I'm sorry about what's happened to you."

A picture flashed before her, of Cade standing sternly beside James Maffitt, and anger and indignation pierced her grief. "Do you expect me to believe that? You have ridiculed me ever since we first met." Her voice hardened. "My uncle has turned me over to—to an enemy!"

"That's not true."

"It is true!" she cried, her hands clenching into fists. "You're taking me away from everyone—from the people I love!"

"Look, you got yourself into this mess, and Tyler has asked me to take you with me to Texas to save you from much worse alternatives. It wasn't my idea and I don't like it any more than you do, but Tyler is my friend, and I owe him a lot."

"Don't say any more mean things to me! I don't deserve any of this, no matter what you think. A tragedy has happened to me and I'm scared." Gabrielle fell silent after this outburst, but her sense of panic intensified with every jolt of the carriage and every faint jingle of the harness. Each mile carried her farther away from her home, from everything that offered her security and warmth. She stared at Cade Montana's shadowy face in the darkness and felt she had to get away from him; she had to go home! Acting on desperation, she gripped the latch and readied herself to jump. Cade seemed to read her mind and in a split second his hand covered hers, squeezing hard and preventing her from moving.

"No, you don't!" he said, pulling her fingers away from the latch. Disgusted, he shoved her back into her seat. "Use your head. Jumping out of the carriage won't accomplish a damned thing except getting yourself hurt. I'll be frank, Gabrielle. If you had managed to get out, I would have come after you. I have no choice in this matter, and you have no choice. You are coming with me to Texas, one way or the other."

"But I don't want to go to Texas," she whispered, tears rolling down her cheeks again.

Cade shook his head and leaned back, more disturbed by her tears than he wanted to admit. How had he let Tyler St. Claire talk him into this mess? Why hadn't he just walked away? He was only beginning to see what a difficult situation it was. The girl had been wrenched away from her family and home, and whether she was guilty or not, she was terrified of leaving and terrified of him. It was the craziest damned thing he'd ever heard of.

"Look," he said, tiredly, "let's call a truce. It's almost daylight. It's been a long night, and we're both exhausted. Let's try to get through the next few hours and we'll talk after we've had some sleep. Will you agree to that?"

It was a long moment before Gabrielle nodded. Cade dropped back against the cushioned seat and began to think of the endless difficulties Gabrielle could cause him politically and socially. Getting her to Texas was a problem, but keeping her in Texas would be an even greater one. He glanced at her, crumpled in the corner, looking forlorn and lost and more like a beautiful, bewildered child than a spy.

She bore no resemblance to the haughty but seductive flirt he'd seen at the ball earlier that night. Cade rubbed his palm against the growth of whiskers on his jaw and reminded himself that he shouldn't feel sorry for her. She deserved her punishment even if she did seem incapable of understanding that what she had done was wrong.

He closed his eyes and relaxed his long frame. It would be good to get back home and out of the rain of Louisiana. Once they arrived, he'd assign someone to watch her day and night. Then she would be out of his hair, and he would be less tempted by her tantalizing curves.

They rode without speaking for the last few miles. Once the carriage turned into the long, oak-lined lane leading to his plantation, Cade straightened up and glanced at Gabrielle.

"I don't know if you are aware of this or not, but I recently bought Metairie Place. We'll be staying there until I can arrange transportation to Texas." He glanced out the window and saw the blur of the big house through the mist. "We'll be arriving in a few minutes. I don't need to remind you that news travels quickly among slaves, and it is in our best interest to keep your identity a secret."

Gabrielle continued to look down at her clasped hands, and he couldn't tell if she was listening to him.

"I purchased the servants along with the plantation. There are also a few loyal slaves of mine here that I can trust. I don't know how trustworthy the others are. I want you to keep the hood covering your face when we enter."

Gabrielle looked up. "But they will still see me—won't they wonder . . ."

"I don't think so. I'll speak bluntly. I've had female company at Metairie before, and they'll assume you're another . . . friend. They won't know you're Gabrielle St. Claire."

When he saw the furious blush that spread across her face at his words, Cade continued, determined that she understand exactly what he had in mind. "You'll be staying in my quarters with me."

Gabrielle looked shocked. "What are you saying?"

"It's my responsibility to get you out of New Orleans quietly and without a scandal. I need your cooperation to accomplish that. Do you want word of what happened last night to get out?"

Gabrielle shook her head.

"Then we must keep your identity a secret. You do not have to worry about your own safety, because I will treat you like a lady."

When they came to a stop, Gabrielle allowed Cade to assist her from the carriage into the gloomy gray morning. She glanced briefly at the white pillars of Metairie and its lush garden and grounds before pulling her hood down to protect her face from the rain and from scrutiny.

A groom stepped forward immediately, and Cade gave him brief instructions before grasping Gabrielle's elbow and ushering her up the wide stairs. A butler held the door open as they swept into the foyer. "Mornin', Mista Montana," the man said. "Weather out there's mighty dreary."

"It sure is, Jeremiah." Cade handed him his cape and gloves. "We would like to have breakfast, please. Have Mattie bring up a couple of trays to my room."

"Yes, sir. I'll tell her right now."

Blushing with humiliation at the implied intimacy, Gabrielle automatically drew back from Cade's tall length. Without changing his expression, he caught her arm firmly and steered her up the stairs. Because her hood had slipped so far down over her face, she could only see emerald carpeting curving upward. With no further protest, she allowed herself to be guided along the hallway and waited silently while he opened the door. He gestured for her to enter, and she looked at him uncertainly before she stepped across the threshold into a spacious and very masculine suite of rooms. Pushing back the hood, she glanced at the fireplace, the two wing-back chairs flanking the sofa, the rich draperies—and the big canopied bed. At the sight of the bed her stomach knotted with apprehension. She whirled at the sound of the key turning in the lock, and color spread over her pale cheeks.

"I can't stay here." Her statement was more a plea than a demand.

"I'm sorry, Gabrielle, but this is how it's got to be." One of the reasons Cade had insisted that they stay together was that it would be easier to watch her. He knew she would try to escape and return to Camden Hill if she got the chance. Maybe it was due to her shock and fatigue, but she still seemed unable to understand the seriousness of her predicament. He walked over and lifted the cape from her shoulders. "Are you hungry?" he asked, laying the wet garment near the hearth.

Gabrielle shook her head and dropped into a chair by the fireplace. Wearily she rubbed her hands over her eyes, feeling cold, exhausted, and numb.

When a knock sounded, Cade nodded toward a side door. "Wait in the dressing room until I call you."

Gabrielle did as she was told. She had no desire to be seen in his room. When she returned she saw that the maid had brought a hearty breakfast tray. Bone weary, she ate mechanically, and when her stomach was full she leaned back and closed her eyes.

"Gabrielle?"

She didn't answer.

"Gabrielle," Cade repeated insistently, "you can sleep on the bed, and if you want to get out of your clothes, I'll give you one of my robes to wear."

His last statement penetrated her sluggishness. "No, no, I'm fine," she assured him, rising unsteadily to her feet. Exhausted, she stumbled over to the bed and lay down in her dress, crinolines and all. She fell asleep as soon as she closed her eyes.

Cade walked over and looked down at Gabrielle. She lay flat on her back, with her head turned to the side. Her corselet and ballgown kept her from sleeping in a more natural position, but he didn't attempt to unlace her. His gaze drifted from her face, down over her shoulders to the swell of her breasts revealed by the low cut of her pink ballgown. How could Tyler be so confident he was an honorable man? He doubted that any man would find it easy to resist such a vision, and Cade rarely resisted lusciously shaped women. If she weren't Tyler's niece he wouldn't even try to resist, but he knew his friend trusted him.

His mouth crimped with cynicism, Cade pulled off her slippers and covered her with a sheet. He planned to make arrangements for their trip to Texas while she slept. He hoped it wouldn't be too hard to find a captain willing to run the blockade for a tidy sum of money.

Although Gabrielle slept deeply, she was troubled by a haunting dream in which Celeste was chasing her in the garden of Camden Hill, calling her name. They were children again, wearing frilly party dresses with matching ribbons in their hair, running fast and dodging through the beautiful bushes and flower beds. Celeste caught up with Gabrielle and grabbed her arm, swinging her around. In the haze of the dream Celeste's angry face was enormous as she shook Gabrielle's shoulders.

"Don't you dare run away from me, Gabrielle! You always get what you want, and Uncle Tyler loves you best. It's my birthday party! My party! Why are your dresses always prettier?" Celeste pushed her down on the soft grass, and Gabrielle continued to fall, down, down until she lost sight of Celeste and could only hear her voice growing weaker in the darkness. "Even at my party you get all the attention! I hate you Gabrielle, I hate you . . . hate you . . ."

Gabrielle woke with a start and stared curiously at the unfamiliar canopied bed. The netting had been drawn about her, and when she parted the wispy white material she saw a strange room with open French doors leading to a balcony. She dropped back on the bed, her heart beating crazily as she realized she was at Metairie. Bolting upright again, she stared through the netting at the glow of dying coals. And then she saw Cade sleeping on a nearby sofa.

Her mind whirled furiously as she wondered what time it was. They had arrived in the early morning, but it was dark out now and still raining. Had she slept through the day? Her gaze fell on the open doors to the balcony, and a flash of distant lightning illuminated the dim edge of the stair rail. A shiver of exhilaration swept through her as she realized it must lead to the ground floor. How easy it would be to slip away!

Her heart beating fiercely, she slid off the bed and pulled on her slippers. Maybe Uncle Tyler already regretted his decision to send her away. He always reacted in anger, then changed his mind. She dismissed James Maffitt and the Committee as a bunch of stuffy officials puffed up with their own power and importance. She was convinced that Uncle Tyler could take care of them if he wanted to.

Gabrielle slipped silently across the room. At the hearth she picked up the black cape in one slow, careful movement. Holding her breath, she glanced briefly at Cade, afraid that even the sweep of her gaze might wake him. His thick, dark brown hair was rumpled, and she thought the day's growth of beard on his chiseled face made him look like a pirate.

Once she was out on the balcony, Gabrielle drew the hood up to cover her head and stepped into the light rain. She listened quietly to the rumble of thunder low over the Gulf, then, with anxious haste, moved stealthily down the stairs into the pitch-dark garden.

Surely Metairie could not be too far from her home—maybe six or seven hours on foot. It would be a long walk, but if she headed east, she'd eventually run into a road she recognized. She knew New Orleans well and would have no difficulty finding her way once she got to the city.

The first hour was chilly but uneventful, and she was elated at the idea that she was going home. Even the sounds of night creatures didn't bother her much because her mind was too occupied with what she would say to Uncle Tyler. Distractedly she hoped the storm that seemed to be brewing would blow itself out, but as the night lengthened lightning flashed continuously all about her, sometimes clearly revealing wet barked trees and thick underbrush. The loud thunder sounded menacingly close, and the wind began to whip her clothing about. Becoming more and more uneasy, Gabrielle looked for some kind of shelter to take refuge in before the brunt of the storm struck.

Suddenly it seemed that the heavens opened up and meant to destroy her. Lightning bolts flashed so furiously that Gabrielle dropped to the ground and huddled in terror, holding her arms over her head. A tree near her snapped and split down the center with a shattering jolt. Gabrielle lay motionless, too frightened to move. It seemed the storm would never end, but finally the intensity slackened and Gabrielle staggered to her feet and started walking again. She was now soaked from head to toe and had to push away the undergrowth that tugged at her wet cape and the branches that slapped against her face.

As the night wore on, Gabrielle realized she was in serious trouble. Somehow she had wandered off the road and headed in the wrong direction. The earth beneath her feet became spongy, and she panicked because that meant she had entered swampland. She turned, heading right in the darkness, hoping to stumble onto firm ground. But whichever way she went, the earth became softer and walking became more difficult. She was wet and cold and ankle-deep in muddy water. Something slithered past her bare leg, and on her right she heard a loud splash. Was it an alligator?

Terrified, Gabrielle struggled through the water that had become knee-high now, but the soggy weight of her water-logged gown depleted her strength. Her breath rasped in her lungs and she stopped, nearly dropping with fatigue. She heard the distant sound of dogs barking, and her heart froze when she remembered the last time she had heard a pack of dogs. She'd been taking a carriage ride with Celeste on a beautiful summer day when they heard wild barking. Men had been tracking a runaway slave, and Uncle Tyler had told her and Celeste to turn away because such a sight was not fit for ladies. She shivered and realized that somewhere along the way she had lost her cape.

When a screech sounded in the trees above her, Gabrielle stumbled and fell into the murky swamp water. She rose to her feet with a cry, spitting out the putrid liquid that had filled her mouth. She reached solid ground and tried to increase her pace, but briars pricked at her skin and finally the brambles became so thick that movement in any direction was impossible.

She closed her eyes, feeling thorns penetrate her clothing. In that instant she felt sure she was going to die. She had heard terrifying stories about people who got lost in the swamps. She hung her head, dragging in air, her lungs aching from her exertion and the cold. Shielding her face with her arms, she sagged to her knees and allowed her head to sink against the earth. Her arm burned from a thorn's long, deep scratch, and cold rain fell on her back.

She lost consciousness for a short time before the sound of baying dogs jerked her back to startled awareness. When she lifted her head, she saw the figures of two men brushing through the dense growth in the dismal early morning light. One man restrained the bounding frenzy of the hounds by pulling tightly on their leashes. Two more men followed on horseback. The fog-shrouded scene seemed to Gabrielle like something out of a nightmare, and she thought for a moment she was dreaming, until she heard Cade's voice and saw the swing of his black cloak.

"We're going to have to cut her out of there, because the bramble is too thick to reach her any other way. Settle those dogs down."

A gravelly voice shouted at the dogs, and they

quieted down somewhat. Cade and a black man started hacking through the thick brush with long knives.

Cade's tight, angry voice sounded so good that she started to cry, weak with relief at being found and saved from a horrid death in the swamp.

The blades of the machetes sliced through the underbrush, and at last Cade, his mouth clamped shut with fury, untangled her from the brambles that ensnarled her hair and clothing. He examined her face impersonally, turning it this way and that, then looked coldly into her eyes.

"You promised we had a truce until morning. I hope this has taught you a lesson."

Gabrielle was too tired to reply.

"Jesus!" he said in disgust as he dragged her along, his gaze dropping to her ragged pink silk gown, now turned a dingy brown. "You are in such bad shape that I hate to put you on my horse. If I thought you could make it, I'd let you walk back."

Gabrielle didn't try to answer. She was so weak she didn't care what he said as long as he let her ride. She knew she could barely walk and her skirt and petticoats felt clammy against her legs. She had lost her slippers somewhere in the swamp, and mud squished between her toes.

She rode in front of him, leaning against his chest, grateful for the feel of his strong arms holding her safe. He used his own cape to protect her from the drizzle, and gradually his warmth penetrated her body. Gabrielle closed her eyes and fell asleep against him.

By the time they reached the plantation the rain had stopped, but a thick fog engulfed them. They rode up to the house through the garden and arrived at the same stairs she had used to escape. Cade dismounted, caught her waist, and lifted her down.

His mouth twisted with distaste at the sulfurous smell of the swamp water soaking her clothes. Grabbing her upper arm, he pulled her to the stairs.

"Don't move," he warned when they reached the balcony outside his room. "Don't even touch the railing. Just wait until I come back for you."

Gabrielle made no protest. She didn't have the energy to move in any case. She hugged her arms about her wet body as she waited and thought that she must look as miserable as she felt. Swamp mud matted her hair, weighed down her dress, and caked her arms and legs.

Minutes passed, and Gabrielle wondered how long Cade meant to leave her on the balcony. By the time he appeared, she was shivering from the cold. "Why did you take so long?"

"I had the maids prepare your bath. Take off your petticoats and leave them out here on the balcony." At her blank look he explained impatiently. "I'm not going to have your muddy skirts drip on the Oriental carpets I just paid a fortune for." He turned his back. "Take them off."

Gabrielle stared at his broad shoulders, then down at the circle of dirty water at her feet. Too weary to argue, she lifted her wet skirt, untied the drawstring of her crinolines, and stepped out of them. "You can turn around," she told him softly.

With a muttered obscenity Cade caught her about the waist and carried her like a sack of feed through his bedroom and into the dressing room where a steaming tub of water sat. He put her down on the bit of marble that protruded from the fireplace. "Time for a bath."

"Don't I have a lady's maid?" Gabrielle demanded anxiously.

"Yes, you do," Cade said, his sapphire-blue eyes blazing. "Me."

Gabrielle snapped out of her exhaustion and straightened abruptly. "That just won't do."

His bronzed features hardened with determination. "It will have to do, my genteel Southern gardenia. I'll unlace you and wait outside the door while you bathe."

"You can't be serious," she breathed, genuinely shocked.

"Oh, but I am. In less than an hour we are getting in my carriage, and by nightfall we'll be on our way to Texas aboard ship. I'm not taking any more chances with you, Gabrielle. When we get there, I'll give you more freedom. I'll turn you loose with ten thousand mean son-of-a-bitch longhorns. I want them to see a creature as ornery as they are."

Gabrielle became still and pale at his mention of a ship. "When did you arrange passage?"

"My mornings and nights are so damned mixed up, I'm not sure when, but I got it done. Now I want you to take a bath."

Gabrielle stared at him. Seeing the fear in her green eyes, Cade sighed. "Look, I plan to unlace you, not seduce you. Now turn around."

When she complied, Cade pushed her foul-smelling hair over her shoulder and with abrupt, angry movements unfastened her dress and untied the lacings of her corselet. Mortified, Gabrielle turned back to Cade slowly, her mud-streaked hands holding up the front of her dress.

"Thank you," she said tightly.

With a look of disgust, Cade dipped his hands into the tub to rinse off the slime. "All right. Be sure to scrub yourself well, Gabrielle. Mattie left four buckets of water for you to rinse with. I hope that will be enough. If I smell any swamp stench in your hair when you come out, I'll bring you back in here and scrub you with a brush myself. I'll be right outside that door and in ten minutes I'm coming in, propriety be damned!''

When the door shut behind him, Gabrielle undressed hurriedly and slipped into the tub. Even though the warm water made her many scratches sting, it felt wonderful. With bristling speed she scrubbed her scalp and body, then rose to her knees, picked up one of the buckets of fresh water, and poured it over her head. She repeated the procedure until her hair was squeaky clean. After stepping out of the tub she dried herself and, conscious of his threat, slipped quickly into the heavy black robe he had left for her. She then wrapped a towel about her head, turban style.

She opened the door and peeked out. Cade sat in one of the chairs facing the door, his expression stony. She noticed he had changed into a crisp white shirt.

''Come here, Gabrielle,'' he ordered, rising. ''I want to look at those scratches on your back.''

She stared at him, thinking she must have heard him wrong. Her gaze dropped to the medical supplies laid out on the table. ''Thank you,'' she said, withdrawing, ''but I can do it myself.''

''You can't reach them.''

She retreated and started to shut the door. In a lightning-fast move he crossed the room, shoved the door open, and grabbed her arm.

''I've got to look at those damned scratches,'' he said, hauling her across the floor. ''Frankly, I would much rather let you suffer than take care of you, but I'm not going to let you get infected. Now sit down.''

''No.''

''Sit down,'' he demanded between clenched teeth.

Realizing she had no choice, she sat.

"Now lift your face to me."

With a cotton swab he smoothed medicine along a scratch on her jaw.

"Oh!" she cried, tears filling her eyes at the stinging it caused. "That burns."

"Good. You deserve it. Now your back."

Gabrielle jumped up and grabbed the front of the robe with both hands. "No, not that," she said, stepping away from him. "That's much too personal. I won't let you."

Cade caught her shoulders and pushed her into the chair. He looked into her startled face. "Yes, you will, by God. It will be your responsibility to make certain I don't see any part of you I shouldn't. You have some deep scratches on your back from rolling around in that damned swamp. This salve will keep them from festering."

Gabrielle saw that there was no use arguing. Blushing scarlet, she adjusted the folds of the robe, and Cade dabbed stinging medicine on the scratches on her back and arms.

"Any other places, *you* can take care of."

"I don't have any other scratches. My skirts protected me."

He nodded, then pulled the towel from her head. "Dry your hair in front of the fire. We only have a few more minutes."

Gabrielle sat on a low stool, crossed her arms over her knees, and rested her head on her arms. Her hair tumbled over her head, glowing deep auburn and gold in the firelight. She thought of big Jacob, her uncle's slave who had repeatedly been punished for his efforts to run away. She knew now how he must have felt. Being helpless and held against your will at the mercy of others was terrible.

Gabrielle lifted her head and pushed her still-damp hair back to fall about her shoulders. She watched as Cade closed and secured the fastenings of the valise he had packed, then stuck a derringer inside his vest pocket. Texas seemed suddenly more real, and she stood up in fear, swaying slightly from light-headedness.

"I don't want to go. Please don't make me go."

"Look. I'm doing what I have to do, not what I want to do." He nodded toward the fireplace. "Just dry your hair and be quiet."

"How can you be angry with me for wanting to go home?"

"If I'm angry at you, it's not because you want to go home."

"Then what is it?"

"What the hell do you think it is? I'm angry because you were stupid enough to help that snake Guillotte, and I'm angry because I can't trust you out of my sight. I'm angry because I've had two sleepless nights, one of which I spent in the swamp. I'm angry because you sold out the South." Cade did not add that he was angry because she was so utterly helpless that it was almost impossible to stay angry with her.

"I did not sell out the South! I told you the truth. I was just delivering letters for Celeste."

Cade turned to her. "I've heard this before. I do not want to hear your declarations of innocence again, is that clear?" He walked over to the bed, tore the wrappings off a big package, and tossed the contents on the bed. "I want you to go into the dressing room and put these clothes on."

Gabrielle stared at the black mourning clothes. "Am I supposed to be a widow?"

"Yes."

"How appropriate," she said.

Chapter 5

Cade and Gabrielle rode in silence throughout
the long, rainy afternoon and into the night,
their carriage headed toward the stretch of deserted
coastline where they would rendezvous with the
ship that would carry them to Texas. Other happier
trips flashed through Gabrielle's mind as she sat opposite Cade. She remembered the family's summer
expeditions from Camden Hill to the St. Claire summer home, and thought how different those excursions had been from this present furtive journey. It
seemed the sun had always been shining then. She
remembered the servants bustling about, packing
trunks and preparing food, as excited as she and her
sister about the trip to the country. At last five carriages were needed to carry the family, personal
slaves, and all the luggage. When Reba was alive,
she had been in charge of the festive annual event,
and had organized everything right down to the contents of the picnic baskets. When she had everything
packed, the servants ready, and the carriages lined
up along the drive in front of Camden Hill, Reba
would climb into the carriage across from Gabrielle
and Celeste. That had always been the signal for
departure. Gabrielle could still hear her admonish-

ing the girls to keep their parasols over their heads
and the sun off their faces to prevent freckles.

Life had been so good back then, so easy and simple. She had thought it would never change, but
nothing had ever been quite the same since Reba
died. Deeply moved by her memory, Gabrielle
forced her thoughts away from the woman who had
been her nurse for sixteen years. She did not want
Cade to see her cry again.

They waited for nearly an hour after they arrived
at their destination before they heard the faint ripple
of oars in the water, and finally the scrape of a boat
against the shoreline. Cade helped Gabrielle from
the carriage and led her through the fog to the water's edge. There he lifted her into his arms and carried her to the waiting longboat. Two silent men
rowed them through the dark waters toward a distant pinpoint of light.

Gradually they could see the murky outline of the
ship against an almost black horizon. When the row-
boat finally bumped against its hull, an indistin-
guishable figure threw a rope ladder over the side
to them. Cade easily climbed up and over the rail,
then called softly for Gabrielle to follow. She climbed
slowly and hesitantly, fearful of the depths of the
inky water heaving beneath her and the dangerous
trip ahead. She realized too well the risk of gunfire
if they were spotted by Yankee patrol boat.

Gabrielle knew the first few hours were the most
perilous. She huddled in the corner of her bunk with
her head pressed against a pillow, imagining a
Northern warship trailing through the dark waters
behind them. At first her heart beat at a frantic pace
because she expected a cannon blast to rip a hole in
the ship at any moment. Nothing happened, however, as they glided silently through the predawn
mists.

A knock at the cabin door awoke Gabrielle with a start. Sunlight slipped in around the edges of the closed window, softly lighting the gloomy interior of the cabin. Hearing Cade call her name, she sat up and swung her legs over the side of the bunk, surprised that she had been able to sleep with the danger of the Yankees a breath away. She smoothed her dress and attempted to arrange her tangled auburn hair.

"Come in," she called softly.

Cade ducked inside and set a tray on the small table anchored to the floor. Gabrielle wrinkled her nose with distaste when she saw the hard rolls and hot coffee.

"Sorry, princess," Cade drawled and grinned sardonically. "I know it's not quite what you're accustomed to." He poured a cup of steaming coffee in a heavy mug and handed it to her. "This should wake you up."

"Are we safe?" she asked anxiously, deciding to ignore his sarcasm.

"There's not much to worry about now," he answered, dropping into the chair opposite her.

Gabrielle glanced at him curiously. He seemed to be in better spirits. Was it because each hour brought him closer and closer to Texas? His hair was windswept, and he smelled of sunshine and salt air. In fact he looked quite tan and handsome with his white shirt open at the neck. His fitness irritated her because she felt hot and disheveled.

"Can I go out on deck?" she asked petulantly. "It's so stuffy down here."

Cade shook his head. "No, there are only men on board. One of them might recognize you."

Gabrielle grimaced at the taste of the bitter coffee. "I don't think we travel in the same circles," she replied testily.

"I'm sure you're right. Still, it's better to be safe. I'll take you up after nightfall."

Her face stony, Gabrielle crossed to the window and unlatched it. Blinking against the brightness, she looked out across the water "What do I have to look forward to in Texas? Confinement in the attic?"

Cade laughed. "I won't need to lock you up."

"Why not?" she asked, turning to him.

"It's a big ranch. You'll have plenty of room."

Feeling out of sorts, Gabrielle returned to the table and stared sullenly at her meager breakfast. "What about the men on board this ship? Don't they think it's strange that I'm locked in?"

"They don't know. I told them you were in mourning."

Gabrielle looked at him in exasperation, annoyed at his good mood and the suspicion that he found her peevishness entertaining. "For whom?"

"I didn't say."

"I'm in mourning for me," she said dramatically, holding on to the table to steady herself against the gentle swells. "Gabrielle St. Claire is dead."

Cade's blue eyes sparkled with amusement, his teeth flashing white against his sun-darkened skin. His easy smile caused an unsettling little flip in Gabrielle's chest.

"Gabrielle St. Claire looks very much alive to me," he countered, standing up and pushing his chair back beneath the table. "I'll check on you later. I've got some work to do."

"Such as basking in a chair by the railing?" she retorted.

Cade laughed and shut the door behind him.

Bored and disgruntled, she looked around the tiny cabin, wondering how she would tolerate being couped up in a place where there was hardly room to stand. It was crammed with furniture, and every available niche and corner had been stacked with boxes. Dispirited at the thought of the long trip, she allowed her gaze to drift over the boxes, then suddenly gave a joyous cry as she realized her own trunk sat in the corner.

Gabrielle started pulling away the boxes piled in front of it. After dragging the trunk to the center of the cabin, she unfastened the latches and threw open the lid. Slowly her enthusiasm faded as she gazed down at the disarray. Her perfume, silver jewelry box, lace hankies, and fans had always been carefully placed in the upper partition. Hetty could not have packed the jumbled mess she saw. She lifted the top section and set it on the floor, dismayed at the pile of roughly folded clothing. Where were her crinolines, her expensive new dresses that should have been wrapped in tissue? One by one, she pulled out the practical cotton undergarments and nightclothes, and last season's dresses until the floor was littered with clothing. They were all old things she had discarded. She searched to the bottom, looking for her matching slippers, silk shifts and lacy chemises. Frantically she searched the entire pile for the gold-handled brush and comb set her uncle had given her for Christmas.

When a brief knock sounded at the door, Gabrielle didn't answer. She didn't even look up when Cade pushed it open and walked in. "What are you doing?" he demanded, his gaze sweeping the disordered mass of apparel.

"Who packed my clothes?" she asked, a catch in her voice.

Cade's brows came together in a frown, "I'm sure Tyler did. Why?"

"All of these are old! Where are all my beautiful things?" Gabrielle felt too defeated to cry. "Uncle Tyler would never be so mean," she whispered, her voice threaded with pain. "He bought me an entire new wardrobe in the early spring." Her gaze dropped to the empty trunk. "He didn't even send my mother's ring."

Cade shook his head, his expression turning grim at her petty concerns. "I think you can manage without your Paris fashions," he said sarcastically.

Hearing the disapproval in his voice, Gabrielle turned on him angrily. "It's not that! I'm not shallow and selfish like you think." Confusion sounded in her voice. "All of this is old. I've even grown out of most of it. Why did Uncle Tyler send it? Why wouldn't he send me what I need? Where's my mother's ring and my favorite things, things that have meaning to me?"

As Cade stared at her face understanding dawned, and his steely gaze softened. He had to remember that Gabrielle's whole life had turned upside down. More than ever she needed proof of Tyler's love. He pushed the door shut. "I'm afraid most of your stuff was packed and sent to your Aunt Emily's."

Gabrielle stared at him in bewilderment. "Why?"

"All your friends and family believe you have left for an extended visit in Georgia. That's what Tyler is telling everyone to explain your absence from the city."

"*Even Celeste?*" Gabrielle asked, horror widening her eyes. "Is that what he's telling her?"

"Yes. She doesn't know anything, not even that the Committee decided your fate. She simply thinks Tyler sent you away to keep you out of trouble."

Gabrielle was struck mute by the elaborate scheme. She had hoped the news of her whereabouts would shame Celeste into telling the truth. But Celeste wouldn't even know of her exile to Texas. Would she now be tempted to keep quiet, thinking her sister safe and maybe even happy with Aunt Emily?

"Tyler had your maid pack your clothes and, to add credibility to the story, he sent her to Georgia with the impression she's joining you there. Everybody saw her leave, especially the slaves at Camden Hill. The news will spread and maybe we can avoid talk—and scandal." Cade glanced down at the clothes. "Tyler packed what was left. I'm sorry."

Seeing Gabrielle's tumbled hair and defeated posture, Cade couldn't suppress the pity he had tried to dismiss earlier. "Let's get these clothes folded up. I'll help you."

Gabrielle sat motionless, stunned by events and terrified by her own powerlessness. All her lovely things weren't in her room anymore. Her cluttered dresser top would be clear, her wardrobe would be empty, her room vacant. Even Hetty wasn't at Camden Hill to miss her.

The rest of the trip did not improve for Gabrielle. The rolling motion of the ship affected her in the worst way, and she felt too sick to move from her bunk. Cade came often to check on her, but nothing made her feel better, not as long as the ship continued to roll.

A couple days later they reached Corpus Christi. During the night they transferred to a packet that would travel the Laguna Madre to Follettville. Without the rolling motion of the ship, Gabrielle immediately began to feel better. There was less need for secrecy with the Texas crew, and Cade allowed her on deck. Still pale from her illness, Gabrielle sat in a chair near the railing, watching with growing interest as they passed coastal bays and inlets. They arrived in Follettville by early afternoon of the following day.

A small crowd had gathered at the foot of the

gangway, and Gabrielle was shocked to discover that
they were there to welcome Cade back home. As
soon as he appeared on deck, a thrill of excitement
rippled through the crowd. A handmade banner was
raised, and a banjo twanged somewhere in the
throng. Individual voices shouted praise at Cade.
"Good to see you home, Montana!" "That's the
way to show those Yankees!"

Cade appeared at her side and snarled beneath his
breath, "That damned Rawlings! I bet he's responsible for this sideshow."

Gabrielle glanced at him, puzzled. "Don't you
want them here?"

He looked down, surprised by her question.
"Certainly not. I'm trying to bring you in as incon-
spicuously as possible." He caught her elbow and
escorted her down the gangplank as soon as the
dockworkers had laid it in place. "Put a smile on
your face, princess. That's all you have to do."

Bewildered, Gabrielle saw that he was grinning
now, exhibiting the confidence of a conquering hero
as he threaded his way through the crowd. Judging
from the comments he made, he knew many of the
people. Gabrielle automatically nodded to the
women who greeted her. As the crowd swarmed
around them, Cade smiled and shook hands like a
veteran politician, as if the adulation was his due.

"Good to see you home," a man's voice called.
"I knew you couldn't stay away from Texas too
long."

"Who's the young woman with you, Mr. Montana? Did you bring home a bride?"

Cade glanced at Gabrielle, seeing her through the
eyes of the crowd. She looked like a shy young wife.
Because he had been busy with the details of their
arrival, he had paid little attention to her that morning, but now he was struck by her beauty. She ap-

peared delicate and almost frail in her plain dark
blue linen dress with a white lace collar. A wide-
brimmed straw hat shaded her classic features, and
her eyes were a clear emerald-green. He shook his
head, amazed again by her tantalizing combination
of purity and sensuousness. Was he the only man
who found the sweet curve of her mouth incongru-
ous with the lush curve of her breast and the way
her lashes fluttered provocatively against the pale
blush of her cheek?

"Mr. Montana?"

Cade gave the persistent woman an uneasy smile.
"Miss St. Claire has been ill, and the humid weather
in Louisiana this season has been hard on her. Her
family is hoping the sunshine of Texas will revitalize
her."

The woman looked at Gabrielle's wan face, "It's
the best climate anywhere for what ails you," she
advised Gabrielle, her voice gentle. "You'll be feeling better in no time."

Gabrielle nodded. "Thank you," she whispered,
her uncertain glance sweeping the curious faces that
crowded close to see her.

Cade had intended that their arrival should go unnoticed, and as a precaution he had sent Billy Williams ahead two days before to inform Tom Rawlings
that he was bringing Gabrielle with him. He had
instructed Billy to tell Tom the entire story, hoping
to prevent just this kind of public spectacle. He
couldn't believe his partner would organize a home-
coming rally if he knew the situation. Perhaps Billy
hadn't made it for some reason, Cade thought with
concern.

From the corner of his eye, he saw Wyatt Fielding
angling through the crowd toward him. "I hope
you've come with a carriage and a way out of this,"

he said as Wyatt broke through the throng and moved up beside him.

Wyatt laughed and tipped his hat to Gabrielle, his gaze lingering appreciatively on her face. "I have. Just follow me." Within moments Cade was lifting Gabrielle into the backseat of a gleaming surrey, and Fielding was maneuvering the vehicle away from the congested dock area. Gabrielle drew a breath of relief and turned her attention to the woman sitting beside Fielding. She had pale blond hair, icy blue eyes, and the bearing of an empress. Gabrielle had never seen such a beautiful woman.

During the hasty introductions Gabrielle learned that the beautiful woman was Wyatt Fielding's sister, Lacy. She also discovered that Lacy Fielding had more than feelings of friendship for Cade Montana. Her manner was forthright and self-contained, but every time she looked at Cade, a hint of vulnerability showed in the depths of her blue eyes.

Lacy turned sideways in her seat to face Gabrielle. "I overheard Cade's explanation for your trip. I do hope the air here will help your condition."

"Thank you," Gabrielle replied after a split-second hesitation. She looked at Lacy thoughtfully. Although her cultured tone had sounded solicitous, her smile was not sincere.

Lacy's white-gloved hand flicked an imaginary speck on her sleeve before she turned to Cade, who sat beside Gabrielle in the backseat. "Wyatt and I have heard all kinds of hair-raising tales about your adventures," she said softly. "I was scared to death. Thank heaven you're back safe and sound. As a matter of fact, I'd like to plan a party in your honor."

Cade grimaced and shifted his weight, stretching his long legs out as far as he could in the confines of the carriage. Without thinking of the intimacy it implied, he rested his arm along the back of the seat behind Gabrielle. "Frankly, Lacy, I'm finding these celebrations a bit embarrassing. If I had done anything exceptionally heroic, I might feel differently."

"How can you say such a thing?" Lacy chided. "You negotiated some difficult contracts with the Europeans—"

"That was my job."

"You ran the blockade—"

Cade laughed. "As have many others on a regular basis."

"Not with a boat loaded with explosives," Lacy protested, her brows drawing together as she frowned slightly.

"Many have."

Lacy smiled, one brow lifting teasingly. "But not all of them look like heroes, and not all are destined to be a senator from Texas. The article in the paper—"

Cade's mouth thinned with ill humor. "Is that how the townspeople found out I was arriving?"

"I suppose so."

"Rawlings is always making everything into a damned circus."

"People are getting to know you," Lacy insisted, ignoring his displeasure.

Wyatt gave his sister a sidelong look. "They'd know him anyway. He owns half of Texas." He was silent for a moment before adding, "How long is Miss St. Claire planning to stay in Follettville?"

"She won't be staying in Follettville," Cade replied easily. "She'll stay at my ranch."

"But, Cade," Lacy objected, glancing quickly at Gabrielle before looking back at him, "What will people think?"

Cade shrugged and said sharply, "As you know, Lacy, I'm not a man who cares about what other people think."

Silence fell over the carriage, and it was Wyatt

who finally spoke. "Have any trouble getting out of New Orleans?"

Cade shook his head. "We left at dawn in a thick fog. By noon we had sunshine and a good trip."

"I hope you plan to stay in town awhile," Wyatt began, then broke off as he guided the matching grays around a buggy stopped in the road. "You've been gone a long time, and there's a lot to catch up on. The town is beginning to bustle since the war started."

"We'll only be staying a couple of days."

"Then you must invite Lacy and me out to the ranch," Wyatt insisted, throwing the words over his shoulder while he watched the road. "Maybe we could all go on a hunt. Sir Henry is still in town and he always loves to come out."

Cade laughed at the mention of Sir Henry and nodded. "I'll arrange something in a couple of weeks. I'll send a rider in to let you know the details."

Preoccupied by the conversation and feeling uneasy at its underlying tension, Gabrielle paid only passing attention to the tree-lined road they followed or the fine homes on either side of the drive. Not until the carriage stopped in front of an impressive brick manor did she realize that they had arrived at their destination. Cade had told her previously that they would be staying with Tom Rawlings during their time in Follettville.

Much to Gabrielle's relief, the farewells were brief. Once they were inside the Rawlings home, a butler ushered them down a long corridor and into a book-lined library much like the one at Camden Hill. A servant offered her tea while Cade, obviously familiar with his surroundings, poured himself a brandy.

A tall, dark-haired man entered the study moments later, and Gabrielle's first thought was that

Tom Rawlings, though older than Cade, seemed cut
from the same cloth. He was definitely not as handsome, but he had the same impressive virility. Like
Cade, he moved as if he were comfortable within
his own skin. The man's swooping dark brows lifted
demonically at the sight of her.

"Well, is this the girl?" he demanded.

Cade glanced up from his brandy. "I see Billy Williams explained the situation to you."

Rawlings's gaze remained on Gabrielle. "He left
less than an hour ago."

Cade nodded, his mouth twisting cynically. "That
little welcoming committee at the dock couldn't have
come at a worse time. Were you behind that?"

Only now did Rawlings turn his attention to Cade.
He held up his hands, palms out, indicating his innocence. "I'm not responsible for your reception,
and I sure as hell would have stopped it if I could
have. I can't believe you came back dragging a traitor with you. Where's your Southern pride?" His
gaze returned to the girl. "I would rather bed down
a rattler than a Union sympathizer!"

Cade set his brandy glass on a small table. "Tom,
this matter is none of your business. But just to set
you straight, Gabrielle and I do not have that sort of
relationship. She's here because the Committee entrusted her into my care."

With a derisive snort Tom walked over to Gabrielle, his mouth curling with contempt. "You realize
the effect her presence could have on your career,
don't you, Cade?"

Gabrielle overcame her momentary speechless-
ness. "I am not a spy, Mr. Rawlings, nor am I deaf
or stupid. Please stop talking about me as if I weren't
here."

Tom met her gaze squarely. "I did not address
you, young woman. I was speaking to Cade." He

turned. "Don't give me any bullshit about what kind of relationship you have with her. It's obvious why you dragged this little chit back here. Just look at her! She's silky as a panther cub and probably just as mean."

Gabrielle couldn't believe her ears. "Sir, how dare you!" she cried, her cheeks flaming, "Who are you, with the manners and breeding of a brute animal, to stand in judgment of me?"

Rawlings regarded her calmly. "In my home I say what I please."

All of Gabrielle's pent-up rage and frustration rose to the surface and fueled her fury. "I will not have you speak to me in such a way!"

"Sit down and hush your mouth, young lady."

"I prefer to stand."

Tom Rawlings seemed to swell with rage. "By God, you arrogant little chit, you are in my house."

When he tried to push her into a chair, Gabrielle slapped him.

To her disbelief, Rawlings raised his own hand to strike her back. An instant later Cade stepped between them, catching the man's uplifted wrist.

"Tom," he warned, his voice steely, "I can't sit back and let you strike Gabrielle." He released his hold. "I think you know that."

Tom drew in a breath and retreated, straightening his black frock coat. "You sure have a hellcat on your hands."

Cade's expression remained uncompromising. "Gabrielle has been raised in a good home, by a fine man. Tyler St. Claire is a close friend of mine. If I'm to stay here, you must treat her with respect."

"I don't see anything to respect about this wild-haired gypsy," Tom flared, waving a hand toward Gabrielle.

"Well, you will."

Tom, his anger seeming to disappear as quickly as it had come, poured himself a drink, "So you're her guardian?"

"I am."

Tom rubbed his jaw. "She sure packs a wallop. Is she any good in bed?"

Gabrielle stared at Tom Rawlings, horrified by her own violent behavior and outraged by his. Even though she had rarely fainted in her life, Gabrielle knew she was going to now. She heard a buzzing in her ears and saw black dots gathering before her eyes. In an instinctive gesture she put her hand to her forehead.

Cade, seeing her sway, caught her in his arms. He carried her to a chair and sat her down. "Take a deep breath," he said softly.

Eyes closed, Gabrielle inhaled, trying to ward off the blackness. She didn't want to show weakness before either one of these men. The heated conversation between Cade and Rawlings drifted about her.

Cade looked up, angered. "Tom, you just scared the hell out of her. Now, watch your manners and your language. You know how to behave like a gentleman. If you continue to carry on like a goddamned fool, we won't be able stay here."

"She's a spy."

"She's a young girl who was infatuated with a son-of-a-bitch."

Rawlings downed the contents of his glass. "Yeah, I know Ruben Guillotte as well as you do."

"Then you know what a tricky bastard he is. I won't allow you to terrorize her. She's gone through a lot in the last few days—she's exhausted and scared. Believe me, she's paying a big price for what she did."

Unmoved, Tom poured himself another shot of brandy. "So are you."

"I'm helping out a friend. I owe him a debt."

Tom shrugged, then walked over close to Gabrielle. "She sure is a pretty thing." He turned. "But being pretty don't keep 'em from acting stupid."

"I want your word that you'll be a gentleman," Cade demanded, unwilling to let Tom skirt the issue.

"All right. You have my word. Now go ahead and take her upstairs. Her room is next to yours and there's a key in the lock. I'll have Ruby stay with her. I'd appreciate it if you'd come down later so we could talk a little business. I've had some problems with the damned Mexicans over in Matamoros."

Amusement warmed Cade's blue eyes. "Do you think perhaps these problems might be due to your charming ways?"

Rawlings laughed, picked up a crystal brandy decanter, and sniffed it. "Could be, Montana. Could be."

Gabrielle had her own room, a consideration she would have appreciated if it had not been locked from the outside. She had to knock when she wanted to leave and wait for a servant to answer her summons. A young black girl accompanied Gabrielle wherever she went; she was never allowed to go anywhere unescorted. What annoyed Gabrielle most was the armed guard who sat at the end of the hallway. The Mexican slouched in a tilted-back chair, holding a rifle across his knees, his wide-brimmed sombrero pulled low on his forehead. Every time she ventured into the hallway, the front legs of his chair would hit the floor, and he'd tighten his grip on the rifle and watch her with insolent brown eyes. Gabrielle was convinced that Tom Rawlings had installed the guard only to humiliate her and reinforce the impression that she was a prisoner, not a guest in his house.

She hated the three days she spent in Follettville. She rarely saw Cade. From conversations she overheard between him and Rawlings, she knew he had business to take care of before leaving for the ranch. Because she wanted to avoid her abrasive host, Gabrielle spent most of the time in her room, going downstairs only for meals. Cade had told her bluntly that if she wanted to eat, she would have to appear at the dinner table. With rather poor grace, she had finally agreed. She dreaded mealtime, however, not only because of her dislike for Tom and her resentment of Cade, but because she found their dinner conversations boring. How long could two men discuss politics, business, and war without tiring of it?

However, she did learn a great deal. She found out that Tom was an extremely wealthy man with a lot of power in Texas, and that he had a high regard for Cade's strong leadership qualities. He was anxious for Cade to enter the senatorial race, as was a group of regional business leaders.

That's what Texas deserved, Gabrielle thought, a hooligan like Cade helping to run the state. He'd probably be elected, too, but Cade flatly refused to run until the war was over. He said too much work needed to be done, and politics was the last place in the world to accomplish it.

Tom seemed to relish Gabrielle's dislike of him, and he even promoted it. He was rude and boorish, and every other word he uttered was a curse. To her disgust, he was inclined to pat the rumps of female servants, and he didn't care who noticed.

As Gabrielle sat at breakfast her last morning in Follettville, she only half listened to the two men talk. She was thinking instead of Lacy and Wyatt's visit the night before. It had not been exactly unpleasant, but it had left her feeling disquieted. Wyatt had been most attentive, and she liked his elegant charm and wry humor. but she didn't like Lacy and it was obvious that Lacy didn't like her. Lacy also didn't like the idea that Cade was the guardian of a "female of marriageable age." She had even suggested, in a cultured and faintly sympathetic voice, that it might be wiser for Gabrielle to stay in Folletville where doctors would be available, and Wyatt had agreed.

After Cade declined, Gabrielle had seen a carefully hidden flare of resentment in Lacy's blue eyes before she took a deep breath, smiled, and changed the subject.

Tom Rawlings had been on his best behavior for the Fieldings, and Gabrielle wondered if he saved his barbarian act just for her. She glanced across the centerpiece of roses to his place at the head of the table. Tom Rawlings had all the trappings of wealth—his servants were well trained and mannerly, his home was tastefully appointed—but he lacked quality. She sighed audibly when she realized they were discussing politics again.

"Why should the Mexican government go along with your plan?" Tom inquired, breaking open a roll and spreading strawberry jam on it.

Cade's mouth slanted ruthlessly. "Money. They can make a lot of money from this transaction."

Having listened to as much of their conversation as she could tolerate, Gabrielle folded her napkin and stood up. "If you'll excuse me, please."

Tom shook his head. "I'd like you to stay. I have something to say that concerns you."

Gabrielle stiffened. "I would rather not."

Without answering, he motioned for her to sit with a wave of his hand. Gabrielle hesitated, then complied only to prevent a scene.

Tom looked at Gabrielle in a way that made her uncomfortable before he turned to Cade. "What do you intend to do with Gabrielle?"

She felt color rise in her face. Tom acted as if he were referring to a house wench. She opened her mouth, an angry retort on her lips, then choked back the words when she saw Cade's reaction. He had started to take a sip of coffee and had stopped in mid-motion. After a split second he set the cup down. Cade was seldom cautious, and his action surprised her.

"I'm going to take her to the ranch. You know that already."

"What happens if she escapes?" Tom persisted.

"I won't stay here and listen to this," Gabrielle said angrily.

"Yes, you will." Tom motioned to the door, and one of the gunmen, who always lingered just out of sight, materialized in the doorway. Gabrielle glanced in disbelief from the Mexican to Cade. He nodded for her to sit down, and she did so.

Tom's dark features were set with determination. "The girl could be an embarrassment and a handicap to you politically, whether you run for the Senate this year or not. You have acted on behalf of the government in areas of diplomacy often in the past, and it would be damaging if it leaked out that you are harboring a traitor to the South."

Cade leaned back in his chair, his expression guarded. "I'll deal with that when it happens."

"She's a traitor," Tom continued. "You're protecting a Yankee spy on one hand, and you're helping the South on the other. The two just don't mix."

"Get on with it, Tom," Cade broke in. "And quit trying to convince me that you have my best interests at heart."

Rawlings nodded. "All right. You're Gabrielle's

guardian. I want you to give me permission to marry her.''

Gabrielle couldn't believe her ears. She leaned forward, hands braced against the table. "But you're old enough to be my father!"

"I am not too old to marry you, girl—"

"You're crazy! You've done nothing but ridicule and humiliate me ever since I arrived."

Rawlings leaned back in his chair, eyes narrowing. "You have some very attractive attributes," he said bluntly. "Marriage to you would suit me and solve Cade's problem and yours." He glanced at Cade. "Lacy doesn't like the idea of this girl going out to your ranch, and she's right. She's thinking what everybody else will be thinking. If Gabrielle is sick, why doesn't she stay where there's a doctor?"

Cade shrugged. "I've made no commitments to Lacy. You know that and she knows it. I don't give a damn what anyone else thinks."

Gabrielle jumped to her feet. "I will not marry him," she said flatly.

"You will marry me if Cade gives me his permission," Rawlings thundered, banging his hand on the table.

"I will not!"

Cade interrupted their heated exchange. "Tom, I plan to take Gabrielle to the ranch."

"And my offer?"

"I'll think about it. You know, of course, I would take Tyler's opinion into consideration."

"What about mine?" Gabrielle demanded.

Cade looked at her. "And yours."

Tom snorted indignantly. "This is an honorable offer of marriage. She's lucky to have even that." He pointed a finger at Gabrielle. "What does the future hold for you, girl? Nothing. You should think about that. With me, you'll have a fine home and a rich husband. I know women are attracted to me, so don't pretend you're not. And as my wife you will have a certain prominence in the community."

"What about my passion for spying?" Gabrielle snapped scathingly. "Aren't you afraid it will taint you?"

Tom laughed. "I'm too rich for that to be a problem. And I'm already tainted; people like me that way." His face sobered. "But there wouldn't be any more spying. Not in this house."

Gabrielle stared at him. "I would *never* marry you, Tom Rawlings. I don't even like you."

"I don't care whether you like me or not. If Montana gives me permission, I'll be your husband." He turned to Cade. "You are a man of honor, and Texas needs you. If this young woman manages to ensnarl you and the truth comes out about her, you're finished. There's something else to consider, too. The girl is tempting, but what happens to her later? She can't go back home for years. Will she continue to live out there on that ranch after you marry Lacy?" He tapped his fingers on the table. "I have something to offer you both. A way out for you, Cade, and a decent life for Gabrielle."

"Decent!" Gabrielle sputtered. "What would be decent about a life here? You've got gunmen standing around as casually as if every home had them. You strike your female servants on the backside. Your speech is deplorable, you drink, and you're willing to marry a woman who hates you!"

Cade glanced at Gabrielle's furious face. Her cheeks were flushed with color, her green eyes snapped, and her hair shimmered and curled about her shoulders, throwing off sparks of light as she moved her head. She was beautiful, but despite the feminine softness of her slim body she looked invincible. He watched as she whirled around with a rustle of skirts and swept past Tom's bodyguard with a look that would have stopped any man. He couldn't help admiring her show of courage. She had held her own just fine.

"It certainly looks like you've made a good impression, Tom," he observed, suppressing his desire to smile. He stood up and dropped his napkin on the table. "I've made a commitment to Tyler to take care of Gabrielle. Just what that will involve, I'm not sure yet, but I do know that I'm not going to turn her over to the first randy gentleman who sees her."

"That may be," Tom retorted, "but my offer stands. I know what I want. I like her; she's feisty. We'd get along just fine after a while."

Cade's mouth twisted at the thought. "I'm sure."

Chapter 6

Six outriders who had arrived from Cade's ranch the night before, escorted them on the last leg of Gabrielle's journey into exile. The small caravan left Follettville midmorning, and by noon Gabrielle drooped in the carriage, already hot, bored to tears, and worn out. She was amazed at the size of Texas. The countryside had seemed enchanting at first, merely because of its difference from Louisiana, but it quickly grew monotonous as it remained unchanged, hour after hour. Gabrielle observed long, undulating sweeps of grassland broken only by clumps of trees along creek beds and ravines. Overhead the high blue skies provided unlimited space for a spiraling hawk, which was her only distraction during the entire morning.

Cade had not ridden with her as she had expected, deciding to ride with the men instead. As the minutes dragged by, Gabrielle envied them their freedom in the saddle. Although heavily armed against the possibility of Mexican bandits or renegade Indians, they seemed unconcerned about any threat. In fact, the men appeared to enjoy the excursion. Cade rode with the grace of a centaur, as if he and the horse were one animal, while she bounced uncomfortably along in the carriage as they followed a bumpy road that consisted of a faint line of wagon tracks.

Infrequent rest stops and bits of occasional fragmented conversation provided her only respite from boredom. The stops, she learned, were solely for her benefit. Apparently these men could ride forever without resting.

Before they left Follettville, Cade had introduced her to his foreman, Sam Fortune. She assumed that his position was similar to that of her uncle's plantation overseer. But the overseer had always been scrupulously polite in her presence, while Fortune's cold gaze made her shiver. She bit her lip, feeling a wave of despair at the scorn she must endure. Then, recognizing her self-pity, she lifted her head defiantly and refused to feel even a twinge of defeat. These uncouth Texans played by different rules from the men she had known. Even Cade seemed to undergo a subtle transformation. He was back to wearing a gunbelt and Western clothes, and carried a rifle in a scabboard on his saddle.

The day dragged by slowly. As the sun dropped on the horizon, a red-gold mist spread across the land, but Gabrielle was too exhausted to appreciate the beauty of the sunset. Her hair straggled from her upswept chignon, and she had long ceased trying to pin it back into place. Her straw hat had been flung on the opposite seat. A simmering resentment accompanied her fatigue as she considered that Uncle Tyler would never expect a woman to undertake such a wearying journey without providing some luxuries, refreshments, and suitable companions to see to her needs. Cade had no right to make her endure such hardship.

The sun had already set by the time they finally stopped for the night. While the men set up camp, Gabrielle wandered along the creek bank. When

Cade suggested she assist in preparing dinner, she gave him a chilling look and walked out of sight among the willows. She would not cook over a campfire for this ragtag bunch of Texans even if she knew how. Finding a spot where the water ran clear and sparkling over a bed of rounded pebbles, Gabrielle washed her hands and face. Still kneeling, she pressed her hands, cold from the water, against her fevered cheeks. Never had she dreamed she'd be brought so low as to wash in a creek like a poor dirt farmer's wife.

When Gabrielle returned to camp, she took one look at the small tent set up about twenty feet from the campfire and set her soft mouth in rebellious lines. She could not even stand upright inside the thing. How could Cade think it would be adequate for her needs?

Cade regarded her impatiently, then motioned to a log drawn up by the fire. "Have a seat, Gabrielle. The food's almost ready."

Deciding not to comment, she sat and glanced resentfully at Cade as he stood talking to Sam Fortune. She watched as he removed his low-crowned hat and ran his long fingers through his hair. The silver that ringed the hat brim caught the firelight, and she stared at it, entranced for a moment, before she looked at him. He was a study in shades of brown, and she shivered slightly at the handsome image he presented. He wore a fawn-colored shirt and leather vest. His rugged features were starkly handsome in the flickering light, and his thick hair, a rich seal-brown color streaked with bronze, fell casually over his forehead. He listened intently as Sam talked, his dark brows drawn together, their swooping arch causing his expression to look most fierce. After a moment he muttered a curse at something Sam said, one that Gabrielle could read on his lips, and she looked away quickly. Cade's powerful presence made her even more uneasy here than it had in New Orleans.

Some beast howled balefully in the distance, followed by a chorus of others. Gabrielle glanced doubtfully at the men, then at the shadowed trees surrounding the camp. A full moon glowed brightly in the night sky. As another howl cut through the still air, a prickle of anxiety crept along her backbone. Pushing a wisp of hair into her untidy chignon, she weakly assured herself that if there were cause for concern, the men wouldn't be lounging about the campfire as they were now.

She crossed her arms over her chest, her annoyed glance sweeping the men who sat about the fire. Exhaustion, discomfort, and an undefined fear made her irritable. She longed to take a bath and then to have Hetty brush out her hair and braid it for the night. She had never realized before how comforting those routines were. She wanted to fall into bed and sleep against clean white sheets edged with lace like the ones on her bed at home. She closed her eyes, engulfed by a longing so intense that it left her weak.

"Ma'am."

The man who had spoken thrust a tin pan of beans and flat bread into her hands, and she accepted it automatically. She stared at its contents in disbelief, recoiling at the thought of eating it. She watched the man's broad back as he walked away, then regarded the tin pan again, angry indignation jolting through her. She rose to her feet and stalked over to where Cade sat eating by the fire with his men.

"I cannot eat this food," she declared, dropping the tin pan, which banged against the ground, spilling the contents in the dirt. "It's not fit to eat!" She glanced around the circle of faces, waiting for their reaction, but only Cade looked up.

"I cannot sleep in that tent," she plunged on recklessly. "I hope you do not expect me to."

Cade tipped is hat back. "Well, you're in a bad spot, aren't you? There is no other food and the tent was set up for your convenience."

"Don't expect me to be *grateful* for that tin pan of beans," she retorted angrily. "You are not without means, Cade Montana. You could have brought decent food. We would not feed our slaves food like this!" she snapped, waving her hand toward the spilled contents. "I know it's not necessary to travel like this! Travel can be a civilized activity if it's done by civilized people!"

Cade rose to his feet and rested his hands on his gunbelt. "I suppose, Gabrielle," he intoned warningly, "that you're going to have to make do."

Her eyes flashed angrily, even though a little voice in the back of her head urged caution. She obviously had no choice but to endure these deplorable conditions as best she could, but she didn't have to be nice about it. "Well, I suppose I *will* have to!" she snapped. She turned to walk away, then whirled back, her skirt flaring around her legs. She could not let him have the last word. "I believe, however," she said tightly, glaring at Cade across the fire, "that you are insulting me deliberately. I should not have to travel under these conditions or without proper companions. I'm quite confident this miserable journey is a deliberate ploy on your part to introduce me to the rigors of your primitive life."

"I think perhaps you're tired—" Cade began, an angry edge in his voice.

"Of course I'm tired," she retorted. "I'm exhausted. I've jolted myself senseless in that carriage. And now you suggest that I rest while wild animals howl all around me . . .'' Her voice broke, her hands clenching as amusement flickered across Cade's face.

"Coyotes," he said.

"What?"

"The creatures you hear are coyotes—and they aren't a threat to you."

Gabrielle stared at him, feeling so exhausted and unnerved that she could not continue. She was scared. Fear of this unfamiliar and threatening land gripped her as irrationally as a child's terror of the dark. Her glance slipped from Cade to the gun-toting cowboys who now watched her curiously, intrigued by her fit of temper but strangely unmoved by it. There was no sympathetic or reassuring face in sight, and her throat tightened with despair as she whirled around to stalk into the darkness.

Sam Fortune watched the swish of Gabrielle's skirts until she disappeared from sight, then he observed laconically, "Looks like your little plantation lady doesn't like us much."

Cade frowned and stared at the spot in the trees where she had disappeared. "She's so worn out she doesn't know what she likes." He clamped his hat on his head and tugged the brim. "I'll be back in a minute."

He walked out of the glow of firelight and listened intently. Past a slight rise he heard a scatter of gravel and followed the sound. Gabrielle was walking quickly, and he increased his pace behind her. Glimpsing her silhouette ahead in the moonlight, he lengthened his strides until he caught up, then slowed his step to match hers. For some reason she seemed smaller to him out in the open, and her profile appeared fragile in the moonlight. The wind blew dark curls across her face and pressed her skirts against her body, making her seem quite vulnerable.

"Let's go back, Gabrielle," he urged softly.

"No."

"It's not safe for you alone out here."

"I don't care about the coyotes," she snapped, her voice brittle.

"There might be an Indian or two."

She angled her steps away from him. "You're just saying that to scare me."

When Cade didn't answer she stopped and turned to him, her hands clenched at her sides. "I have never been so angry with anyone before in my life. I didn't like you the first night I met you, and I don't like you now. You're always so remote, so detached from others' misery. You're arrogant, Cade Montana, and you don't care about anybody but yourself!"

Her hand was lifted to the side of her head, holding back the tumbling curls that the breeze blew forward. Her bare arm was slim and shapely, and Cade thought of reaching out for it and grabbing her to find out what she felt like in his arms.

"What's the matter?" she taunted. "Cat got your tongue? Has nobody ever had the courage to confront you?"

He grinned, unmoved by her harsh words. "Well, I have to admit that you do it better than anyone else ever has. Tell me, who is it you want me to care about?"

"I don't want you to care about me personally, if that's what you think, but if you're Uncle Tyler's friend, you could show some concern for my welfare!" Gabrielle drew in a ragged breath. "I hate being treated like some detestable object. I hate being so tired I can't walk. I hate being hungry. I hate being ignored. I hate being alone, and most of all I hate you for making all this happen to me!"

Cade could have told her that *she* was responsible for what had happened to her, but he didn't bother.

The fact was, he didn't hear hate in her voice; he heard childlike desperation.

He let his gaze drift over the rolling hills, silvered by moonlight, then sighed. "Gabrielle, life here will take some getting use to," he said softly. "Give yourself time. The trip has been hard for you. After you've had some rest, you'll feel better about a lot of things."

He was moved by the expression of hopelessness that crossed her face, and instinctively he reached out and touched her cheek. The moment he did so, he knew he shouldn't have. Moonlight played over her, drawing his attention to her tender curves. His fingers trailed across the satiny skin of her cheek, traced her jawline, then dropped down to feel the pulse beat in her throat. It seemed like the most natural thing in the world to reach out and pull her close to him. Her lips were warm and soft, her breath was sweet, and her mouth trembled beneath his lips. The innocence of her kiss reminded him of her inexperience, and he knew he should stop, but he let his mouth continue to play over hers.

It was Gabrielle who broke the contact of their lips. Her breathing sounded shallow and fast, and her heart was beating like a frightened bird's, but Cade noticed that she didn't pull away. He kissed her closed eyes, her forehead, her neck, and the hollow of her throat. Her eyes fluttered open, and her delicate brows drew together in confusion for a moment before she moved away from him. Finally she spoke.

"Were I not . . . so unsettled," she informed him shakily, "I wouldn't have allowed you to kiss me." She turned and looked at him. "I suppose you forgot yourself, too."

Cade shook his head, thinking he would never understand the female mind. Everything had to be put in its proper place; even a kiss had to be categorized and labeled as a slip in judgment. "I suppose I did," he said softly.

Gabrielle still felt unsatisfied and wanted to establish an emotional distance from him. "I think I'll be going home pretty soon, so it's a shame everybody is going to so much trouble. Celeste told me she will tell Uncle Tyler the truth after Ruben escapes. Some of his acquaintances are going to break him out of jail, you know."

Cade paused to light a cheroot. "Is that right?"

"Yes." Her face seemed very solemn in the moonlight. Her slender hands unconsciously twisted together. "Aren't you beginning to believe me a little bit? I've told you over and over that I'm telling the truth."

Cade shrugged and gazed out at the darkened landscape. "It doesn't matter what I think, or what Tyler thinks. The Committee is in control now. If they tell me to send you back, I will. But until they do, you have to stay here."

"But what about *you*?"

"Look," Cade flared, his voice turning harsh, "don't put me on the spot, because I don't think you want to hear what I have to say."

"I want to know," she persisted.

"Your own uncle isn't even sure about your involvement in what happened. The Committee doesn't believe you. The facts say you did it. We found documents on you, and Ruben says you helped him. Still you want me to believe that you're innocent because you say you are?"

"I do."

Cade laughed softly. "Well, I can't do that."

Without a word, Gabrielle turned on her heel and headed back to camp.

* * *

Half asleep, Gabrielle rolled onto her stomach, burrowing in the warmth her body had left against the sheet. The cool air seemed to caress her skin as she stretched, waking up slowly. Remembering suddenly that she wasn't home she snapped her eyes open and sat up. They had arrived at Cade's ranch late the night before. She stared around the room, examining the peculiar Spanish architecture. Knowing Cade was a man of means, she had assumed he lived comfortably, but the style of his home had astonished her. It was lovely, even luxurious, but different from anything she had ever seen before. It had white stucco walls, arched doorways, patterned tiles, long verandas, and lots of plants and potted trees. Even as exhausted as she had been when they walked through the arched promenade into the central garden, she had been struck by its beauty. Its fountain and sweet-smelling flowers rivaled any she had seen in New Orleans.

She stacked her pillows against the headboard and leaned back. As unusual as it was, she liked the large upstairs room she had been given. It was airy and cheerful, with French doors that opened onto a lovely balcony that seemed to invite her to stroll down its shaded length. Large baskets of ivy hung from the rafters, and the scent of honeysuckle perfumed the air. It pleased her to see the vase of brightly colored flowers on the small table near the balcony. She loved flowers and loved to have them around her. She grimaced when she caught sight of her reflection in the mirror over the dresser. Normally her hair was brushed into a long braid at night, but now it billowed in a tangled auburn cloud around her shoulders, and she knew it would take forever to brush the snarls out.

She looked out the window, guessed that it was late morning, then dropped back against the pillows. How wonderful it was to sleep in a bed again instead of on that dreadful bedroll on the bare ground. In her mind she relived again the incident when Cade had kissed her in the darkness out of sight of the men gathered at the campfire. To her relief, she could remember it without shame. She could not deny her reaction to Cade's kiss. The fact was, she had gone limp with wonder and it had taken all the will she possessed to pull away. From now on she must be careful not to spend time alone with Cade. He was one of those men with handsome looks and a way about him that made women act foolishly.

At St. Teresa's Ladies' Academy she had heard plenty of talk about his kind, in hushed whispers late at night. Her friends had scorned such men, though they had seemed strangely fascinated by them, too. Then last spring one of her classmates had been sent home. Gabrielle had caught a glimpse of the poor girl as she had left, escorted down the stairs by her grim-faced parents. She had been pale, her eyes swollen from tears. The rumors had been that she was going to have a child, and the man responsible already had a wife. Gabrielle had felt contempt for her, as well as pity. Any woman who made such a mistake must be a simpleminded creature indeed.

But Cade's touch had had a frightening effect on her. Her mind had ceased to function, and a dizzying current had swept through every inch of her. For a few moments she had been utterly helpless. She shivered and turned over on her side, pushing the pillow away to lay her cheek against the bed. To prevent such "helplessness" from happening again, she must avoid Cade.

A knock sounded and Gabrielle sat up, staring at the heavy carved door. "Who is it?" she asked,

her brows coming together in slight irritation. At
Camden Hill, nobody disturbed her until she rang.

A Mexican girl opened the door. "Good morning,
senorita." She smiled faintly. "I am Maria. Senor
Montana is waiting downstairs. He wishes to speak
with you."

Gabrielle slid to the side of the bed and looked at
the brightly woven rug at her feet. "Tell him I cannot come down," she advised curtly. "I have only
just awakened. As a matter of fact, please arrange a
bath for me as soon as possible."

The girl stared at her wonderingly, then shook her
head. "You will have to tell him that yourself, senorita," she answered. Without another word she
pulled the door shut behind her.

Gabrielle stared at the door, then closed her eyes
in exasperation. With a softly muttered exclamation
she slipped out of bed and padded barefoot to her
trunk. "I might as well go down to breakfast," she
grumbled as she lifted the lid and searched through
the wrinkled contents for a dress to wear. It would
probably be impossible to get one of Cade's high-
handed servants to press something for her. Besides, now that she was awake, she was curious to
see her new surroundings in the light of day.

Some time later, Gabrielle was seated in the dining room across the table from Cade, listening with
growing confusion as he explained what he expected of her while she remained at the ranch. Her
breakfast sat untouched in front of her. Everything
Cade said made less and less sense to her.

"You are not a guest on this ranch, Gabrielle," he
went on, his tone reasonable and paternalistic. "You
live here now. I want you to feel at home, and if you
need anything, let me know." He put down his coffee cup. "Are you satisfied with your room?"

"Yes, it's fine." She nodded distractedly. "Thank you. But there is something I need." She watched his dark brows slant upward in question. "A personal servant."

He didn't move, but his eyes narrowed, and Gabrielle shifted uncomfortably. "I am accustomed to having my own. Hetty was born at Camden Hill, you know."

His mouth thinned. "Yes, I remember Hetty," he replied dryly.

Remembering the circumstances of their meeting, Gabrielle felt heat burn in her cheeks, but she kept her silence.

Cade leaned back in his chair, his blue eyes intent. "Tell me what she did for you."

Gabrielle was confounded by his question. Did he truly not know the services a lady's maid performed? "She was my servant," she answered slowly. "She did everything."

"Like what?"

Gabrielle searched his face for signs of mockery, but she saw that he was serious. "She knew the flowers I liked in my room and kept them fresh. She was a skilled hairdresser, although Celeste never thought so. She brought my breakfast, kept my dresses pressed, kept my jewelry in order . . ."

Cade lit a cheroot before returning his attention to her. "You don't need a servant," he assured her briefly. "All the things you mentioned you can easily do for yourself. I realize it will take time for you to settle into the routine of the ranch, so I'll assign you to different tasks. Once you find one you like and are good at, that will become your job while you're here. You'll start by helping Helen in the kitchen."

Gabrielle's fingers threaded tightly together in her

lap, her expression confused. "I'm not sure I know what you're talking about."

"This ranch is a functioning unit. Everybody has a job."

Gabrielle hesitated. "Are you talking about work?'

"Yes, I am."

She stared at him in bewilderment and responded sincerely, "But servants work."

His eyes darkened. "Gabrielle, there's a lot to be done, and you have a lot to offer. If kitchen work doesn't suit you, there's laundry and mending, or gardening and housecleaning. Helen has been my housekeeper for years. She'll help us decide what suits you best." He tapped his long fingers against the table top, regarding her thoughtfully. "In your spare time maybe you could teach some of the ranch children to read."

She shook her head in confusion. "But I'm not a governess," she objected. "Uncle Tyler hired a Creole woman to tutor Celeste and me."

Cade's mouth quivered, and for a moment Gabrielle thought he was going to smile. Instead his face became stern. "Gabrielle, this is Texas, and it's a different world from the one you're used to. You won't be allowed to idle your time away like you did in New Orleans."

"I did not idle my time away!" she denied heatedly.

Cade pushed his chair back and stood up. "All you did was entertain yourself—at teas, at the races, at picnics," he said flatly, dropping his napkin on the table. "You had so much idle time you were capable of getting yourself into a lot of trouble that was probably the result of pure boredom, and it will not happen here."

Stunned, Gabrielle could only stare at the clear-cut lines of his profile as he raised his voice and called to the young maid who had awakened her earlier. "Maria, send Zeke in, please."

Offended by Cade's unfair assessment of her life in New Orleans, Gabrielle gave the young cowboy who entered only a cursory glance.

Cade looked at Gabrielle as she sat rigidly at the end of the table. Her demeanor clearly revealed that she considered herself the victim of outrageous insult. "I'd like you to meet Zeke."

Gabrielle glanced briefly at the young man; he looked as out of sorts and sullen as she felt.

"I have asked him to accompany you wherever you wish to go."

"Oh, I see," she exploded bitterly. "I am to have a guard, is that it?"

"Let's just say you have protection," Cade stated calmly. "I've told Zeke what happened in New Orleans, because I felt I had to. If you wish to go riding, he will escort you." Cade turned to his young cowhand. "There'll be no exceptions to that rule. Do you understand?"

Zeke nodded. "Where she goes, I'll go."

"Well, it hardly matters, because I don't ride," Gabrielle answered leadenly, rising to her feet with the intention of ending the interview.

Cade frowned, and Zeke gaped at her. "You don't ride?" the young man asked incredulously. "But everybody knows how to ride a horse. It's easier than walking."

Gabrielle gave him a quelling look. "I don't ride," she repeated.

Shaking his head, Cade picked up his gunbelt and buckled it on with quick, efficient movements. "Then you'll have to learn. Zeke can teach you."

Observing Zeke's vindictive expression, Cade changed his mind. The boy would put her on a horse that would scare the hell out of her just for the fun

of it. "On second thought, I'll teach you myself.
We'll start this afternoon." Seeing the storm of reaction building in Gabrielle's green eyes, Cade held
up a hand to forestall her objections. "In this country, you must learn to ride, Gabrielle. That's final.
Out here the distances are too great to walk anywhere, and your survival may depend on the ability
to ride. Besides, it's a diversion you may welcome
as time goes by."

With that, to Gabrielle's chagrin, he strode from
the room.

"Senorita, it's time to wake up," a distressed
voice urged softly. "You're supposed to be helping
Helen in the kitchen. Don't you remember?"

Gabrielle's eyes fluttered open for an instant, and
she saw that it was barely daylight. With a groan
she pulled the pillow over her head, feeling the ache
of her sore muscles every time she moved. "Go
away," she moaned.

"Please wake up," the soft voice beseeched, "or
Senor Montana will be very angry."

"Leave me alone," Gabrielle muttered, easing
over onto her side and pulling the sheet up to her
chin. She had had her first riding lesson yesterday
afternoon, and the muscles in her thighs and hips
ached terribly. It would take days to recuperate and
it was impossible for her to help Helen in the
kitchen. A moment later she heard the soft click as
the door closed behind the young maid named
Juana. Gabrielle's body relaxed as she drifted once
more into sound sleep.

Cade watched Juana descend the stairs, her young
face troubled. She took things much more seriously
than her older sister, Maria. "Did you tell her to get
up?" he demanded.

Juana nodded. "I did."

"And?"

Juana wrung her hands. "She is still sleeping."

Cade stared up the flight of stairs, his mouth taking on an unpleasant twist. "Is she decent?"

Juana's eyes widened, "No, senor. She is wearing only nightclothes."

He brushed past her and took the stairs two at a time. "That's decent enough. You tell Helen that Gabrielle will be down in a few minutes. Tell her that my orders stand. She is not to start breakfast until Gabrielle arrives to help her."

Juana stared up at him. "But it's already an hour past due. Helen will be most upset." He didn't answer, and she watched as he disappeared down the corridor. Turning, Juana started slowly toward the kitchen.

Cade paused at the entrance to Gabrielle's room, then pushed the door open. She lay on her back with her head turned to the side, her face as serene as if she knew a dozen angels stood guard over her. Trust her to call his bluff and force him to take action, he thought. She was as contrary as any woman he had ever known. Her riding lesson yesterday had been merely a contest of his will against hers. His mouth tightening, he walked over to the bed and gazed down at her. Her hair curled silkily across the pillow, gleaming deep red and gold. Her lashes swept gently against her cheekbones. Her skin was fine-textured and dewy peach in color, and he wondered suddenly if the skin beneath her embroidered gown could possibly be as beautiful. It was enough to drive a man mad. He drew in a deep breath and silently cursed Tyler one more time for giving him such a temptation. Leaning over, he placed his hands on either side of her head. "Gabrielle."

Her eyelids flickered.

"Wake up."

The stern voice reached into the depths of her sleep. Gabrielle's eyes opened and closed sleepily, then opened again. At the sight of Cade's face she inhaled sharply, her emerald eyes widening in confusion. "What . . ."

"Gabrielle," Cade said, a muscle flexing along his jaw, "you have to be downstairs in the kitchen to help Helen in ten minutes. Do you understand?"

Her slim brows came together in bewilderment. Her hand caught the sheet and pulled it up to her chin.

"Gabrielle!" he said sharply, his expression harsh. "I meant what I said yesterday. You will work today, do you understand?"

She nodded.

"I will not come up here after you again. Do you understand that also?"

"Yes," she whispered.

"Fine. Then we have an agreement, do we not?"

"Yes."

Cade straightened, and Gabrielle stared at him, paralyzed with shock. No man had ever been in her bedroom in her entire life, not even Uncle Tyler. Without another word, Cade turned to leave, and she watched the swing of his broad shoulders as he walked out of the room. When the door banged shut behind him, she stared at it without moving for several long moments, her heart beating frantically. She wasn't sure why she had agreed so readily to his demands, but he had startled her by barging into her room. She pushed tumbling curls over her shoulder and slipped hurriedly out of bed.

She pressed her hands against her cheeks and looked around the room, her thoughts coming fast. When Uncle Tyler found out that she was being threatened, that she was forced to perform the work

of servants, he would be furious. She stumbled over
to the armoire and threw open the door. In fumbling
haste she drew her petticoats over her head and tied
them at the waist, listening for Cade's booted steps
in the hallway. Had he said ten minutes? She
reached for a blue cotton print dress, struggled into
it, and fumbled with the tiny buttons up the front.
As soon as she finished, she turned to the dresser
and grabbed her brush. She smoothed her hair,
poured water into a bowl, and washed her face.
Even before it was dry, she headed across the room
and jerked open the door. She ran down the hallway, then came to an instant stop at the head of the
stairs. Cade was waiting at the bottom.

"I'm ready," she said, shifting nervously.

"Good."

The sting of pride prompted her to protest. "It
was terrible for you to come into my room and
threaten me." She moved quickly down the stairs,
pressing her body against the railing in an effort to
stay as far away from him as possible. "One
shouldn't have to suffer such abuse," she accused
breathlessly, slipping past him and turning toward
the kitchen.

Cade's eyes glinted with amusement. Gabrielle St.
Claire had been so flustered that she had forgotten
her slippers. When she realized that, he imagined
she would be quite embarrassed. Midway down the
hall she halted abruptly. Cade arranged his features
into severe lines as she turned slowly, confused.

"What's the matter now?"

"Nothing's the matter," she retorted, lifting her
chin. "Nothing at all." Moving quickly, she headed
barefoot down the back hallway.

Cade shook his head and turned down the corridor, seeking the haven of his study. Everybody in
the house was angry and upset, and he wanted to

get away for a while. He had realized he would have problems with Gabrielle, but the difficulties involved in integrating her into the routine of the ranch and into the lives of the others were staggering. He knew she had been pampered and waited on all her life, but he had never anticipated the ramifications of that fact.

She had been dressed by maids, her hair had been combed and arranged by Hetty; she hadn't even fanned herself when she got hot. His mouth twisted sardonically. Apparently the only exercise she'd ever gotten was in the pursuit of something she shouldn't be doing—like climbing down the trellis to meet that slug, Guillotte. Good God, he wouldn't be surprised to learn that Hetty had slept in her room just in case she needed a drink of water during the night! Cade entered his study and stood scowling at the paperwork atop his desk. Parties were fine, as were shopping and socials, but to have a constant life of it, spiced with nothing but a little embroidery on the veranda, would bore anyone, especially someone as bright and intelligent as Gabrielle. His dark brows swooped together in a frown. He had decided that during her first few months on the ranch she should be too busy to think about mischief. Once she had accepted the fact that she had to stay, he would soften his stance, but only after he had established that his word was law, and only after she had established that she could be responsible and reliable.

As Gabrielle walked into the kitchen she looked uncertainly at the housekeeper, who was pacing back and forth on the floor. Seeing Gabrielle, the woman stopped. "We are over an hour late with breakfast," she announced. "I don't think this has happened once in the five years I've been here."

"You needn't have waited—"

Helen placed a pan over the fire, her mouth tight. "It was an order," she declared. "Mr. Montana refused to let me start work until you came down. All the servants are waiting to be fed, Sam Fortune has been sitting at the table drinking coffee and scowling, and even Mr. Montana hasn't eaten yet. I don't know why he had to let others suffer just because you were still upstairs sleeping." She started pouring flour into a wooden bowl. "I was able to manage this kitchen before you arrived. I don't know why I'm not allowed to do a thing without you now." She measured ingredients for biscuits and started mixing dough. "My whole day is going to be thrown off and so is everybody else's."

Helen dumped the contents of the bowl onto the floured counter. "Where are your shoes?"

Gabrielle felt her face color, but she shrugged. "Sometimes I don't wear shoes. It's good for the feet, you know."

"No, I wasn't aware of that."

By the time the meal was served, Helen and Gabrielle were well aware of the enormous task that lay ahead for them. Gabrielle had never cooked in her entire life. She had never set a table, stirred a cake, or lit a fire. She knew absolutely nothing about the kitchen, and Helen was not the best teacher for her reluctant student. Helen had a lot to do, and taking the time to teach Gabrielle only made her own job harder.

In the next few days Gabrielle learned to dread certain aspects of her job more than others. What she hated most was touching raw meat. She hated seeing the plucked carcasses of chickens, and fried chicken quickly lost its appeal for her. She had never known that the wonderful roasts she had savored at home had oozed blood before they were cooked.

The work that went into cooking meals over-whelmed her. It was a never-ending cycle: planning, cooking, setting the table, serving, clearing, cleaning up in a hurry so one could start the entire process all over again for the next meal. The only time she was excused from her duties was for the riding les-sons she detested. All in all, her life was miserable. She could only pray that a reprieve would come from her sister before she was worn and broken and her hands permanently callused.

In that entire first week of work, there was only one afternoon of enjoyment. She helped Helen make a cake and put a wonderful thick frosting on it, dec-orating it with intricate roses around the bottom. Gabrielle had never seen anyone do that even though the chefs in New Orleans were extremely accomplished. She had to admit she wouldn't mind learning how to form those pretty frosting roses.

Numerous afternoons of riding lessons had also left Gabrielle sullen and resentful. Now another les-son had begun, and her nerves were stretched taut. She clung to the saddle horn with not a tad of the horsemanship Cade seemed to expect of her, but she didn't care. She didn't feel one bit more secure atop a horse now than she had before her first lesson.

"I want to get off. I don't like this." To her vex-ation, Cade continued to lead her mount around the corral, ignoring her demand. "Let me down," she fumed. "There's something wrong with this animal. His gait is impossible. He's jumpy and he's going to throw me."

Cade caught the bridle and brought the chestnut to a stop. "This mare is fifteen years old," he pointed out with exaggerated patience. "She hasn't ever thrown anyone, and there is nothing wrong with her gait." He gave the brim of his hat an irritated tug. "You're the one who's jumpy. Now just relax and ride."

Gabrielle gritted her teeth. "Let me down."

Swearing beneath his breath, Cade walked up to her side. "Gabrielle, you will ride today. We have been at this for days and you have learned nothing. If you don't get the feel of the horse—"

"I have the feel of the horse, I just don't like it!"

A muscle flexed along his jaw. "You have done nothing but crawl on the horse, and once you accomplish that feat, you demand to get down. Not today. You are going to ride around this corral until you can stay on the damned horse by yourself."

"I can't."

"It's that goddamned sidesaddle. If you can't stay on that thing, ride astride—"

"No! I will not ride like a man."

Her billowing yellow skirt rustled with the breeze, and the chestnut sidestepped nervously. With undignified fear Gabrielle leaned forward, clutching the horse's mane. "I want to get off," she insisted stubbornly, her voice trembling.

"No! You won't get over your fear until you give it a chance." He caught up the reins and forced them into her hands. "Now try it once again," he advised, slapping the horse's flank.

The horse trotted about the corral, Gabrielle bouncing about on its back with as much decorum as a clinging monkey. Her hat fell off her head from all the jolting, and her hair slipped from its pins, spilling around her shoulders.

Cade picked up her wide-brimmed hat and dusted it off against his leg while he watched her progress. After the horse had circled the corral once, he caught the reins she had dropped and brought the animal to a stop. "Now that wasn't so bad. You did just fine."

Anger flushed Gabrielle's face as she glared down at him. "Yes it was bad! I had not given you permission to do that!"

Twisting onto her stomach, she slid off the horse with ungraceful haste, slapped away Cade's steadying hand when she staggered off balance, and caught up her full skirts to walk away. "I don't need your help when I am on solid ground. I can manage that by myself," she spat.

"Let her break old Fireball," a man's voice called out. "She's good enough now to tame that old son-of-a-gun."

Gabrielle whirled, fire flashing from her green eyes. Five of Cade's men lined the fence railing like crows along a washline. From the grins on their faces she knew they were enjoying her clumsy attempts at riding.

Irate, and as imperious as an empress, Gabrielle stared from one to the other, her mouth compressed tightly. She did not say a word, but her displeasure was clearly evident. One by one the men stepped back from the fence and drifted away as Cade watched with surprise. These men were tough. Not one of them would cower from a band of renegade Indians, yet they slunk away from this fiery redhead like scolded children.

Gabrielle spun on Cade as if there had been no interruption. "You insufferable, mean, contemptible, arrogant ass!" She did not raise her voice but snapped out the words like ice. The only clue to her fury was the trembling emotion beneath every word.

With a disgusted sigh Cade turned to lead the chestnut into the barn.

"I will not allow you to ignore me," Gabrielle threatened, following close on his heels. "You are *not* going to perch me on top of a horse that I obviously cannot ride every afternoon for the rest of my stay here and then threaten me like a nasty-tempered child." As she caught her breath, Cade lifted the saddle from the horse and dropped it across a stall.

When he walked over to get feed she followed angrily. "If I want to get down, I want to get down! Do you understand?" Still he didn't acknowledge her, and Gabrielle grabbed the back of his shirt in frustration. "Listen to me when I'm talking to you!"

Cade whirled around so suddenly that Gabrielle stumbled backward. He caught her upper arms and stared into her startled green eyes. "No, you listen to me, Gabrielle St. Claire. You *will* learn to ride. You can get as goddamned ornery as you wish and make yourself as miserable as you can, but you will learn. I don't care if you trot around that corral for the next year." He released her and stepped back. "However, your lessons will be with Zeke from now on. I don't have the goddamned patience, and if I continue, I'm sure I'll wring your neck."

Taken aback but refusing to be defeated, Gabrielle lifted her chin. "Why are you doing this?" she asked, her voice low and taunting. "Just to best me, to prove that you can?"

Cade's gaze was level and direct. "Why are you resisting with such vehemence? You've learned nothing so far because you didn't *want* to. *You* made it a contest of wills."

Gabrielle clamped her mouth shut, unsure whether she recognized truth in his words or not. She did realize, however, that she would not get out out of her riding lessons. He seemed quite set on it. "Should I decide to learn, I won't have those men lining the fence to watch," she conceded grudgingly. To save her pride, she wanted to force a concession from him.

Cade laughed. "Why? Because you don't want

anyone to know how muleheaded and cantankerous you are?''

Gabrielle sucked in a sharp breath, the skin around her mouth paling. ''I would slap you for that if I didn't think you were the kind of man who would slap a lady back.''

Cade turned back to his work. ''Go on up to the house.''

''I will not,'' she responded, stiffening her posture. ''You are not going to order me about like one of your servants. Do you really expect me to jump when you say jump?''

He turned, his eyes narrowing. ''Yes, I expect you to do what I say. The fact is,'' he said, ''I expect less of you than I expect of anyone on this ranch. Do you know why? Because you don't know how to do a damned thing. If you didn't have someone to take care of you, Gabrielle, you couldn't survive a day out here. You couldn't survive anywhere. You are the most helpless female I have ever known,''

''I am not helpless in my own world,'' she thrust back. ''I am quite accomplished in polite society.''

''Your world is gone, and I'm trying to teach you how to live in this one.'' He started to turn away, then swung back, his gaze dropping to her face.

''What is it?'' she snapped.

''You've got dirt on your face.''

Gabrielle's hand flew to her cheek.

With a look of impatience, Cade stepped nearer. ''Here.'' He caught her chin and began to wipe the smudge from the side of her mouth.

The contact of his hand against her flesh caused electricity to jolt through her. Head lifted, she stared at the place where his shirt opened at the neck, reminded too late of his intoxicating virility and her own treacherous reaction to him. Pulse spinning, she saw the suntanned skin of his chest and the strength of his shoulders rising to his throat. The warmth of his fingertips near her mouth spread across her skin like a fever. Flustered, she looked up to meet his midnight-blue eyes.

"I must go," she whispered in a choked voice. But her words did not connect with her brain, and she did not move.

With agonizing slowness, Cade's hand flattened against her cheek. Almost reluctantly his gaze dropped to her mouth, and his thumb moved slowly to trace her lips. Mesmerized, Gabrielle sighed and leaned toward him, her mouth softening with expectation of his kiss.

"Good God, Gabrielle," he whispered as his arms went around her. "What are we doing?"

She shuddered as a crazy forbidden excitement swept through her at the warmth of his body against hers. She melted in his embrace and when his mouth touched hers, her heart stopped beating at the incredible sweetness of his kiss.

His hands spread out against the small of her back, and her arms lifted of their own accord to rest around his neck. Nothing had ever felt so right. In those wonderful moments rapture curled all the way to her toes and back up to wind itself around her heart. When Cade lifted his head, Gabrielle unraveled slowly from the tendrils of desire, her eyes dreamy, her cheeks flushed.

Then reality intruded with dizzying swiftness. Pulling away, she stepped back, replaying in her head what had happened and marveling at her own actions. She had made the advance, not him. She had invited his touch. Bewildered by her own nature, she stared at his handsome, tanned face. Breathing fast, she retreated until she bumped into the barn door. Then, feeling despair at her own lack of will, she turned and fled from the barn.

Cade watched her go, then shook his head, every bit as confused by the electricity that sparked between them as Gabrielle was. He leaned against one of the thick stable posts and bowed his head. Why had he told Tyler he would take Gabrielle? He had known right away it wouldn't work. Although he hadn't admitted it to himself, he had wanted Gabrielle since their first encounter on Tyler's balcony, and he never should have agreed to be her guardian when he wanted her as a woman.

Cade sighed and walked into the square of light coming in the open door. Even if Tyler had had doubts about the situation, he didn't have any other options. Cade squinted against the sunlight. Maybe all he needed was a distraction. Maybe he should invite Lacy and Wyatt out to the ranch for an early summer rodeo. The men on the neighboring ranches would enjoy it, and the women would love the chance to get together.

Over the next couple of weeks Gabrielle worked hard at learning to ride, but not because Cade wanted her to. Something Zeke had said set her to thinking. He had complained endlessly about spending time with her when he should be doing a man's work, and then he added, "I don't know why Mr. Montana bothers to teach you to ride. If you don't know how, you can't get off the ranch, and then he wouldn't have to worry about you. His reasoning doesn't make any sense to me."

It was true, and it had hit Gabrielle with startling clarity. She had said nothing, but from that moment on she had listened and learned. Zeke was continually critical of her progress, of course, but within a week they were taking short rides down along the creek. When she managed to ignore his sarcastic comments about her "darn-fool saddle" and about her timidity with the horse, Gabrielle found she enjoyed the excursions and, most of all, they got her out of the kitchen and away from Helen's demands.

Cade and Sam Fortune walked down the front steps of the ranch in the soft light of early morning. Cade took a moment to buckle his gunbelt about his hips while Sam rolled a cigarette, flicked a match with his thumbnail, held it to the tip, and inhaled. Once he had a smoke going, he fell into step beside Cade.

"The boys have got most of the strays rounded up, and they've been branding 'em for the last week. They're working up north of here near Maplewood Springs."

Cade angled his steps toward the stables. "What kind of numbers are they working with?"

Sam pulled a bit of tobacco from the tip of his tongue. "I'd say there's a thousand head at least."

Cade nodded. "I thought the calving would go pretty well."

Sam slowed his step and pushed his hat back on his head. "Ain't that Miss High-and-Mighty over there?"

Cade squinted in the light. The early morning sun formed a halo about the small figure, transforming the tumbled mass of her unbound hair into a brilliant red circle around her head. It was Gabrielle all right. No one else on the ranch had hair like that.

"What's she up to?" Sam asked.

Cade snorted. "Don't ask," he said. "When she has a problem it tends to tie you up for three days, at least."

Sam chuckled. "Looks like something's got the best of her."

Cade stopped and scowled in her direction. Gabrielle sat with her elbows on her knees and her hands propped against her dejected face. Her posture was very unlike her usual regal carriage.

Cade shook his head. "Well, dammit, Fortune, let's find out."

As they got closer, Cade could see that Gabrielle was perched on a stump, staring at a wooden crate that held two chickens. A small hand ax lay at her feet.

Hearing their approach, Gabrielle only glanced up briefly. Cade thought he had never seen anyone look so miserable before. "What are you doing?" he asked when it was evident that she wasn't going to speak.

She compressed her mouth glumly but didn't move. "I'm supposed to kill these chickens."

Her answer was so totally unexpected that it took a second to sink in. Cade met Sam's amused glance. The thought of Gabrielle St. Claire, who was raised to be Southern royalty, killing chickens was so ludicrous that Cade laughed in spite of himself.

Gabrielle looked up at him, offended. "I'm just not going to do it. I can't do it. I don't care what you say!"

Sam began to laugh. Cade looked at him, then at Gabrielle, then at the chickens in the cage, and had to walk away to hide his snickers. He wiped tears from his eyes before he turned back. "I'm sorry for laughing, Gabrielle. I really am."

Sam reached for the ax and held it in his hand. "Were you going to use this?"

Gabrielle's green eyes flashed with suspicion. She looked from one to the other before nodding.

Sam dropped down on a nearby log, threw his head back, and guffawed, unable to control his mirth. Seeing Gabrielle's growing indignation, Cade kept a straight face with difficulty.

"Who told you to do this? Helen?"

She looked accusingly at Sam. "Yes. She said Juana has been preparing chickens for the table since she was thirteen years old."

Cade rubbed a hand along his jaw. "Have you ever seen the, ah, process?"

Gabrielle nodded, and her expression paled. "A couple of days ago I did. Helen wrung their necks."

The thought of Gabrielle watching Helen wring a chicken's neck started Sam laughing again. Gabrielle jumped to her feet. "What's so funny about killing chickens?" she demanded. She looked in bewilderment from one man to the other. Their eyes were watering, and they looked as if they were about to explode with laughter.

"Nothing," Cade answered shakily. He took a deep breath, then walked over to the crate and opened the lid.

Gabrielle backed up in alarm. "You're not going to do it, are you?"

Sam started laughing again, and Cade shook his head. He tilted the cage forward, and the chickens tumbled out. Unaware of their close call with death, they ruffled their white feathers and strutted and clucked across the yard.

"I don't much like this kind of job, either," Cade told her.

Only slightly relieved, Gabrielle nodded.

Cade eyed her thoughtfully. Gabrielle had seemed withdrawn over the last few days. Maybe she needed a break from her routine. "How'd you like to ride out and see the herd today?"

She lifted her hand, shielding her face from the sun. "Now?"

Cade nodded. He watched her troubled features undergo a pleasant transformation as her face brightened. "I'd like to," she said, brushing tumbling curls from her face in a feminine gesture.

"Then go tell Helen you're coming with me. I'll harness up the buggy and meet you at the front door."

He watched as she took off, noticing a buoyancy in her step that he hadn't seen for days.

Sam tilted his head back, watching her go. "What'd you reckon Helen was thinking?"

Cade shrugged. "Helen's been a farm girl all her life. She doesn't have any idea how Gabrielle was raised."

Chapter 7

After that day Gabrielle didn't see much of Cade. He was busy with the branding and ranch affairs and was gone from morning till night. But that day stuck in her mind, and she vividly remembered every detail. Not just the branding, and the cattle, and the men as they worked, but things about Cade. What he said and how he said it. It had been one of the most exciting days of her life because it had felt as if they were courting. Every time he had smiled at her, or laughed, or brushed against her, her heart had either slowed or pounded. He had a very masculine manner, and it thrilled her to hear him give orders to the hands so confidently. She had to admit that he frightened her just a bit, but on the other hand, she wanted to touch him, to reach out and run her hands over him.

During the next week Gabrielle was too busy to think about much of anything. The entire housekeeping staff was preparing for guests. The Fieldings were expected, as was Tom Rawlings and various neighbors. An elaborate annual festival was planned. A rodeo was to be held—she learned from Zeke that a rodeo was an exhibition of skill on horseback. There would also be a barbecue and a dance, during which they would be serenaded by the Mexicans who worked on the ranch. It would be a rowdy affair, she surmised. Gabrielle thought of the beautiful, elegant balls she had attended back home, and in comparison the Texas socials seemed pitifully barbaric.

On the morning after the first of the guests arrived, Gabrielle was walking briskly along the flagstone path of the patio toward the kitchen, planning to have a glass of lemonade. At the sound of voices she halted beside the fountain, her mouth pursed with displeasure as she saw who was sitting on the veranda. Cade and Tom Rawlings appeared to be having a late breakfast. She had purposely waited until midmorning just to avoid running into Cade's guests.

Tom, the Fieldings, and a fat little Englishman named Sir Henry had arrived last evening, two days before the other guests. She had joined them for dinner, and it had been pleasant enough. She found Wyatt quite nice, and his attention was flattering. And in spite of her unfavorable first impression of both Lacy and Tom, the two had been in good humor and their conversation lively. Tom had said nothing more about his ridiculous marriage proposal. As a gentlewoman, Gabrielle could only pretend that the incident had never happened and hope that Tom would mind his manners in the future. She glanced back along the path, looking for an avenue of escape. Perhaps she could retrace her steps without Tom seeing her this morning. But that soon proved impossible.

"Don't run away, Gabrielle," Tom yelled out.

Her shoulder blades tensed at the sound of his voice, and she uttered one of Cade's favorite swearwords. Drawing a deep breath, she turned to face them.

"We've just finished feeding and don't devour little girls until lunch.'' Tom gave her a sardonic and knowing smile, as if he understood exactly how she felt about him. Without waiting for her agreement, he rose to his feet and pulled out a chair, looking her over in a way that made her blush. ''Come join us. I have something to tell you that I think you'll find most interesting.''

She lifted her skirt and maneuvered past the rose bushes. ''I wasn't running away,'' she retorted with a tilt of her chin.

Tom laughed, amused by her refusal to be intimidated. He rubbed his hands together with pleasure, as if he took personal pride in her undaunted spirit. ''I have word from your uncle, my pretty princess. If you'll mind your manners and be a good girl, I'll tell you what I know.''

Gabrielle's heart leaped at the mention of Tyler. All she could think of was that a reprieve had come. She forced herself to move sedately when in truth she felt giddy and lighthearted. She saw Cade glance at Tom questioningly.

At her approach Cade rose to his feet, and Gabrielle nodded in greeting. She took her seat quickly and busied herself with folding her napkin in her lap, just to hide her trembling hands. ''How did you happen to hear from my uncle?'' she asked. ''I wasn't aware you knew each other.''

Tom poured her a cup of coffee, then dropped back in his chair. ''I've known Tyler St. Claire for years, but I must tell you I didn't hear from him personally. One of my associates, Marv Delwoody, met with him in New Orleans last week. Delwoody is not on the Committee, but he is aware of your difficulty.''

Gabrielle felt a rush of heat stain her cheeks at the mention of her ''difficulty.'' ''Did Mr. Delwoody have news for me?''

"Yes, he did," Tom said. "Tyler told him to pass along his regard and tell you that everything is fine at Camden Hill. Tyler can't send you a letter yet, of course, but as soon as things cool down, he will."

Gabrielle shifted impatiently. "And what else?" she prompted. There had to be more. Uncle Tyler wouldn't be so impersonal as to inquire after her like an old-maid aunt.

Tom puffed on his cigar, divulging his information with slow relish. "It seems your sister is getting married in the spring."

Gabrielle's startled eyes widened. "To whom?" she asked, breathless.

"A neighbor by the name of Bienville."

Gabrielle's mouth opened in disbelief. "Phillip?"

"No, the older boy, Paul."

"She wouldn't marry him!" Gabrielle blurted out, her voice emphatic. She looked from Tom to Cade. "Celeste has never even liked Paul Bienville! Why on earth would she marry him?"

Cade shrugged. "Women have a way of changing their minds about things."

His complacence jarred Gabrielle's nerves. "That's not the case here," she returned sharply. She pressed her fingers against her forehead, her thoughts racing. Something was wrong, terribly wrong. "What about Ruben Guillotte?" she demanded suddenly. "What happened to him?"

Tom's face darkened with contempt. "The son-of-a-bitch escaped."

Gabrielle gripped the arm of her chair. "Oh, dear God! I knew it!" She leaned toward Cade. "I told you she was going to help him escape! I told you! Don't you remember? While we were alone in the stateroom Celeste told me she would tell Uncle Tyler the truth when Ruben was safe. She told me she had never meant me any harm but she couldn't let the man she loved hang. Don't you see, this is the proof I need. This is what I've been waiting for. Now she'll tell my uncle.''

"Nobody helped Guillotte escape," Tom broke in bluntly. "He hit a drunken guard over the head with the man's own gun, took his keys, and let himself out. It was as simple as that."

Gabrielle shook her head vehemently. "It only looked simple. I'm sure my sister helped him." She turned to Cade. "Don't you see this isn't a coincidence? Now she can tell Uncle Tyler." She leaned back in her chair, feeling as if a crushing weight had been lifted off her shoulders. "Thank God, it's all over."

Cade's penetrating glance brushed Gabrielle's flushed features. "Celeste hasn't told Tyler anything. It's still just your word against hers. And because she's marrying another man, the case seems even worse for you."

"No, no," she said. "The marriage must just be a rumor. Celeste will tell Uncle Tyler the truth now," she insisted. "I know she will." Suddenly her gaze faltered, and she sat up very straight. "Tom, had Ruben already escaped when Mr. Delwoody talked to Uncle Tyler?"

He nodded.

"How many days before?"

"A week, maybe more."

So a week after Ruben's escape, Celeste still hadn't said a word. Gabrielle shivered, suddenly cold despite the warmth of the day. Why would Celeste say she was going to marry Paul Bienville? Why would she withhold the truth? Gabrielle closed her eyes, feeling faint. Over the roaring in her ears, she heard Celeste's childhood voice. *I hate you, Gabrielle. I hate you because Uncle Tyler loves you best. I hate you.*

You're not even clean. You have a dirty face. He shouldn't love you best!

Seeing the blood drain from her face, Cade leaned forward. "Are you all right?"

Gabrielle took a deep breath and nodded, looking away from the question in his eyes. Celeste was going to keep the secret and let her bear the shame, she now realized. For the rest of her life people would think she was a traitor, no matter how many times she denied it. Devastated by the realization of what her sister had done, Gabrielle barely heard Wyatt Fielding as he strode through the archway.

"Hope I made it down in time for breakfast," he called jovially.

Gabrielle felt as if she were carved of ice. She watched as Wyatt lifted his arms in an expansive gesture, sunlight glinting in his well-groomed blond hair.

"My God, Montana, you've got the best place in the world. Every time I come here, I swear I'm going to buy a ranch of my own and run cattle. All I need to make this morning perfect is a cup of coffee." He pulled out a chair and sat down. "Are you going on the hunt with us today, Gabrielle?" he said, but then his smile faded. "Are you feeling well?"

"I'm fine, just a little tired," she answered woodenly. "I don't think I'll be going on the hunt, Wyatt. I—I have so much to do." She rose to her feet. "If you'll excuse me, please," she whispered leadenly before turning and walking carefully down the steps and into the garden. She felt such despair that she couldn't even cry. Ruben had escaped and Celeste hadn't kept her promise. Now the truth might never come out. She would be an outcast forever.

Hours later, Gabrielle stood at the window of her room and watched a dozen or so riders start off from the stables. The Fieldings, Tom Rawlings, Sir Henry, and a few of Sir Henry's English friends were in the party, along with a few ranch hands to help in case they shot anything. Zeke had gone along, so she knew she would be spared a riding lesson. Maria had said they wouldn't be back until late afternoon.

Gabrielle turned, her shoulders sagging. How could Celeste sink so low, she wondered. It was dishonorable and unfair to let someone else bear one's punishment. How could Celeste live with herself? Didn't the guilt torment her?

Gabrielle stopped suddenly, her pain turning to intent concentration at the thought that had come to her. She turned back to the window, eyes narrowing at the dust trail that was all she could see of the disappearing riders. It was time to go home. Today. She had to convince Uncle Tyler of the truth. She had to do that or accept the situation as it was. And living with Cade was driving her crazy.

Her mouth tightened with determination as a plan evolved in her head. Thanks to Cade's insistence that she learn to ride, she could manage well enough, and she thought she knew how to get to Follettville. With a little luck, and a lot of courage, she could make it. No one would stop her.

Gabrielle glanced around the room and decided she would take nothing with her. She didn't want to arouse the suspicion of the old man at the stables. Suddenly she twirled in a circle, feeling a wave of exhilaration. The timing couldn't be more perfect. The hunting party would be gone most of the day. Zeke, who usually hung about like an old hound dog, had gone on the hunt. Best of all, Tom Rawlings wouldn't be in Follettville to spot her by chance as she attempted to make travel arrangements. She didn't know exactly what she would do once she

reached Follettville. She would simply have to worry
about one thing at a time.

In less than an hour she was on her way. The old
man at the stables had saddled her horse without
question, talking about the heat the whole time. In
Cade's study she had found a hundred dollars and
took it without feeling the least bit guilty. She had
to have money for the trip, and her uncle would
reimburse Cade later.

As she turned from the lane to angle toward the
low line of hills, she kept the horse at a slow trot.
Thank heaven for Zeke's big mouth. He had mentioned during one of their rides that the rolling ridge
of hills lay on the right all the way to Follettville.
She knew that if she kept them in sight, she couldn't
get lost.

But by noon she began to think of important
things she might have brought along, like water. Her
mouth was dry, but her thirst didn't concern her
very much. On her journey inland they had passed
a small creek midway, and somewhere along the line
she, too, would cross it. Still, the sun was hot. Her
wide-brimmed hat protected her face, but the hot
rays seemed to burn across her back and shoulders.
Thank heaven she had remembered to wear her lace
gloves and her white blouse with the long sleeves
and high-buttoned neck. Otherwise she'd be sun-
burned like a farmer's daughter. She looked down
at her royal-blue skirt spread across heavy petticoats, thinking how miserably uncomfortable they
were. Her mouth crimped with bitter comfort at the
thought that it wouldn't be long before she'd be back
to the luxury of Camden Hill and enjoying the attention of decent servants.

She saw no one during the entire afternoon. As
the hours passed, worry began to plague her. How
long would it take before Cade discovered she had

gone? Would he notice right away, or would he be preoccupied with guests? She felt saddened by the thought that she might never see Cade again, but she was also relieved. Something about him made her weak in the knees—and in the head, too. How could a handsome, virile man make her act so silly? And how could her Uncle Tyler have thought that Cade would make an acceptable guardian?

Although exhausted by nightfall, Gabrielle did not stop to rest. She couldn't forget the howling coyotes she had heard before, and she felt safer riding through the night. For a while she planned what she would say to Tyler, and she played out her desperate entreaty to Celeste in her mind. Eventually, even her plans could not keep her awake. As the chestnut plodded onward, Gabrielle fell asleep many times, only to awake instants later, startled and panicky. Each time it happened, her glance sought out the moonswept hills, and her panic would subside when she saw them. As long as they stayed in sight, she would know she had not strayed off course.

As the black of night changed to dull gray, Gabrielle topped a rise and saw the dark line of willows that edged the creek bank. Relief spread through her exhausted body. The mare, smelling water, perked her ears forward and increased her plodding pace. A half hour later, as dawn turned the horizon a glowing pink, Gabrielle slid off her horse just before the weary animal waded into the water. Gabrielle's knees buckled when she hit solid ground, her legs too weak to support her. Stifling a groan, she lifted herself to her feet and stumbled upstream from the horse, then knelt and drank the clear, cold water from her cupped hands.

After quenching her thirst, she caught the horse's reins and pulled it back up on the bank. "We made it, didn't we girl," she whispered softly. Tying the

chestnut to a nearby log, she glanced up and down
the willow-lined bank. Reassured by the peaceful-
ness, she dropped to the ground with a sigh. A small
brown bird chirped overhead as Gabrielle leaned
against the grassy bank; she found its presence comforting. The sparrow wouldn't be carrying on quite
so contentedly if there were danger about.

With that thought in mind, Gabrielle fell asleep.

Hours later, she awoke and sat straight up in
panic. Frightened by her unfamiliar surroundings
she jumped to her feet, her heart pounding. Several
seconds passed before she remembered that she had
left the ranch and was going home. The horse stood
nearby, the sun was midway up in the sky, and the
stream rushed pleasantly over the rocks. She drew
a deep breath and let it out slowly. She had made it
through the night, and everything was just fine. She
estimated she could reach Follettville by nightfall.
Immediately upon her arrival, she was determined
to get transportation home. If Cade did come looking for her, she certainly didn't want to be found.
No doubt about it, he would be furious with her for
breaking his trust.

Disturbed by the thought, she turned on her heel
and looked westward toward the ranch. ''You
should have believed me, Cade Montana,'' she said
aloud. ''Trust is a two-way street. Ruben's escape
should have proven something to you. It should at
least have made you doubt Celeste.''

Feeling better, Gabrielle washed her face and
hands, then walked around a bit to ease her stiff-
ness. Using a rock, she managed to mount the mare
without too much difficulty. Keeping the hills to her
right, she headed off again.

About noon, she heard a peculiar clanking and
rattling. Indians! Her heart began to thud painfully.
After a few terrifying moments, it occurred to her

that Indians wouldn't be very smart to make such an awful racket. As she listened, she decided that the sound she heard had a rhythmic quality that wasn't very alarming. She reined the chestnut around and headed toward the rise that obscured her view. She saw a covered wagon so laden with goods that it seemed the wheels would surely sink into the ground. Mops and brooms and plows and harness were tied to the side, and the many pots and pans and spades and shovels glittered in the sun. A bearded old man and a young boy sat on the wagon seat. Gabrielle clucked to her mount and angled her course to intercept them.

"Hello there," the old man called out. "Where you headed?"

"Follettville."

He pushed his hat back on his head and nodded. "You're welcome to ride along with us, ma'am. That's where we're headed, too." He peered at her from under bushy gray eyebrows. "This here's my grandson, Josh. My name's Amos."

She nodded, her spirits soaring. "My name's Gabrielle, and I would welcome the opportunity for company."

She rode silently, listening to the old man ramble on about the early wild days when Indians were a constant threat. "You couldn't have ridden alone then, ma'am. You'd never have made it. Indians would have taken your scalp. They would have loved that red hair."

Gabrielle shivered at the thought. The old man fell quiet, and for a while the only sound was the clinking of pots and pans. He flicked the reins. "Mind if I ask what you're doin' out here alone?"

She hesitated, suddenly unsure just how much to tell him. "I'm on my way home," she said finally. "To New Orleans."

The old man nodded, sensing, perhaps, that she had said all she wanted to say. The boy, however, didn't have his grandpa's reticence. "How'd you wind up in Texas?"

Gabrielle shifted her weight, trying to ease a cramp in her thigh. "My uncle sent me here for safety, because of the war."

"So why you goin' back?" Josh questioned bluntly.

The old man nudged the boy with his arm. "That's the lady's business, not yours," he chided.

"Well, she ain't travelin' with nothing, like she mighta left in a hurry. I weren't bein' nosy. I was just thinkin' that if she's in trouble, we could help."

Gabrielle smiled down at his serious young face. "I appreciate your concern."

"Are you runnin' away?" Josh persisted.

She sighed. "In a way. My guardian is . . ." She hesitated, searching for words to explain. Before she could continue, the boy interrupted.

"What's a guardian?"

Her green eyes darkened. "Someone responsible for me while I'm here."

"Does he have say over what you do?"

"Yes," she answered flatly.

"You don't like him, do you?"

She wished suddenly that she had not been so forthright in her answers to Josh's questions. She was beginning to feel uncomfortable. "We see things differently," she said carefully.

Josh's brown eyes stared intently at her as she rode beside the wagon. "Did he know you wanted to leave?"

"Yes."

"But still you had to run away?" he asked, his voice rising with indignation.

"Kind of . . ." she paused, her voice trailing off.

She felt more than a little deceitful. Cade had not been cruel to her, and she knew the boy had the impression that he had been.

Josh's mouth tightened with determination. "If he ain't kin, then he ain't got no right to do a thing. You stay with us. We'll get you to town. Won't we, Grandpa?"

"She's welcome to ride along, boy," the old man answered, as if taking care not to commit himself.

Josh ignored the caution in his grandfather's statement. "You don't have to worry none." He lifted his rifle and grinned at her. "I know how to use this good, don't I, Grandpa?"

Amos looked at Gabrielle. "You'll have a hard time gettin' back into New Orleans. The Yankees have got it bottled up pretty tight."

"I'm aware that they have the city blockaded. But people are going in and out all the time," she told him. One way or the other, she meant to go home. If it were too dangerous to go by boat, she would journey over land.

For the next hour they traveled with only desultory talk. The boy bragged about his horsemanship and prowess with a gun in comparison to his friend in Follettville. Then, unexpectedly, a rider appeared at the top of a rise and reined up, his horse prancing nervously.

Her heart catapulting in her chest, Gabrielle recognized the buckskin horse with black mane and tail that Cade road. "Oh, my God," she whispered, "it's him! How did he find me?"

"Is that the man you're runnin' from?" Josh asked, straightening up on the wagon seat.

White-faced, Gabrielle nodded.

Josh caught up his rifle. "You don't have to worry about him none," he promised as he sighted down the barrel. "I'll scare him off real fast."

It took Gabrielle an instant to realize what he meant to do. "No!" she gasped in horror.

"Wait a minute, here!" old Amos yelled, pulling back on the lines.

But his words of caution came too late. In disbelief Gabrielle heard the gunshot and saw the spurt of flame from the barrel, and her frantic gaze flew to the man on horseback. The old man cuffed the boy and grabbed the rifle from him.

"That's Cade Montana, you young fool! Don't you recognize the horse he rides?" Swearing frightfully, he stood up and waved the rifle over his head. "Montana! It's Amos. The gunfire was a mistake!"

A moment later there was an answering salute, and the buckskin leaped forward.

Amos turned and scowled at Gabrielle. "He the man you runnin' from?"

She nodded without looking at him, then watched as Cade covered the grassland between them, his horse galloping. She swallowed hard when he reined up in front of them.

"Josh here did the shootin'," Amos apologized, his voice harsh, "and I'm sorry. He was all caught up with this young woman's story. She said a man was after her and Josh was tryin' to protect her. She didn't say nothin' about the man bein' you, Cade."

Grim-faced, Cade braced his hand against the saddle horn, his blue eyes fixed on Gabrielle. "Well, that's interesting to know," he said.

Amos, too, turned to her. "Ma'am, I've known Montana for years, and I have to say, even if you're a lady, I don't believe your story. This man would never harm you."

Gabrielle flinched from the coldness of Cade's expression, her heart aching from the scare she had experienced. "I wanted to go home," she explained, feeling a numbing disappointment that she had failed. "I didn't want anything to happen to you. I . . ." her voice trailed off as her vision swam and her distance from Cade seemed to grow. Leaning forward, she tried to draw air into her lungs. "I think . . . I'm going to . . . faint."

Cade slipped off his horse and caught Gabrielle as she doubled over and tumbled into his arms. He carried her over to the shady side of the wagon and laid her down. "You got some water, Amos?" he asked while he loosened the top buttons of her blouse.

Amos poured water from his canteen onto a rag and watched silently as Cade bathed her face. "These New Orleans ladies are sure different, ain't they?" he observed dispassionately.

Cade's mouth curled in a grimace. "They sure are," he agreed. As angry as he was, he couldn't help noticing how long Gabrielle's lashes were and how fine-textured the skin of her face was. A few freckles dotted the bridge of her nose, making her look young and vulnerable.

Josh edged closer, his face every bit as pale as Gabrielle's. "Mr. Montana, I'm real sorry about shootin' at you. I'm glad I didn't kill you or nothin'."

"Let it be a lesson to you. Know who you're facing before you fire a gun. It's a good thing to learn young."

"Yes, sir," the boy answered solemnly.

Most of the afternoon passed in miserable silence for Gabrielle. She hated the rush of emotions that made her angry and on the verge of tears. She hated feeling as if she had done something wrong even though she knew she hadn't, and most of all, she hated the humiliation of being caught and returned home like a runaway child. Cade's angry silence wore at her nerves, until finally she could stand it no longer. As tired as she was, and even though she told herself it didn't matter what Cade thought, she had to talk to him. She preferred arguing to silence.

"I need a drink of water," she called out irritably.

Without a word Cade reined in and removed the stopper of his canteen, then handed it over to her.

She drank, frowned at the metallic taste, then regarded him sullenly. "I suppose you're angry."

His steely gaze settled on her with uncompromising intensity. "What do you think?"

She returned the canteen. "I think you are," she stated matter-of-factly. "But I don't think you have a right to be." She pushed a silky auburn curl from her face. "I felt I had to get back home, and I tried to do it in the only way I could."

"You picked a hell of a time to leave," Cade retorted, unmoved by her reasoning. "I have a house full of guests."

She bristled. "Oh, I'm sorry I didn't choose a more convenient time for you. It seemed a perfect opportunity to me. You were occupied with guests, Zeke wasn't trailing me like a nasty-tempered hound dog, and I thought I had a good chance of success. I'll try to seek your opinion the next time."

The line of Cade's mouth was hard. "What the hell do I tell the Fieldings now? How do I explain your abrupt departure?"

Gabrielle glared at him, but his anger caused her gaze to waver. "You haven't told them yet?" A tinge of embarrassment pinkened her cheeks.

"They know you rode off and didn't come back," he answered coldly. "They know Sam Fortune and I are out looking for you." He remained silent a moment before adding cynically, "I'm sure they assume you are a very unhappy house guest, don't you?"

Gabrielle shrugged and looked away from him.

"I thought we had an agreement, Gabrielle. You're forcing me into a bad position. I don't want everybody wondering why the hell I'm keeping you against your will."

"That's your problem," she retorted, hating the guilt that assailed her. "I'm not a guest. I'm a prisoner, and I have a right to try to get away. I'm certainly not going to worry if I'm hurting your feelings."

"Goddammit!" Cade's features turned to stone. "I ought to lock you in your room when we get back and be done with this nonsense."

Gabrielle's heart tripped in her chest. "You won't do that," she challenged.

"Don't push me."

"Don't you think that would cause talk?"

Cade laughed cynically. "Before you took off, Lacy and Wyatt thought you were here for your health. What they think now is anyone's guess." His angry blue gaze swept over her. "I'll tell you one thing, Gabrielle. I'm not going to chase you every time you decide to take off. I've had it. If I find I have to lock you up to keep you put, I will. You asked me if I'm angry. Yes, by God, I am."

At nightfall they camped along the same creek where Gabrielle had stayed the night before. They had ridden all afternoon with only the most necessary words spoken between them. For supper Cade had given her some tough strips of meat that she had to tear at and chew like an animal. Even after she had eaten them, her stomach growled with hunger. By the time Cade spread out his bedroll it was dark, and the evening had turned chilly. Arms hugged around her, Gabrielle stared at the fire, pointedly ignoring him. He dropped onto the blanket, repositioned his saddle, and lay back against it, tilting his hat over his eyes.

Realizing that he meant to go to sleep, Gabrielle rose uncertainly to her feet. "What about me?" she demanded peevishly.

Cade didn't move. "You managed to get by last night," he said. "You can do the same tonight."

Gabrielle sat down in sulky silence, arms crossed over her chest. She knew Cade was grouchy, but no matter how angry he was, she felt certain he would not let her sit alone in the cold all night. He had a point to make and then he would relent. Determinedly she prepared to wait him out.

Wrapping her arms around her knees, she stared into the dying fire, hoping to get the last of its warmth. She must have dozed off for a moment, for she came alert suddenly, her heart thumping. Her gaze swept the dark trees ringing the camp. The night had grown intensely and forbiddingly quiet, and a shudder of apprehension traveled up her spine.

Cade lay motionless, and she realized he was sleeping. The brute! She could see the slow rise and fall of his chest. He didn't have any concern for her welfare. She dropped her head on her knees and closed her eyes, trying to fall asleep. Nothing bad was out there, she told herself. She had just dozed off again when a faint sound in the brush jerked her to wakefulness.

Holding her breath, she listened. Again she heard it—it sounded like a snapping twig. She rose to her knees, staring hard into the darkness. Was someone or something sneaking about? Gabrielle pivoted slowly, studying the trees behind her for movement. She turned back to the fire, realizing it had burned low and would go out if she didn't find more wood. Another twig snapped and she froze. She couldn't go into those trees to find wood if something was out there.

Gabrielle inched closer to Cade, her eyes searching the looming black trees. She heard no other sounds. Was somebody out there watching her? Or was her imagination playing tricks on her jittery nerves? An owl screeched, and she gasped aloud. Too scared to be proud, she crept over beside Cade and listened again.

"Cade," she whispered, teeth chattering with cold and fright, "I think there's something out there." She touched his shoulder, and when he didn't respond grew bolder and shook his arm.

He stirred only slightly.

"Cade, wake up. I keep hearing something."

His voice sounded muffled beneath his hat. "It's nothing," he muttered. "Go back to sleep."

As Gabrielle stared into the shadows, indignation began to mingle with her fear. Cade didn't have any right to let her suffer on purpose.

She nudged him again. "Wake up!"

With a scowl he pushed his hat back off his face and lifted his head. "What do you want?"

"I'm cold."

His blue eyes filled with disgust. "I can't do anything about that," he said, dropping back. "I've only got one blanket."

"Can I have it?"

"No. You wouldn't appreciate it if I gave it to you. I'm not going out of my way for you anymore."

"I *would* appreciate it," she assured him.

"I don't think so," he said, leaning on his elbow to study her. "You haven't appreciated a damned thing so far."

Gabrielle had no intention of getting into a quarrel. "Can I share?"

When Cade shook his head she clenched her fists,

her voice rising. "I know what you're doing. You're just being mean and trying to make me suffer. But you're going too far. It won't hurt you to share that blanket. It's cold and I'll probably catch pneumonia by morning."

"It's hardly proper that you sleep with me," Cade observed sarcastically. "Didn't your Southern up-bringing teach you that girls are not supposed to sleep with men who are not their husbands?"

She gritted her teeth. "It's hardly proper that I freeze to death, Cade Montana."

After giving her a doubtful glance he lifted the blanket and she slid in beside him. She snuggled greedily against his warmth, not caring if he despised her. Tucking the blanket tight around her, she huddled her arms against her chest, then closed her eyes with a sigh, savoring the heat from his body.

Cade stared up at the dark leaves overhead. If he had suggested sharing the blanket, she would have frozen to death before agreeing to sleep beside him. But because it was her idea, she had gotten damned persistent about it. A few minutes after she had fallen asleep, he turned toward her and dropped an arm across her waist. He sighed with resignation at the fragrant scent of her hair just beneath his chin. His earlier anger had disappeared, and he fell asleep thinking how good it felt to have her sleeping next to him.

By midmorning the sun slanted harshly through the willows and cottonwoods, promising a hot day. Cade had been up for hours, but he hadn't awakened Gabrielle. Despite his anger the day before, the bluish tinge of exhaustion beneath her eyes had worried him. It wouldn't hurt to let her have a couple hours of extra rest.

While she slept he had shot a wild turkey and was now roasting it over the fire. It had been sizzling and browning for about an hour and was beginning to smell quite tantalizing in the fresh morning air. He glanced at Gabrielle. Her breathing was deep and even, her face as innocent as a child's. Sunlight dappled through the leaves, catching fire in the rich texture of her hair.

Cade lit a cheroot, his face reflective. She shifted and rolled onto her back, waking slowly. She reminded him of a doe, fine-boned and exquisite, yet softly feminine. Even as beautiful as Lacy Fielding was, she seemed harsh and unappealing compared to Gabrielle. What did the girl have that made her so damned irresistible? Just looking at her gave him pleasure. She had pretty little ears and a long slender neck, and when she wore her hair on top of her head, he wondered what it would be like to press a kiss to the tender skin behind her ear.

Her movements in sleep became disturbingly provocative for Cade, so he turned and knelt by the fire to adjust the makeshift spit on which the turkey roasted. His mouth twisted cynically. Maybe sleeping beside her last night had been more temptation than he could withstand. If he didn't watch his step he'd be writing her poetry and swearing to avenge her honor like a foolish schoolboy.

He frowned and thought that as much as he didn't want to, he found himself believing her story. She had told him Guillotte would escape, and he had. He rubbed his palm along the black stubble on his jaw. Of course, what he thought didn't change a thing. As long as the Committee was convinced she was guilty, she'd have to stay in Texas. It was his responsibility to make sure she didn't leave. Turning, Cade watched as she stretched and blinked sleepily, looking charmingly mussed and refreshed from sleep. He planned to keep his opinion to himself until he knew for sure, but instinct told him she was innocent.

Gabrielle sat up and pushed her tumbling hair from her face. She saw Cade, observed that his features didn't look quite so uncompromising, and figured that his anger had diminished somewhat. Feeling a rumble of hunger in her stomach, she turned her attention to the meat roasting over the fire. "Um, that smells good."

She slid out from under the blanket and stood, no longer feeling the animosity of the night before, then walked over to the fire to investigate.

"What is it?"

"Turkey."

She nodded, her face intent. "Is it done?"

Cade suppressed a grin. "Almost."

"Good. I'm hungry." Gabrielle shot him a sudden suspicious glance. "Or are you going to eat it all and not let me have any?"

Cade stood up. "I'll give you a very small piece."

Her green eyes darkened, then a glint appeared in their depths. "You're teasing, aren't you?"

Tiny lines crinkled the corners of his eyes as he smiled. "Yes." Gabrielle laughed, and Cade found he liked the sound.

"Good, because I'm really hungry."

She ate with relish, consuming almost as much as Cade. When she was finished she sat back and sighed. "It tasted wonderful." Quite content, she looked about her. "It's really very pretty and peaceful here, isn't it? I like Texas. Not the servitude you force me to endure," she amended quickly, "but I like the openness. This big land makes me feel significant."

"It's not bad," Cade answered, kicking dirt over

the fire until it was out. He picked up his saddle and walked over to the buckskin.

Gabrielle followed, watching him thoughtfully as he saddled up. "What time will we get back?"

"Late afternoon," he said, pulling the bridle over the horse's ears.

"Are you going to lock me in my room?" she asked without changing her tone.

Cade hesitated, then threw the saddle blanket over the horse's back. "I don't seem to be able to get it through your head that you must stay in Texas."

Gabrielle stared at his broad shoulders and glossy dark hair. "We had a pleasant morning."

He turned. "And because you have been *gracious* for about one hour, I'm supposed to forget that you broke your promise to me and that I nearly got my head shot off?"

Gabrielle shrugged lamely. "It's a start. I find all this hostility uncomfortable, and it'll seem a long trip if we don't talk."

Cade flashed a taunting smile. "Well, we wouldn't want you to be uncomfortable. Not for a minute."

He helped her mount, and Gabrielle followed as he led the way, walking his horse along the creek bank, looking for a crossing. Finding shallow water that was easily forded, he headed up through the cottonwoods, ducking low-hanging branches. Gabrielle followed, allowing the chestnut to find the way while she thought about Cade. She knew he was trying to prove a point. Her exile could be pleasant or miserable, it was up to her. She also knew he usually did what he said he would do.

Without warning a furious flutter of flapping wings sounded and a black shape sprang from a tree branch directly in front of her. The creature flew so close over her head that she saw the claws curled against its chest and felt the rush of its beating wings. Instinctively she lifted her hands to protect her face at the same moment that her horse half reared. Unable to keep her balance, she toppled backward, rolling off her mount and landing on the ground with a bone-jarring thud.

Cade sucked in his breath with concern when he heard her scream. He pivoted the buckskin and galloped back, dismounting before the horse came to a full stop. He saw her roll over on her side, trying to pull air into her lungs, and he sighed with relief that she wasn't seriously hurt.

"You'll be all right," he told her gently. "You've just got the breath knocked out of you."

Straddling her, he caught his hands about her ribs and lifted her chest quickly. The second time he did so, Gabrielle sucked in a shuddering breath. Cade knelt at her side and supported her as she struggled to sit up.

"What was it?" she gasped, her face white.

He grinned. "You scared up a hawk."

"I tore my blouse on something," she said, her fingers touching the tear at her shoulder. Weak from fright and the jar of her tumble, she leaned against his strength. "It happened so suddenly."

"Is anything broken? You practically somersaulted off the back of that horse."

She shook her head. "I don't think so."

She started to rise, but Cade held her back. "Give yourself a minute. You've just taken a nasty fall." He brushed her auburn hair off her face. "This is why it's important for you to learn to really ride, not just sit on a horse. You have to be accomplished enough to handle the unexpected."

Closing her eyes, Gabrielle allowed herself to relax in his arms. She could feel the beat of his heart, hear the rumble of his voice as he talked.

"When I saw you fall I was afraid you had broken your neck."

Gabrielle shuddered, then opened her eyes and saw his hand on her arm. It was square and strong, his skin darker than hers. Why did she find it so compelling? Her gaze slipped along the length of his muscular thigh, and she realized with a shiver how much bigger he was than she. An unexpected flush spread across her skin. Being so near him made her feel female, and she was strangely conscious of her blouse rubbing over her tightened nipples. She went still and felt strange little chills rippling from each point of contact with him. She turned to look at him, afraid he might read her thoughts. An instant later her gaze dropped to his mouth.

Cade saw the flickering change in her expression, and his body reacted like gunpowder at the touch of flame. With a swift intake of breath, he drew back. "No you don't. I'm not interested in you playing passionate virgin again." His voice had turned ragged and a little angry.

Despite her innocence, Gabrielle moistened her lips with the tip of her tongue, knowing instinctively the ways of seduction. "What are you talking about?" she asked, her voice a breathless whisper.

Her compulsion to touch Cade became irresistible, like the need to stroke a dangerous animal that was too beautiful to resist.

"Please don't look at me so fiercely," she murmured. Amazed by her own boldness, she reached up her hand and touched his cheek, noting how pale her fingers were against his skin. Her gaze returned to his mouth and then she rose to her knees and leaned forward, pressing her lips ever so softly against his.

"Don't do this, Gabrielle," Cade warned, holding her away. "Don't push me too far."

"Why?" she murmured with thoughtless daring, her feeling of power escalating. "What happens when you're pushed too far?"

"You don't know what the hell you're doing."

"Do you?"

"Yes."

"Show me."

Cade searched her fine-boned features, now flushed, and his hands tightened on her upper arms. With his heart pounding a maddening rhythm, he pulled her close, her soft sigh sounding like a siren's song in his ears.

Eyes closed, Gabrielle surrendered to a melting world of sensation. Her mind seemed sluggish, and only her body reacted. She didn't know when she lay back on the grass, or when his length half covered hers. She felt his hands on her and the roughness of his clothes. His weight molded to her, and the subtle aggression became his, not hers. Gentle endearments sounded in her ears, exciting and soothing at the same time. When his hand lifted to the first button of her high-necked blouse, she lifted her chin, her heart fluttering. He undid the other buttons in rapid succession, his experienced fingers moving quickly between her breasts and down her midriff. She heard his breath catch as he brushed aside the fabric of her bodice and viewed the soft mounds of flesh faintly visible through her chemise. Even this flimsy fabric was drawn aside, and thrills rippled across her skin when his fingers stroked a tantalizing circle around each peak. Then his hand slipped upward, closing warmly over her softness.

"You're beautiful, Gabrielle. God, unbelievably beautiful."

The words sent a wave of pleasure through her. His breath fluttered warm against her throat, and her toes curled as his mouth traveled closer and closer to her breast. Gabrielle shuddered at the touch of his mouth, but fire curled in her belly when his tongue slowly stroked her nipple. His hands and whispers seemed to take possession of her. Each moment carried the excitement of a new sensation, and she found the confidence of his touch thrilling. Every unfamiliar caress caused her to stiffen with breathless apprehension, but each time Cade would hold her and kiss her until she melted in his embrace once more. When he finally lifted her and pulled her petticoats and skirt up over her hips, Gabrielle opened her eyes in sudden alarm.

"Cade," she whispered, her voice shaking.

"Don't be frightened, sweetheart," he soothed, pushing her petticoats underneath her as a cushion. "I want to feel your skin against mine." His words sounded muffled against her throat as his arms slipped around her again, his body warm and strong.

His hand moved up under her short chemise, slipping over the curve of her hip. Gabrielle bit her lip in pleasure as his tongue circled her nipple once again. Shamelessly she arched her body upward. His fingers were tracing patterns on the inside of her thigh, moving closer and closer. His tongue slipped inside her mouth just as he touched her. She whimpered at the spiraling sensation that swept over her. His tongue mimicked the movement of his fingers, and Gabrielle's whole body began to quiver at his touch, her hips arching toward the wondrous sensations his fingers created.

Faintly she became aware that his body had moved over hers. She felt the tickle of his chest hair against her tender, sensitive breasts and the exciting pressure of his hard man's body against the soft warmth of hers. Instinctively she knew he could satisfy the aching need inside her, and she was almost mindless with desire. Then she felt his knees nudge her legs apart. The unexpected and frightening action caused her to draw a sharp breath.

"It's all right, sweetheart," he whispered, softly and slowly kissing her forehead, her nose, the corner of her mouth. His strong body trembled, and she wondered at the intensity of his need.

He smoothed her hair back from her forehead, and she closed her eyes, calmed by his gentle touch. His mouth covered hers, and his hand lifted her hips. But the disturbing, probing pressure scared her. She felt a sharp, tearing lunge as part of his body slipped into hers. She gasped in pain and turned her mouth from his.

Cade dragged in a shuddering breath. "I'm sorry, Gabrielle, I didn't want you to feel pain." He kissed her eyelids, her mouth, her throat. "It won't hurt anymore," he promised softly.

He didn't lift away from her but instead remained motionless, and she felt only a fullness inside her. Then he began to move slowly, ever so slowly. She stiffened, afraid of more pain, but his movement felt surprisingly good, like warm honey flowing deep inside her, and soon the hurt was forgotten. She held her breath as each slow, steady thrust ignited a liquid fire within her. Her arms slipped around his back, and she clung to him, pressing her breasts against his chest, arching toward the growing sensation. Her mouth opened, and her kisses became as greedy and demanding as his. Shamelessly she responded to the rhythm of his body, until the passion inside her gathered tighter and tighter and her small, striving body could not contain it. It seemed to explode in waves, leaving her gasping and shaking from pleasure.

Cade lay over her, breathing raggedly. When his heartbeat finally slowed, he looked down at Gabrielle. Her long lashes stood out against her skin, and a scattering of freckles crossed her small nose. Her pleasure had been obvious.

"You're beautiful, Gabrielle. So warm and soft and responsive. You were made for loving," he said softly, kissing the tip of her nose.

A faint smile curved the corners of her mouth. "Yes. It was . . . wonderful."

Cade chuckled softly, then, lifting away from her, he shifted to his side. Gently he ran his hand over the rounded contour of her breasts. They were beautiful, with unusual delicate pale pink tips that made them look incredibly tender. Brimming with contentment, he allowed his gaze to drift down over her, marveling at how curvy such a slim form could be. He reluctantly pulled the edges of her intricately embroidered chemise across her breasts, his lips brushing the tip of each one before he fastened the tiny pearl buttons. Her dress had been bunched about her rib cage, and he drew it down to cover her hips. If he continued to look at her, he would be aching to make love again.

Gabrielle sighed, finding the moment too precious to disturb. Her bones seemed to have melted, and she felt heavy and languorous. She heard Cade rise to his feet and a faint rustle as he dressed, but she didn't want to move. "You've got leaves in your hair, princess," he teased, dropping down beside her. His low voice sounded wonderful to her.

Gabrielle brought her hand up to her chest, feeling the thin cotton of her chemise. Then the image of her former classmate at St. Teresa's Ladies' Academy intruded on the soft haze of her mind. She couldn't remember the girl's name, but she could vividly remember her shamed posture as she crossed the foyer with her parents. As swiftly as a lightning bolt, the implication of what she had done struck her. She had lost her virginity, forever. She sat up so suddenly that her head spun. Sweeping the tumble of hair away from her face, she stared through the leafy shade of the trees. She had been so smugly superior to the poor girl's plight at the time, but now she, too, had fallen.

Cade saw the stricken look on her face. "Are you all right?"

"I'm never going to do that again."

One eyebrow rose. "Is that right?"

"Never," she repeated with conviction. Drawing in a deep breath, she forced herself to look into his eyes, knowing that if she didn't, she would never be able to look at him again. "I forgot myself. I simply wasn't thinking."

A half-mocking expression crossed his face. "Well, it isn't much of a thinking activity," he drawled.

"And it was not what I expected." A slight quaking had started in her voice.

"Oh? What did you expect?"

"I don't know," she stated simply. Her cheeks flushed with color, and an explosive feeling of vulnerability welled up inside her chest. It suddenly became very important to her to maintain her dignity and control. She had to prove to him, and to herself, that she had not given away some vital and integral part of herself, that she was still Gabrielle. It would help to put the episode in the proper perspective. "I think what we did was much too personal to be quite right. Taking off one's clothes is—well, I just don't think one should."

Cade nodded, his mouth curving with unconscious tenderness. "No one ever told you anything about what happens between a man and woman?"

Showing a bit of her natural arrogance, Gabrielle regarded him indignantly. "Of course not. I was properly raised."

"I see." Cade grinned, amused by her naivete. "I rather enjoyed being . . . too personal with you. I think you're quite wonderful."

Gabrielle heard the amusement in his voice and saw the sparkle in his blue eyes, and her fragile façade of control collapsed. Humiliation and loss dropped over her like a shroud. She clapped both hands over her face, took a long, shuddering breath, and held it so long that Cade grew concerned.

"Gabrielle?"

Her cry sounded like that of a wounded animal, then she began to sob, rocking back and forth. Cade stared at her in growing horror, then rose to his feet, running his hands through his thick dark hair. He looked around the shady spot that moments before had been a perfect lover's hideaway and wished he were someplace else.

Her sobs intensified and he scowled down at her, observing with great discomfort that tears were dripping through her fingers and dropping on the soft rise of her breasts. Jesus Christ! He stalked over to the buckskin, then paced back to her. Each shudder doubled the guilt that gnawed at his conscience. How could he have found her so sensual and exciting before when now she seemed so distressingly helpless and vulnerable?

Cade lit a cheroot, then grimaced at the acrid taste and flicked the cigar toward the creek. He picked up his hat and settled it on his head, waiting for her fit of remorse to play itself out. What a price to pay for a few moments of pleasure, he thought uncomfortably. He drew in a deep breath of relief when she began to calm down.

Gabrielle dropped her hands into her lap. Cade gazed uncertainly at her. Her eyes were red and swollen from crying, and she didn't look exciting and sultry anymore; she looked young. She glanced

up at him and saw his annoyance, and her face
crumpled. She gulped as if she were choking,
pressed her hand against her mouth, then started
weeping again.

"Gabrielle . . ." he began after a moment.

"Oh, be quiet," she sobbed and struggled awkwardly to her feet.

Sunlight cut through the fabric of her chemise as
if were translucent and revealed the thrust of her
breasts. He glanced away in embarrassment. Her
enticing shape seemed out of place with her tear-
streaked young face.

Feeling as awkward as a schoolboy, he reached
down, picked up his gunbelt, and buckled it around
his hips. He had never found the aftermath of lovemaking difficult before. Why did he go dry-mouthed
and speechless with an inexperienced girl like Gabrielle?

"Are you going to be all right?" he inquired
lamely.

"Yes," she whispered, wiping tears from her
cheeks.

Cade stared at her and was struck by the magnitude of what he had done. This tantalizing creature
happened to be the favorite and cherished niece of
his best friend, she had been born to a life tanta-
mount to Southern royalty, and he had just taken
her with all the casualness with which he would take
a tavern wench. He was paralyzed by the responsibility of having bedded someone like Gabrielle St.
Claire.

He had forgotten all notions of honor, responsibility, and Southern gentility when he had taken
Gabrielle in his arms earlier. It had seemed as if they
were the only two people in the world, alone in a
desert paradise, and he had thought only of the softness of her skin, the gentle fragrance of her hair,

and the warm, passionate way she responded to his touch. But he was a man of honor, and Tyler trusted and respected him. He had breached that trust, and now he had no choice but to accept full responsibility for his actions by offering to marry Gabrielle.

"I'll get in touch with Tyler right away," he said heavily. She turned and looked at him. He noticed that a tear glistened on the tip of her lashes and fell to her cheek when she blinked. "Why?" The question had a weighted quality and a stillness that made Cade uneasy.

"To tell him I'll marry you." He watched her mouth drop open. She looked so stunned that Cade felt it necessary to explain. "Tyler is my friend and I respect him." Still she stared at him. "I will not dishonor you by failing to offer marriage."

Bewildered, he watched white-hot fury flame over her young face. Her eyes narrowed, and her lips compressed until they turned white around the edges.

"You—you polecat!"

Cade frowned at her. "What's the matter with you?"

"How dare you!" She sucked in an outraged breath and clenched her fists. "How dare you! Do you think I'm some old-maid aunt who has to press a man into marriage? How dare you look at me like I'm the last thing on earth you want and then ask me to marry you! You rat! Cade Montana, you'd better hear this. When I marry a man, he'll love me." Her mouth thinned with loathing. "I wouldn't marry you, anyway."

She turned to stalk away, then whirled back. Cade noticed with a flip in his stomach how her breasts jiggled beneath her white cotton chemise.

"I want a man from my world, one who's gentle, who listens. I want a life in which things are refined and planned out properly." She observed the rugged planes of his handsome face and thought that all his attributes now seemed like shortcomings. "You're too big and too wild, like this stupid, primitive country you live in. This would never have happened to me in New Orleans. I would have had a courtship and flowers. A man would have *asked* to kiss me, even to kiss my hand." Her nostrils flared with fury. "You don't understand any of that. You're too impatient. You made me forget who I am and what I was born to. You're overpowering, and I don't like that." Her mouth trembled, and to avoid the threat of tears, she grabbed her blouse, pulled it on, and began to button it up with quick, angry movements.

Taken aback by her refusal and intimidating temper, Cade glowered at her. "Sounds to me like you want a man who does embroidery, too. With a husband that goddamned weak, you'll have to wear the pants in the family." His gaze dropped to her blouse—it was torn, grass-stained, and fastened up wrong. "You'd better check your buttons."

"Oh, just hush," she gasped, an angry flush burning on her cheeks. Tears started flowing down her cheeks again as she attempted to button her blouse correctly. "I've gone through too much . . . to have you . . . mock me now," she choked out brokenly.

Cade watched her slim fingers thoughtfully, noticing that they were trembling. The alienation he'd felt seemed to drift away, and he felt sorry for her. He also thought she looked quite beautiful. Her green eyes were bright with tears, her hair was tangled wildly about her shoulders, and her nipples pressed against her chemise, reminding him of delights he had been too quick to dismiss. The view was covered as she fastened her blouse again. Marriage to someone like Gabrielle St. Claire might be a damned sight more interesting than he had first thought. Any man in his right mind would want her, and he would have no difficulty getting used to having her in his bed at night. Suddenly he felt a peace settle over him as if some missing pieces had settled into place. No doubt about it, they would marry. As he walked toward her, Gabrielle looked up and, unable to read his expression, began to back away.

"Come here," he cajoled, reaching out and catching her arm.

Looking cornered and unsure, she shook her head.

Ignoring her efforts to get away, Cade pulled her against him, imprisoning her struggling body. "I'm sorry if I've hurt you," he whispered. "I truly am." He knew that with some rest, she would change her mind. She was overwrought and exhausted and couldn't think clearly.

His soothing words seemed to open the floodgates again. Gabrielle stood in the circle of his arms and wept again like a child.

"It's all right, Gabrielle. Go ahead and cry."

Chapter 8

Night had fallen by the time they saw the glow of the lights at the ranch. Music and laughter floated in the still air, and Gabrielle could see dozens of buggies and carriages in the moonlight. The festivities they had been planning for weeks appeared to be in full swing. Her heart quaked at the thought of so many people. All the surrounding neighbors and many friends of Cade's from Follettville had been invited. But she couldn't face anyone now. Not a single soul.

Cade, his face shadowed beneath the brim of his hat, caught the reins of her horse and drew the animal to a stop beside his buckskin. Gabrielle's manner during the afternoon had disturbed him. She had flung up a wall around herself, one he had been unable to penetrate.

"We'll ride in the back lane."

In the moonlight he saw her nod. He wanted to say more, but he didn't want to risk shattering the fragile control that seemed to hold her together.

"All the guests will be at the dance, but if we should run into anyone, I'll tell them you went out for a ride and lost your way. They may not believe it, but you don't owe them an explanation."

She nodded again. She wanted nothing more than

to get away from Cade. She couldn't look at him without burning with shame and regret. Maybe she couldn't blame him, because he had tried to push her away at first, but, dear God, how could she have known where it would lead? How could she have known that the sweet, warm yearning that laced her heart and soul and body would result in such a shameful act? But *he* had known, she thought bitterly. He had known that she would be gripped by some sleepy, numbing sensuousness that would make her a willing partner to his masculine desires. With heart-stopping vividness, she remembered Cade's touch and her uninhibited responses. Her face flamed. She hated him, pure and simple.

She squeezed her eyes shut for a moment. All she wanted to do was go to sleep and forget it had ever happened. The day had been scorching hot. Heat waves had risen above the prairie, distorting her vision, and with each passing hour the elements had seemed to sap more energy. Even now, in the cool of evening, she could feel the tremble of exhaustion in her legs, and her eyes felt gritty when she blinked.

They traveled in silence along the dark lane of trees behind the ranch, the horses' hooves sounding muted against the earth. When they reached the back entrance, Cade dismounted and came around to help her down.

"Gabrielle, we need to talk," he insisted, his tone worried.

She lowered her head and slipped from his hands. "I can't." A fleeting shadow in the darkness, she ducked inside the doorway.

Cade caught the door before it closed. "Wait, please."

She hurried along the unlit corridor toward the servants' stairway, praying Cade would let her go.

A voice at the head of the stairs stopped her in her tracks.

"Who's there?"

Gabrielle peered upward and pressed her hands against her heart with dismay. It was Lacy. The wall lantern reflected the silvery blond of her hair and outlined her profile as she moved closer to the banister. "Gabrielle!" her gaze shifted to Cade as he emerged from the shadows. "I'm so glad you found her!" Then she frowned and asked, "Did you have an accident?"

Cade swore silently. "She's fine . . . she just had a bit of a fall." Without a thought of the intimacy it implied, he touched Gabrielle's arm and ushered her to the foot of the stairs. "All she needs is some rest."

Lacy stared at the two of them. "When did you find her?" she asked, her voice faltering.

"This morning," Cade answered.

"My dear child," Lacy murmured, insincerely, "how terrifying it must have been out there . . . all alone." Her gaze flicked over Gabrielle's dust-stained face and clothes again. "If you will send Maria up," she suggested, glancing at Cade, "and ask one of the servants to prepare a bath, I'll stay with her. I don't think she should be alone."

Lacy's words roused Gabrielle from her exhausted stupor. She didn't want to spend a single moment with Lacy, especially now. "Please," she begged, "don't feel that you must miss the party on my account."

"Nonsense," Lacy answered, dismissing her objection. "I've been there all evening. Nobody will miss me the few minutes I'm away." She glanced at Cade with faint reproach. "The same doesn't apply to you, however. You should get cleaned up, Cade. Your guests outside are wondering if their host plans to make an appearance at his own party."

She smiled at Gabrielle. "Come on, my dear. You look as if you're ready to drop."

As Gabrielle ascended the stairs, Lacy's blue eyes met Cade's. "Don't worry about a thing. I'll take care of her."

With a doubtful glance at Gabrielle, Cade nodded. He saw no way to avoid Lacy's offer without arousing suspicion. "Thank you."

Maria washed the grit and dust from Gabrielle's hair and rinsed it clean with fresh water. She worked quickly, helping with a minimum of words. Completing the bath in short order, Gabrielle dried herself and allowed Maria to slip a soft gown over her head. Her face pale and strained, she dreaded having to deal with Lacy, who waited for her just beyond the Chinese folding screen. Why had the woman insisted on staying? Kindness seemed an unlikely motivation.

As if she understood Gabrielle's dilemma, Maria smiled sympathetically. "I'll dry your hair and brush it out," she offered, following Gabrielle into the bedroom. "Then you can get to bed. You look asleep on your feet."

Gabrielle nodded and sat down at her dressing table. She gripped the arms of the chair while Maria briskly towel-dried the mass of tangled curls.

Lacy's blue taffeta frock rustled like crackling ice as she rose to her feet. "Maria," she said pleasantly, "you've had a long day, and it must be near midnight. Please go on to the celebration. I'll stay with Gabrielle."

When Gabrielle nodded her agreement, Maria handed the brush to Lacy.

"I've been concerned about you," Lacy said. She lifted a strand of Gabrielle's wet hair and drew it through her fingers. "Tom and Wyatt wanted to go

out looking for you, but Cade wouldn't let them."
She laughed softly. "He said he and Sam would be
more successful without anyone spoiling the tracks.
He told them to play host until he returned."

She lifted the mass of Gabrielle's hair high on her
head and studied the girl's reflection in the mirror.
"You have wonderful coloring, my dear. I've always
admired red hair."

Gabrielle shifted uneasily. "Thank you."

The slender lines of Gabrielle's neck and shoulders and the fine texture of her peach-hued skin
stood out in the mirror. Lacy's mouth twisted bitterly and she let the damp curls fall. "Were you trying to run away?" she inquired casually.

Gabrielle felt her heart stop. "No, of course not,"
she objected too quickly. "I only meant to go for a
short ride. This country is so big that I got lost."

Lacy pursed her lips. "Fortunately for you, Cade
found you."

"Yes."

"All the while you were gone," Lacy continued,
"I kept wondering why Cade didn't send a search
party. I swear he seemed to know exactly where you
were headed." She shrugged carelessly, her voice
light. "Just between the two of us, I thought perhaps you had gotten homesick . . . and I thought
maybe you had . . . run away. I thought maybe you
wanted to go back home."

Gabrielle winced as the brush caught at a snarl in
her hair. She could almost see Camden Hill and the
serenity of its moss-hung oaks. Her heart ached with
yearning. "No, no, I'm quite content here. But I do
get homesick sometimes," she admitted wistfully.

"Maybe you'll be able to go home soon," Lacy
suggested.

"I can't."

"You can't?" Lacy's gaze sharpened on Gabrielle's reflected image. "Why not?"

Gabrielle saw the burning inquiry in Lacy's brilliant blue eyes. "I'm not supposed to," she hedged. "Not for a while. Not until I'm stronger physically."

"Oh, I see." Lacy replied, smiling coldly. Brushing out the length of damp hair, lustrous with fiery highlights, Lacy remained silent. Finally she laid the brush on the dresser.

"Come on, my dear. Time for bed. Sleep is just what you need," she said as if she were speaking to a child.

Lacy tucked Gabrielle in bed and pulled the sheet up to her chin. The minute Gabrielle's head hit the pillow, her eyes closed, and with a soft sigh she drifted into sleep, her thick auburn hair spread damply over the pillow.

Lacy glanced across the room at her own image in the mirror. She appeared almost as young as Gabrielle. The difference lay in a degree of sophistication. Her own face possessed a fine bone structure, but it lacked the softness of youth. Gabrielle's movements were more vibrant and energetic than Lacy's without the elegance and refinement she would have after a few years. For a moment Lacy felt sadness sweep over her. She didn't want to lose Cade to this young woman. Then her face hardened. No matter what it took, she would not let Cade go. Her expression grew thoughtful as she turned the lamp down and left the room, closing the door without a sound.

Stepping onto the veranda, Lacy stared toward the lights of the barn dance. Her mouth twisted sharply in disapproval as one of Cade's men made his way haltingly across the front lawn. Give a man enough to drink and he always kept on until he made an ass of himself, she thought. It was disgraceful.

Suddenly her expression cleared as she recognized Zeke, the young man who always seemed to be trailing after Gabrielle.

"Zeke," she called out.

He stopped, weaved unsteadily, and with some effort swung around to face her. "Yes, ma'am?"

"I want to talk to you for a moment."

He ambled toward her. "What do you want, Miss Fielding?"

Lacy smiled. "How about walking me over to the dance?"

Zeke swept his hat from his head. "I'd be honored to, ma'am."

"Pretty night, isn't it?"

"Sure is, Miss Fielding," he agreed, falling into step beside her.

"It's such a shame Gabrielle is going to miss it. She and Cade just got back, you know."

Zeke nodded sullenly. "It's her own durn fault."

"For getting lost?"

"She weren't lost. She was headed for Follettville," he muttered. "That's where she was going."

He stumbled and Lacy caught his arm, steadying him. "Don't you like her, Zeke?" she asked innocently.

"Oh, she's all right. Except ever since she got here I been keepin' an eye on her. No real man should be pussyfootin' around after a female. I'm goin' to miss the brandin' this year."

"You mean you have to keep her company?" Lacy prompted. "Why?"

"Oh, I can't tell."

"It's a secret, hmm? Sounds to me like she fell in love with the wrong kind of man and her family is getting her out of harm's way."

"No, ma'am. Nothin' innocent like that." Zeke pressed his palm against his forehead. "Think I drank . . . too much. My head's buzzin' like a hornet's nest.''

Lacy prayed he would not pass out before she could learn what he knew. ''Just lean against this buggy wheel for a moment and you'll be all right. I bet a pretty girl is waiting for you at the dance.''

''Yep. Real purty.'' He caught hold of the wheel rim with both hands and dropped his head.

''Why don't you like Gabrielle?''

Zeke shook his head as if to clear his foggy thoughts. ''Mr. Montana ain't been the same since she came. She's messed up everything.''

''How'd she do that?''

''She's a spy.''

Lacy gripped his arm and pulled him around to face her. ''Zeke, what are you talking about? She's just a young woman.''

''I know, but she was helping the North anyway. Cade said she was in ex . . . ex . . . I can't remember the word. When someone is sent away in disgrace and can't come back.''

''Exile?''

''Yep. The Southern politicians are gentlemen, you know, and they couldn't abide puttin' a woman in jail, so they sent her out here.''

''So she's forced to stay here?''

''Yep, but she ain't no prisoner. I've seen Mr. Montana lookin' at her sometimes.'' He shook his head forlornly. ''I just don't think nothin' good is goin' to come of it all. She's purty, you know?''

''Yes, I know.'' Lacy said thoughtfully, the spark of an idea already forming in her mind.

Chapter 9

C ade sat at his desk with his arms crossed over his chest, a dark scowl on his face. After dinner he had talked to Sam Fortune about some ranch business. When his foreman had left, he turned his attention to Gabrielle. She hadn't left her room for three days.

It angered him that she'd turned down his marriage proposal as if he were some out-of-luck, enamored cowboy whose boots were run down at the heels. Dammit, his proposal had been an act of chivalry. He was considered an eligible bachelor in New Orleans, he owned a big part of Texas, and women found him attractive. Yet this redheaded New Orleans princess refused his offer and even had the audacity to list his drawbacks. Cade scowled down at his desk top. It was just this kind of snooty, unjustified arrogance that made him itch to turn her over his knee and teach her a lesson.

Today Maria had said Gabrielle seemed terribly sad. The young Mexican woman had shaken her head worriedly. ''Something bad must have happened when she was lost to make her so unhappy.''

Cade muttered an oath beneath his breath. She'd endured a painful separation from her family and exile in an unfamiliar, wild land far from home with a stubborn spirit that Cade had always admired despite the inconvenience it caused him, but now she took to her bed for three days because they had made love!

He knew exactly what was bothering Gabrielle. She had a straitlaced, puritanical mind, and she was hell-bent on punishing herself and him for her fall from grace. She was wallowing in self-pity and determined to make him feel guilty.

He had tried repeatedly to talk to her and had become so frustrated that he had left the room before he lost his temper. She had sat there silently, playing the pathetic, soiled virgin dying of shame, and refused to discuss his offer of marriage. Tears had rolled down her cheeks when he had mentioned anything about what had happened at the creek.

He'd expected some remorse; he even felt some regret about the situation himself. He and Gabrielle had been tossed together in a volatile, unconventional situation. They had been caught up by the war and they didn't have the social fabric of New Orleans with family, tradition, and chaperons acting as a buffer. This was exactly what he had feared would happen when Tyler had asked him to take her to Texas. But now he knew he could not resist Gabrielle St. Claire, and the distance between them made each day a misery. He had lived most of his life by instinct, and he couldn't change now. He knew he wanted her, he had decided they should marry, and he wasn't putting up with any more nonsense.

After he made his decision he stood up, unbuckled his gunbelt, and dropped it on his desk. Enough was enough. His face was dark as a thundercloud as he stalked out of his study and turned down the lighted corridor toward the wide stairs, then took the steps two at a time. He didn't knock at the door of Gabrielle's room, he just threw it open.

She sat in the middle of her bed, staring out the darkened window like a doomed saint. Burnished curls cascaded over the shoulders of her white lace-trimmed gown. At the sight of him looming in the doorway, her mouth dropped open in surprise. Seconds later, her expression hardened. "Go away. I don't want to see you."

"Too bad."

As he stalked toward the bed, Gabrielle stared at him in astonishment, taking too long to register the determined set of his jaw. He was only a few feet from her bed when she seemed to realize his intent. Too late she tried to scramble away from him. Cade reached across and grabbed her, pulled her back, then lifted her into his arms.

Gabrielle gasped. "What are you doing?"

Cade looked down at her briefly before turning and heading for the door. "I'm taking you to my room. You're going to sleep in my bed from now on. While there you can decide whether you want to marry me, but I won't tolerate any more moping and feeling sorry for yourself."

"Cade!" Gabrielle grabbed the door jamb when he shifted sideways to get her through. "Stop this!" Her fingers caught, slowing their progress. Cade merely tugged and she lost her hold.

Gabrielle struggled wildly in his arms as he carried her down the hallway. Maria turned the corner with an armload of linens and stopped in her tracks.

"Excuse us, Maria," Cade said, stepping past her. Maria's blank expression didn't change even though she pressed back against the wall to give them room to pass. Mortified, Gabrielle renewed her effort to get free. Cade continued along the corridor undaunted.

He kicked open the door to his room, walked inside, and dumped Gabrielle unceremoniously on his bed.

"There, sweetheart." Her shocked face and tousled hair made her appear so surprised and appealing that he grinned. "Take a look around your new quarters."

She slid quickly over to the side of the bed and watched him warily as he slammed the door shut. When the key turned in the lock, her eyes flared with anger. "Cade, have you lost your mind?"

"Yes."

She shrank back as he returned. "Stay away from me."

His mouth quirked with something like humor. "I want you to know what to expect. I'm going to sleep with you here every night and I'm going to make love to you every night." With a surprisingly quick move, he seized her upper arms with strong hands and lifted her up like a rag doll, kissing her soundly on the mouth. "What do you think of that, Gabrielle?" He released her suddenly and her backside bounced on the bed.

Gabrielle brushed tumbling hair from her face, her cheeks flushing with color. "Are you drunk?" she demanded. She thought he looked positively wicked in the soft lamplight, but he also looked handsome and very male.

Cade laughed. "No, I'm not."

She slid off the bed, her slim legs showing briefly before she stood up. "I'm not staying here, Cade. You can't make me." Her voice had turned imperious—it was the same tone she used with Hetty when she wanted her to know she meant business. Disregarding him, she started for the door, her posture ramrod straight.

In a swift move Cade blocked her way. "Oh, yes,

I can. I'm bigger and stronger, and there's not a damned thing you can do about it.''

"You *have* lost your mind,'' she whispered with almost savage satisfaction.

"Maybe. But tonight I'm going to take that gown off you, and I'm going to run my hands all over your sweet body. All over,'' he reiterated with a significant lift of his dark brows. "I'm going to kiss your throat, and your pretty pink ears, and the tight little buds of your breasts until you cry out for me to make love to you.''

Gabrielle gasped, horrified to be hearing such intimacies spoken aloud. "I would never do that!''

"Yes, you will. Your body always betrays you. Always.'' He moved toward her and she backed away, her emerald eyes wide.

"I'll make love to you tonight and again tomorrow morning when we wake up. And tomorrow night and the next night and the next.''

Gabrielle retreated across the room, never taking her eyes from him. "Cade, stop it!'' She cried out when his arm snaked out to catch her but she narrowly escaped. Moving sideways, she managed to get the table between them. Cade chuckled, still circling to find a better advantage.

"Come here.''

"No!''

Wit a sudden move he caught her and swept her up in his arms. Even though Gabrielle fought, Cade easily carried her to the bed and dropped her on it. Not giving her a chance to recover, he came down over her, pinning her beneath him. Capturing her face between his hands, he kissed the corner of her mouth with quick, soft kisses.

"Cade, you don't know what you're doing—'' His mouth stopped her words for a moment. "The servants—'' She gasped as his hand slid along her hip

and her fury gave her the strength to free her hand
and slap him on the face as hard as she could. "You
big brute. Stop it!"

At the sound of the slap, and the stinging pain on
his cheek, Cade suddenly stopped kissing her and
pulled away. He looked down, glowering in anger,
but what he saw surprised him. Gabrielle had started
to cry, and she looked more like a scared little girl
than the haughty tease he had imagined her to be a
few moments before. She had covered her face with
her hands, and her nightgown was torn a bit at the
neck. Shame flooded through him.

"Princess, I'm sorry. I didn't want to scare you,
but I just didn't know what else to do. I was afraid
you would stay holed up in your room forever, feeling sorry for yourself and angry at me. You are so
damn stubborn, and I want you here with me. You
belong here now," he said.

"You think you can have anything you want just
because you're big and strong. You think you can
just take me and use me at your pleasure like I'm
some kind of serving wench, like I'm some kind of
toy! You're a monster, Cade Montana. Now let me
go. I'm returning to my own room this minute."
She struggled to pull herself up off the bed.

"Please, Gabrielle, stay here with me tonight," he
said, reaching out to touch her shoulder. She pushed
his hand aside furiously and scrambled away from
him. "I won't try anything. I won't make you do
anything you don't want to do, if you will just stay
here with me. Just let me hold you, please?" he
asked softly, as if he were trying to calm a frightened chid.

The gentle tone in his voice caught her attention,
and she looked at him suspiciously. He appeared
almost vulnerable, sitting on the side of his rumpled
bed, begging her to stay with him, and she was

struck again by how handsome he was. She thought suddenly of how easily he had picked her up and carried her into his room, how firm his arms were when they were wrapped around her body. Sighing, she hesitantly approached him.

"I'll stay a little while, but not the whole night," she said as she sat down on the edge of the bed.

Cade laughed softly and moved closer to her. "You always have to have the last word, don't you, Gabrielle? You can never just give in."

"Well, if that isn't a case of the pot calling the kettle black! You're the one who always has to have his way," she said, smiling in spite of herself. Cade was sitting next to her now, and he pulled her gently against him. His embrace felt comforting after her days of solitude, and she nuzzled her face in his chest, feeling the hard muscles beneath the soft fabric of his shirt. She was amazed at how quickly her anger had evaporated. How could he drive her to murderous fury one moment and make her melt in his arms the next? She never felt in control of herself when she was around him.

He continued to hold her in silence for a long while, rocking back and forth silently, stroking her back. She felt warm and protected, almost drowsy. Finally he pulled away from her.

"You *are* exciting when you're angry, you know," he said, grinning at her mischievously. "Your eyes flash like jewels, and your cheeks flush with color." He trailed his finger across her cheekbones, and they turned red, as if in answer to him.

"That's no excuse for your behavior earlier, Cade," she said chidingly, a small tinge of her anger returning.

"I already said I was sorry for that." He leaned over to kiss her cheek where his finger had been only a second before. She moved her head slightly, so that her mouth met his, and then slowly wrapped her arm around his neck. They kissed slowly and leisurely, their tongues touching and exploring as they lost all track of time.

Gabrielle felt as if she were sinking deep into Cade's arms, enveloped by the soft luxury of his lips and the velvet recesses of his mouth. She hardly noticed when he moved his hand slowly down her back and around to cup her breast over her night-gown, but a jolt of sharp pleasure roused her when he brushed her nipple with his thumb.

"Cade, no," she murmured, trying weakly to pull her mouth away from his. "We shouldn't, we can't . . ."

"Shhh, love, don't say it. I want you, Gabrielle. You're so beautiful, so beautiful. I've wanted you since the first moment I saw you on the balcony, dripping wet, your clothes molded to your gorgeous body." His voice was little more than a whisper, his breath hot on her face as he kissed her chin, her nose, her eyelids. "Say you want me, too, Gabri-elle," he said softly, beseechingly. He licked the sensitive flesh behind her ear and she moaned as he nibbled gently.

She felt the familiar madness return as he moved his hand down the length of her body until it rested on her thigh. When he reached the bare skin past her nightgown he clutched her with new intensity, slipping his hand under the fabric to caress the silky curve of her hip.

"You have such beautiful legs, Gabrielle. Tell me you want to wrap those long legs around me and make love to me," he whispered as he kissed her neck and the base of her throat, moving down to the gentle swell of her breast. With slow, relentless persistence, Cade seemed to turn all movements into

caresses. He pulled her nightgown over her head
and flung it across the room.

He stroked her body with wonderful tenderness
as his lips touched an aching nipple, and his tongue
circled the peak, causing her to cry out with pleasure. Her heart beat maddingly as her veins filled
with heavy warmth rushing downward.

"Say it. Say you want me," he demanded,
spreading his hand over her belly.

The sensation of his touch left her almost breathless, but finally she gasped, "Yes, yes, I do want
you," as she started to pull off his shirt.

He tossed it away and quickly unfastened his
trousers while she played with the dark curls covering his chest. She ran her hands up and down the
rippling muscles of his chest and stomach, delight-
ing in their power. As her touch moved down his
body, it became tentative and unsure, but Cade
guided her hand, teaching and encouraging her. His
skin was warm and smooth, and everything about
him tantalized her—his strength, the darker hue of
his skin, and his chiseled, hard-planed face, so
starkly handsome and masculine.

She no longer felt that she belonged to herself;
she belonged to him and to the hazy warm world of
desire. She heard only breathless, mingled whispers, and felt only the moving poetry of one body
melding to another.

Then his body joined with hers, loving and
strong, ruthless and possessive . . . and incredibly
tender. Gabrielle gasped as he entered, sure and
deep, and then withdrew with delicious slowness,
the sensation so dazzling that she was robbed of
breath. His tongue traced the outline of her mouth
and flicked against her tongue, and then he entered
again, over and over. Gabrielle felt her body begin
to tremble as she was driven to distraction by the

slow, exquisite torture that brought heightened feelings but not release.

"Cade," she gasped, her breath jerking in her lungs. "Please."

"Not yet. No, not yet." He kissed her, his words smothered against her throat. "Don't be greedy, my impatient little lover."

The softly spoken words were a caress in her ears. His hands circled her breasts, gently kneading, and then he dropped his head, pressed the nipple between thumb and forefinger, and flicked his tongue across the tight little bud. Gabrielle whimpered as the sensation inside her seemed to heighten. Arching against him, she drew in a ragged breath and tried to still her trembling. "Please, Cade, please."

He chuckled softly and withdrew. Before she could protest, he flipped her onto her stomach. Gabrielle was suddenly staring down at the white sheet. Confused, she lifted up on her arms just as a strong arm circled her waist and pulled her lower in the bed.

"What—" she began.

Cade settled over her, nudged her legs apart, and entered again. Gabrielle closed her eyes at the sensation. His fingers came around to touch her and she felt a roaring in her ears as the ecstasy grew beyond what she could endure. She pressed her face into the bed, her fingers knotting the sheets. His thrusts became stronger, more purposeful, driving her relentlessly toward that tantalizing pinnacle. And then came the shattering, trembling, melting release, and ever so slowly, the quaking, golden return. She felt his weight on her body, pressing her against the bed, his breathing rasping in her ears, but still she seemed to be floating in a warm sea of contentment.

After a few minutes, Cade supported his weight

on his arms and looked down at Gabrielle. With a wondering shake of his head, he kissed her cheek and shifted to her side. What a marvelous, healthy passion she had, and what a lucky man he was!

Gabrielle didn't move for a long time. When her breathing had slowed, she turned onto her side, cheek against the pillow, her gaze on his profile. He had almost drifted off to sleep when she spoke.

"I should go back to my own room now," she said softly.

Cade's eyes snapped open, and he pulled her close to him. "You aren't going anywhere," he answered.

"Cade, I can't stay here. People will talk."

"I don't care."

"Well, I do."

"Do you really? Then I guess we'll have to get married." His eyes glinted in the moonlight coming through the window.

Gabrielle sighed. She had no energy to argue with him now.

"We'll talk about it later, I suppose," she said, resigned. "You know that you and Celeste have ruined me."

"I know."

"First a spy, and now a fallen woman."

Cade said nothing, just reached over and pulled her up against him. He no longer thought she was guilty. He didn't have any proof, but he simply believed she was telling the truth. In fact, he decided to hire a man to investigate Celeste's activities. If Gabrielle was innocent, then the answers lay with her sister. He wanted proof in order to clear Gabrielle's name. But in his heart, he knew it wasn't necessary.

* * *

Over the next week Gabrielle was alternately entertained, shocked, and horrified by the rakehell man she found herself falling in love with. Mesmerized by his presence, she lived moment to moment. Still, she held a tiny bit of herself away from Cade. Just a bit, so something would belong to her. But it was hard, so compelling and forceful was his personality, so completely did it envelop her. He was irreverent one moment, then properly responsible and high-principled the next. She loved everything about him, especially the sudden bursts of laughter from deep inside his chest that thrilled her heart.

A week after they began their new sleeping arrangement, Cade woke her out of a sound sleep early one morning, insisting that she come outside with him, barely giving her time to dress. She had only half brushed her hair when he caught her hand, drew her down the stairs and out of the house. Once on the veranda, she saw that the sun had just risen and that in the distance, softened by the gentle morning haze, the ranch crew was filing into the cook shack for breakfast. Cade ignored her mutterings that he had awakened her too early. He merely hurried her along, practically forcing her to run to keep up with his long strides.

"You can go back to sleep soon, princess," he advised with a remorseless grin. "But I want to show you something before I leave today."

He dragged her all the way down to the corral, braced an arm against the top railing, and nodded. "Take a look at that."

Gabrielle stepped up on the lower pole. The corral was empty except for two calves. "I don't see anything."

"Take a look at the brand."

She peered closer, still unimpressed as she saw that a "G" had been burned onto each flank. "I see it."

"That's your brand."

Her mouth curved with a hint of sarcasm. "Well, thank you, Cade. I'm sure that will look nice on a critical part of my anatomy."

"That's what I thought." He laughed, sliding a hand over her hip.

"Stop that," she gasped, bolting from his touch. With a scandalized glance at him, she looked around to see if anyone had observed the intimacy. Then with a sigh she faced him, holding a hand over her eyes to block the sun. "Tell me what this is all about," she insisted. "I don't want to guess. What I really want to do is go back to bed."

"These calves are yours. I'm giving them to you."

She stared at him for a long moment, then turned and headed for the house. "Thank you, very much. What a lovely, thoughtful gift."

Cade caught her arm and pulled her back. "Gabrielle, I'm offering you a game to play, and a business of sorts. You will have an assistant, too, as long as you mind your manners and don't get bossy with him."

Gabrielle closed her eyes. "Just let me guess who that assistant would be." She feigned puzzlement. "Could it be Zeke?"

"Yes."

She shook her head in mild exasperation. "What do you want me to do?"

"You may have every unbranded stray you and Zeke find. We'll put your brand on it. Your brand has been registered and is legal."

She touched a hand to her forehead. "Am I up too early? Am I not understanding you? Why would I want to hunt down stray cattle?" Her green eyes darkened. "I'm not even a good rider, and my ideas of a good time involve shopping trips and tea parties."

"Now you have a reason to become a good rider."

"To hunt strays?" The ridiculousness of the idea sounded in her tone.

"Over the next few months I'm going to be gone quite a bit. The social life here is limited, and I've wondered how you might occupy your time, and I hit upon this. You don't have to do it, of course. It's entirely up to you. But the cattle you find will belong to you. You will own something. All you have to do is point your pretty little gloved finger at a stray and Zeke will round it up. Then it's yours."

"I plan on going back to New Orleans. You know that."

"You're free to go back as soon as the Committee says you may. I'll buy your cattle from you then."

Gabrielle looked at the two calves. They seemed to watch her with the same skepticism she felt. "What if I find a lot? Are you going to change your mind?"

"No."

Gabrielle stepped up on the bottom rung of the fence and put her arms over the top, her thoughts racing. She had to admit that she was a bit intrigued. "You won't change your mind no matter how many I get?"

"No."

"I can't take care of them by myself."

"We'll run 'em with my herd."

Gabrielle turned and looked at him, her expression intent. "I'll try it." A ruthless smile touched her pretty face. Cade was so high-handed, wanting to find a "game" for her to occupy her time. She'd show him how many strays she'd find. "But you'd better watch out. You may not be the biggest rancher in these parts for long."

After Gabrielle returned to the house, Cade lit a cheroot and propped his arms on the top rung of the corral, enjoying the early morning quiet. He was pleased with Gabrielle's acceptance. He wanted her to be drawn into the life of the ranch, to become a part of it, and to understand its workings. Maybe in time she would grow to appreciate Texas as he did rather than feeling like an outcast. He wanted to occupy her mind with thoughts other than New Orleans and what had happened there.

He watched smoke from the tip of his cheroot drift into the still morning air, turning his thoughts to another issue. Over the course of the last week, he had noticed a definite cooling toward him from the servants. He grinned, remembering with a bit of embarrassment how he had carried Gabrielle, fighting like a wildcat, to his room. It probably hadn't taken Maria ten minutes to tell the rest of the servants.

Sam Fortune told him that the ranch hands were talking about it, too. Some said it was none of their business what their boss did. Others argued that, boss or no, it was wrong to treat a lady like that. Without a doubt, everyone's sympathies lay with Gabrielle, which rather pleased Cade. He didn't like all the speculation into his affairs, but he preferred to bear the brunt of condemnation rather than have it fall on Gabrielle's shoulders. The present situation couldn't continue indefinitely, but the solution lay with Gabrielle. He flicked the last of his cigar onto the ground and headed for the stable. There was a day's work to be done.

A few nights later, Cade informed Gabrielle that he planned to leave for Mexico and would be gone for two or three weeks. He would sail from Follettville to meet with Mexican officials in Matamoros. When she heard the news, Gabrielle felt a sudden, puzzling sense of loss. To hide her emotions, she moved over to the open door of the balcony and stared out. A soft evening breeze rustled her skirts. "Will your trip be dangerous?" she asked after a moment.

"Mostly boring." Cade stared at her slim back curiously, then walked up behind her. "What's the matter?"

Gabrielle couldn't tell him the truth—that she would miss him. She hated to admit it, but life on the ranch was filled with adventure compared to the routine of her old life in New Orleans, and Cade was a big part of the excitement. She knew it would be lonely without him, and the thought of something happening to him terrified her. Somehow she couldn't admit how much her heart was involved. Instead she spoke of commonplace concerns to answer his question. "Oh, I was just thinking about your trip and the places you'll be seeing. It's exciting to travel, isn't it?"

Cade put his arms around her, pulling her back against him. "Are you getting bored at the ranch?"

Gabrielle shrugged, making no comment. Cade's hand about her waist drifted automatically toward her breasts. Without thinking, Gabrielle stopped the movement. Cade's chin touched the top of her head, and he grinned. "Tell you what, we'll plan a trip for you. Sam can bring you and Maria into Follettville, and I'll meet you there on my way back from Mexico. We'll stay a few days, then travel back together." He kissed the top of her head. "It's about time you had a shopping trip, don't you think?"

Gabrielle turned in his arms, the prospect of a trip bringing a sparkle to her eyes. "I would love it. That would be in about three weeks, wouldn't it?"

Cade nodded, his hands roaming her back. "You can stay with Rawlings."

Gabrielle drew back instantly. "I can't. He's even worse than you."

Cade laughed. "Worse than me?"

"You know what I mean," Gabrielle returned, pulling impatiently away. "He's always looking at me like he's fixing to buy a horse."

"And I look at you like that?"

Gabrielle sniffed. "Not anymore. You already made the purchase."

As soon as the words were out of her mouth, Gabrielle blushed, shocked at herself for such an indelicate statement. She covered her mouth with her fingers. "See what you make me do?" she accused. "You make me say things before I think. You make me *do* things before I think! I don't even sound like a lady anymore."

Cade took her resisting body into his arms. "Don't you worry about that. You are a lady, Gabrielle. Clear through to your tender little heart." He kissed her forehead. "You just came in contact with a scoundrel, that's all."

Gabrielle looked up. "You *are* a scoundrel."

"I know."

He kissed her mouth, and her body became yielding and responsive. Eyes cloudy with growing passion, she pushed him away, one issue unresolved. "I'll stay with Tom Rawlings, but only if I can take Zeke as a bodyguard."

"That's fine." Cade bent and kissed her mouth. "No more talking," he murmured.

The weeks during Cade's absence passed quickly for Gabrielle. To her surprise, she enjoyed her new enterprise and set about the hunt with diligence. When she drew up a section map the third day to keep a record of her search, even Zeke was impressed. Privately he told the ranch hands that Cade Montana might be destitute by the end of the year if Gabrielle's current interest continued. Within days a thriving gambling industry had been generated in the bunkhouse. The men found endless combinations of bets, from how many strays the lady would find in one day, to how long Cade would allow the game to continue. Money changed hands nightly. Over the weeks the men grew used to seeing Gabrielle's slim figure, riding sidesaddle, parasol in hand, heading out from the ranch.

By nighttime, Gabrielle would fall into bed exhausted, but not too exhausted to miss the warmth of Cade's body beside her, or the excitement of his possessive touch.

During Cade's absence, Gabrielle found twenty-five head of unbranded cattle. Before she left for Follettville, she insisted that Sam Fortune have one of his men brand them. After working as hard as she had, she wanted to make sure her brand was clearly marked on all of them.

Chapter 10

On his way to Matamoros, Cade had stopped overnight in Follettville. He wanted to talk to Tom about Gabrielle. Because Lacy and Wyatt had been invited for dinner and had stayed late to chat, it was almost midnight before the two men sat alone in the study.

Tom refilled Cade's brandy glass and placed the decanter within easy reach on a nearby table. Selecting a cigar from an ornate silver box, Tom went through an elaborate ritual of sniffing it, biting off the tip, then puffing rhythmically until he had it going. Even though he seemed absorbed in his task, he gave Cade several probing glances.

"What's on your mind?" he demanded bluntly, sitting down in the big wing-back chair across from Cade. "Seems to me there's been something chewing on you all evening."

Cade nodded. "Yeah, I guess so. I want to talk to you about Gabrielle."

"What's going on?" Tom waved smoke away from his face. "She didn't take off again, did she?"

"No, nothing like that." Cade rubbed his hand along his jaw, and when he looked at Tom, his expression had turned thoughtful. "You know, I don't think Gabrielle is guilty of a damned thing anymore." His mouth curled with a touch of irony. "Except maybe being more headstrong and arrogant than a woman has a right to be. But I don't have any proof, and that's where I need your help. I want to prove she's innocent."

Snorting with disgust, Tom leaned back in his chair, puffing furiously on his cigar. After a few moments he scowled through the smoke haze at Cade. "Why the hell would I want to help you do that? If she's proven innocent, I won't stand a chance of getting her to marry me."

Cade laughed in spite of how strongly he felt about the topic. "What is this obsession with Gabrielle? It's absurd."

Tom shrugged. "I like her. She's got spunk."

"Well, I think you're out of luck on this one," Cade advised him dryly.

Tom's eyes darkened with suspicion. "You sleeping with her?"

"That's none of your business, but I'd say yes if I thought it'd end your preoccupation with her."

"By God, I know you are! Here I am offering marriage for that privilege and you take her out to the ranch and bed her down without so much as a by-your-leave. You have a lot of nerve. Tyler St. Claire is going to do some reassessing of your character, and I wouldn't want to be there when he does."

"I didn't set out on a campaign to seduce Gabrielle."

"Are you going to marry her?" Tom challenged. When Cade hesitated, he slammed his fist down on the arm of his chair. "See," he jeered, leaning forward and jabbing the tip of his cigar toward Cade. "You see, you *are* using her. But *I* am willing to marry—"

"Hold on a minute," Cade interrupted. "I didn't say I wasn't going to marry her. But I'm talking about real reasons for marriage, which require some thought and consideration, while you're talking about a pretty possession. You don't give a damn what she thinks about the idea."

Tom threw up his hands in defeat. "What the hell could she think about it? I'd treat her well. She'd have anything she wants."

Cade grinned and shook his head, amused as always by Tom's Old World attitude toward marriage. Then thinking of Gabrielle, his features sobered. "I thought Gabrielle was too self-centered to amount to anything when I first met her, but considering what she's gone through, she's handled herself pretty well." He looked up at Tom. "She's got more fiber and backbone in that pretty little body than you'd expect, and she's no spy."

Tom's mouth quirked. "Oh, yeah?"

"Yeah. I know it's easy to be swayed by a pretty face, and I guarded against that. But I have a feeling she's telling the truth. Her story is always the same, and if she were lying, she'd get her facts mixed up sometimes."

Tom shrugged. "I don't think I ever really cared whether she was guilty or not. With her blackened past, I stood a chance of getting her, and it didn't matter to me if the whole world knew what she'd done." Tom downed his brandy in one gulp, then frowned at Cade. "With your political goals, however, you have to care what people think."

Cade shook his head. "Politics has always been an extra for me. If it works out later, fine. But I'm a cattleman, that's my work. I refuse to live my life according to public opinion."

"What about Lacy?"

"We've never discussed marriage."

Rawlings's mouth twisted with sarcasm. "Well,

that certainly relieves you of any responsibility to her, doesn't it?''

''No, it doesn't,'' Cade returned sharply. ''I've known she wanted us to marry, but she knows I'm not interested, and I've made that clear. Lacy's beautiful, she's intelligent, but she has a toughness that I don't find attractive.''

Tom stubbed his cigar out and leaned back in the big leather chair. ''I had my mind set on Gabrielle,'' he said with a sullen wistfulness, ''but now you've beat me to it.'' He looked up, his dark eyes gleaming. ''I bet that spunky little redhead is something in bed.'' Chuckling, he held up his hands to forestall Cade's angry retort. ''Sorry. Just couldn't keep from speculating.'' He pursed his mouth. ''You were saying you needed some help. What kind of help do you need?''

''I want to hire an investigator to follow Celeste St. Claire. If Gabrielle is telling the truth, that's where we'll find the answers. Also, I'd like to know what's happening with the Committee.''

Tom nodded. ''You take care of business in Mexico, and I'll see to this.'' He rubbed his hands together, dark eyes sparkling. ''I love this secret intrigue.''

Cade grinned. ''I knew I could count on you.''

''Of course,'' Rawlings's mouth twisted downward. ''I've always been such a gracious loser,'' he said sarcastically. For a long moment he stared down at his brandy, then his heavy black brows arched in an evil scowl. ''I was serious about Gabrielle.''

''I know.''

''If it were any other man but you, I'd shoot him and take her. You know I would, don't you?''

''I know that, too.''

''What do you think makes you the exception?'' Rawlings persisted.

Cade stared at him, his face solemn. "First of all, I'm not that easy to kill, and I believe you know that. And I think maybe you riled up the situation on purpose just to see the sparks fly."

"Maybe. Maybe not. But I think you're a son-of-a-bitch anyway. You want another drink?"

Lacy folded her hands in her lap and looked at the woman who was as out of place in her parlor as a crow in a canary cage. She still wore the black hood and cape that had concealed her identity as she exited her carriage and entered the Fielding home. She sat motionless, totally self-possessed, showing not one hint of discomfort at finding herself with one of the town's most admired and respected women, while she occupied the position of most scorned.

"What do you want, Miss Fielding?" The woman's smile turned cynical. "I don't suppose your invitation was social."

Lacy ignored her sarcasm and dropped a stack of bills on the table between them. "There's a hundred dollars there."

Nora Petridge glanced at the money and then lifted her gaze to Lacy, unimpressed. "And what do I have to do to earn it?"

"A young woman is coming into town in about three weeks. I want you to spread a story, a true story, about her. I want you to tell your girls, and I want them to tell their customers. I want the whole town to know."

"To know what?"

Lacy's mouth thinned, and for an instant her beautiful face looked old with bitterness. "I want the town to know that she's a spy."

Nora Petridge observed her cynically. "You're trying to help the South?"

A smile played over Lacy's mouth. "I'm patriotic."

Nora nodded, reached for the money, and dropped it into her black drawstring purse. "And your personal reason?" she inquired, one brow lifting in skepticism.

"Cade Montana."

Shaking her head with a jaded world-weariness, Nora rose to her feet. "He's a man hard to corral, isn't he?"

Lacy ignored her. "I want you to come back next week at the same time. I'll have all my plans put together by then."

The madam of Follettville's rowdiest whorehouse walked over to the door and pulled the black hood up over her head. "If you want me to do more than spread rumors," she said, turning to look at Lacy, "you better come up with more money."

"Don't worry," Lacy said flatly. "You'll be paid well."

Gabrielle had kept herself busy during the three weeks of Cade's absence so that the time would pass quickly. The activity helped, but she still was impatient for his return. Finally the day came for the trip to Follettville, and she settled herself into the carriage. Maria and Zeke traveled with her, in addition to the outriders assigned for protection. To her delight, she found that Maria had a most pleasing, light personality, and her witty and entertaining stories of her Mexican ancestors provided a wonderful diversion during the monotony of the trip.

Gabrielle also found she liked Zeke better the more she got to know him, especially when he wasn't showing off and trying to prove he was the toughest cowboy around. He cast sidelong glances at Maria, and Gabrielle suspected that Zeke was sweet on her. Maria also did not seem to discourage his very subtle attention.

Once they arrived in Follettville, Gabrielle asked that a cot be brought to her room for Maria. She did not trust Tom Rawlings, even with Zeke standing guard at her door.

"You afraid of the dark, little girl?" Tom had wanted to know. "Is that why you have to have a maid sleep in your room?"

"I am not afraid of the dark," Gabrielle responded tartly. "I don't trust you, and I'm not taking any chances."

Tom laughed, pleased by her retort. He swaggered down the corridor, and at the patio door he turned back. "Lunch is at twelve sharp. I look forward to your company." Still chuckling, he disappeared from view.

Their lunch together turned out to be quite pleasant. Tom had a raunchy vocabulary, of course, but Gabrielle found that she became desensitized to his language after a time. She also found that her concern about her own welfare had been unnecessary because Cade arrived that afternoon.

She and Tom were sitting on the shaded veranda when a carriage stopped in the street. Moments later Cade stepped down, and Gabrielle's heart started an erratic rhythm at the sight of his tall, broad-shouldered body. Rising, she followed Tom to the stairs and watched as Cade made his way along the flagstone path. At the top of the stairs he shook hands with Tom and grinned at her.

"Good afternoon, Gabrielle," he said, one brow lifting as he looked her over.

Blushing, Gabrielle inclined her head, disconcerted by the open admiration in his gaze. "Did you have a nice trip?" she inquired politely.

Cade smiled, a hint of humor touching his mouth. "Yes, I did. Thank you."

Much to Gabrielle's relief, Rawlings's barrage of questions regarding Cade's negotiations shifted the focus away from her. She felt as flustered as a schoolgirl with her first beau.

"You get the Mexican officials to agree to your proposal or are those bastards as ornery as usual?" Rawlings demanded.

Cade nodded, his gaze drifting to Gabrielle as he walked onto the shaded porch. "Old Vasquez jumped at the chance. They'll buy all the cotton we manage to get to Brownsville."

"By damn, that's great," Tom declared, clapping him on the back. Turning, he looked around impatiently for a servant. "Those gals I got working for me are only good for one thing. You have a seat and I'll get you a drink. It's hotter than a son-of-a-bitch today."

As soon as Tom left, Cade caught Gabrielle's hand and pulled her toward the porch swing partially shielded behind climbing ivy. "My," he observed with a possessive grin, "don't you look pretty today." He bent and kissed her lightly on the lips, then sat down in the swing. "I missed you."

Seeing her blush again, Cade drew her closer, so that she stood between his long legs, her hands in his. "How'd you manage to get by without me?" he teased.

"I worked," she said proudly.

"Oh?" His grin widened, and Gabrielle thought her heart would burst. Cade was the handsomest man she had ever seen.

"Tell me, am I poor man now?"

"We found twenty-five unbranded cattle."

Cade laughed, his hands releasing hers and slipping about her waist. "You have been busy."

"Yes, I have." She smiled, his banter easing her uncharacteristic moment of shyness. "And I know where there's a ravine with nearly ten, all just waiting until I get back." She did not add that they were in quadrant four of her map or that she had turned the game into a search that entailed precision and diligence.

"I can see I'm headed for financial ruin." Cade watched her thoughtfully for a moment, his blue eyes shaded with amusement. "Did Rawlings mind his manners?"

Gabrielle nodded. Cade watched her mouth, all pink with a hint of pearly-white teeth showing when she smiled, and he felt desire curl inside him. Distracted, he listened to her explanation.

"We only arrived this afternoon. But Tom has been on his best behavior. Did you talk to him?"

"Oh, a bit," Cade admitted.

Hearing Tom's footsteps coming down the corridor, Gabrielle pulled quickly away. Rawlings stepped out on the veranda and directed the hip-swinging Mexican girl to to put the tray of refreshments on the white wicker table. Over the next hour, the conversation was mostly about financial arrangements with the Mexicans, but Gabrielle didn't mind. She found it a pleasure to sit beside Cade again and to listen to his deep voice and easy laugh. She suspected that he felt the same about her.

Over the next few days their stay in Follettville seemed like a courtship to Gabrielle. Knowing Cade as well as she did, she knew he wanted to be with her and to hold her at night. Sometimes when she turned suddenly she caught him watching her with that smoldering interest that made her heart knock, but he didn't come to her room, nor did he exhibit any sign of excessive familiarity. He never embarrassed her in even the smallest way or revealed in a single gesture or utterance that there had been intimacy between them. He might be a "scoundrel," as he had referred to himself, but in public at least he was also a man of principle, and for that she was thankful.

The days flew by quickly, filled with shopping trips, picnics on the beach, and carriage rides. Every evening Tom had guests for dinner, and the assortment of people he knew astonished Gabrielle. She met people as varied as politicians, Confederate officers, a riverboat captain, and two actors from the theater troupe. The only people she did not see were Lacy and Wyatt, and she wondered if their omission had been deliberate on Tom's part.

During the day she occupied her time with one of her favorite pursuits, shopping. She knew some men disliked shopping trips, but Cade didn't appear to mind. In fact, he seemed to enjoy it. Gabrielle interviewed a couple of dressmakers he recommended, and the one she decided to use seemed quite knowledgeable about fashion, for such an out of the way place as Follettville. She examined bolt after bolt of fabric and pattern sketch after pattern sketch before she made a decision. Cade, she discovered, had a good eye for color and fashion, and she found herself asking for his opinion quite often.

Gabrielle knew she had never been so happy. The trouble in New Orleans seemed distant and remote compared to the golden light of falling in love in Texas, and she wanted nothing to change.

On the last day of their stay, Gabrielle awoke later than usual. It must have been midmorning by the time she left her room. From the top of the stairs she caught sight of Cade in the foyer, preparing to leave. Tom's voice echoed from the veranda as he shouted instructions to the gardener. She smiled. How typical of Tom to yell and bluster when he could summon the man to the front porch and offer suggestions in a civilized way.

"Are you going out?" Gabrielle called softly.

Cade turned and smiled when he saw her. He walked to the foot of the stairs, propped a shiny black boot on the first step, and let his gaze drift appreciatively over her. She wore a dress of green-sprigged white muslin with short puffed sleeves. Its low, rounded neckline revealed just the beginning swell of her breasts. A matching green ribbon had been threaded through the auburn curls piled high on the back of her head. Cade sighed as he watched her descent, once again admiring the enchanting woman he had fallen in love with. She looked fresh-scrubbed and young, her beautiful face glowing with happiness.

He caught her hand when she reached the foot of the stairs. "I hope you slept well." His smile quirked wickedly, and Gabrielle blushed.

"I did," she answered coyly. "Did you?"

"Cade, are you coming or not?" Tom yelled as he entered the foyer. Seeing Gabrielle, he stopped. "Well, what do you know. Her grace has decided to make an appearance."

"Good morning, Tom."

"I have some banking business to take care of before we leave town," Cade told her. "We should be back by early afternoon." At the flicker of disappointment in her green eyes, he grinned. "Does that interfere with your plans?"

"Oh, no," Gabrielle protested quickly. After a moment she tilted her head to the side, reconsidering. "Well, maybe. Would you mind if Maria and I go in to see Mrs. Maybank this morning? I want to make a change on one of the patterns I picked out."

Cade laughed, then turned. "Tom, do you think your driver could take Gabrielle and Maria to the dressmaker's this morning?"

"Of course," he agreed, pulling on his gloves. "I'll let Manuel know before we leave."

"Would you mind if Zeke drove us in?" Gabrielle asked quickly.

Cade's brows lifted. "I thought you didn't like Zeke."

She shrugged lightly. "I've gotten used to him."

"Sure, he can take you in. As a matter of fact," Cade added, considering, "there are a few items he can pick up for me at the feed store."

Gabrielle finished her business with the dressmaker as quickly as she could. For some reason the woman's manner had undergone a change overnight. She had turned rude and abrupt, and after having promised Cade that she'd have the dresses finished within a month, she told Gabrielle that she didn't know when she could get to them.

"I don't like her much, do you?" Maria muttered beneath her breath as they walked out of the shop.

Gabrielle lifted her parasol over her head, her expression puzzled. "It's the strangest thing. Yesterday Mrs. Maybank couldn't possibly have been any more pleasant and helpful." Her brows came together in a slight frown. Then she shrugged and looked at Maria. "Well, we shan't let her upset us. We have a few minutes before we're supposed to meet Zeke. Shall we walk down to the Emporium and look at their ribbons?"

Maria nodded and fell into step beside her. "Seems like there's a lot of people in town, doesn't it?"

Gabrielle nodded. "There must be something special happening."

As they made their way down the street, Gabrielle grew uneasy. There was something disturbing about the people who stood around on the street, clustered in small groups, not talking much. She felt a sinister and charged energy beneath their surface.

A small gathering of townswomen fell silent as Gabrielle and Maria approached. When her smile was met with stony glances, a chill traveled down Gabrielle's spine in spite of the heat.

Maria pressed close, her voice low. "What's the matter with everybody?"

"I don't know." Unconsciously, Gabrielle increased her pace. "I have one other item to pick up, and then maybe Zeke will be back." She looked over her shoulder at the women and realized they were still watching her. "I hope it doesn't take Zeke too long," she whispered nervously. After closing her parasol, Gabrielle opened the door to the Emporium.

A dark-haired woman walked out from behind the counter, her heavy features sullen with hate. "You ain't welcome in this establishment, missy. We don't allow traitors in here."

As the words registered in her mind, Gabrielle's face drained of color. For a moment she stared at the woman without moving.

Maria caught her hand, pulling her back. "Let's go."

The woman edged forward threateningly, gripping her broom as if she meant to strike them. "Go on. Get out."

Gabrielle whirled around so quickly that her skirts flared out, briefly brushing against the woman's. Once outside, she stopped and pressed her hand against her breast. Her heart pounded as if it would leap from her chest.

"Oh, dear God," she whispered. Somehow word

of what had happened in New Orleans had spread
to Follettville. The people standing about on the
street were talking about her! She turned and saw
fear and bewilderment in Maria's brown eyes, but
she didn't have time to explain now.

"Maria," she whispered urgently, catching the
girl's hand, "we must find Zeke. You look in Ste-
ven's Merchandise, and I'll check at the feed store.
I'll meet you back here in five minutes. Please
hurry."

Without waiting for a reply, Gabrielle walked
briskly along the boardwalk toward the corner.
Drawing a quick breath of relief, she saw that the
narrow side street was empty. She held her skirts
from the dusty ground to keep from tripping as she
scurried down the street. Chaotic, fearful thoughts
whirled in her head, shattering her concentration.
Where was the feed store? She thought it was on a
backstreet . . . by the blacksmith. They had driven
past it a couple of days before, and Tom had mentioned that the man who owned it owed him money.
At the far corner she stopped, her hands knotting in
anxious frustration. She had found the feed store
she was looking for and there were several buck-
boards parked along the front, but the surrey Zeke
had driven wasn't in sight.

Feeling panicky, she turned to retrace her steps,
then hesitated at the sight of two men walking down
the narrow street toward her. She started forward,
then stopped again uncertainly when something
about them caused the hair to raise on the back of
her neck. Their faces were shadowed beneath the
brims of their hats, and they walked about four feet
apart, their arms slightly out from their bodies as if
poised for attack. A chill traveled down her spine.
Overwhelmed by a premonition of danger, Gabrielle
turned and ran as hard as she could, but their foot-

steps thudded on the hard ground behind her, coming closer and closer. One of the men grabbed her about the waist, silently jerking her off her feet, while his left hand covered her mouth, stifling her scream. The other caught her flailing hands and tied them behind her back, then stuffed a gag in her mouth. Her frenzied struggles were futile against the strength of her attackers.

A blanket came down over her head, and one of the men wrapped it tightly around her upper body. Gabrielle felt herself lifted and tossed roughly over one man's shoulder, knocking the breath from her.

A masculine voice floated into her consciousness. "You sure we take her to the jail?"

"Yeah," a raspy voice answered. "The sheriff's on a manhunt and the deputy's off on a wild-goose chase."

In the next few minutes she was aware only of the movement of the man's body, the lift of three wooden steps, the echo of a long damp corridor, and the clang and rasp of rusty hinges. Then suddenly the man stopped.

"Did you get her?" a coarse female voice demanded. Apparently one of the men nodded, for she spoke again. "Unwrap her. Let's see."

Gabrielle landed on the cot with a hard jolt. The blanket was caught and jerked from her, rolling her onto her stomach.

"That's her," another woman muttered in low-voiced triumph. "Take the gag out of her mouth."

Gabrielle opened her eyes and stared at the coarse pillow and further on, to the bars that separated the cells. She recognized the woman's voice as Lacy's. She tried to twist over on her back.

"You men go on now," a third woman ordered. "You've done your job."

Gabrielle heard their heavy booted steps retreating as rough hands flipped her over and pulled the gag from her mouth. The sight before her caused her to cringe in horror. She was surrounded by women dressed in black, wearing masks. Only their eyes gleamed through the ragged holes cut in the grotesque black hoods.

She struggled to a half-sitting position, trying to control her terror. "What do you want?" she gasped.

One of them stepped forward, her finger pointed toward Gabrielle's face. "We're aiming to teach you a lesson," she announced. "You spying slut. You've been prancing about our streets like a high-toned lady, but now you'll see how we Texans treat the likes of you."

A streak of silver gleamed in her uplifted hand, and Gabrielle recoiled from the flash of a blade. Then she saw that it was a pair of scissors the woman held, not a knife.

"Get it done," came an impatient order." Again, it was Lacy's muffled voice.

The women swarmed over Gabrielle, fingers pinching, nails scratching. One caught a handful of hair close to her scalp and jerked her head forward. Only then did Gabrielle realize that they were going to cut her hair. She closed her eyes when she heard the sawing of the blades through a thick strand. Seconds later she felt a feathery touch as the long curl drifted over her shoulder and along her arm. At that moment she quit fighting and kept her eyes closed. The ordeal went on and on. *Whisk. Whisk. Whisk.* Their hateful voices echoed in her ears as they called her a Yankee whore, a traitor, and other things so horrible that her mind refused to register them. Finally the women's clamor faded into a strained silence. Her passivity gave them nothing to fuel their hate.

"Now, Yankee whore," a voice rasped, striving for the earlier bravado, "you may waltz up and down Main Street to your heart's content. You have a crowd awaiting you."

It was over. One of them shoved her, and Gabrielle fell on her side. She felt the silky pile of her loose hair against her arm, her cheek, and even her shoulder.

"Come on," the same voice hissed. "Let's get out of here."

She heard their running feet but didn't open her eyes. There was no place to hide, no place to go. She wanted to die.

Maria had found Zeke within minutes, but they couldn't find Gabrielle. During their brief search they discovered her parasol in an alley, still open, two of its spokes broken. Zeke's face was young and scared. "Cade's at the bank, let's go get him."

They reached the Exchange Bank just in time to meet Cade and Tom as they walked out the door. In frantic bits and pieces, Maria told Cade what had happened.

He started off at a run before she could finish. He didn't have to look for Gabrielle. It seemed the whole town had gathered on the street in front of the jail. He shouldered his way through, pushing townspeople ruthlessly aside. The fragments of sentences he heard caused his blood to run cold.

"A spy," they said. "This'll teach her a lesson." They were the kind of distorted rumors that fed a mob's hate.

Just inside the jail entrance, Cade stopped, his eyes adjusting to the dim interior. Tom, Zeke, and Maria crowded behind him. The desk where the sheriff usually sat was empty. The jail was deathly silent.

"Wait here," Cade told them.

His heart filled with dread, he headed toward the corridor of the individual cells that angled off the main room. His footsteps sounded abnormally loud as he crossed the hardwood floor and the angry shouting of the crowd dimmed. The first cell was empty. Slowly he moved to the second. There was a slight mound on the cot of the third cell. At the door he stopped, his chest feeling as if giant hand were crushing the life from him. Shimmering strands of auburn hair covered the floor, catching the rays of sunlight slanting through the small barred window. Gabrielle lay motionless, eyes closed, hands tied behind her. Her hair had been chopped off inches from her scalp.

"Gabrielle."

She seemed to cringe from his voice, but he saw that she was alive. Only then did his heart start beating again. Weak with relief, he knelt beside the cot, untied her hands, and drew her limp body into his arms. He pressed her head into the hollow of his neck. "Dear God, Gabrielle. How did this happen to you?" Rage and pain seemed to tear at his insides.

His long fingers threaded through the ragged, spiky lengths of her hair. He kissed her forehead and the top of her head, then studied her pale face. Her fine-boned features seemed unbearably fragile. She shuddered and covered her face.

"It'll grow back, sweetheart."

She started to cry in loud body-shuddering sobs, and Cade folded her in his arms.

Tom stepped to the doorway, his voice low. "Cade, we have to get the hell out of here. That crowd's getting nasty."

"Is Zeke with you?"

"Yeah. He's still at the door."

"Keep them back for a few minutes, that's all I need."

Tom gave him a doubtful glance, and his gaze dropped over the scattered curls. "I'll do what I can."

After Tom left, Cade caught Gabrielle's shoulders and held her away from him. "Listen to me. There's only one way out of here and that's out the front door. You've got to walk out beside me."

Gabrielle bowed her head, tears flowing down her cheeks. "I can't."

Cade's voice filled with emotion. "Are you guilty of spying, Gabrielle?"

She went still, and then her bright green eyes, shadowed by incredibly long lashes, met his. "No."

"Then you'll walk out, and you'll do it with all the grace and dignity you possess. Do you understand?"

Her eyes clung to his as if she would draw some magic strength from him. She looked so incredibly young, so shattered, that Cade's heart twisted with pity and hatred—a fierce, fiery hatred for whoever had done this to her.

He stood up. "You don't have to say anything, only stay beside me."

The crowd rumbled as they waited for Gabrielle to emerge from the jail. When she stepped through the door with Cade's arm protectively around her shoulders, they grew silent. She fell short of their expectations. With her hair ragged about her pale, beautiful face, she looked too young and tender to be the coldblooded spy they had heard about. Her body seemed slight beside Cade's, vunerable and defenseless. Hardened hearts twisted with shock at the sight of her frailty. A few dropped their eyes and turned away, ashamed to see what had been done.

Cade stared at the assembled throng, his face flint-hard with fury. "Had Gabrielle been hurt," he announced, his words spaced for emphasis, "I would have burned this town to the ground."

A petulant voice whined from their midst. "She's a traitor, Mr. Montana. We were just givin' her what she deserves. We weren't meanin' no disrespect to you."

The words provoked a rustle of movement in the crowd, and Cade's mouth twisted with anger, "Gabrielle St. Claire is going to be my wife. What you have done to her you have done to me, and I will never forget or forgive it. This woman is not a traitor to the South, you are. You have betrayed every principle the South stands for," he declared, his voice strained with rage. "If ever a man or woman touches her again with harm in mind, I will kill him."

Tom Rawlings stepped up beside Gabrielle. "You bunch of sons-of-bitches. I, too, plan to protect Gabrielle St. Claire. If any of you even sneers at her name, I'll shoot your ass with my shotgun."

Dignified and handsome, Wyatt Fielding stepped up on the boardwalk, his white suit and white Panama hat bright in the strong light of midday. "Those are my sentiments exactly," he stated, turning to face the crowd.

The townspeople shifted uneasily as another figure circled around the outside of the throng. A brassy-haired woman of middle age walked up on the boardwalk beside Fielding. The men in the crowd knew her as Lorna, the madam of the Golden Slipper. Her gaudy, low-cut dress appeared absurdly out of place. She looked at Gabrielle a moment, then turned to the crowd. "I'm a good judge of character. I meet so many lowlife bastards, I ought to have some insight. This little wisp of a gal you call a spy ain't too many years away from her mama's tit, and she ain't no traitor."

A man advanced a few steps out of the crush of people, hat held nervously in front of him. "Mr. Montana, we didn't mean to offend you. We heard that you were near forced to keep the girl at your ranch. Nobody here realized your feelings for her." There were nods of agreement in the throng about him. "Besides, most of us are just onlookers. We heard about what was happening and just wandered down here out of curiosity."

"Onlookers, my ass!" Tom exploded. "Ten minutes ago you were calling her a Yankee whore and trying to push your way through that door."

Lorna turned to Cade. "Take her home, Montana. I don't think there's going to be any more trouble from this bunch of yokels."

Cade guided Gabrielle down the three wooden steps of the jail. The crowd, now silent, made an aisle through which they passed.

Chapter 11

Cade knocked lightly on Gabrielle's bedroom door and waited. A second knock brought no response. Thinking she must have fallen asleep, he opened the door and walked silently inside. Catching sight of her, he stopped in the dim shadows outside the reach of lamplight. She sat on the side of the bed, head bowed in contemplation, her bare toes just touching the floor. Her hair, still slightly damp from her bath, curled in thick auburn strands around her head. He knew Maria had trimmed it earlier to even up its ragged lengths.

She wore only her white shift, and her hands were folded in her lap. She appeared quite childlike in the circle of light. All during the trip back from Follettville, she had been withdrawn and remote, and upon returning to the ranch she had gone directly to her own room. Cade didn't understand her behavior. She refused to talk about what had happened, and she didn't cry.

How had the damned story gotten out, anyway? Cade's scowl made his handsome face look demonic in the dim light. No one on the Committee would have told, and he had learned that there had been no scandal in New Orleans. Even Ruben Guillotte had escaped before the public learned of his treason.

Someone had had to dig for the information, purposely looking for it. But to hurt Gabrielle, or him?

She straightened suddenly, causing the light to fall full on her face, and a fleeting agitation replaced the sadness Cade had observed before. She rose restlessly to her feet, and saw Cade as she turned.

"I didn't hear you come in," she said, automatically reaching for her robe. She slipped into it quickly but not before Cade saw the ugly bruise on her shoulder and the scratch down her arm.

Something twisted hard inside him. He felt frustrated that she wouldn't talk about what had happened. He knew only that two men had abducted her and that a group of women had cut her hair. She refused to say anything more. He imagined the scene over and over in his head, and the thought of it made him sick with rage. Seeing Gabrielle shift uneasily under his scrutiny, he walked further into the circle of lamplight.

"Tell me what happened."

She half turned away from him. "I can't. I didn't see anything," she said, her tone lifeless.

He ran his fingers through his hair in bewilderment. "I want to find out who's responsible, Gabrielle. I want them to pay for what they did to you. Please help me do that."

She looked over her shoulder, bitterness sounding in her voice. "They're women. You can't shoot them or fight them. Nothing will ever happen to them no matter who they are."

"Let me make that decision."

To tell him would be so simple, Gabrielle thought, staring down at her hands. But no words could describe what had happened in her heart and mind, because she didn't understand it herself. They hadn't just cut her hair—it seemed as if they had cut her soul. She didn't think Cade would understand that, and she knew she couldn't tell him about Lacy, not yet anyway. Lacy had witnessed her shame, had seen her defenseless and pitiful, and had reveled in it. Gabrielle knew she wasn't ready to talk about that.

She turned to face Cade. "Thank you for what you said to the crowd. It was noble and it took a lot of courage. Those people were really angry."

A muscle flexed along Cade's jaw. "I'm not being noble, Gabrielle. I told them what I believe. I think you're innocent."

She nodded. "It's been a long time since someone said they believed in me." She bit her lip, wishing her tears weren't so close to the surface. "I'm glad that it's you."

Despite her seeming courage, Gabrielle's manner disturbed Cade. He paced over to the window, then turned back abruptly. "Let's stop this, for God's sake. I feel as though I'm talking to a stranger." He started toward her, but stopped when Gabrielle flinched. "Please don't hold yourself from me anymore. I don't give a damn that your hair's been cut. Sleep with me tonight. Let me hold you; let me know what you're going through."

When he reached for her, she drew back. "Cade, don't!" she declared sharply. She braced a hand against a chair back and drew in a shuddering breath. "If you touch me, I won't be able to stay strong."

"I don't want you to stay strong. I want you to cry or do whatever the hell it is you need to do."

"This is what I need to do," she cried. She closed her eyes, her face pale. "I'm doing what I need to do. Please just let me be."

Gabrielle felt crumbled to ashes inside. She wanted to close the door and hide forever. She didn't want anyone to see her, and she didn't want anyone to talk to her. Feeling desperate and near the end of her strength, she walked out onto the balcony.

Cade followed. "Gabrielle, we will get through this and the hard times will pass."

She spun around, voicing the thought that had come repeatedly to her mind. "I want to leave here, Cade." Her voice turned pleading. "I could go to Europe. I know Uncle Tyler will be willing to pay for the trip. If he knew what I've gone through, I know he'd do it. No one would know me there, and I wouldn't have to go through this agony."

Cade studied her silently for a long moment. "Gabrielle, it's never good to run away. You're innocent. Let's prove it."

"How?" Desperation filled her softly voiced question.

"I've hired a detective. He's been in New Orleans now for about three weeks."

She turned, her expression guarded. "Have you heard from him?"

He shook his head. "It's too soon."

She stood very still. "Have you told Uncle Tyler?"

"No. I don't want Celeste to find out anything. Besides, this could take some time."

Gabrielle threaded her fingers together, clenching them tightly. "How long?"

"The break we need might come tomorrow . . . or it could be a year. There's no way of knowing."

The hope that had briefly animated Gabrielle's face faded, and she turned to gaze out across the moonlit hills. "A year's a long time."

"Maybe, but you've got your whole life to live, and I want it to be a life with honor. I'll get the proof we need, just give me time. Ruben Guillotte is a fool. I know he made a mistake somewhere along the line, and I'll find it. You can count on it."

She sighed. "I wish I felt as sure of everything as you do."

"You're tired," he told her gently. "I think you should get some rest."

She nodded, then stood on tiptoe and kissed his cheek. "Thank you."

Cade wanted to take her in his arms, but he didn't. That wasn't what she wanted. He turned at the door and said, "Good night, Gabrielle."

"Good night."

Cade took the stairs two at a time and turned down the corridor toward Gabrielle's room, his face set with determination. Over the last ten days she had grown more and more despondent. She declined all Cade's invitations and requested meals in her room. When he tried to reason with her, she told him that she needed more time. But each day brought no improvement. This morning he had made up his mind that her days of seclusion had come to an end.

He halted and rapped sharply at her door. When Gabrielle didn't answer he turned the knob, pushed the door open, and stepped inside. The drapes were drawn tightly across the windows, shrouding the bedroom in gloom even though the sun shone brightly outside. Gabrielle lay on the chaise longue, but she sat up with a start when she saw him.

"Good morning," he said briefly, walking over and opening her drapes, allowing the sunlight to flood the room.

"The light hurts my eyes," she protested.

"We have company for breakfast," Cade advised her, his face unsympathetic. "I told you last night that Sam Fortune would be joining us."

Gabrielle rose to her feet, disturbed by his manner. "I'm not hungry."

Cade noticed the wilted roses in the vase on the table. In the past, Gabrielle had always loved to have flowers around her. "You can have a cup of coffee," he told her briefly.

Her face, thinner than before, revealed a hint of petulance. "I don't want coffee."

"Then come down and just sit at the table."

"I would prefer not to," she said, crossing her arms over her chest. "I appreciate that you thought of me, however."

"I'm afraid you have no choice in the matter," Cade informed her flatly. "If you are not in your chair in the dining room in ten minutes, I'm coming after you." He walked to the door before turning back to her. "I will not allow you to hide away in this room any longer, and that's final." He left without bothering to shut the door.

Stunned, Gabrielle stared after Cade, a riot of emotion churning through the depression that gripped her. Cade had been so thoughtful and considerate ever since the incident at Follettville, but she should have known it wouldn't last. The old, arrogant Cade had resurfaced. Her soft mouth compressed tightly as she thought about his ultimatum. Unconsciously her hands knotted the fabric of her skirt. She had to go downstairs or he would come and drag her down. She knew he would do it. The normal code of decent behavior meant nothing to him.

When Gabrielle entered the dining room a few minutes later, Cade and Sam Fortune were engrossed in conversation, and only Maria noticed her arrival. "Good morning, senorita."

"Good morning, Maria."

Noting her presence, both men rose to their feet,

and Cade stepped around the table to hold her chair for her. The animosity Gabrielle felt toward him was almost a physical pain.

"How nice to have you join us," Cade greeted her pleasantly. One would never be able to tell from his affable manner that he had just stormed out of her room, leaving a threat to settle over her head.

Gabrielle did not answer. She would not strive to make this breakfast tolerable for the sake of convention. She would let him handle the awkwardness.

Seemingly unaware of her festering mood, Sam continued to tell Cade about a new man who had been hired within the last few weeks. He had a checkered past, apparently, but he knew cattle and could ride like a Comanche.

As she sat listening, Gabrielle's indignation escalated. Sam Fortune could not be considered company. He ate at the main house often, and his presence did not justify Cade's insistence that she come down. He was only bullying her, just as he had done in the past. The thought made her furious. After what she had been through she didn't deserve such callous treatment.

The men made no attempt to draw her into their discussion of business. Sam suggested moving the cattle up to the north range. What did she care if recent rains had improved the grass? Too agitated to sit still, she arose. "Excuse me, please," she said, her tone as brittle as breaking ice.

Cade's brows swooped upward with displeasure. "Sit down."

Gabrielle stared at his stubborn, arrogant face. It took only the space of a heartbeat for her shock to change to fury. "I will not," she snapped, holding her back ramrod straight.

"You are not going back to your room."

Disbelieving his capacity for rudeness, she found

herself again unable to respond for a moment. "That's fine," she replied sharply, recovering her composure. "I will not go back to my room." She stalked out of the dining room and didn't stop until she reached the front door. Hearing Cade's boot steps behind her, she walked onto the veranda, then whirled to confront him.

"How could you humiliate me so?" she demanded, her voice low with fury. "After what I've been through, how can you be so cruel? I told you I needed time!"

Cade shifted his weight, his hands resting on his gunbelt. "You've *had* time and it hasn't helped. I won't have you hiding in your room anymore."

She spun and ran down the front stairs. With his long strides, Cade easily caught up with her. "Keep away from me," she cried.

"I can't do that."

"Why are you acting like this?" she demanded. "Last week you were so sensitive and understanding, and I thought you were wonderful. Why do you have to destroy everything by being a brute?"

"I'm not destroying anything. You are."

Recognizing the futility of trying to make Cade understand, Gabrielle pivoted and angled her steps toward the stables. Too late she saw the men leaning against the corral fence, and her pace faltered. Inside the corral a rider was taking a wild mustang to the end of its strength. The animal crow-hopped about, its neck lathered with sweat. Even as she watched, the animal ceased bucking. Its head hung and it breathed in great gasps of air.

She closed her eyes for a moment, then continued to walk. She didn't want the men to see her, but pride kept her from turning back. She would not give Cade reason to accuse her of hiding.

"You don't want them to see you, do you?" he taunted.

"Leave me alone."

"You want to go back to your room, don't you, Gabrielle, and never let anyone see you again."

"I do not."

Cade caught her hand and pulled her to an abrupt stop. "You're ashamed, aren't you?"

Jerking her wrist from his grip, she glared at him. "Of course I'm ashamed," she said. "My hair is chopped off. My very name has become a curse on everyone's tongue! How in the name of God do you expect me to feel?"

Unmoved by her desperate outburst, Cade responded levelly, "I expect you to do what you have to do to go on with your life."

"Ohhh!" His insensitivity caused tears to burn her eyes, and the dam that held in her pain finally broke. "I can't look at myself in the mirror without cringing," she cried, oblivious to the men who turned to stare.

"Why is that?" Cade demanded, grabbing hold of her wrist. "Are you guilty? Is that why you can't look at yourself?"

"No, I'm not guilty!" she tried to jerk her arm away, but Cade held it firmly. She tugged at his fingers, then realizing he would not release her, she went still. Tears ran down her cheeks.

"I'll tell you why I can't look in the mirror," she said, her eyes shooting sparks of fire. "With my hair chopped off, I don't feel pretty anymore. I don't feel like a woman. And you want to know why I hide? Because I'm scared. I'm being scorned like some kind of vermin." Her eyes narrowed, and her hands clenched into fists. "How dare you ask me if I'm guilty. How dare you! You said you believed me. You gave me hope that one person in this whole world believed me!'' Overcome, she pressed her hands against her face, sobbing so hard her shoulders shook.

''Others believe in you,'' Cade charged, his tone unrelenting. ''Or have you forgotten that fact while you wallow in self-pity?''

Gabrielle jerked her hands away from her face and stared at him as if he had turned into a monster. ''I am not wallowing in self-pity!''

''Tom told the whole damned town that he believed you. So did Wyatt Fielding.''

''They said that for your sake,''

Cade's brows lifted. ''So you think they're liars?''

''I didn't say that!''

''Well, either they lied or they told the truth. If they were telling the truth, then they believe in you.''

A young cowboy stepped off the fence and walked toward Cade. ''Mr. Montana, my name is Kiley. I know you're my boss, sir, but I don't think you should upset Miss St. Claire like this.''

''What I say to Miss St. Claire is none of your business,'' Cade answered grimly.

''Well, maybe not, but I think she's been through enough,'' Kiley persisted. He nodded toward the men who stood along the corral fence. ''Me and the boys heard about what happened in town, and we sort of made a pact to watch out for her.''

Cade scowled. ''Is that right?''

''Yes, sir.''

''And you think I mean her harm?''

''Well, we overheard what you said about self-pity, and yes, sir, I think it's cruel. What happened in town was real bad, and I don't think it's self-pitying for her to be sad. Even real sad.'' He looked Gabrielle's stunned face. ''Frankly, ma'am, I promised myself I wouldn't stare the first time I saw you 'cause I imagined your hair to be all straggly. But you're ever' bit as pretty as you used to be. Just different, that's all. So you don't have to worry about not looking like a woman, 'cause you do. And I bet every one of the fellas back there agrees." He blushed as if unaccustomed to so many effusive words. "The boys and I feel pretty strongly about this," he added, turning back to Cade.

Cade glanced over at Sam Fortune, who had wandered down to stand watching, then squinted down at the young man. "I don't take kindly to advice. You know that, don't you?"

"I know that, sir. And I don't mean to be disrespectful."

Gabrielle stepped closer, fearing Cade might hurt the young cowboy. "Cade, please, just let the matter drop." The smile she bestowed on Kiley was strained but gracious. "Thank you and the others for your offers of protection. I appreciate your support." She gave Cade a scathing look, then turned on her heel and walked toward the house with head held high.

The young man shifted uncertainly. After a moment Cade pulled his gaze from Gabrielle's departing figure and glared at him. "Go on back to work."

The boy fidgeted nervously. "Are you going to fire me?"

"No."

"Thank you, sir." Kiley started to walk away, but Cade's voice stopped him.

"Don't make a habit of offering me criticism. You understand, Kiley?"

"Yes, sir."

Sam Fortune sauntered over, a matchstick held between his teeth and an ironic smile on his mouth.

"That's mighty fine acting, Montana. You pay Kiley
to say that?

Cade shifted his gunbelt about his lean hips and
grimaced. "No, but I would have if I'd thought of
it. It's good for Gabrielle to know people are behind
her." He shook his head. "I tell you, she's got a
temper. I'd hate to see her really riled."

"You did the right thing, boss," Fortune observed
laconically. "Some womenfolks get kind of dazed
when they go through something bad, and it takes
a shock to get 'em back. I figure it's like spanking a
new baby to get him breathing. It hurts, but it
works."

Cade cast him a humorous sidelong lock. "You
turning into a philosopher, Sam?"

"Hell, no. If I'm beginning to sound like one, I
guess I better get to work."

Over the next few days Gabrielle's spirits improved considerably. She found it comforting to
know that Cade's men were on her side—that they
felt so strongly about her plight they were willing to
confront Cade. And Kiley's heartfelt compliment had
not gone unnoticed, either. For the first time Gabrielle had taken a long, honest look at herself in the
mirror. She didn't look so terrible, and she could do
a lot with her hair. After experimenting a bit, she
found if she used flowers and ribbons, she could
give it the illusion of length.

But the problem with Cade remained. She had not
spoken to him since their argument and she doubted
she would ever forgive him for being so cruel. But
gradually Gabrielle's anger subsided, and she began
to think rationally. In truth, Cade didn't have much
patience, even for those who had suffered. But how
could she expect a man like him, accustomed to
Western ways, to understand a woman's more del-

icate nature? And he had been very kind and understanding to her at times. Was it fair to think only
of his bad points?

That night as she was getting ready for bed, Gabrielle's fingers stopped while she was unfastening
the buttons of her dress. Her thoughts swirled and
her emerald eyes glinted with decision. The standoff
with Cade had gone on long enough. Fastening the
tiny pearl buttons again, she glanced at herself in
the mirror. Knowing Cade was working late in his
study, she headed downstairs. At least she could tell
him how she felt. She would tell him honestly, and
if he got angry, well, he got angry.

The study door had been left open to allow a
breeze, and Gabrielle stopped in the doorway. Cade
looked up from his writing and returned his pen to
the inkwell when he saw her.

"Please, come in."

Gabrielle walked inside and closed the door. She
stood silent for a moment, then spoke quietly. "I
have thought about our conflict quite a bit over the
last few days," she admitted, advancing to the center of the room, "and I've decided to forgive you."

"Oh?"

"Yes. I realize men don't have the sensibilities that
women do, and perhaps you couldn't know the pain
I've felt. Even though I've been angry, I've remembered the things you've done for me. You stood up
to the crowd, and I consider that a very courageous
act. You've been considerate in the last few weeks,
and you even hired a detective. That's why I didn't
understand your cruel behavior the other day. But
despite that, I'm willing to drop the matter if you
are."

Cade looked down at his desk and thought for a
moment before he looked up. "Well, I'm certainly
willing to drop hostilities. I'm glad you've found it

in your heart to forgive me," he said with a touch of sarcasm.

"You can be frightfully difficult and grumpy, Cade." Her mouth pursed prettily as she observed him like a mother with a difficult child. "I thought you were going to shoot Kiley."

Cade leaned back in his chair, one brow arching upward. "Thankfully *you* intervened."

"Are you mocking me?" she asked suspiciously.

"Certainly not," he replied, his face solemn. "I think you're quite magnanimous. Since we are now on speaking terms," he said, his blue eyes glinting, "how would you like to go for a ride tomorrow? The first cotton wagons are coming through, and I thought you might want to have a look."

Gabrielle was undecided. She hadn't expected the discussion to go as easily as it had. "I think that might be nice," she answered slowly.

Cade stood up. "Tomorrow then."

Gabrielle nodded. "Tomorrow." She walked out, shut the door, and stared at the painting on the opposite wall without really seeing it. Why did she feel that their conversation had gone exactly as Cade had wanted it to?

The following morning Cade and Gabrielle set out on horseback immediately after breakfast. During their ride he conducted himself so pleasantly, and Gabrielle found him so charming and attentive, that all her leftover resentments gradually evaporated. The hazy early morning turned into a beautiful day. Knee-high grass undulated like ocean waves in the breeze, and overhead not a single cloud marred the clear, blue sky. The heat that had been unbearable the day before had lessened.

Reaching a tree-topped knoll, Gabrielle was the first to catch sight of a distant wagon train as it meandered down the grass-covered hillside. Dismounting, she watched in silence, counting nearly a hundred wagons heavily loaded with cotton bales. Cotton pulled loose from the wagons and clung to the tall grass and underbrush close to the way of access. The train seemed endless, and she could see that a trail of cotton bolls would be left to mark its passage.

"It must be all the cotton in the South," she breathed, impressed by the magnitude of the venture.

Cade shook his head. "There'll be a wagon train that big coming through quite often—as long as the North doesn't find out," he added darkly.

She turned and looked at him suddenly, happiness filling her heart as she realized that Cade must really believe she was innocent if he was trusting her with this information. It was as if he had brought her here to show her the wagon trail as proof of his faith in her.

Cade caught her waist and lifted her bodily onto her saddle. "There's a stream just east of us where we can water the horses. Then we'll ride over to the wagon train, if you'd like."

As they rode across the stretch of grassland, Cade answered Gabrielle's questions about the cotton train and its contribution to the Southern war effort. After a few minutes they both fell silent, grimly reminded of the specter of the distant war. It made them both appreciate the relative peace in which they lived.

When they were within sight of the tree-lined creek, Gabrielle shrugged off her ponderous thoughts and kicked her horse into a run. "I'll race you," she yelled to him over her shoulder.

She beat Cade by a length, breathless from her exertion. Her green eyes sparkling with devilment, she taunted, "You're going to have to ask Zeke to give you riding lessons."

Cade laughed. "I let you win."

"No, you didn't," she retorted. "I won fair and square." She slid off her horse without waiting for Cade's help, caught the reins, and led the animal through the trees toward the water. Willows shaded the creek banks, and she walked toward a hollowed-out place where water spilled over the rocks and formed a shallow basin.

Ducking low-hanging branches, Cade nudged his horse behind her. Idly he let his gaze drop over Gabrielle's slender back and, without meaning to, his attention focused on the prim, but provocative swing of her hips. He could almost feel the silkiness of her skin against his palm as he imagined running his hand over the firm curve of her hip. Drawing a deep breath, he dismounted. Even the location seemed erotic to his already stimulated thoughts. It had privacy, a thick carpet of green grass, and trees to provide an arbor over their heads.

His mouth crimping into a grin at his thoughts, he led his horse down to the water. When he glanced around, he saw that Gabrielle had plopped down on a rock and was tugging off her riding boots. "I'm going wading," she announced. "You want to come?"

"No, thanks."

A log had fallen across the narrow end of the hollowed-out pool, and she started walking across it. Cade watched her as she balanced, vividly remembering their first intimate encounter. She had been a graceful little cat, seducing him with the innocent jiggle of her breasts beneath her chemise and her bold responsiveness. His hungry gaze slid over her now. She wore a wide-brimmed straw hat which hid her hair, a blue skirt, and a soft white blouse. A glimpse of slender ankles and bare feet flashed briefly as Gabrielle held her skirt and chose her footing with care. The ruffles of her petticoats peaked demurely from beneath the dark blue fabric of her skirt as she stepped along the log, a vivid reminder to Cade of her lacy underclothes.

When she reached the other side, she turned back, laughing. "Why don't you try it, Cade?" Her brows lifted in a playful challenge. "Or are you afraid you'll fall in?"

"I'm afraid I'll fall in," he agreed easily, dropping down and leaning back against the trunk of a cottonwood. He pulled a cheroot from his vest pocket. "You can be the daring one."

Her cheeks flushed, she started back across, placing one foot in front of the other, her slender body swaying and posing for balance. Cade swallowed, his eyes turning midnight-blue with his thoughts.

Stopping midway, she lifted her hand to her forehead, blocking the glare of sunbeams. "I bet you can't catch me." She smiled at him and raised one slim brow suggestively.

The tantalizing implication behind that dare brought Cade to his feet, and he tossed his cheroot away, half smoked. He could think of nothing he wanted more than to catch Gabrielle right now. He easily jumped the stones scattered across the shallow pond, which were spaced too far apart for Gabrielle. She giggled, surprised at how close he had come to capturing her, and retreated to the middle of the log. Bending on one knee and balancing precariously on one foot, she dipped the other foot in the water and tried to splash him.

"Come here, Gabrielle," Cade coaxed, avoiding the spray of water. He grinned slowly. "I want to tell you a secret."

She heard the husky timbre of his voice and shook

her head. "I don't think you have a secret," she responded coyly. "And you're not going to catch me through trickery." She crossed to the bank and turned to taunt Cade, only to see him jumping the last stone a few feet from her. With a shriek she ran across the bank and managed to put the cottonwood between them. Its vee-shaped trunk gave her the advantage, for she could easily tell which way he meant to move.

"What are you going to do when you catch me?" she teased, her eyes sparkling with merriment.

He grinned wickedly. "Would you like to know in detail?" He suddenly lunged for her, but she eluded him. Laughing and out of breath, she gazed at him through the split tree trunk. "I thought you didn't find me desirable anymore."

"Because of your hair?" He unbuckled his gunbelt and laid it on the ground.

She remained motionless, standing on tiptoe to watch his actions. "Yes."

He straightened and looked at her. "Short and curly the way it is, your hair always looks slightly disheveled, as if someone's been tossing you about in the hay. It makes me think about making love to you . . . all the time."

"Oh, you!" Gabrielle blushed.

Impatient with the game, Cade feigned a move to the right, and when she miscalculated his direction, he caught her. Seizing her wrist, he pulled her squealing into his arms, forcibly subduing her and kissing her mouth. A second later she relaxed in his arms. He held her gently.

After a long interval, Gabrielle pulled away, her gaze softening. "You weren't going to touch me until I wanted you to, were you?"

"No," he answered huskily.

She smiled, comforted by that knowledge. She

rose up on tiptoe and kissed his mouth, but resisted his embrace. Slowly, with trembling fingers, she unbuttoned the first two buttons of his shirt and slid a hand inside. With a sigh she ran her fingers through the crisp, curling hair, then laid her palm against his chest, feeling the strong beat of his heart. She touched her lips against his bronzed skin and felt his heartbeat quicken. Longing to be close to him, she unfastened the other buttons down to his belt and slid her arms around his lean, hard-muscled body. "I love the feel of you," she whispered, pressing her face against his chest. "Your warmth and strength." Her words were muffled against his body. "You make me feel shivery . . . and helpless . . . and strong . . . and female." She felt his heart begin to pound.

"Gabrielle . . ."

Cade set her away from him and quickly began to unbutton her blouse. The sight beneath caused a muscle to flex along his jaw. A frilly white corselet cupped her breasts, leaving the creamy upper portion uncovered. Unable to resist, he kissed each beginning swell, then dipped a finger beneath the lace to pop out a quivering peak, taut with excitement. With a groan he dropped his mouth over it, and he felt it tighten into a hard bud against his tongue. His mouth returned to hers in a fierce, demanding kiss, and this time when he lifted his head, his experienced fingers flew to the lacings of her corselet. In seconds it was undone, and he tossed her blouse and corselet to the ground, his eyes on Gabrielle. Dappled sunlight played sensuously over her upper body.

He tore off his shirt. "God, Gabrielle, you're beautiful."

His eyes dark and smoldering, he impatiently lowered her to the ground onto their discarded clothing. His mouth covered hers, while his hands drew up her skirt and petticoats. Unfastening her pantaloons, he pulled them from her without a word. After savoring the taste of her mouth and each pink nipple, Cade bypassed her bunched-up skirt to brush his lips against her stomach. Gabrielle's hand touched his hair, and she shook her head, unable to utter a word. Her breath was trapped in her throat. His breathing fluttered against the skin of her stomach and against her thighs, the exciting sensation causing her toes to curl. Slowly he moved lower, closer to the intimate part of her. His fingers touched her, and then his mouth, and Gabrielle felt as if she had turned to melted honey. That warm sensation soon grew to more insistent need.

Muttering an oath at the time it took, Cade jerked his boots and socks off and kicked free from his trousers. Then he pulled Gabrielle against him with raw urgency. Holding his body over hers he pressed her legs apart and thrust into her velvety warmth. He remained motionless for a moment, then shuddered at the sensation rocketing through his body. Drawing a ragged breath, and gaining some control, he slipped his hand beneath her hips. He moved to the rhythm that drummed through him, matching the beat of her heart.

Gabrielle thought completion only a breath away when Cade stopped moving. Disappointment clouded her emerald eyes when Cade suddenly rolled, carrying her with him, until she found herself on top, her hands pressed against his bare chest. She stared down at him in round-eyed surprise. Her skirt and petticoats covered them both, but Gabrielle felt him deep inside her.

Cade lifted, attempting to kiss each pink nipple thrust so delectably before him. After he had accomplished the feat, he glanced up at Gabrielle. "Now you can move the way you want to."

Gabrielle blushed and shook her head, but Cade caught her waist and lifted her, teaching her how to move. Gabrielle closed her eyes as the gentle, deep movements carried her into ecstasy.

After a bit Cade pulled her down against his chest and kissed her mouth. Then he turned with her until he again lay on top. His mouth covered hers, and his hands on her body tightened while his movements became strong and deliberate. Gabrielle felt herself spiraling with each hard thrust until the tightening knot at her center shattered into a million brightly colored pieces, and then shattered into a million more, over and over. After an interminable, breathless moment, the colors came floating down, mingling together like a watercolor painting in the rain. She lay for long moments, her eyes closed, replete. When Cade lifted from her, she was too enervated to move.

A soft breeze blew against their bodies, bringing her slowly back to the present. She felt happy and content, and she never wanted to live one day without Cade Montana.

Gabrielle was half dressed, wearing her pantaloons and corselet, while Cade was dressed only in trousers, his shirt dangling from his fingers, when he looked at her and asked, "When are you going to marry me?"

Gabrielle put her hand to her heart as a variety of expressions flickered across her face. Then she smiled tenderly and tossed her head. "Don't you think it might have been a bit more proper to mention marriage before . . . we were together?" she chided.

Cade laughed. "No, my little conventional miss,

I think it's very proper right now." Gabrielle turned away, smarting at his gentle teasing, and Cade caught her and held her against him. He kissed her neck. "I love you, Gabrielle," he said seriously. "I want you to be my wife."

Gabrielle heard his tone change and turned slowly in his arms, her gaze lifting to meet his. "And I love you, Cade. With all my heart and soul. I can't imagine living my life without you in it." Her fingers lifted to trail across his cheek. "You've taught me so much since I met you." She frowned slightly, and then her expression cleared. "I will never be the same, and I'm glad." Gabrielle laid her head against his chest and closed her eyes. Rapture flowed through her, filling her with a newfound peace as Cade's arms tightened around her.

Chapter 12

Gabrielle peered at herself closely in the mirror. Her hair seemed longer—only a little bit, of course, but every bit counted. Feeling more light-hearted than before, she brushed the short strands vigorously, and when they glowed with copper fire, pulled back one side and pinned a white lace flower over her ear. The rest of her hair curled with an unruly will of its own about her face, the longest part at the neck barely reaching her collarbone when she pulled it straight. Cade told her he found her tousled hair provocative. Maybe he did, she thought, smiling secretly as she straightened the perfume bottles on her dresser. Almost every night he slipped down to her room and stayed until dawn. He wanted her to move into his room, but she refused to share a room unless they were married.

Gabrielle touched a bit of perfume behind her ears and on each wrist, and thoughtfully returned the stopper to its crystal decanter. Cade had mentioned that he'd be gone all morning. But where? Her delicate brows drew together. Oh, yes, he and Sam Fortune had some sort of business to attend to at a neighboring ranch.

Humming snatches of a childhood tune, Gabrielle searched through her jewelry. Suddenly her hand stilled in its motion, coming to rest on a letter from Uncle Tyler that she had tucked away in her jewelry box. Cade had shown it to her when it had arrived the week before, and she had asked him if she could keep it because it comforted her to have something from her uncle. She knew the disturbing contents by heart, but still she unfolded the paper and reread the message scrawled in Tyler's blocky hand and addressed to Cade.

My friend, I want you to be aware of recent events here. A reporter from Follettville wrote an article about what happened to Gabrielle. I've seen a copy of the paper, in fact. He reported that she had been accused of providing vital information to the North.

The story has spread to Louisiana. No one has mentioned it to me personally, but I have friends who have told me it's being discussed behind closed doors.

My concern, of course, is how this will affect Gabrielle. The Committee is bound to hear of it, perhaps already has. I'm hoping public opinion will not cause them to change their minds about her exile in Texas.

Gabrielle folded the letter carefully and slipped it into her pocket. Sometimes she liked to carry it with her as a reminder of home and family, despite its distressing news. She selected a short string of pearls and fastened them around her neck, then glanced in the mirror. Cade had told her not to worry and teasingly assured her that the Committee had more serious concerns than an auburn-haired Southern girl. Then he had caught her shoulders and pulled her around to face him.

"I'll never let them take you from me." His gaze

had drifted over her cropped curls before he met her eyes again. "There'll be no more indignities. If the damned fools change their minds, which I doubt, I'll take you to Europe where you'll be safe. That's a promise."

Gabrielle's heart lightened as her thoughts turned to Cade. She had never known love could be so wonderful, or bring such a sense of well-being. Suddenly she laughed. "Gabrielle, get busy," she scolded herself, "and quit dreaming about your man!"

A busy morning lay before her, but she had mentioned none of her plans to Cade. Not because she wanted to keep them from him exactly, but because she still felt too nervous to share them with him. Fifteen of Cade's crew were married and lived in their own homes on sections of land Cade provided. Gabrielle had never met any of their wives, but as time had gone by, she had felt more inclined to make their acquaintance. This morning, with Maria along as interpreter if needed, she planned to pay a social call on the first wife on her list, a young Mexican woman who lived only a couple of miles away. Guadalupe Ortega—Lupe as she was called—had married one of Cade's Mexican wranglers and expected her first baby within a week or so.

Gabrielle cocked her head to the side, listening to a faint popping sound in the clear morning air. Distant gunfire. Must be target practice, she concluded. Turning her thoughts back to her own plans, she considered the reservations that still lingered in her mind. Without a doubt, she and Guadalupe would not have been friends in New Orleans, and she would certainly not have visited her home. But in Texas, women were so scarce that not visiting each other because of social standing seemed ridiculous. Frankly, she missed the company of women and the social events they planned, like teas and coffees. Even the knitting parties she had dreaded so much in New Orleans would be welcome now.

The sound of gunfire seemed much closer, and she shook her head, thinking Cade would not approve of his men firing their guns so close to the house. Returning to her thoughts, she mulled over the conversation she had had with Maria a week ago. Quite a few school-aged children lived on the ranch, and none of them, as far as she knew, were receiving any kind of education.

Last night she had mentioned the problem to Cade and had gone on to propose that he build a school and hire a teacher. After a long pause he said he would build the school if she would teach, and despite her initial shock that he would suggest she take up a profession, she had found herself agreeing to do so. Strangely enough, this morning she had been excited by the idea and was determined to ask Maria to teach her Spanish. She would have to be able to communicate with all the children. But first she must meet the wives.

After opening her bureau drawer Gabrielle selected a pair of dainty embroidered gloves and a lace handkerchief, then donned her wide-brimmed straw hat. Heading down the hallway, she thought of her friends in New Orleans and wondered what they would think of her new life. A smile played on her mouth as she considered all the changes in her life. She had been rounding up strays for dollars a head, she had learned to ride with an expertise almost unbecoming to a woman, and now she had agreed to teach school. Her face softened as she thought that she was happy now with the work her friends would consider common, with the wide open spaces of Texas, and especially with Cade.

Halfway down the stairs Gabrielle stopped

abruptly, her hand tightening on the balustrade. Quick staccato bursts of gunfire sounded across the front of the house, and men shouted back and forth, their voices harsh with urgency. The hair rose on the back of her neck, and her first wild thought was of a stampede. She had heard too many times that when they were spooked, cattle overran everything, like a floodtide. Her heart pounding a furious rhythm, she flew down the steps and lifting her full skirts in both hands, ran down the carpeted corridor toward the foyer. Through the lace curtains she saw men riding their horses across the front lawn.

No one ever did that. Pulling the curtains aside, she peered out, then gasped in horror. Diego, a young Mexican she knew only slightly, fired wildly at an approaching rider. Even as she watched, Diego went motionless, then slumped to his knees, a red-black stain appearing on his chest before he fell backward. It took her a stunned second to realize he'd been shot. Two riders careened across the yard, one reining his mount in a tight circle around the fallen man. Gabrielle's face drained of color. They were Yankees!

She fell back against the wall, her hand pressed against her chest. It was like a nightmare come true! Edging back from the window, she squeezed her eyes shut, trying to block out the grisly reality of what she'd seen. From the back of the house a woman screamed. The sound of shrieks of shrill panic coming from down the corridor slowly penetrated Gabrielle's terror-stunned mind. She must help. Without thinking, she picked up the heavy brass candlestick from the foyer table and ran toward the dining room. A woman's screams ended abruptly, followed by a sudden deathly silence.

Entering the dining room, Gabrielle stared at the kitchen door, fearing what she'd find on the other side. Then the door burst open and Helen, her face wild with terror, ran through. With violent suddenness a Yankee soldier appeared behind her and lifted his revolver, bringing it smashing down on her head. Helen crumpled to the floor at Gabrielle's feet, her green print skirt and white apron spreading around her like a flower.

The soldier's face was grimly composed, his brutal features stamped with blood-lust. Gabrielle whirled and fled from his pounding footsteps. Too late, she saw another blue-clad soldier step out of the study, directly into her path. Apparently startled by her headlong flight, he reacted slowly, and Gabrielle almost eluded his reaching hands.

"Get her!" the soldier yelled behind her.

With a muttered oath the startled man galvanized into action, moving quickly for a man of his large size. Scooping an arm about her waist he literally jerked her off her feet and pulled her against his body.

"Well, now, Jacob," he scolded the soldier who came to a panting, leering stop, "no use scaring this little lady with your rough ways." He laughed hoarsely as he wrenched the candlestick from her hands. "You'll hurt somebody with that, miss," he warned, allowing his hands to wander over her breasts as she struggled. "You wouldn't want to do that, would you now?"

"Let me go!" Gabrielle cried, hitting him.

The man's laughter suddenly died in his throat. "Son-of-a-bitch," he muttered, releasing her. "Looks like the fun's over. Captain McDaniels is on his way in."

The men called Jacob sobered instantly. "Yeah, if anybody's going to get some, it'll be that horny bastard."

Although Gabrielle couldn't see the officer they

referred to, she could hear the rumble of his deep voice as he issued orders from the veranda. Straightening her disordered clothing and flicking the two men a glance of utter revulsion, she said a prayer of thanks that the two were afraid of their captain.

"Take all prisoners into the library for questioning. I can't find that Rebel son-of-a-bitch anywhere."

Gabrielle allowed herself to be shoved into Cade's study. Maria stumbled in next, then Helen, a crimson smear of blood congealing behind her ear. In the next few minutes everyone was herded into the room and pushed up against the bookshelves. The young maids on the housekeeping staff, terrified and weeping, pressed close to Gabrielle. Mr. Murphy, Cade's bookkeeper, entered next, followed by the gardener and his assistant. Zeke, his young face looking both furious and insolent, took his place in front of Gabrielle.

The Yankee officer halted just outside the door, keeping his back to them. Gabrielle could see the hated gold stripe that ran down the length of his leg.

"Any casualties, corporal?" he demanded.

"None, sir."

"What about the Rebels? How many of the ranch hands were killed?"

"Only two. We're holding the rest of them in the stable."

One of the maids started to cry, and Gabrielle swallowed back her own tears. She had seen Diego die.

"And what about Montana?" the officer snapped, resting his hand on his revolver. "Anybody find him?"

Gabrielle froze.

"No, sir."

In the silence that followed, Gabrielle thought the

beating of her heart could surely be heard. Without another word the tall Yankee officer spun on his heel and stalked into the study. He stood for a moment, observing the assembled group with displeasure.

"My name is Captain McDaniels," he informed them coldly.

Gabrielle shivered at the sight of his narrow, wolfish face. She had never been so frightened in her life, and Juana's muffled sobbing only undermined what little courage she had left.

"Where's Cade Montana?" the Yankee demanded, his gaze raking the group.

The question hung in the stillness. Gabrielle bowed her head, her terrified mind spinning. They wanted Cade. She saw his face in her mind, with the sudden flashing smile that made him so handsome it caused an ache in her chest. Her panic escalated. This wasn't a random attack; the Yankees had come so deep into Texas just to find Cade. With both terror and grief, she watched the captain walk over to Maria.

"You," he barked. "Do you know Montana's whereabouts?"

Maria flinched as if he had stuck her. "I don't know," she blubbered. "I don't know where he is."

"Did you see him this morning?"

"No, sir, I didn't see him," she whimpered.

Captain McDaniels's mouth curled with contempt. "We are at war. My orders are to find this bastard." He crossed in front of Juana, then turned back, his tone chillingly reasonable. "You may protect him if you wish. You may choose not to say a word. But you must remember the men we hold prisoner." He looked at his sergeant, his mouth pursed. "How many did you say we have?"

"Fourteen, sir."

"Thank you." The captain laced his hands together behind him, paced to the center, and whirled to face the prisoners. "Fourteen men," he said with chilling calm. A dark brow lifted, making his face look fiercely predatory. "Could they be husbands? Fathers? Brothers? You think about it." He smiled malevolently. "I want you to know that although I have qualms about using violence on women, I have no such compunction about using violence to get your men to talk."

A chill traveled down Gabrielle's spine as he continued. "We stopped one of Mr. Montana's cotton trains this morning. Seventy-five wagons, along with the contents, were set on fire"—his voice took on a low savagery—"and by now my men have seen to it that every damned cotton boll has burned." He sucked a deep breath into his lungs, his gaze drifting over their faces. "And I guarantee each future train will be stopped. None of them will reach the Rio Grande." He paused to remove his gloves. "Now, I would like one of you to tell me where Mr. Montana is hiding out." He approached Zeke, gave him a cursory glance, then swung toward Gabrielle. "Which one of you will volunteer? Who will save the men from the whip? Do you want to see their backs lashed to raw meat?" He pursed his mouth thoughtfully. "They will talk in the end. They always do."

Gabrielle stood motionless, her breath trapped in her throat, not daring to look at the captain even though he came to a stop beside her. With her eyes cast downward she saw the hair on the back of his hands as he slapped his gloves against the side of his leg. She felt his glance settle on her, and her heart fluttered with agitation.

"Well, well," he observed with amusement, "what have we here? Sergeant Clancy, take a look at this redheaded woman."

"She's redheaded all right," the sergeant agreed with a leering grin.

When the captain reached out to touch her hair, Gabrielle shrank away from him with a shudder.

Zeke whirled around furiously. "You leave her alone!" he threatened. "Cade Montana will kill you for touching her."

The captain laughed softly, his gaze never leaving Gabrielle's face. "And why would he do that?"

Zeke squared his shoulders, incensed by the Yankee's taunting tone. "Because she's going to marry him, that's why."

"Is that right?" McDaniels mused silkily. His glance drifted over her slim form, then rose to her face. Her long lashes brushed against the pale skin of her cheekbones, and her profile was delicate. He saw the slight rise of her creamy breasts peeking out of her dress.

He stepped closer. "Maybe you can tell me where Montana is?" he prompted, his voice low. With the tip of his finger he lifted the string of pearls around her neck, shifted them back and forth a couple of times, then let them drop. The tension in the room intensified.

Gabrielle swallowed. "He's gone to Mexico on a trip—" Her voice broke and died.

"Mexico?"

"Yes," she whispered.

Captain McDaniels spun around abruptly and walked over to Cade's desk. Deliberately he knocked the inkwell over and watched idly as ink spread across the papers on the desk. Scratching his cheek, he turned back to Gabrielle. "How long do you think he'll be gone?"

She wet her lips and glanced sidelong at Helen. "A month, maybe longer."

McDaniels laughed and looked over at his sergeant. "Isn't this interesting? We heard he was here only yesterday. Surely such a pretty little lady wouldn't lie to us."

Gabrielle looked up to deny his words and froze at the lust in his eyes that he didn't bother to conceal.

The tense moment was shattered by a commotion in the foyer. A Yankee soldier staggered to the study doorway. "Got to talk to the captain," he gasped. His face was stained almost black by gunpowder, his breathing came in great gulps, and sweat soaked his uniform.

"What is it, private?"

The soldier wiped his face with the back of his sleeve. "We engaged Confederate troops . . . at the wagons," he rasped out. "A big force . . . We couldn't stop them, sir!" He ducked his head and drew air into his lungs. "They're right behind me, sir. Maybe an hour, two at the most."

McDaniels's lazy insolence underwent a lightning change as he bristled into command. "Sergeant Clancy," he ordered sharply, "prepare to pull out. Take a few men and create a delaying action for the Rebels. I'll head north."

"What about the prisoners, sir?"

"Leave them be." McDaniels started pulling on his gloves as he headed across the marble floor of the foyer. At the door he stopped and turned back. "Sergeant Clancy, bring the redheaded woman."

Gabrielle watched with horror as Clancy approached.

"You dirty son-of-a-bitch," Zeke yelled, throwing himself at the giant black-haired man. Clancy turned, lifted his rifle, and brought the stock down with a smashing blow against Zeke's head. The boy crumpled to the floor without a sound.

"Nooo!" Gabrielle reached for Zeke but the ser-

geant caught her arm and dragged her into the foyer.
When her struggles became an annoyance, he lifted
her over his shoulder and carried her out on the veranda and down the stairs as if she weighed nothing. He set her on the ground in front of the
mounted soldiers.

Gabrielle, her face drained of color, stared at the
troops.

She noticed that the grass was trampled and that
the ornamental shrubs and rose bushes had been
trodden beneath the horses' hooves. A soldier led a
horse up beside her, while another pulled a grimy
bandana from his pocket and tied it around her
mouth. Her nose wrinkled in disgust at the filthy
gag.

"Sorry, ma'am. Captain's orders. It seems he
doesn't want you to get ideas about crying for help
if we pass any houses. Now, you can either ride that
horse by yourself, or I'll have you tied across the
saddle," Clancy informed her bluntly. "You decide."

Without waiting for an answer, he caught her
around the waist and lifted her into the saddle. With
a grin he pressed the reins into her hand and leaned
briefly against her leg. "You're going to have all the
riding you want, ma'am." He tipped his hat to her,
his gaze dropping insolently to her bosom.

"Want us to burn the place, captain?" a nasal
Yankee voice called out.

"Leave it," McDaniels answered sourly. "I want
him to have a home to return to, so I know where
to find him the next time I come looking. "Stay beside me," he advised Gabrielle darkly. "It's going
to be a rough ride." His mouth curled thoughtfully.
"You wouldn't want to get lost somewhere alone
with one of my boys, now would you?"

Her glance flicked across the troops and she shuddered.

McDaniels kicked his mount into motion and they set off.

The Confederate officer walked briskly up the walk and shook hands with the tall Texan he had heard so much about. "Mr. Montana, I'm sorry we have to meet under these conditions. I'm Lieutenant Sutherland D. Harris." He looked around briefly. "I can see that they've been here already." He slapped his riding whip impatiently against his leg. "We heard they came for you."

Cade nodded, his expression unreadable. "I was warned, but I didn't expect them to come this far south."

"It was foolhardy," Lieutenant Harris agreed. "We're going after them. We'll close off their avenue of escape and trap 'em." He shook his head. "They must have wanted you real bad. Did you suffer any casualties?"

"Two of my men were killed," Cade answered grimly. He thumbed cartridges into the chamber of his pistol. "And a woman was taken hostage."

Lieutenant Harris turned from his inspection of the ranch. "Hostage? I hadn't heard."

Cade nodded, his expression ruthless. "I want to ride with you."

The lieutenant took a second look at his grim expression. "Yes, sir. You've a right to. I'll be honored to have you ride along with us."

It was hours after nightfall, and pouring rain, when the Yankee troops stopped at the small farmhouse.

Gabrielle, wearing a raincoat McDaniels had given her, watched as the frightened family who lived there was herded at gunpoint toward the barn. Concerned about their welfare, she glanced at the captain. "Don't worry, ma'am," he advised her sardonically. "They'll be back in their home come morning, all safe and sound."

Gabrielle's nerves grated at the taunting, mocking tone of his voice. The troops dismounted and busily hauled canvas and poles from the supply wagon to begin setting up tents. One of the soldiers finally noticed her sitting on her horse in the rain and led her into the farmhouse.

A short time later, she sat wrapped in a blanket before the fire, half listening to the low voices of the captain and his staff, who were gathered around the table, coffee mugs in their hands, studying the map spread out in front of them. She was still gagged and had no doubt in her mind about the reason the soldiers had dragged her along. As the evening progressed and they began drinking, Gabrielle was aware that more than an occasional glance lingered on her body. Her blood turned to ice when she overheard one of the soldiers say that Captain McDaniels was a lucky bastard, because he was going to "get some" that night.

She turned to face the fire, staring into the flames with growing apprehension and fear. She racked her brain to think of some way to escape, but it seemed hopeless. An army of men surrounded her, both in the house and camped all over in the woods outside. As her terror escalated she began to think that perhaps the soldiers would kill her, after her body had been pawed by dozens of pairs of Yankee hands. Sadness washed over her when she pictured Cade's handsome bronzed face and imagined that she might never feel the touch of his hand on hers or see the warmth of his flashing smile ever again. Images of Camden Hill floated through her mind; Reba scolding her for getting her dress all dirty for the third time that day and then smiling conspiratorially as she offered her a fresh-baked cookie; chasing frogs with Philip Bienville at Uncle Tyler's annual garden party. Memories of Uncle Tyler caused her tears to gently overflow, blurring her vision of the flames into patches of orange and gold. She had always relied on Uncle Tyler to get her out of any mess she got into, at school and at home, but he couldn't help her now.

Suddenly she remembered the letter from Uncle Tyler that she still carried in her pocket, and she shook the tears from her eyes. If she told the Yankees she was a spy for the North and used her uncle's letter as proof, maybe she could protect herself from their lust and buy herself time to escape. Her mind was racing feverishly when she heard chairs scrape across the wooden floor as the soldiers prepared to go. She would be left alone with Captain McDaniels. He shut the door behind the last of his men and then walked over to where she sat on the other side of the room and leaned against the wall.

"I think it's time we got to know each other better, don't you?" he asked. The flickering lamplight formed deep shadows along the grooves of his face, making him look brutal and sinister. Gabrielle swallowed her rising panic and forced herself to appear calm.

McDaniels swaggered toward her, his mouth twisting downward as he looked her over. He grinned wolfishly as he leaned closer, reached behind her neck, and removed the bandana that gagged her. He dragged a three-legged stool up beside her and, still grinning, bent forward with his elbows resting on his knees.

"What's your name, pretty one?"

"Gabrielle St. Clair," she said with pride, despite her fear.

His smile widened. "You don't sound like a Texas girl to me." He raised his forefinger so that just the tip of it touched her knee.

She jerked reflexively from his touch, then wet her lips nervously. "I'm from New Orleans," she said in a frightened whisper.

Leaning so close to her that she could smell the damp wool of his uniform, he began to finger the fabric of her skirt as he leered at her face, and then he moved his hand onto her knee.

"Well, Gabrielle, I won't waste time talking. I mean to have you, right now, and I mean to enjoy it, so you can either relax and enjoy it, too, or I can use a little force, whichever you prefer." His hand began to move up her thigh.

Gabrielle's heart pounded in her chest, and her throat went dry at his words. She forced her voice to remain level.

"Captain McDaniels," she began, mustering all the strength and authority she could, "I believe you have made a grave mistake. I happen to be a very important Union spy, and I am hardly a plaything for you or your men."

Confusion spread over the Yankee's face and then turned to amusement.

"You, a spy? Let's not waste time, sweetheart, I'm not a patient man." He stood up and braced his hands on either side of the rocker. When he moved in to try to kiss her, Gabrielle slid down in the seat until she was half out of it, then boldly pushed at his chest and shoved him away.

"I'm not patient either, captain, and I think you should listen to what I have to say. I can't imagine that your superiors would like to hear about your methods of interrogating female prisoners, and I wouldn't be afraid to report you."

McDaniels sighed and sat back down on the stool. "What kind of a spy are you, then?"

"I took critical documents from my uncle's safe and gave them to Ruben Guillotte, who passed them to a Yankee courier. It was valuable information, and I was exiled to Texas as my punishment. Guillotte was sentenced to hang," she said, raising one eyebrow to emphasize the severity of his punishment.

"I suppose you have some proof of this?" the captain asked.

"As a matter of fact, I have a letter my uncle just sent that should convince you I'm telling the truth." She reached into the pocket of her dress and handed him the folded paper.

McDaniels scowled as he read it. Gabrielle's legs were shaking, and she crossed the fingers of one hand hoping her uncle's words indeed convince him.

"What was this incident in Follettville he mentions?"

"They cut my hair off to shame me because word got out that I was a spy," she answered, gesturing toward her short curls."

McDaniels bit his lip as he considered. "You still don't look like a spy to me," he said, shaking his head.

"Please, captain, use your head. I come from a wealthy and influential New Orleans family. I am an effective spy because my uncle is a very important member of a secret war committee and I appear both loyal to the South and very innocent-looking," Gabrielle said, trying to sound exasperated.

"Why didn't they hang you, or put you in jail?" McDaniels asked.

"They didn't know what to do with me, because

I'm a woman, and at least in the South, men are gentlemen,'' she said, regarding him accusingly. ''My uncle believed I was merely the victim of a youthful infatuation, so he asked Cade Montana, a good friend of his, to take me to Texas with him as an exile.''

''If Montana is your jailer, why are you going to marry him?'' McDaniels asked skeptically.

''He fell in love with me.'' Gabrielle sighed casually. ''And then he began to believe me when I maintained my innocence. I always told him I was framed by my sister, Celeste. He's a source of lots of important secrets, since he works for the Southern war effort, and I decided to use my time in exile to gather more information for the North as best I could.'' She looked him square in the eye and prayed that her act was working.

Captain McDaniels walked over to the table, poured himself a glass of whiskey, and sat down heavily. ''Well, Miss St. Claire, I may have misjudged you. Why didn't you tell me all this before?'' he asked, swirling his glass thoughtfully.

''You didn't exactly give me an opportunity, now did you, captain?'' she said slowly.

Captain McDaniels sighed. ''No, I suppose I didn't.''

Cade made his way soundlessly through the trees and underbrush that grew beneath the ridge. A Yankee sentry he had encountered lay bound and gagged a few feet behind him. Rain poured from the brim of his hat and the ground had long since turned slippery with mud.

Cade had carefully scouted the enemy camp and decided that they must be holding Gabrielle in the farmhouse. A guard stood at the door, and light showed dimly through the small windows. Tents for the troops dotted the cleared area in the front yard. Surprisely few sentries had been posted; worn out from their ride and made even more miserable by the weather, they had long since relaxed their vigil. They huddled under their slickers, hats pulled down to shield their faces and keep the rain from running down their necks.

Reaching the edge of the clearing, Cade ran across the open space and flattened his length against the back of the house. As he caught his breath he scanned the dark ridge that shielded the farm and knew that even now, Confederate troops were silently edging their way down the wooded embankment. He had managed to convince Lieutenant Harris to hold off his attack for ten minutes while he rescued Gabrielle.

Two soldiers passed by before Cade started moving again, the thick shrubbery next to the house making his progress difficult. He did not allow himself to think of what might have already happened to Gabrielle, but he could think of only one reason for the Yankees to take a woman hostage.

Eventually he stumbled upon a narrow side entrance. The knob turned under his grip, and he pushed the door open half an inch. The room was dark except for a narrow crack of light coming from the kitchen. Slipping silently inside, he closed the door behind him and stood perfectly still, waiting. Water dripped from his clothes onto the floor, but the volume of rain outside and the murmur of voices in the kitchen covered the sound. One of the voices he heard was Gabrielle's. Cade closed his eyes and drew in a deep breath of thanks. Hearing her low and controlled tones, he knew she faced no immediate danger.

Cade moved forward, wincing when a floorboard squeaked beneath his boots. Peering around the cor-

ner, he could see Gabrielle sitting in a rocker near
the fire, her head dropped against the cushioned
back. Her face was pale, and she looked weary. A
man in a blue uniform sat at a table. Cade could see
the back of his head as he stood up and walked over
to the fire, one hand holding a glass while the other
was clasped behind him. Cade frowned. Something
was very wrong with the scene. Gabrielle and the
soldier looked almost companionable together. Why?
He tilted his head, straining to hear what they were
saying.

"How long have you been in Texas?" the Yankee
captain asked.

"For several months," Gabrielle answered, her
tone brisk. "Needless to say it seems like years. You
don't know how difficult it has been for me down
here in this barren land, separated from all my con-
tacts, completely surrounded by Confederate dogs
like Cade Montana."

"I can imagine. To think you came close to marrying him for the Cause. For that alone you deserve
a medal. Tell me again how you convinced him you
were innocent," the captain said, his boots scraping
the floor as he paced back and forth in front of her.

"Oh, it really wasn't very hard," she said, laughing briefly. "He's actually pretty gullible. With
Southern heroes like him the North won't have any
trouble winning the war. I just told him over and
over again that I was innocent and batted my eye-
lashes a little. He fell for it, even though he caught
me trying to escape twice. I told him Celeste was
going to help rescue Ruben, and then when my own
men finally got him out of jail, Montana accepted
that as proof that I had been telling the truth. Ironic,
isn't it?"

Her voice became more serious as she continued.
"That almost backfired, however, because he de-

ceided to hire a private detective to follow Celeste
and gather proof of my innocence. I was very nervous, knowing that all the detective would discover
was further evidence of my spying. However, it
seems that he hired an incompetent man, because
there's been no word from him in weeks."

"That's a lucky break." The captain stopped pacing. "What were you planning to do next, actually
marry Montana?"

"I was hoping it wouldn't come to that. As he
began to believe me, and to love me, he relaxed his
guard substantially. I was planning to attempt another escape as soon as he left town again. But
thankfully you came along to rescue me instead,"
she concluded.

"Well, it was my honor, of course, to, ah, rescue
you," the captain said, clearing his throat nervously.

"Believe me, Captain McDaniels, I won't forget to
mention your kindness to people who can be very
helpful to your career," she said in a low, conspir-
atorial tone. "Once you see me safely back up
North."

"That will be my first priority, I assure you. You
won't disclose the details of your rescue, will you? I
like to keep some of my most effective, ah, actions
secret even from my superiors, if you know what I
mean."

"Of course, captain. Now that we understand
each other, I don't see any need to go into particu-
lars. If you will excuse me," Gabrielle said wearily,
standing up. "I'm sure you realize that I'm very
tired. We can talk further in the morning."

"Certainly. I will see you then." The Yankee
turned abruptly and left the room.

From his hiding place, Cade leaned back against
the wall, feeling as if a horse had kicked him in the

stomach. How could he have been so stupid? How could he have let Gabrielle's pretty face and enticing body cloud his mind, when it had all been so obvious? His blood boiled with anger when he remembered their encounter by the stream when he had told her that he loved her. To think that she had been lying all along . . .

Gabrielle breathed with relief as soon as McDaniels left the room. She sank back down into the rocker, her knees suddenly weak. She had done it; she had fooled him into thinking she was a spy. But she still wasn't safe. She had only a few hours before morning to think of a way to escape from an armed camp of Yankees and make it back to Cade's ranch. Suddenly a man's hand came around from behind to cover her mouth, and she was lifted up off the rocker with violent force. A strong arm twisted her around and shoved her up against a wall. Gabrielle gasped for the air that had been knocked from her lungs. When she opened her eyes, she saw Cade, his face twisted with rage.

"You were right," he said dangerously. "I've been a fool for a pretty face. You damned lying little bitch."

A knock sounded on the door, and a moment later the startled pair heard the captain's voice above the patter of rain. "Miss St. Claire?"

Cade pulled his gun from its holster and lifted it against Gabrielle's chin. "I hate to use you as a shield, princess, but I don't have a choice." His mouth curled unpleasantly. "I have a feeling they won't take the chance of hurting their little heroine."

Captain McDaniels pushed the door open. "Sorry to interrupt you, but we've detected what might be enemy activity—" His voice broke off when he saw the gun held against the smooth line of Gabrielle's throat. His gaze lifted to Cade's ruthless face. "What do you want with her?"

Cade shoved Gabrielle forward. "If you try to stop me, captain, I'll shoot your pretty little spy."

McDaniels retreated slowly, his hands lifted. "You're Montana, aren't you? Leave the woman here and I swear no one will harm you." The captain pivoted slowly as Cade moved toward the door with Gabrielle. "Sir, I appeal to you as a Southern gentleman. Miss St. Claire has been through enough. Let her go."

Cade laughed. "Order your men to let us by," he demanded.

The captain edged past them onto the small porch. A lamp glowed forlornly in the gloom. The troops, apparently having heard some disturbance, had already slipped from their tents and stood in the rain, watching curiously. When Cade walked out onto the porch, still holding Gabrielle in front of him, they straightened.

Captain McDaniels lifted his voice. "Let them pass. I don't want a single shot fired."

Chapter 13

In the darkness Gabrielle caught only a glimpse of the surprised faces of the Yankee soldiers as Cade dragged her across the clearing, holding his gun to her throat. A soldier ran forward, dropped on one knee, and leveled his gun. Again came McDaniels's order. "Hold your fire!"

Reaching the shelter of the trees, Cade half carried, half pushed her up the muddy hillside toward the crest. It took only minutes for rain to soak her clothing and mud caked her skirt from the knees down after only a few steps. Lightning cracked overhead, and in between each burst of thunder, Cade cursed her for being slow, for falling, for anything he could think of. The hill became so steep at times that Gabrielle had to claw her way up using her hands. Leafy branches slapped her in the face, and the smell of wet earth and decaying wood offended her nostrils.

Cade finally grabbed her around the waist and carried her to the top like a sack of potatoes, then dropped her in the mud. Collapsing in a heap on the ground, Gabrielle tried to catch her breath and make sense of all that was going on. Gunfire sounded below at a steady pace, and indistinct voices yelled out orders. Already the acrid smell of gunpowder permeated the air. Despite the darkness Gabrielle could see the shadowy figures of Confederate soldiers as they disappeared into the trees. She shuddered, thinking of the dangerous embankment they must slide down before they could join the skirmish.

When she caught her breath she looked up at Cade. "Let me explain . . . to you . . . what happened," she pleaded. "You're acting crazy . . ."

"I overheard your conversation with the captain," he snarled. He grabbed her wrist and jerked her to her feet. "Damn you, Gabrielle."

"Cade, for heaven's sake! Give me a chance to explain. He meant to rape me! Don't you see? To save myself I told him the only thing that would make him stop."

"You never quit trying, do you Gabrielle?" He shook his head. "Do you expect me to believe anything out of your mouth now? Jesus Christ, you've been lying to me all along."

"Cade!" she gasped, "That's not true!"

A Confederate soldier, unable to see in the downpour, blundered into them. "Sorry, sir." Seeing Gabrielle, he came to attention. "Glad to see you safe, ma'am."

Gabrielle could not speak. Her mind was whirling chaotically. Dear God, when would the insanity end?

"What's your name?" Cade demanded of the youth.

"Morgan, sir. Willy Morgan."

Cade turned Gabrielle around and tied her hands behind her. Morgan shifted uneasily, observing the process with growing concern. "What're you doing, sir?" he asked finally.

"Morgan, I want you to watch her." To Gabrielle's dismay, Cade tied a gag around her mouth.

"If she's gone when I return, I'll see that you're court-martialed. You understand?"

The boy's face contorted with the effort to choose between conflicting loyalties as he looked from Gabrielle to Cade. "I don't even know who you are . . ."

"Cade Montana."

The boy wiped the rain from his eyes. "Yes, sir," he announced, the worry vanishing from his face. "You're a neighbor of ours. We live south of you a hun'erd miles or so. I just joined up about a month ago." He watched curiously as Cade checked his revolver. "Nice gun," he said, moving closer. "You going back down?"

Cade nodded. "Can I count on you?"

"Yes, sir. She'll be right here."

Gabrielle spent a miserable night huddled against the base of a tree. The rain never let up. All through those long, lonely hours, she heard intermittent fighting and could only surmise that the troops had scattered and the battle had become a hunt to track down the enemy. The boy who watched her seemed nervous. He twisted around at every sound and peered into the night as if he expected a Yankee to jump out and cut his throat. He was a big boy, taller than she was, but Gabrielle figured he couldn't be more than sixteen years old.

By the time the eerie light of dawn penetrated the darkness, the firing became more sporadic and a cease-fire was called . The Yankee soldiers who had survived had scattered into the woods, and tracking them wasn't worth the effort. Slowly the men in gray straggled wearily back into camp. Cade appeared out of the heavy wet fog as quietly as a wisp of smoke.

"Thanks, Willy," he said. "I'll be sure and mention you to Lieutenant Harris."

"Thank you, sir."

Gabrielle regretfully watched the boy disappear into the mist, feeling chilled by Cade's presence. He didn't speak, only took the gag from her mouth and untied her hands. Blood streaked his shoulder, but she didn't even feel concern for him.

"Keep your mouth shut and stay put," he said. "You make a run for it and I'll shoot you."

She closed her eyes and rubbed her hand against her forehead, thinking his threat was ludicrous. She had no place to run. Listening to Cade walk away, she wondered what he planned to do with her. Would he take her back to the ranch, or turn her over to the military?

Sensing that someone was watching her, she looked up to see an officer standing close by. He leaned against a straggly oak with his foot propped against its trunk and regarded her closely, his gaze seeming to penetrate her wet dress. Warily she turned away, and, although she doubted Cade would protect her from an untoward advance, she searched the gauzy fog until she saw him. A soldier was wrapping a bandage around Cade's upper arm, and she saw him grimace as it was pulled tight.

Aware of the officer's scrutiny but too tired to really care, Gabrielle observed the smooth brown strength of Cade's shoulders and arms and the dark curling hair on his chest. As he sat hunched over, she saw the tight ripple of his stomach muscles and shivered, remembering exactly what it felt like to touch him. How powerfully built he was in comparison to most men. The white skin of the wounded soldier beside him seemed pallid against the healthy bronze of Cade's skin.

The officer next to her spoke up suddenly. "Cade told me they took a woman hostage and he wanted to get her back." Pausing, he tried to light a cigarette, but finding the tobacco wet and the matches damp, he finally gave up. He peered down at her. "What happened inside the house?" he asked curiously. "He went in to save you. Why'd he use you as a shield when he came out?"

"What do you think happened?" she asked after a moment.

"I don't know."

She observed Cade's long-legged stride and the gentle shift of his broad shoulders as he walked toward her. "He heard me tell the Yankee captain I was a spy," she answered simply.

The lieutenant gaped at her in disbelief, then pushed away from the tree. He stepped forward at Cade's approach. "I hope that shoulder doesn't give you too much trouble, Montana."

"It won't. It's nothing serious." Cade extended his hand. "Thank you, Lieutenant Harris."

Harris glanced briefly around the camp. "Are you headed back home?"

Cade nodded.

"I'd keep some men posted," Harris advised. He pulled a brandy flask from his pocket and held it out to Cade. When the Texan shook his head, the lieutenant took a swallow and returned it to his pocket. "I imagine they'll come looking for you again."

Cade nodded. "I'll be ready if they do."

They rode for hours in silence through an eerie blanket of fog. When Cade stopped to rest, Gabrielle slid wearily to the ground. He thrust his canteen into her hands and she drank, then glanced at the stony lines of his profile. She wanted to feel sorry that circumstances had led him to misunderstand her encounter with the Yankee, but his failure to believe her had profoundly hurt her. After what they had meant to each other, she felt betrayed by his mistrust. She might as well save her sympathy for herself, because she would be the one to suffer. But once again sadness wrapped around her heart as she remembered the warmth they had shared only a few nights before.

She turned impulsively to him. "Cade, I know you're angry and hurt, but if you'll only listen—"

His mouth twisted menacingly. "I want you to shut up."

She pressed her hands against her face, knowing that in his present mood, nothing she said would do any good. "I must have some rest. I've been up all night."

"We're going back to the ranch now," he answered flatly.

"Cade," she said softly, "those troops just appeared at the ranch. They forced me to go with them!"

He tightened the cinch on his horse. "Gabrielle, if you don't shut up," he said, "I'm going to gag you."

"Cade, just give me a chance."

He turned, his face furious, the skin white around his mouth. "Don't say another word," he spat out between clenched teeth.

"And don't threaten me!" she cried. She watched in disbelief as he came toward her menacingly. She started backing away, and then turned and ran. He caught her before she'd taken ten steps and kicked her feet out from under her. She fell breathless to the ground, staring at him, unable to believe his brutality. In short order he pulled her up onto her feet, dragged her across to the horses, and lifted her into the saddle.

"If you don't ride," he warned, ignoring the tears in her eyes, "I'll tie you across your saddle. Now I don't want to hear another word out of you, do you understand?'' He swung effortlessly into his saddle and they rode off together in silence.

When Gabrielle crawled into her bed that night, she pulled the covers up to her chin and closed her eyes. Maria fussed over her, scolded her for not eating her soup, and worried about the flush in her cheeks. Not until she fell asleep did Maria leave her. She knew what soldiers usually did to women, and she suspected something horrible had happened to Gabrielle. The girl seemed completely devastated. Exhaustion couldn't fully account for the despair in her young face.

Gabrielle did not wake during the night, but her sleep was tormented by fragmented and frightening dreams. Celeste, beckoning with thin white arms, coaxed her deeper and deeper into a thick fog. Gabrielle couldn't breathe, she couldn't see her hands in front of her face, and Celeste wouldn't answer her frightened calls. The danger that pressed in on all sides was so tangible that it seemed alive. Sounds echoed in the thick mist, but no matter how hard she looked, she could see nothing.

Suddenly Gabrielle sat bolt upright in bed, her emerald eyes wide. Finally she realized that she was in her own bed, but she drew in a ragged breath as the feeling of suffocation lingered. A knock sounded at the door. Without waiting for her permission, Cade swung the door open and strode in. He advanced to the foot of her bed, his expression as he braced a hand against the post of her canopy offering her no hope that his heart had softened.

"I want to tell you what I've decided." A muscle flexed along his jaw as he tried not to notice the wild disarray of her auburn hair or the soft shape of her body beneath her gown. "I made Tyler a promise and I will keep it. You will remain at the ranch until the Committee decides you should be moved. It's not your uncle's fault that I became personally involved with you."

"Cade," Gabrielle pleaded, "please listen to me. I didn't do anything. You only have to listen to me to understand!"

He flung his hand out angrily. "Don't say anything. I don't want to hear it."

She came to a stop just out of his reach. "I love you," she cried. "Please give me a chance to explain. It's breaking my heart to be lost from you. There's no reason for this pain. We should be happy we're together again."

"You're really good at this, Gabrielle," he muttered contemptuously. "Really good. But don't expect me to fall for it again."

She refused to give up. "Don't you see? I told that story to protect myself. If you weren't so blind with anger, you'd see it's the truth!"

Cade's mouth curved downward with loathing. "You weren't in any danger that I could see. You and the captain looked quite comfortable to me in front of your damned fire!" Without another word, he turned and stalked away.

Gabrielle ran after him into the corridor. "Cade, please! Don't ruin what we have. Please!"

Despair spread through her heart, and tears streamed down her cheeks as she watched him walk away.

After that, she didn't wonder anymore if Cade still loved her; she wondered if he loathed her as much as he seemed to. The next few weeks were filled with disillusionment and isolation for her. Everything reminded her of her broken dreams with Cade. Her plans for the school fell by the wayside. The mavericks she and Zake had rounded up had been run out of the corral and she didn't know, or care, if her brand had ever been put on them. And, worst of all, she began to experience disturbing physical changes that aroused even greater fears: her regular monthly flow of blood never arrived, and she suffered recurring bouts of nausea in the mornings. Unable to accept what these changes might mean, she tried to push them from her thoughts.

Cade avoided her completely, keeping busy away from the ranch. At first Gabrielle hardly felt like living, then slowly one thought gave her tortured mind comfort: freedom. Even if there was no hope of regaining Cade's faith and love, she had to have freedom from the web of lies that Celeste had spun around her. Gabrielle swore to herself that she would prove her innocence even if it took a lifetime. She would depend only on herself, because everyone she had trusted and relied on had failed her. If no one would help her redeem her reputation, then she would do it alone.

Her new attitude gave her a quiet strength she had never known before. She started to keep a journal in which she wrote down everything that had happened to her in the last year. She thought of several different means of escape, but decided to try the fastest and simplest remedy first. It was possible that if Uncle Tyler knew how miserable she was in Texas, he would send her the money to get away. She wasn't sure where she would go, but she knew she had to find a refuge from scandal and to get away from Cade and the memory of their broken love. Somehow she had to send a letter to Tyler.

She refused to dwell on Cade's inexplicable behavior. It seemed that he detested her presence, yet he thwarted her every attempt to explain or leave.

The weeks passed slowly and miserably. Ironically, the only relief she found now was in her work in the kitchen. One day just before dusk, Helen sent her to the well for water. As she lowered the bucket, Gabrielle took a moment to view the red-gold glow that spread across the western horizon. As she watched, the black silhouette of a rider appeared in the beautiful, burning light. The rider had a slender female body, and from her hat arched a feather that bounced jauntily with the horse's movements. The bucket fell from Gabrielle's frozen fingers and fell to the bottom of the well with a splash. Her blood turned to ice. As the rider angled away from the sunset, Gabrielle could see Lacy Fielding's blond hair and blue riding habit.

Gabrielle turned away blindly. Lacy was at the ranch!

Details of the attack in Follettville returned to Gabrielle with haunting clarity. She pressed her hands against her face, trying to block out the memory of the *whisking* sound of the scissors as those vicious women cut her hair. God Almighty, she should have known Cade would invite Lacy to the ranch. After all, she had never told Cade that Lacy had been involved in the incident.

Gabrielle wandered slowly back to the kitchen, feeling numb, her face drained of color. She told Helen that she felt sick and would spend the rest of the evening in her room. She barely heard Maria's knock at the door when she came up later with a bowl of soup and some dry toast that Helen had prepared. Gabrielle asked her to leave the tray on a table. She was sitting at the window, looking blankly at the darkness, and she only shook her head when Maria asked her if she needed anything else. She could not bring herself to talk to anyone.

Sleep would not come to her that night. She lay wide awake, reliving what had happened in Follettville over and over until she dropped her head in her hands and cried out in despair. It was unbelievable that Lacy Fielding was in the same house, under the same roof, an honored guest at the ranch. No disgrace had fallen on her for her misdeed. Perhaps Cade was even sleeping with her.

It was nearing dawn and the house lay quiet when Gabrielle made her way down the back stairs and entered the still darkened kitchen to begin her daily chores. Moving quietly, she lit a lamp and sat down at the big kitchen table. It wouldn't be long before Helen and Juana came in to start breakfast. At the thought of food her stomach twisted with nausea. Swallowing hard, she dropped her head down on her crossed arms, feeling sweat break out on her forehead.

Whisper-soft footsteps sounded in the hallway, and she straightened, an irrational fright sweeping over her. The kitchen door swung open, and she stared wordlessly at Lacy.

The corners of Lacy's mouth curled upward like that of a cat with cream. "Couldn't sleep, hmm?" she said with malice, rubbing her slim hands together as if to warm them.

Gabrielle could barely breathe as she saw that Lacy was wearing Cade's dark brown robe and, judging from the vee of snowy skin showing at the neck, nothing beneath. Her hair had fallen in tumbling disarray around her shoulders, and all at once Gabrielle knew that she had just left Cade's bed.

Gabrielle felt as if an invisible force lifted her from her chair. Clenching her shaking hands against her body, she circled the table, knowing she had to get away.

"What's the matter?" Lacy inquired, her eyes glinting.

"I know you were there in Follettville," Gabrielle said, stopping at the door. Raw emotion underscored her words. "I recognized your voice at the jail."

Lacy lifted the cover of the bread bin and peered inside. "But you're the only one who knows." She looked up, smiling. "And it won't do you much good, will it?"

The injustice of the situation twisted Gabrielle's heart. "I didn't betray the South," she whispered. She reached up, threading her fingers through the short lengths of her hair. "I didn't deserve this."

Lacy shook her head, her mouth curling with false pity. "Cutting your hair wasn't punishment for betraying the South, my dear," she informed her contemptuously. "It was retaliation for trying to take Cade away from me. I wanted you to pay."

Gabrielle stared at her, disbelieving that even Lacy could be so coldbloodedly cruel. Repelled and frightened by such viciousness, she shrank away as the woman stepped forward.

"I'm glad we had this little talk," Lacy confided, lifting her delicate brows. "Maybe in the future you'll watch your step more carefully. Hmm?"

Gabrielle looked at Lacy in horror for one frozen moment before she fled into the hall and back upstairs.

Cade was standing at the window of his room, looking out at the distant sunrise, when he heard a knock at his door. His heart leaped at the thought that it might be Gabrielle, but then he realized that was impossible.

"Come in," he said absently, turning to see Lacy enter.

"You're up early," she said softly.

He shrugged. "I had some things on my mind," he said, his gaze dropping over her and lifting again to her face. "May I ask what you're doing in my robe?"

She smiled, her fingers trailing downward from the base of her throat to the cleft between her breasts, where her hand fisted in the material. "I thought you might come to my room last night. I waited for you."

Cade stared at her for a minute, then shook his head. "Lacy," he sighed, "when you invited yourself out here, I made it plain that our relationship, such as it was, was over."

Her face hardened. "Isn't it over with the girl?"

Cade approached her and pushed her gently through the doorway into the hall. "That, Lacy Fielding, is none of your business. Now get going so I can get my work done."

Undaunted, Lacy tossed her shimmering blond hair back over one shoulder. "Cade, it's time for us to be together. I want to be with you, really be with you."

He laughed softly, "You're an insatiable woman. Rumor has it you've been keeping company with a certain gambler for the last two months."

"That's not true," Lacy whispered in a shocked breath, looking up and down the hallway.

Cade's dark brows lifted with amusement. "I have proof."

She shrugged. "Well, maybe he has sneaked into my bedroom a time or two. But he doesn't matter to me. Only you matter." She smiled, flicking Cade a quick upward glance. "You'll think about my offer, won't you?" She touched her forefinger to his mouth. "Won't you?"

He watched as she walked away, then stepped back into his room and closed the door. "I don't think so," he said aloud, his easygoing manner abruptly disappearing. He had awakened hours before, dreaming of Gabrielle. It had been so vivid that he could still feel her and smell her and hear her soft breathing. He walked over and stared down at the letter lying on his bureau. Ever since it had arrived yesterday he had had no peace.

Dear Cade,
I am writing to inform you of what has happened here at Camden Hill. After reading this, draw what conclusions you wish. I have come to the opinion that it was Celeste who helped Ruben Guillotte, just as Gabrielle has always maintained. Here are my reasons:
Night before last, Celeste packed a few clothes, her jewels, and the contents of my safe, and left this house. Although I instigated a search, I could find no trace of her. As much as it saddens me, I suspect that she has gone to join Ruben Guillotte. Paul Bienville, her betrothed, is devastated . . .

Cade swung away, unable to read further. He walked over to the window and braced a hand against the frame, scowling at the beauty of the early morning. Celeste had run away . . . but what the hell did that mean? She could have eloped with some joker from Kansas.

His hand clenched into a fist as frustration pounded through him. Frustration and thwarted passion had become his constant companions ever since the night he had followed Gabrielle to the Yankee camp. He turned, muttering a vicious oath as he remembered what he had seen and overheard there. She had sat in the rocker before the fire, talking to McDaniels as if she'd known him forever. She certainly hadn't acted like a frightened kidnap victim. Goddammit, he didn't know what the truth was, and worst of all, he didn't trust his own instincts anymore. One thing was sure. He was miserable, and he wanted to get rid of Lacy and all the other guests who were wandering around his house. He wanted to open a bottle of whiskey and drink until he was so drunk he couldn't be tormented by doubts any longer. Then he wanted to go down to Gabrielle's room and crawl into the frilly canopied bed and make love to her.

Muttering an oath, Cade strode from his room and slammed the door, hoping it woke everyone in the house.

That night, when Maria was summoned to bring dessert and coffee to the guests, her glance paused briefly on Lacy as she thought about what Gabrielle had asked her to do. Then she looked around quickly to Wyatt, Tom Rawlings, and finally to Cade. There were three other individuals, two men and another woman, whom she had never seen before.

Maria deftly placed in front of the guests crystal dessert plates laden with delicious pastries that she and Helen had spent the entire afternoon baking, and cups of steaming coffee. Keeping her expression carefully blank, she watched as Lacy lifted her fork and placed a small bite in her mouth, then sipped her coffee.

Lacy closed her eyes as if in ecstasy. "Maria," she exclaimed in a silky voice, "this is just exquisite! My goodness, Cade, these deserts are as good as my chef prepares, and he spent three years in Paris. Even the coffee tastes especially good—different, but good."

"Thank you, ma'am," Maria replied before she left the dining room. She couldn't suppress a smile. No one suspected a thing.

* * *

Shortly after midnight Gabrielle made her way through the darkened house. She felt no nervousness, nor did she doubt the success of her plan. She waited a moment, listening. Hearing only the sounds of a sleeping house, she drifted quietly down the corridor and paused at the foot of the stairs. It was as still as death. She continued upward to Lacy's room and stopped outside the door, her face tranquil. She turned the knob, slipped inside, then pushed the door shut and locked it quietly. Her gaze swept the shadowed interior. "Lacy?"

Through the moonlight Gabrielle could see the slight rise and fall of Lacy's chest. She walked to the foot of the bed and rested her hands on the wooden footrail. "Are you awake?" she called softly.

Lacy didn't move. Her breathing sounded deep and even.

Gabrielle glanced about the darkened room, then gazed again at Lacy, who lay on her back, the satin folds of her cream-colored gown reflecting a liquid light.

"What you did to me was brutal and unforgivable," she whispered, "and now I'm going to pay you back."

She reached into the pocket of her apron and withdrew a pair of scissors she had taken from Helen's sewing basket. She snapped them open and shut, remembering the horror of that sound when she had heard it in the jail cell.

Her eyes sparkled with ruthlessness. "It's a shame you're not awake, Lacy, but I don't have an army of harlots to hold you while I cut your hair. I only have Maria and the sleeping potion she gave you in your coffee." The corners of her mouth tilted upward in a pleased smile. "Cade and all the others will sleep well, too. I wanted to make sure they didn't hear anything out of the ordinary tonight."

She walked around to the side of the bed, picked

up a strand of Lacy's hair near the forehead, and whacked it off. "Oh, by the way, Lacy, Cade didn't mind my short hair at all. Maybe, if you're lucky, he won't mind yours."

The next morning Cade opened his eyes to see the sun slanting through the window and groaned. Jesus, he had slept a long time, and in addition he felt like hell. He swung his legs over to the side of the bed and sat up. Propping his elbows on his knees, he cradled his head in his hands, trying to remember what the hell he had had to drink the night before. His temples pounding, he stood up slowly.

Carefully he pulled on his trousers, then his socks, and stomped into his boots. He was just tucking his shirt in when he heard the commotion down the hall. "Son-of-a-bitch!" he muttered.

As he swung his door open, he heard Wyatt yelling and a woman screaming, but his head hurt too bad to try to make sense of it. He stumbled out into the hallway just in time to glimpse Lacy, still in a champagne-colored dressing gown, running down the stairway. The two young French maids she had brought from Follettville ran after her, one screaming, the other wildly calling her name.

Cade stared after Wyatt as he raced pell-mell down the stairs. "What the hell is going on?" he demanded to an empty corridor.

Turning around, Cade glared into his empty room, muttered a few expletives, then finished tucking in his shirt. Running a hand through his hair, he followed the rest of them down the hall. By the time he got to the front door the entire retinue had circled the front lawn and headed down the path along the west side of the house. Cade started after them, wondering if the whole bunch had lost their minds. He paused a moment, allowing the wave of pain that attacked his temples to pass, then followed his crazy guests.

Helen emerged from the rose garden, appearing horrified. "What happened to Miss Fielding?" she asked, her hands clasped together as if she had been praying.

"Hell, I don't know," Cade retorted disgustedly. "She left the house screaming like a snake bit her, with her maids and Wyatt right behind." He put his hand to his head and closed his eyes, making a mental note to throw his aged brandy out. Any drink that could cause such pain had to be bad.

"Sir, are you all right?" Helen asked anxiously.

"Yes." Cade looked up to see the yard was empty. "Where the hell did they go?"

"Miss Fielding's looking for Gabrielle," Helen said. "I told her she had gone for a walk early this morning."

Squinting against the early morning sun, Cade staggered past the garden and the laundry. Freshly washed sheets hung on the line, a fire blazed under a washtub, and two young women stood nearby, aprons caught up as if they had been in the middle of drying their hands and had suddenly forgotten what they were doing. Everyone stood still, gazing toward the west. Cade lengthened his stride.

When he rounded the workshed he saw Lacy, then Gabrielle in the distance. The sun seemed to caress her, glowing red in her hair and outlining her willowy body. His heart lifted at the sight.

Lacy had begun to run, her satin gown floating out behind her, gleaming richly. Cade watched in astonishment as she literally threw herself on Gabrielle and the two women sprawled on the ground. "Damn," he muttered, beginning to sprint despite the pain in his temples. He saw Sam Fortune heading from the barn and the hired hands, awakened from sleep, tumbled out of the bunkhouse to see what the shouting was all about. Wyatt stood by helplessly, looking as if he wanted to stop them but wasn't sure how. The women rolled back and forth in the dust, their arms and legs flashing. "Get Gabrielle," Cade yelled at Sam. He saw a bare foot and grabbed it, pulling Lacy away from Gabrielle. Sam ducked in, caught Gabrielle around the waist with one hand, and with the other loosened her fingers from Lacy's robe.

Although the satin material was slippery, Cade managed to grip Lacy around her middle and drag her from the melee. When he stood up and got a good look at her, he literally lost his breath. Her hair had been shorn close to her head.

"Jesus Christ," he gasped. His gaze went in horror to Gabrielle. Lacy struggled free and he caught her again, using all his strength to hold her.

"I'll kill you, Gabrielle!" Lacy screamed. "I'll kill you, I swear it, you bloody little bitch!"

Gabrielle went still in Sam's arms, her dusty face calm.

"You conniving, vicious little hypocrite!" Lacy choked with rage.

Fury rippled through Cade's veins. "Did you do this, Gabrielle?" he demanded, but he could tell from the look on her face that she had.

Gabrielle met his angry gaze. "Yes, I did. I never told you, but Lacy was there when they cut my hair. She hired the men who abducted me off the street and those vicious women who terrorized me." Gabrielle leaned her head back against Sam as if she were suddenly weak, then after drawing a deep breath she told Lacy, "You're a mean-spirited woman. It's high time someone paid you back for your cruelty."

Shrugging out of Sam's arms, Gabrielle looked at

Cade one last time, then turned and walked away. He stared after her, unable to believe what had happened. He studied the ragged lengths of Lacy's hair and slowly released her. "Is she telling the truth?" he demanded.

"Of course not!" Lacy spat. "She's a liar."

Wyatt shook his head sorrowfully. "You might as well admit it, Lacy. The story's already out in town. It's just a matter of time before Cade hears it."

"Shut up, damn you," Lacy hissed, whirling on him. "Shut up!"

Wyatt squinted toward the morning sun, then sighed heavily. "It wouldn't do any good for me to keep quiet. Some of the *ladies*—he stressed the word sarcastically—"you hired are beginning to talk." He glanced at Cade. "I heard about it in one of the gaming houses a couple of nights ago." He rubbed a hand along his jaw morosely. "I hated to hear it because I knew it was true."

"She's a traitor," Lacy cried, her gaze sweeping the stony expressions of first Cade, then Sam, then Wyatt. "She deserved what she got, she betrayed the South!" Her lips thinned with bitterness.

As Cade stared into Lacy's glittering pale blue eyes, he remembered the pain he had seen in Gabrielle's after her hair had been cut. "What you did was wicked," he said flatly. Repulsed, he turned from her. "As soon as you pack your bags, I want you off this ranch."

"Cade . . ."

"I mean it." He looked up. "Wyatt, you're welcome any time, but not Lacy."

Lacy's mouth twisted. "To hell with you." She jerked her dusty satin robe around her body and stalked toward the house.

Chapter 14

Cade watched Lacy walk away, followed by Wyatt, then turned to look in the direction that Gabrielle had headed earlier. He wanted to go after her, he wanted to take her in his arms and tell her how sorry he was, how wrong he had been. He realized now that she had been innocent all along. Celeste's sudden departure following Ruben's escape spoke for itself, and now he knew that the incident in Folletville had been the result of Lacy's jealousy and had had nothing to do with Gabrielle's spying. He shuddered to think what she must have gone through while Lacy was visiting the ranch. If only she had told him that Lacy had been responsible, he would have gone after her and taught her a lesson long ago. If only Gabrielle hadn't kept all her pain inside her, lying in bed for days while he had tried to get her to talk about it.

He shook his head in an attempt to clear his thoughts. He and Gabrielle had a lot of things to talk over, but first he had to make sure Lacy left immediately, and without abusing his servants with her imperious demands. He scowled when he thought of Lacy, wishing he could throw her bodily from his home, but she was still a woman. He strode back into the house at a furious pace, barely noticing the sultry, unnatural calm of the air or the ominous blue-black clouds gathering on the horizon.

A half hour later, after he had personally watched Lacy and her two French maids pile into a carriage and rattle off, Cade stepped through the kitchen door intending to find Gabrielle. She had not returned since the scene with Lacy, and Cade grew more and more concerned as dark clouds continued to spread across the sky. The air had a heavy, still feeling, and everything was tinged a green-gray color. Cade knew that a serious storm was moving in fast, and he had to find Gabrielle before it hit.

Gabrielle sat with her back to a tree, out past the corral. She was still shaken by the confrontation with Lacy, but an odd calm had settled over her while she had sat there. For the first time since she had left New Orleans she felt she had some kind of control over her life. She had taken action against Lacy, and she had gotten her revenge. Perhaps Cade was so disgusted with her now that he would let her leave in peace and go to Europe. He was probably consoling Lacy right now as she told him lie after lie about her innocence and Gabrielle's deceit. The thought of Cade holding Lacy in his arms made her eyes fill with tears, breaking her calm. She had to get away from the ranch before the pain of seeing Cade and Lacy together became unbearable, and she had to leave before Cade noticed her increasing morning sickness. If he knew she was carrying his child he would never let her go, no matter how much he hated her.

The dark clouds she had noticed earlier now completely filled the sky and made her feel as if something ominous was about to happen. It looked as if it was going to rain, but she had never seen weather like this before. In the distance she could see the ranch hands running back and forth, leading horses into the barns and shouting at one another. Finally one tall figure emerged from the confusion, striding purposefully toward her.

It was Cade. She thought about trying to escape him, but she knew he would be able to catch her no matter how fast she ran, so she remained sitting against the tree.

"Gabrielle!" he called out. "I've been looking all over for you."

"I don't want to talk to you," she answered. "Just leave me alone. Please."

Cade crossed the distance between them. He stood with his legs spread slightly apart, his hands held out in appeal. "Gabrielle, we have to talk. You have to listen to me. I've been an idiot, and I want to make it up to you."

Towering over her, Cade looked ten feet tall. Gabrielle's blood ran hot with fury. How dare he chase her down out here to bully her again. She had had enough. She leaped to her feet.

"No, you listen to me, Cade Montana. You've pushed me around since the day I met you and I'm tired of it. You *have* been an idiot, but I don't want to hear about it. I just want to leave. I want to leave you, I want to leave this ranch, and I want to leave Texas. I'm going to Europe and you can't stop me." She spun around and started to walk away from him.

He stared after her in surprise, then began to follow her. A strong wind whipped at her skirt, pulling it tight against her hips, and her hair blew around her face. She pushed her auburn curls back behind her ears.

"Please give me a chance to explain!" Cade shouted. "I know you're innocent, Gabrielle. I was wrong before. I believe now it *was* an act you put on

for the Yankee to save yourself. Stop, right now!"
he ordered in frustration as he grabbed her wrist
and swung her around to face him.

Her face flamed as she wrenched her arm from his
grasp. "Don't touch me! I don't want to hear your
apologies, and I don't want to hear your explana-
tions. You didn't believe me, and I can't forgive you
for that. If you loved me, you would have believed
me." She was crying now, and she wiped her eyes
as the increasing wind swirled her hair all around
her face.

Lightning flashed and thunder boomed loudly in
the distance, and drops of rain blended with her
tears as they fell on her cheek. Cade's heart ached
for her even as the thunder reminded him of the
coming storm. They had to get to shelter immediately. Gabrielle turned and ran away again as another bolt of lightning flashed nearby. Cade chased
her while the wind blew sharp dirt on his face. It
was almost pitch-dark now, and the entire sky
seemed to rumble overhead.

"Gabrielle, we have to get inside." His words
were drowned out by a tremendous clap of thunder.
"Before the storm really hits."

She continued to run ahead of him, and he muttered an oath under his breath as he broke into full
speed. He caught up with her quickly, swept her up
in his arms, and threw her over his shoulder. He
held her legs firmly as he continued to run toward
the ranch.

Bouncing along on his shoulder, she beat fiercely
at his back with her fists. "Put me down! Put me
down!" he thought he heard her yell, but her voice
was drowned out by the wind and the rain, which
fell heavily now. Cade could barely see through the
dark sheets of wind-driven water. He pressed on
against the strong gusts, praying that they would

make it to the ranch before his legs gave out. It seemed that the ranch was miles away in the black of the storm when he suddenly remembered the small abandoned barn near the corral. He had been planning to tear it down for months, but luckily none of his men had had the time.

They reached the rickety old barn just as the sky seemed to fall down around them. Cade practically threw Gabrielle down in a pile of hay before he turned to secure the door. As he was closing the latch they heard a powerful crash and a heavy thud as something fell against the door. Breathing hard from exertion, Cade felt in the corner for a lamp. He found it and lit the wick with matches lying next to it. A warm yellow glow illuminated the barn.

Gabrielle sat on the hay, her wildly disordered hair flaming in the lamplight. She looked up at him in confusion and surprise, still trying to catch her breath from the rough ride on his shoulder. Her breasts rose and fell rapidly, pressing against her wet dress.

"I'm sorry, princess, but I couldn't let you die out there, no matter how stubborn you are," he said, smiling dryly. He looked at her intently, his gaze fixed on her glinting emerald eyes. "It seems we might be here awhile, because something just fell against the door. It looks like we are going to have a talk whether you like it or not."

"Just because I'm trapped in here doesn't mean I have to listen to—"

"No, Gabrielle," Cade said firmly, dropping to his knees beside her. "You *are* going to listen. I need to tell you something. I got a letter from Tyler the day before yesterday."

At the mention of Tyler's name, Gabrielle's anger evaporated. "What did he say?"

"He wrote that Celeste ran off last week, taking a

lot of luggage and the entire contents of his safe. He assumes she means to join Guillotte, and he assured me that he believes you're innocent." Dropping his voice, he added, "So do I."

Gabrielle regarded him in astonishment, then it was as if a lead weight had been lifted from her chest. She began to cry with relief that Uncle Tyler believed in her innocence. He still cared, he still loved her. She covered her face with her hands and sobbed.

"Gabrielle, why are you crying? Didn't you hear me? Tyler believes you and so do I. I thought that would make you happy," Cade said softly.

She looked up at him as if she had forgotten he was there at all. In her relief that Uncle Tyler believed her, she had barely noticed that Cade had said *he* believed her. He was kneeling next to her, his wet hair raked back by his fingers, his strong face full of concern. She thought she had never seen a more beautiful man. His body was so powerful, yet he held his hand out to her so gently. Her desire to touch him was so strong that she was tempted to take his hand, but then she remembered Lacy, and her heart grew cold again.

"Why should I care whether you believe me or not?" she asked acidly. "All I care about is getting away from you. Go back to the house and tell Lacy you believe *her*. If you want her, you can have her. You don't need to keep up any charade with me for Uncle Tyler's sake. He doesn't need to know anything about what happened between us. I told you before that I'm no old maid who needs to force herself on a man." She held her head high with pride.

"What are you talking about, Gabrielle? If Lacy were a man I would challenge her for what she did to you. I'm just sorry for what I put you through

when Lacy came to visit. I don't want her here,"
Cade said.

"It's fine to say that now, but I notice you were
only too happy to have her warm your bed before
you found out she cut my hair. I cut her hair, so
now we're even. You can have her."

Cade's face darkened. He grabbed her shoulders
and looked deep into her eyes. "Gabrielle, will you
listen to me? I never wanted Lacy, and she has never
been in my bed. I don't want anyone but you."

Gabrielle looked at him suspiciously. His blue eyes
appeared black in the low light, and she realized
that she cared very much whether he was sincere.
"Don't try to fool me, Cade. I saw her wearing your
brown robe early yesterday morning after she had
just left your room."

Cade sighed loudly. "That's where you got this
idea? Lacy took my robe and was wearing it so you
would think we had been together. I know she
wanted to spend the night with me, but I refused.
No other woman appeals to me, Gabrielle, especially not Lacy. She's made of ice, but you're made
of fire. The same morning you saw her in my robe I
had been up for hours thinking about you. Even
when I thought you had lied to me I couldn't forget
how you felt in my arms. I want you, princess."

A silence fell between them, and Gabrielle suddenly noticed the sound of the rain whipping at the
windows and the howling wind that shook the walls
of the small barn. She felt Cade's hand stroking her
cheek, and she shut her eyes, torn by confusion.
Cade wanted her, and she in turn wanted him . . .
so desperately. But still she wasn't sure. His thumb
traveled over her lips and she ached to kiss it, but
she remained motionless.

All at once the windows were illuminated by
lightning and a tremendous clap of thunder boomed.

Another boom sounded and another until she felt that the whole sky must be crashing down around them. The light from the lamp flickered weakly as wind blew in the cracks of the door. Gabrielle shivered with fear.

"Cade," she whispered, her eyes wide.

He moved his hand to the back of her neck and pulled her into his arms. She began to shake as she felt his strong muscles wrap around her. Her breasts pushed against his hard chest, and she almost cried out from the joy of touching him. Nothing bad could ever happen to her while he held her, while she was enveloped by his power and strength.

She lifted her head slightly and met his lips with her own. Desire overcame her fear and uncertainty until all she felt was the insistent force of his kiss. He pulled her down onto the hay and held her even more tightly against him while his hand stroked her back and inched downward. Thick warmth flowed through her veins when his mouth left the velvet softness of her lips, and he began to kiss her ear and then her neck and the base of her throat.

"Gabrielle," Cade murmured, his breath hot against her, "I want you so much. I love you, and I don't plan to ever let you leave."

"I won't leave," she said. "I don't want to leave. I love you, Cade. I could never stop loving you."

"Marry me, Gabrielle. Say you'll marry me," he whispered in her ear, kissing the sensitive skin.

She pushed abruptly against his chest. " Oh, Cade, please don't ruin things now. Isn't it enough that I said I love you? I don't know about getting married. I'm not saying no, but you have to give me time to think about it."

"You are so stubborn, Gabrielle," Cade said. "You know you—" He was cut off by a loud knocking on the barn door and Sam Fortune's voice.

"Is there anyone in there?" he yelled as he pounded on the side of the barn again.

Gabrielle, listening, was surprised to realize that the wind and rain had stopped. The storm had lifted as quickly as it had hit.

"Sam," Cade called out, "it's me. Gabrielle and I are trapped in here. Do you think you can get us out?"

Sam's voice was muffled. "It's going to take a while. We've got to break through the wall. The door's completely blocked by a supporting beam. Good thing you planned on tearing this shack down anyway."

"Did the storm do much damage?" Cade called out.

Sam's voice sounded closer. "Toolshed was blown away. Some of the roofs were damaged. The stable got hit the worst. It's the only building that suffered structural damage."

"What about the horses?"

"Looks like they weren't touched."

Gabrielle and Cade said little during the twenty minutes it took Sam and the men to free them. The damage to the stable was extensive, but it could be repaired. A few tree limbs had fallen, the bunkhouse roof needed repair, and the toolshed had to be replaced, but considering what could have happened, they were lucky.

When the two of them walked into the house, Helen took one look at Gabrielle and ushered her into the kitchen. "You need something warm in your stomach after all that excitement."

Helen placed mugs of steaming coffee in front of them and settled her hands on her hips while they sipped gingerly. "I just thank the Lord that we all made it through. I heard the storm coming, and I got down on my knees and prayed."

Cade leaned back in his chair and feigned astonishment. "By God, Helen, sure as the world, you saved us all."

Helen regarded him with disgust. "Don't be blasphemous," she warned him. "I know for a fact that my prayers didn't hurt us none."

Gabrielle listened to their banter as if from a distance. She set her coffee mug back on the table, her hand shaking slightly. The strong coffee scent was making her stomach churn alarmingly. Oh, no, not now, she thought. Don't let me be sick now.

Helen saw her face turn pale. "What's the matter, honey?"

Gabrielle lifted her head, seeking a breath of fresh air.

"Are you going to be sick?" Helen demanded.

Gabrielle nodded, rose from her chair with a moan, and ran from the room. Helen followed, close on her heels.

Cade watched their disappearing backs in surprise. Now, what was that all about? It wasn't like Gabrielle to be sick. She'd seemed fine all during the storm and rescue . . . fine until they'd sat down for coffee. Was some kind of stomach ailment going around? Not as far as he knew. Unless . . .

As another shocking possibility entered his head, Cade sat bolt upright. It couldn't be . . . or could it? She hadn't said anything, but then, knowing Gabrielle, he wouldn't be surprised to learn she was keeping it a secret from him. Goddammit, if it was true, all the more reason for her to accept his marriage proposal! But had the little chit said yes yet? No. Well, she soon would!

Cade took the stairs two at a time and hurried down the corridor to Gabrielle's room. He rapped softly and scowled when Helen opened the door.

"I just got her into bed," she informed him reproachfully. "She needs her rest."

Cade shook his head, unmoved by her efforts to deter him. "Helen, I appreciate that you want to protect Gabrielle, but I have to talk to her. If you'll excuse me, please."

Cade watched her bristle angrily away, then pushed the door open and entered the bedroom. Gabrielle lay in the big canopied bed, looking small, a wet cloth over her forehead and eyes.

"I'd like to talk to you for a minute," he said quietly.

Startled at hearing his deep voice, Gabrielle pulled the cloth from her face. "What do you want?" she asked faintly.

Cade walked nearer, feeling suddenly ill-at-ease surrounded by all the feminine flounces. He had never realized before how hard-edged and roughly male he was compared to Gabrielle's fragile beauty. Her auburn hair and green eyes were the only colors against the white lace sheets and bedhangings. "How're you feeling?" he asked, pulling a chair up close to the bed and sitting down.

"Better." Gabrielle wished he hadn't come to her now. He hadn't been in her room since Captain McDaniels had taken her from the ranch. She slid upward, pulling the sheet with her. And then, to her horror, she felt her stomach revolt once more. She sat up in bed, threw back the sheet, and scrambled over to the side. "Oh," she gasped. "I'm going to be sick again."

She leaned over the chamber pot. There was no food in her stomach, but still she retched, her stomach convulsing over and over.

"Go . . ." she panted, waving Cade away. But he stayed, then washed her face when she finally lifted her head.

"Are you finished?" he asked gently.

She nodded weakly, allowing him to help settle her back in bed.

"Have you been sick a lot lately?" he asked, pulling the sheet up to cover her.

Gabrielle nodded, eyes closed. "Just in the mornings . . ." She curled on her side away from him, not wanting him to read the truth in her eyes. "I've been upset . . ."

"I think you have morning sickness because you're going to have a child."

She stared at him, unmoving, still not wanting to give herself away.

"Hadn't you realized that?" he asked, closing his fingers around her small hand.

"Yes, I knew," she admitted faintly. Her hand moved unconsciously over her flat stomach and she sat up in bed, suddenly frightened. "Uncle Tyler is going to be furious."

Cade laughed softly. "Yeah. I think we better plan a wedding, don't you?"

Gabrielle's expression turned wary. "Why are you laughing? It's not funny."

He shrugged. "I feel good about it. I like the idea of our having a baby together."

Gabrielle was still trying to take in his reaction when a fresh wave of nausea swept over her. "Ohhh . . ." She dropped back against the pillow. Cade caught up a clean cloth, poured fresh water from the pitcher over it, and wiped her face.

"Feeling better?"

She nodded, eyes closed, her long lashes brushing her pale skin.

"I want to marry you, Gabrielle."

She turned on her side with a soft moan. Cade brushed the hair back from her face. "This ranch needs a woman. I need you. The baby needs you. Surely you see that now.''

Gabrielle clenched her eyes shut and reached for his hand. ''Oh, Cade, I'm too sick and confused to see anything straight right now. Please be patient with me.''

And with another moan she leaned over the side of the bed and retched again while Cade tenderly held her head.

Chapter 15

I t was late in the afternoon when, with a restless sigh, Gabrielle dropped her needlework on the small garden bench beside her and looked up at the wispy trails of fairweather clouds. The thought that she was carrying a child was still incomprehensible to her. But not to Cade. The spark of life inside her had immediately become a reality to him. And he was so excited! Her delicate brows came together in thought. How could he adapt so easily when she still couldn't take it all in? How could he be altogether certain of their future together when she was consumed with doubts and questions?

Rising to her feet, she walked slowly toward the gate. Cade wanted to marry right away, and didn't seem to doubt that it would work out just fine. But she felt bewildered by the enormous changes marriage would entail, and frightened by the thought of being pregnant, giving birth, assuming the responsibility of caring for a child. More than anything, she needed time to put things in perspective.

Preoccupied, she automatically turned her footsteps toward the creek, wandering aimlessly until the serenity of late afternoon was shattered with an abrupt clattering of hooves and jangling of harness. Turning, she saw one of the riders split from the others and angle toward her. Cade. Warmth filled her despite her determination to resist his entreaties to marry him.

He rode a beautiful buckskin mare with a black mane and tail, handling the animal with virile grace, his broad-shouldered body lifting and falling with the horse's gallop.

He reined up beside her. "Where're you going?" He grinned as he slid off the horse.

"Down to the creek," she answered, taking in his dusty length. With his day-old growth of beard and the gun on his hip, he looked like an outlaw—a charming one whose long-legged swagger could make the ladies catch their breath, whose smile could charm the birds out of the trees. Good Lord, how could she marry him? Even with a child on the way, how could she surrender her life to a man like him? In some ways he was bigger than life. Could she be her own person with him, or would she wither in his shadow?

"Are you feeling better?" Cade asked, lifting his hat and running his fingers through his tousled hair.

"Fine, thank you," she answered, embarrassed by his reference to her condition. Turning, she began to walk and Cade fell into step by her side.

"I had a visitor this morning," he mentioned casually.

"Oh?"

"Rudolf Adler."

Gabrielle's steps faltered slightly. "Isn't he the investigator you hired to follow Celeste?"

"Yes. I never did pull him off the job."

She stopped. "I thought you fired him. You were so certain I was guilty."

Cade shook his head. "No." He took her hand and kissed it, then gave her a smile that made her heart flip. "I think I wanted to be proven wrong."

Gabrielle felt hope blossom in her heart. Maybe Adler had found final proof of her innocence. "What did he say?" she asked, her voice catching.

He hesitated. "Part of it we already knew from Tyler's letter—that your sister left home and disappeared, probably to join Ruben Guillotte. Adler suspects Celeste is headed for Mexico. He was able to trace her as far as Brownsville."

Gabrielle shook her head, horrified by her sister's deeds. "How can she do this to Uncle Tyler? How can she hurt others without even caring?"

Cade shrugged. "I don't know. I just want to get *you* out of this mess. I told Adler to go to Mexico to see what he can find out. He left this morning." He smiled down at her. "Maybe we're going to find proof of your innocence sooner that we thought."

Cade leaned over, tilted her chin, and kissed her on the mouth. "I feel damned good about everything," he announced. "If you weren't in such a delicate state, I'd swing you around and throw you in the air."

Gabrielle regarded him uneasily. "Why? Because you think I'm innocent?"

He laughed. "Yes. But I also want to free you of this shadow . . . and I don't want our children or our marriage to suffer, either." He saw her face go still. "What's the matter?"

"I haven't told you I'd marry you yet."

"Gabrielle, you're going to have *my* child."

She clasped her hands in her lap and took a deep, even breath. "There's an attraction between us, Cade," she began calmly. "I admit it. But I'm not sure I'd have any freedom with you. The truth is, you're used to having your own way. Well, I'm used to having my way, too, and I don't wish to lose that . . . privilege. I want my marriage to be a partner-

ship. You're a strong man. I don't want you to overcome me by sheer energy and force of will."

Cade shook his head. "That won't happen. The
circumstances of our getting to know each other have
been insane all along, and that's why you've gotten
the wrong impression of me."

"Cade—"

He held up a hand to stop her. "Gabrielle, look
at it from my side, just once. When I first met you,
I thought you were beautiful, but I also thought you
were a spoiled brat and one woman a man should
stay clear of. Then I learned you were apparently a
spy . . . and not only that, but your uncle wanted
me to assume responsibility for you. That's quite a
series of events. I accepted, reluctantly. Then that
damned Committee laid out strict guidelines that
made me a prisoner of my promise. You were to
behave yourself. No hint of scandal was to filter back
to New Orleans to embarrass them. Well, hell, you
were just like one of those calves out there. You
balked at every damned thing, ran off every time
someone wasn't looking. I had to be tough and
domineering. I didn't have a choice."

She nodded, her expression unchanged. "I know
that. But I'm not talking about what you had to do.
I'm talking about the way you *are*, with everybody."

"Well, then, we will just have to work through
our differences," he said equably. "With a child on
the way there's no choice. We're going to get married."

Gabrielle's mouth firmed stubbornly. She knew
she loved this man, but he would have to stop ordering her around like a child or she wouldn't marry
him. "But there *is* a choice, Cade. My choice. And I
haven't decided yet."

In a lightning-fast move Cade caught her wrist,

his handsome face indignant. "The child you carry is mine!"

Gabrielle lifted her chin. "The child is mine, Cade." She looked down at his hand on her wrist. "And this is what I'm talking about. Now turn my hand loose and mind your manners."

As if burned, Cade released her wrist and scowled after her as she walked away. His expression thunderous, he strode back to his horse, caught up the reins, and threw himself into the saddle. "Son-of-a-bitch," he muttered, heading toward the bunkhouse. Gabrielle might be in a delicate state, but she was as muleheaded and ornery as ever.

That night Sam took a drink out of the bottle, handed it back to Cade, then tilted his straight-backed chair precariously against the bunkhouse. A rising moon hung low in the sky, providing ample light for them to see by. Morose, Sam gazed at his boss, who sat on the porch steps a few feet away.

"She thinks you're autocratic?" At Cade's nod, Sam's brows furrowed in thought. "What exactly does she mean by that?" he asked after a moment.

Cade stared down at the bottle. "Well, it's someone who has power and who uses it without asking anybody else his opinion."

"Well, hell," Sam muttered laconically, "that's what my father was. Autocratic," he mused, rolling the word on his tongue. "My mother didn't think much about it, though. She just did what he said."

"Yeah," Cade agreed. "But Gabrielle is stubborn. "She looks all soft and tender, but she's strong-minded, believe me. She'll go along and be as sweet as honey, a man's dream of a woman, and suddenly she'll want something, and by God, it becomes important to her. And that's when the trouble starts, because when Gabrielle decides something's important, she digs in her heels. And she won't budge. That's the way she is about marrying me. Something's got to get straight in her head, and then she'll do it, but not before." He shook his head. "She doesn't want anybody doing her thinking for her."

"Well that doesn't sound so unreasonable," Sam observed, reaching for the bottle. "You just have to give her time."

Cade nodded. "I know." His brows came together in a frown. "Ordinarily I wouldn't mind, but she's so damned . . . arrogant about it."

The next day Gabrielle walked into Cade's study without bothering to knock. He looked up and straightened. He couldn't help thinking how pretty she looked. Her dress was the color of sunshine with a close-fitting bodice of snow-white lace. He tried to control his lustful thoughts and his surprise at her unexpected appearance. "Yes?" he asked, one brow lifting.

"I've decided to marry you," Gabrielle informed him. "If you will agree to certain conditions."

He eyed her indulgently. "What are they?"

"I want to go to Europe every couple of years."

His eyes narrowed. "For how long?"

"Three months."

Her pretty face was set with determination, but he could tell she was prepared to bargain. He shook his head, his blue eyes darkening with calculation. "I'll agree to every three years, but for only two months."

"Fine," she agreed quickly.

"What's the next condition?" he asked, leaning back in his chair and crossing his arms over his chest.

"That you start a school here," she replied. "And hire a teacher. I can't do it all myself and have a baby, too."

He nodded. "I agree." He leaned forward with an air of implicit dismissal. "Is that all?"

"No." Her emerald eyes began to gleam. "When this war is over, I want my wardrobe to be designed in Paris. I love clothes and I don't want to suffer because I live in Texas."

"Suffer?" Cade barked indignantly. "Living in Texas is a hardship?"

"Cade," Gabrielle reminded him, "don't lapse into boorish behavior now. I've seen you act the gentleman and know you can be sophisticated and cosmopolitan when you want to."

He settled back in his chair, grinning at her. "What else?"

"We do not sleep together until after our wedding."

His grin deepened as his gaze traveled slowly down her body and back up again to her flushed face. "Fine. What else?"

"I get to name our baby."

"No."

"That's one of my conditions," Gabrielle insisted with a note of finality.

"I won't do it."

When she turned and walked toward the door, Cade leaped to his feet. "All right!" he bellowed. "What the hell else do you have in mind? Do you want to run the goddamned ranch, too?"

"I don't want you to curse in front of me."

He leaned forward, placing both hands on his desk. "Listen here, you little redheaded wench, are you going to marry me or not? Those are all the concessions I'm going to make."

Gabrielle smiled sweetly at him. "I'm going to marry you. I told you I was."

His expression surly, he sat down. "All right." He waited a moment for her to leave, and when she continued to stand before his desk, he said, "What is it now?"

"I want to ask you about the wedding."

"What about it?" he snapped, irritated at the way this slip of a girl was ordering him around as if he were a schoolboy. "As soon as we can make the arrangements for a big celebration, we'll get married."

"Celebration?" Gabrielle shuddered delicately. "Cade, this has to be a small wedding. After all, I'm going to have a baby in an indecent amount of time."

Cade shot out of his chair. "What the hell is indecent about it? We don't have to announce it's coming, but I'm damned happy about this baby. We're going to have a celebration like you've never seen. People would think I'd lost my mind if I slunk off somewhere and married you. I won't do it."

"What about what happened in Follettville?"

Cade laughed. "Most of those sons-of-bitches will show up here, hats in their hands, bowing and scraping and hoping I didn't see them in the crowd."

Gabrielle was horrified to think that those awful people who had reviled her would come to her wedding. "Cade, I won't have it!"

"Yes, you will," he insisted. "By God, terrible things happen and people eventually get over them. You will, too. We're going to be living here for a good long time. Our sons and daughters and their sons and daughters will grow up in this area. We're established. We don't want bitterness and conflict ahead for us or for them." He perched on the edge of his desk. "Now I admit, Gabrielle, that what I'm asking you to do is hard, but it's the only way. We have to set the standard. The people in Follettville will appreciate the fact that you're the kind of person who can forgive and forget."

Gabrielle acknowledged that there might be truth in his words and acquiesced reluctantly. At the door she turned. "I won't have Lacy here."

Cade nodded. "Of course not."

Cade had not been exaggerating when he'd used the word *celebration*. He hired additional servants in Brownsville, and while there he ordered enough lace, ribbons, and satin to make at least three wedding dresses, not just one. He hired a Spanish dressmaker from Mexico City and brought her back for a month's stay at the ranch.

A rodeo and barbecue were part of any festival in Texas, at least as far as Cade was concerned. He also hired a skilled Mexican carpenter from Brownsville to build a pavilion with a wooden dance floor.

The wedding was set for a month hence. Gabrielle viewed the enormity of the proceedings with disbelief. A Frenchwoman by the name of Madam Borghese was retained to orchestrate the preparation of food and entertainment and to handle the guests who would stay at the ranch. Madam Borghese had a talent for organization, along with an impatient temperament. Gabrielle found her trying. Typical of a man, Cade left it up to Gabrielle to smooth Helen's and Maria's ruffled feathers; neither of them liked being ordered about by the Frenchwoman.

Gabrielle's reluctance to have a big wedding didn't last long. In short order she was caught up in the preparations. Cade, on the other hand, after setting things in motion turned all the details over to the hired help and involved himself only when they sought his opinion. Gabrielle kept him informed of their progress. It pleased her that not once during that month did they have a single argument.

Gabrielle enjoyed the hustle and bustle of those days. She was increasingly reassured as time passed and Cade continued to respect her demands for independence. She began to believe they could have a strong, lasting marriage after all.

Somehow, the reality that she would be a married woman, and a mother, seemed to slip past her until the night before the wedding. At dinner that evening Tom Rawlings stood up to make a toast.

"To Gabrielle and Cade, wishes for a long and happy life together."

She and Cade rose to their feet from opposite ends of the long table and acknowledged the well-wishes of their guests. Gazing at Cade, splendidly handsome in formal black, his shirt brilliant white against his suntanned skin, she felt her heart flip in her chest. Tomorrow she would marry him! She remembered the girl she had been in New Orleans, and all the wicked things she had heard about Cade Montana, plus the girlish fantasies that had gone through her head about him. Now, months later, she was to marry the very same man. Not only that but he was the father of her child.

That night when she went to bed Gabrielle could hardly contain her excitement. The house was already filled with guests, and even more—a total of two hundred—would arrive in the morning. And they were all coming to see her marry Cade Montana. Shivering with pleasure, she closed her eyes.

The following day dawned bright and clear, with not even a hazy cloud to mar the blue sky overhead. The ceremony had been set for late afternoon. As the day wore on, Gabrielle began to think that such a late hour might have been a mistake. The laughter from the veranda and patio downstairs seemed to be getting louder, and she suspected many of their guests had already had too much to drink.

Madam Borghese had insisted that all the guests remain far away from the upstairs of the west wing. The bride needed peace and quiet for a few hours before the ceremony. Without the hubbub, it seemed eerily silent to Gabrielle. She had been ordered to rest but didn't feel tired. In an hour or so Maria would arrive to help her dress and the hairdresser would come to do her hair. But for now she was alone. Glancing at her reflection in the mirror, she laughed softly, remembering Antoinette's shocked expression when she'd first seen her short hair. She'd recovered quickly, however, thanking heaven that at least what Gabrielle did have was thick and curly and of a vibrant color.

Her thoughts drifted over the events of the morning. The rodeo had been the worst. She had watched with her heart in her mouth as Cade had ridden a mean-looking brute of a horse. The animal had bucked and crow-hopped viciously until Cade had been thrown. The guests had loved it, but Gabrielle had been merely thankful to see him get to his feet and walk from the arena without assistance.

How people loved Cade. She was beginning to accept the idea that someday he would run for public office and win. She laughed, remembering the big old clumsy hound that had leaped up and muddied Cade's clothes in his exuberance to welcome him. A young boy, from whom the dog had escaped, had apologized profusely.

Cade had a generous heart and not a snobbish bone in his body. Today she'd seen small ranchers, townspeople, and servants mingle with senators, the governor, wealthy ranchers, and businessmen from all over the state.

The sound of a lively Mexican folk dance drew her
attention. Barefoot, she stepped onto the balcony,
leaning far over the railing in a futile effort to see
the pavilion below. Maria had described it this
morning, explaining that it was decorated with white
ribbons, greenery, and brightly colored lanterns.

A breeze ruffled the lace at the neck of Gabrielle's
wrap, and with a little shiver she wandered back
inside and down the hallway, her hand trailing along
the banister at the top of the stairs. Even from the
big floor-length windows in the foyer, she couldn't
see the pavilion. Returning to the corridor, she
glanced idly past Cade's room toward the window
at the end of the hall. The pavilion would certainly
be visible from there.

But she had just walked past Cade's room, when,
on impulse, she stopped. Frowning slightly, she re-
traced her steps and tilted her head to listen. She
heard no sound coming from inside. Of course he
was probably outdoors, sharing toasts with Tom
Rawlings and his crowd of hooligans.

Piqued by sudden curiosity, Gabrielle opened the
door and looked inside. She had never paid much
attention to his room before, although she had been
there many times. It was big, much like hers, but
decorated to his taste, of course. A little nervous,
she walked inside and glanced about. Cade was very
neat, almost spartan. Motivated by boredom more
than anything, she opened the door to his wardrobe
and studied the contents—it was filled with finely
polished boots and suits on hangers and hat boxes
on the top shelf. She smiled. And he thought she
was frivolous when it came to clothes.

Beginning to enjoy herself, she looked inside a
matching wardrobe alongside the first. Ranch
clothes, work shirts, gunbelts, boxes of bullets, and
other Western paraphernalia filled it. She shook her

head, marveling at the two different worlds in which he lived. Her fingers ran along his gunbelt, trailing over the row of shells. The man who wore these clothes would be the man she married. She would seldom see the man who wore the black frock coat and gold-brocaded vest.

Hearing a slight noise, Gabrielle walked to the center of the room and listened. The sound came again, like pebbles scattering across water, and she realized it was coming from Cade's dressing room. She tiptoed over to the door and, holding her breath, pressed the tip of her finger against it until it moved.

Her emerald eyes widened and her teeth came down on her lower lip as she stared through the narrow opening. Cade, with his back to her, was taking a bath in a big oval copper tub. Intrigued, she watched as his fingers curled around the bar of soap and scrubbed across his shoulders. She shivered, moved by the sight of his bronze skin and corded muscles. He was lean and masculine and beautiful, and she had a crazy, irresistible desire to touch him and find out what his wet skin felt like.

Then she heard footsteps coming down the hallway, and a moment later a knock sounded on Cade's door.

"Montana," Rawlings yelled.

Gabrielle stared at Cade in horror, wondering how in the world she had managed to get herself into such a ridiculous, awkward situation.

"Come on in," Cade answered as, unaware of her presence, he soaped his upper arms.

Gabrielle was forced to make an instant decision. Without another thought she slipped into Cade's dressing room and edged behind the door. Pressing her fingers against her mouth, she listened as Rawlings walked across the bedroom and stopped in the doorway.

"Helen sent me up to see if you need anything," he said, his voice slurred with drink. "She says since I'm your best man, I'm supposed to see that your needs are met."

"I'm fine," Cade said, turning. "Tell Helen—" He stopped, his gaze slipping past Tom to Gabrielle pressed against the wall. "Tell Helen not to worry about me."

"Well, I'm going back down and see if I can corner that prissy Mrs. Andrews in the barn. I think I know a cure for her affliction. If I have a smile on my face when you come down, you'll know it worked."

Cade grinned. "Good luck."

Tom's footsteps retreated, and a moment later the door slammed shut. Only then did Cade's glance shift again to Gabrielle, his eyes brimming with wicked amusement. A furious blush spread across her cheeks as she stepped forward. "I didn't want him to know I was here."

"Oh?" Cade grinned slowly, his teeth white against his dark skin. "Why don't you close the door . . . just in case he comes back?" His dark brow lifted sardonically as she complied. "Mind if I ask what you're doing?"

"I—I didn't realize you were here," she explained, her blush deepening. "I thought you would be downstairs."

He nodded, not understanding but not really caring. He was becoming acutely aware of her slim curves beneath her robe.

Gabrielle moved closer. "It was so quiet in my room . . ."

"Don't you women consider seeing the groom before the wedding bad luck?"

She swallowed. His eyes were very blue, and little droplets of water had caught in the hair on his chest, where they glistened brightly. "It's only bad luck," she said, wetting her lips nervously, "if one is seen . . . in a wedding dress."

His gaze dropped to her mouth. "So it doesn't matter if I see you . . . in this?" He reached out and caught the hem of her robe, twisting it around his fingers.

Gabrielle shivered as the fabric pulled tighter around her and, highly sensitized, her nipples hardened. Her senses reeled at the sight of him, at his hard mouth curled with amusement. "Want to take a bath with me?"

"Heavens no." Her glance dropped to where the hair on his broad chest narrowed to a thin line and disappeared beneath the water. She heaved a breathless sigh. It had been so long since they had been together. "I really must go . . ."

She willed her feet to move, but they refused to obey her. Cade laughed softly. "I don't think you want to go, Gabrielle." To her surprise he stood up, looming over her as water cascaded from his tall body to the floor. She inhaled sharply—he was hard and lean and brown . . . She saw immediately that he wanted her.

Before she could come to her senses, Cade caught her around the waist and lifted her into the tub, pulling her hard against him. Water dripped onto her cheeks as his arms tightened and their gazes met, mesmerizing her into stillness. He touched her mouth, his fingers leaving a wet imprint on her lips. "I love your mouth," he whispered, his voice husky. "The corners tilt up . . . like a sassy cat's with cream." He bent his head, his wet mouth brushing hers ever so lightly. "I've missed you, Gabrielle."

His tongue traced the soft contour of her lips while one hand explored the curves of her breasts, his touch feather-light through her clothes. With a low groan, his mouth captured hers. Gabrielle's senses reeled, and she was hardly aware when he slipped the robe from her shoulders and tossed it to the floor. She began to tremble as his hands moved over her in the old ways she remembered so well.

Scooping her into his arms, Cade dropped deeper in the water, settling her onto his lap. She twisted until she managed to face him. The warm water in the big tub reached to just below her breasts. "We shouldn't," she whispered. "I shouldn't . . ."

Cade kissed her forehead, then let his finger trail down her cheeks, along her throat, and between her breasts. "I know," he murmured, leaning forward to kiss her mouth. He found the soap, lathered his hands, and slid them slowly over her shoulders. "It's just a bath."

Gabrielle closed her eyes as his hands moved firmly and silkily over her body. They circled her breasts, smoothed along her back, traced her hip, delved along the inside of her thigh and then higher.

She opened her eyes, which had grown heavy-lidded with passion. She leaned forward, arms braced on either side of the tub, and kissed his mouth. Disbelieving her own audacity, she traced his mouth with her tongue, and her hand slipped farther down, over the tight, hard muscles of his stomach. A shiver traveled down her spine at his sharp intake of breath as her hand closed around him.

"It's been a long time, hasn't it?" she whispered against his ear, then nipped his earlobe, and traced its outline with the tip of her tongue. She could feel his heart thudding as she molded herself against the slippery wetness of him. Cade caught her waist and pulled her forward, her legs astride him, his kisses hungry and impatient. Gabrielle gasped as she felt his hard length find entrance, then ever so slowly fill her. The warm water rippled about her nipples as they moved together.

She closed her eyes, rocking slightly, as magic curled from Cade into her and spread throughout her being. He caressed her breasts and his tongue moved into her mouth, and an electricity arced through her. Their arms entwined, their bodies strained, their mouths came together as one.

With a faint cry Gabrielle broke their kiss, arching her breasts against him as sensation after sensation spiraled up inside her. Her head dropped back and Cade's hands encircled her, his mouth at the pounding pulse in her throat. Ecstasy crashed blindingly through her. It seemed to go on and on, the exquisite feelings ebbing slowly. When her muscles finally relaxed, she bowed her head, drawing in deep breaths. Eyes closed, she dropped her forehead against Cade's, feeling his breathing slow in rhythm with hers.

They lay together, unmoving, while the water cooled around them. Gabrielle felt half drugged when Cade stirred again. He caught her face between his palms and kissed her mouth. Then his blue eyes met hers, and he smiled. "I love you."

The corners of her mouth tipped up. "I love you, too," she whispered.

He kissed her nose. "Do you think we should get ready for our wedding?" he asked, his voice still husky from their lovemaking.

Gabrielle nodded. "I suppose so."

Drawing a deep breath, Cade rose from the water, lifting her with him. He grabbed a towel, wrapped it about his lean hips, and caught up his robe. "Dry off and you can wear this back to your room. It's less than an hour before the ceremony."

He shook his head, grinning as she slipped into the robe and, with a little wave at the door, disappeared.

Chapter 16

The wedding was a wondrously happy affair. Whenever Gabrielle thought of it during the following months, she remembered one moment most often. At the dance Cade had taken her hand and led her onto the floor of the pavilion. At the time she had been barely aware of her neighbors and friends, but now she remembered their happy expressions. They had applauded and laughed and insisted the wedding couple should have the first dance alone.

It had been a violin solo, a sentimental melody that touched her heart. She had lifted her arms to Cade, and as he swung her about, his eyes, as blue as sapphires, crinkled at the corners. Then he smiled, teeth flashing white against his skin. He was so handsome that he took her breath away. That moment seemed burned into her memory—a moment of love, of exuberance and excitement, of swiftly moving events, of a man who was irrepressibly vital and full of life. That moment of joy seemed to epitomize their marriage.

The next time Zeke went into Follettville after the wedding, he brought back a package from Uncle Tyler. He had sent a cash gift and a small keepsake box that had belonged to Gabrielle's mother. It con-

tained some pieces of jewelry and various letters,
poetry, and notes that she had written. Nothing
could have pleased Gabrielle more. She spent hours
examining each article and written message, trying
to imagine what her mother had been like. It was a
marvelous wedding gift.

The early months of Gabrielle's pregnancy passed
quickly, like a wonderful holiday. Cade was thoughtful and attentive, and Gabrielle couldn't believe she
had ever worried that he would dominate her life. He
was the perfect husband.

Not only her marriage, but other areas of her life,
flowed smoothly during those days. At her urging,
Cade started construction of the schoolhouse. She
had chosen a location about a half mile from the
ranch, on a gentle rise. The structure itself would be
situated to the right of two huge old oak trees whose
trunks had grown together over the years. Gabrielle
found their giant size impressive and beautiful, and
they suggested to her a name for her school: the
Twisted Oaks Schoolhouse.

She wondered if other children in the area, besides those on the ranch, might wish to attend the
school. When she mentioned the idea to Cade, he
said why not find out. Over the next few weeks Gabrielle and Zeke took periodic trips to their outlying
neighbors, telling them about the school that would
open in the fall. She enjoyed meeting the wives
again, some of whom she'd met for the first time at
the wedding. From the promises she received from
parents, she guessed that eighteen children would
attend the first day of school.

Gabrielle spent many nights curled up in a big
overstuffed leather chair in Cade's study, making
lists of what must be done. She ordered supplies,
knowing that with a war going on her chances of
getting anything were slim. She arranged to have

notices placed in Southern papers, announcing a
teaching post in Texas, but no one seemed interested in moving to such a remote area. Finally a
young woman from Alabama wrote that she would
come. Gabrielle was thrilled. Maybe her excitement
about the school stemmed from the fact that her own
child would one day attend and be able to tell classmates that his mama had started it. The thought
made her feel proud. She had never known her own
mother, but she wanted to be an exemplary parent
to her child.

In the spring, Gabrielle received disturbing news.
Yankee Admiral Farragut had captured the city of
New Orleans. After heavy fighting, fourteen of his
warships had sailed past Forts Jackson and St. Phillip and taken the city. Defenses were almost non-
existent, and all he had had to do was go ashore,
haul down the flag, and formally take possession.

As ignominious as that seemed, Gabrielle thanked
God that no fighting had taken place in the city.
From what she could learn, although her uncle had
been imprisoned for several weeks, he had not been
harmed. When the Yankees could find no reason to
hold him, they had deported him across Lake Pont-
chartrain. Uncle Tyler didn't think he would lose
Camden Hill. Judge Dahlman and James Maffitt escaped altogether and were ordered by the Confederacy to new posts in Richmond.

Gabrielle's mouth crimped at hearing of their good
fortune. She detested James Maffitt and was still
haunted by the nightmare he had put her through
on the riverboat that fateful night. Nasty, grim-faced
man. He had seemed to enjoy tormenting her.

Rudolf Adler sent periodic communications to
Cade, telling of his progress in Mexico. Gabrielle
thought *progress* too positive a word for the little he
accomplished. When he had first gone down there,

he had learned that a Southerner matching Ruben's description had inquired about the possibility of buying cattle to stock a ranch. The man had been seen in one of the border towns off and on for a month or so, then he had disappeared. No one had seen Celeste, but Adler felt if he kept looking, he would eventually find her. Despite the slim evidence, Gabrielle hoped Adler's hunch proved right.

Everything flowed smoothly for a while until John Freemont came to talk to Cade. Gabrielle knew him vaguely, having met him once at Camden Hill. In his satchel he carried a letter from the War Department requesting that Cade continue diplomatic excursions into Mexico.

After Freemont's visit Cade was gone periodically, usually for a couple of weeks at a time. Although Gabrielle hated his absences, she understood why he had to go and didn't object. She asked only one thing of him: that no matter what, he be present at the baby's birth. Cade promised he would be.

Gabrielle was well into her pregnancy when John Freemont appeared at her door a second time. With an eerie sense of dread, she escorted him into the study where Cade had been working all morning. After chatting for a few minutes about the weather and other inconsequential subjects, Gabrielle withdrew, pulling the door shut behind her.

The meeting lasted long into the night. Gabrielle lay in bed waiting, unable to sleep. She knew Cade would be leaving again. She just hoped it wouldn't be a dangerous trip. She knew how badly the Yankees wanted to stop Cade because of his influence with certain Mexican officials, and she always worried that some lone gun would trail him and shoot him down. Cade had laughed at her fears and told her she had an overactive imagination.

Hearing the door open, Gabrielle sat up in bed.

Cade turned to her. "Why aren't you sleeping? It's so late." His gaze drifted to her rounded stomach, and he smiled. Placing his hands on either side of her, he leaned over and kissed her mouth. "You need your rest."

Gabrielle dismissed his concerns with a wave of her hand. "Does he want you to leave again?"

At Cade's troubled look, Gabrielle slid out of bed. "Cade, it's something serious, isn't it? What did he want?"

Cade hesitated. "He asked me to go to Europe."

A look of alarm spread over her face. "When?"

"I leave tomorrow."

She sank down on the side of the bed. Almost protectively her arm circled the small mound of her stomach. "If you go, you won't be here when the baby comes." She looked up, her expression stricken. "You promised you would be."

"Sweetheart, I know this is hard for you." Running his hands through his hair in frustration, Cade crossed to the open French doors. "He came on special request from the President."

"Can't they send somebody else? Surely you aren't the only man who can go."

"No, I'm not," Cade conceded, turning to her. "But I've been there before, and I'm available. I know who to talk to. The South desperately needs arms and ammunition. We need support from the Europeans."

Gabrielle felt the swell of a pain beyond tears. "I don't care! You've done enough!" She bit her lip, realizing she sounded hysterical. In a softer voice she continued. "I'm going to have a baby. I don't want to be alone when the time comes. It's dangerous, and I don't want to be wondering if you've been killed or drowned at sea. I just can't go through any more."

"I don't want to leave you, Gabrielle," Cade said, his voice deep with emotion. "But as hard as this is, I have to go. This is my way of contributing to the war. Otherwise I would have been a soldier, and that would have involved hand-to-hand combat. My risk is minimal compared to what it could have been."

Gabrielle closed her eyes in despair.

Cade stared at her pale face. "It's not as though I'm leaving you alone. You have the servants, and a doctor will be here when the baby comes. Sam Fortune will take charge of running the ranch." He closed the distance between them and grasped her shoulders. "Gabrielle, in wartime a man's got to do a lot of things he doesn't want to do."

"You won't be here when I need you," Gabrielle whispered, her voice breaking.

"Sweetheart, there's nothing more I can say. I have to go."

Gabrielle allowed him to pull her against his chest. "Oh, Cade, I'm so afraid," she whispered. "I have an awful feeling that something terrible is going to happen."

The next morning Gabrielle sat in her room, her face pale as marble, and prayed Cade would change his mind. But she knew he wouldn't. He had come up earlier and explained again how important the mission was. She understood completely, but still she didn't want him to leave. She was terrified of giving birth without him, fearing it in a way she herself didn't understand. Finally Cade went back downstairs to make the final preparations for his journey.

When he returned to say goodbye, walking over and kissing her cheek, her heart stilled.

"Goodbye, Gabrielle. I love you."

She stared straight ahead, unmoving.

"I don't want to leave with it like this between us."

She looked into his eyes, seeing there a grief that matched her own, and suddenly she was in his arms, clinging to him, trying to imprint upon her memory the scent and feel of him, the strength and bulk for all the months that they would be apart. At last he reluctantly pulled away, touched her cheek, then turned and walked out the door. Hot tears rolled down her cheeks, and finally she gave in to her grief, sobbing so hard her shoulders shook.

Weeks passed with no word from Cade. Although Gabrielle knew that the war made communication difficult, she worried more with each passing day. Gradually a numbness set in. As life at the ranch flowed on as usual, she began to feel that Cade was never coming back, as if he was part of a beautiful but fading dream. She felt she had never really known him, married him, loved him. The child she carried was her own and had nothing to do with Cade Montana. She'd lost him—just as she'd lost her parents and Uncle Tyler and even Celeste and her old nurse, Reba. Often she was consumed with loneliness.

Her fear of giving birth intensified. One night she dreamed she was going to die. The next morning, pale and shaken, she told Maria what had upset her and made her promise not to tell anyone. Several days before the baby was due Dr. Harper Chapman arrived at the ranch with Tom Rawlings in anticipation of the birth. The doctor expected no problems. Despite Gabrielle's slender build, she was healthy and strong. In his experience, he had found that fine-boned women had an easier time in childbirth than their stockier counterparts.

Despite his optimism, however, when Gabrielle went into labor a week later, in the middle of the night, things did not go well with her. By the following night, after long hours of labor, Dr.Chapman began to be concerned.

Helen walked out of Gabrielle's room, shutting the door behind her. Seeing the bleakness of her expression, Maria shivered and settled into the straight-backed chair where she maintained her vigil. "No change?" she asked softly.

Helen shook her head, fatigue making her look suddenly old. "I just can't bear to see her suffer so."

Maria hugged her arms to her chest, unable to stop the trembling that seized her. "What are we going to do?"

"I don't know," Helen said, her shoulders slumping wearily. "Dr. Chapman's worried. Gabrielle's been in labor a long time and she's worn out." Pity darkened her eyes. "She's not making sense anymore. Even when I tell her Cade's gone, she still asks for him over and over. It breaks my heart to hear her."

Maria shook her head. "Gabrielle had a feeling something bad would happen." She shuddered and crossed herself. "She dreamed she would die in childbirth," she said bleakly.

Helen stared at her in horror. "Dear God, woman, don't tell me that." She turned away. "I don't want to hear it!"

"It's true. That's why she was so scared."

Helen dropped her head in her hands. "Why does the good Lord make a woman suffer so?" She turned when the door opened.

Dr. Chapman stepped into the hallway, his face shadowed by the stubble of his beard. "Would you get me some more coffee, please," he said, speaking to Maria. "I could sure use it." He looked up and down the hallway. "Where's Rawlings?"

"He went down just now for some fresh air," Maria replied.

Dr. Chapman scowled at her from beneath shaggy brows. "Fetch him. I want him to go in there and let Gabrielle think he's Cade.

Helen's mouth sagged. "Dr. Chapman, she'll know better. You can't trick that poor girl."

"She won't know—she's been talking out of her head. Go get him. If it works, it works."

The three looked at one another, their faces strained, silently aware of how serious the situation had become. Maria nodded. "I'll find Mr. Rawlings right now."

Early the next morning Gabrielle gave birth to a baby girl and fell into a deep, exhausted sleep. Dr.Chapman gazed down at her, then out the window at the faint blush of dawn. He touched his fingers to his forehead in a weary salute to an unseen presence. "Thank you."

Shoulders slumping, he walked out into the hall and confronted the anxious, tired faces of those who had waited throughout the night. "She's real weak," he stated.

"Is she going to die?" Tom asked gruffly. " 'Cause if she is, you're not going to keep me out. Gabrielle is not going to be alone when she dies."

Dr. Chapman shook his head. "I think she's going to make it," he said, rubbing his whiskers. "She was very comforted by your impersonation of Cade, Mr. Rawlings. I think that's what got her through it. But we're going to have to find a wet nurse for the baby. The girl can't feed a child, she's too weak." He shuffled down the hall, his voice trailing back over his shoulder. "I'm going to bed. Call me . . ."

Gabrielle slept through the entire day. It was almost dark when her eyes fluttered open. Helen, who had been waiting by her bedside, leaned close, concern marking her features. "How're you feeling, Gabrielle?"

"My baby," she whispered.

Smiling, Helen took Gabrielle's hand between hers. "She's a girl, a beautiful little girl, Gabrielle. And she's perfect. Just like you. Wait a minute." She stepped over to the bassinet and picked up the baby, holding her for Gabrielle to see.

Gabrielle nodded, tears glistening in her eyes. "I want . . . to hold . . . her."

Helen shook her head. "Oh, honey, you're too weak. Wait till morning."

Gabrielle closed her eyes. "No . . . now."

"Okay." She propped a pillow against Gabrielle's side so that her arm was supported, then laid the baby in her arms.

Gabrielle looked up. "Her name is Laurel Marie."

Helen nodded, feeling a clutch in her heart. "That's a beautiful name."

When Gabrielle's eyes closed, Helen lifted the baby and put her back in the bassinet, then sat down in the rocker and dropped her head back. She closed her eyes, thinking that she hadn't slept in a long time. A smile touched her face. Laurel Marie Montana had raven-black hair and blue eyes, and she was a healthy little baby. Thank the Lord.

As more time passed, Gabrielle's feelings toward Cade hardened into anger. At the gravest crisis of her life, he had not been there for her. After all those months he had, in effect, deserted them all—abdicated his responsibility to the ranch, to his child, and, most of all, to her, his wife. When he returned, *if* he returned, she doubted they would be able to repair the damage he had done to their marriage.

Laurel Marie was four weeks old, and Gabrielle still had not regained her full strength, when Cade unexpectedly arrived home.

Gabrielle was standing by her bedroom window when he rode slowly, almost casually, into the yard—as if he'd been gone a couple of hours instead of months, she thought. She watched as ranch hands and servants ran to welcome him, surrounding his horse until he was swallowed up in the crowd.

Gabrielle had no intention of welcoming him home. Still, her heart thudded in her chest as she waited, sitting motionless in the rocker. He would come to her, she knew he would. And she was right. A few minutes later Cade appeared in the open doorway. He stood looking at her for a long time without speaking. His face was leaner, and more darkly tanned, and there was knowledge and experience in that handsome face that had not been there when he'd left.

"Aren't you going to welcome me home, sweetheart?" he said with a wry smile. "I had hoped you'd have gotten over your anger by now."

Bitter tears welled up in her eyes. Even though she had sworn she would be cold as ice, hurt, love, and relief swept her like a floodtide. "You weren't here when I needed you. I almost died."

"I know. Sam just told me. I'm so sorry I wasn't able to be here." He picked up the straight-backed chair from the desk and pulled it up closer to her, sitting silent for a long time. "Why don't you tell me about it. Tell me about when the baby was born."

Gabrielle thought of those terrifying hours when

nothing in her life existed except the pain and the precious moments of respite in between. She remembered thinking she was going to die and being so scared she couldn't breathe. Fearing tears, she lowered her face from him. "I was so frightened."

"I know you had a hard time. I wish I could have been here for you."

"But you weren't."

Cade met her look and knew that winning back her trust would be a slow process. "I'm home now, Gabrielle. I want to be a good husband to you, and I want to see my daughter."

Gabrielle's posture remained uncompromisingly straight. A war was going on inside her mind. "You may see Laurel Marie," she said finally, knowing she couldn't stop him. Without waiting for Cade's reply, she led the way into the nursery. A lamp burned on the table, its light illuminating the bassinet. Laurel Marie lay on her stomach, looking warm in sleep, her cheeks flushed pink. Gabrielle pulled the light blanket off her.

Cade swallowed, awed by the perfection of the tiny bit of humanity that was his daughter. "She's beautiful," he said.

Gabrielle nodded, her expression softening as she gazed down at the baby.

"I'd like to hold her."

"Of course," Gabrielle said stiffly. Reaching down, she picked up the warm little bundle. Without looking at Cade, she put Laurel into his arms, then turned abruptly and left the room.

Cade examined the baby's features in detail. He saw skin so delicate it was almost translucent, and realized she was breathing through her softly parted mouth. Laurie Marie jerked suddenly, waving a tiny fist before settling back into sleep. He laughed softly, touching his cheek against hers. "You're beautiful.

And don't you worry, your mother will come around," he whispered. "She's just stubborn, and she's been through a lot." He sat down in a rocker and stared at her face. His child.

Within a few hours, Cade reasserted his authority on the ranch and support from the servants and ranch hands swung in his favor. Some of the men were dismayed to see their boss tolerating Gabrielle's cold shoulder and thought he should put his spurs to what they called a nasty-tongued little filly. Even Sam, who thought highly of Gabrielle and understood that Cade was trying to soothe her feathers, was surprised that Cade could remain so patient with her.

That he had a loyal following, and that opinion favored him, had not escaped Gabrielle's notice. It hurt her feelings, although she'd die before she'd admit it. Cade could go off, desert everybody, leave his wife to hold the ranch together, then come back and take up where he left off, without losing anybody's respect.

And men thought women were fickle! she fumed as she headed toward the stables before breakfast the next morning. Last night Cade's mouth had tightened grimly when Sam had mentioned that the golden buckskin had been confined until she foaled. Gabrielle had given that order to protect the beautiful mare. She was hoping that its offspring would have the same wonderful coloring—she wanted to perpetuate the line.

She slipped in a side door of the stable and stood still for a moment, letting her eyes adjust to the shadowy interior.

"Is that buckskin still in here?" came Cade's voice from several stalls over.

"Yeah," Sam answered.

"It's too early for her to foal. Take her out in the corral," he ordered.

Fury trapped Gabrielle's breath in her throat and she spun around the end of the stall to confront him. "I have already given Sam instructions regarding that mare," she snapped.

Both men turned to look at her. A look of cold warning settled over Cade's face as he nodded toward the mare. "Take her on out, Sam."

A deadly quiet fell as the foreman followed Cade's instructions. Once the stable door closed behind him, Gabrielle whirled on Cade. "How dare you countermand my orders!"

"That is my mare," he answered, "and this is my ranch. I will not have you embarrass me in front of my men. Is that clear?"

Gabrielle practically shook with the force of the feeling that welled up in her. "I've been giving the orders. You ran off and left this place untended! God knows what would've happened if I hadn't been here."

Cade's mouth was tight and grim. "I'm going to tell you this once more, and I won't repeat it again. I did not run off. I was sent to Europe by President Jefferson Davis, during wartime. I regret that I left you at a critical time. I did not leave this ranch untended. I left it in the care of Sam Fortune, not you. I've done that many times in the past. That's why I retain a foreman of his caliber and pay him the kind of salary I do."

Gabrielle glared at him with burning, reproachful eyes. "I hate you."

When she started for the door, Cade blocked her way, a muscle flicking angrily in his jaw. "You don't hate me. You might *wish* you did, but you don't. You're angry—downright stinking, ugly mad. Your problem is that you don't know how the hell to *stop* being mad. You're pigheaded and you're too stubborn to admit that you're wrong."

Gabrielle's green eyes darkened with fury. "Let me pass."

Cade reached out and grabbed her wrist, pulling her against him. His arm encircled her waist. "I haven't touched you since I've been home."

His hand tangled in her hair, holding her head immobilized as his mouth settled over hers. He kissed her until she was breathless, then released her abruptly. Gabrielle stumbled backward and wiped her mouth with the back of her hand.

Cade merely stared at her. With a disgusted sigh he turned to leave. Gabrielle felt something twist inside her, as if something was breaking. Tears ran down her cheeks, and pain split her anger like a shell. "Why did you go?" She wailed the words like a child at his retreating back. "Why did you go off and leave me alone? Everybody left me. My mother died, Reba died, my sister is lost to me, and I can't even see Uncle Tyler anymore. I thought when I married you I wouldn't be alone anymore!"

Cade turned back to her. "I left because I had to, Gabrielle," he said softly. "I didn't want to, and it was one of the hardest things I've ever done. I loved you, I still love you, but I had to go."

She stared at him, then dropped down on a bale of hay, feeling suddenly tired. Her shoulders slumped, she stared down at the hands in her lap. "How will I get over feeling betrayed?"

"I don't know."

Gabrielle's thoughts whirled inward, and it was a moment before she spoke. "I guess I'll eventually have to forgive you," she said, wiping tears from her cheeks before looking up. "But I don't think I can do that just yet."

"Then I'll wait until you can."

Gabrielle stared at him. "Why?"

"Why?" He laughed softly. "Because I love you. I think you're very courageous and strong. I think you've done a wonderful job with Laurel."

She glanced down at her interlaced fingers. She felt lighter, as if the burden of resentment had been lifted from her shoulders. "I never asked . . . about your trip. Was it successful?"

He nodded. "In some respects. We got the promise of more arms. But the support we hoped for is going to be long in coming, if it ever comes."

"Were you in danger?"

He shrugged. "Sometimes."

To Gabrielle's disappointment, Zeke opened the barn door just then and walked into the dim interior. "Mr. Montana," he called out, "are you in here?"

Frowning, Cade turned. "Yeah, I'm here. What do you need?"

"There's a man who wants to talk to you about a job."

With a quick glance at Cade, Gabrielle rose to her feet and headed toward the door. "That's all right. I want to give Laurel her bath, anyway."

Over the next few days, Gabrielle's tension seemed to ebb away. She didn't feel that knot of anger and hurt in her heart anymore. She considered this change one morning after breakfast as she returned to the bedroom she had platonically shared with Cade since his return. Sam had informed her moments before that the buckskin had foaled during the night, and she was pleased about it. Thunder rumbled overhead, and she could see through the window at the end of the corridor how heavily it was raining. She knew Cade had wanted to move a herd down to better pastures, but he wouldn't get far in this weather.

Cade was getting dressed in the bedroom, wearing only trousers and socks. "You slept late today," she said.

He ran a hand through his hair, picked up his boots, and carried them over to a chair. "Yeah. There's something about this rain . . ." He rested his elbows on his knees. "What can I do for you?"

"I wanted to tell you—" Her voice broke off as she stared at him, noticing mannerisms that had made him so compelling to her in the first place. He had a lean exciting face, keen blue eyes, and a mobile mouth that could twist with humor, sarcasm, anger. He had a wide-shouldered strength and virility that gave her goosebumps. His hands were strong and nicely shaped, with long fingers. But best of all he had a wonderful chest, with curling hair that narrowed down over a lean, muscled body.

Realizing he was watching her curiously, she sought to cover her distraction. "Sam just told me the buckskin had her colt," she said shakily. "I thought you'd like to know."

"I do. Thank you."

Thunder reverberated outside, and Cade crossed to the window. "The weather in Texas puts on a powerful show, doesn't it?"

Gabrielle felt as if an unseen force was drawing her to him. Clasping her hands tightly together, she looked out across the rainswept yard, so aware of his nearness that she tingled all over. "Yes . . . It doesn't rain often," she agreed inanely, "but when it does . . ."

Cade looked down at her. Her hair was long enough now to be swept up into a mass of curls on the back of her head. Wispy auburn tendrils had slipped down on the tender peach-colored skin of

her neck. Without wondering why, he pulled a pin
from her hair and watched as a shimmering ringlet
slipped down her shoulder.

She spun nervously. "What—what are you doing?" she whispered.

"I'm taking the pins from your hair."

"Oh . . ."

Desire curled inside him. "Listen," he said huskily, "I love you, I've been away from you a long
time, and I want you. If you don't feel that way, I
think it would be in your best interest to leave the
room. Right now, all I want to do is kiss your neck
. . . right here." His fingers traced a burning trail at
the base of her throat, and Gabrielle closed her eyes
in response.

She swallowed, meeting his glance with a drugged
look. "I love you, too," she began haltingly, "but if
all you want to do is kiss my neck . . . then perhaps
I had better leave." She wet her lips with a pink
tongue. "I really had much more in mind."

She turned as if to walk away, but with a low
laugh Cade scooped her up in his arms. "No, you
don't," he warned, dropping her on the bed with a
flash of white petticoats.

Just as quickly she rolled off the other side. "You
are not a savage, so behave yourself," she scolded
teasingly as she attempted to unbutton her dress.

"Yes, I am," he said, circling the bed. "I don't
have an ounce of civilization left in me. I want you
so bad I think I could howl like a coyote."

Gabrielle laughed, amused by the thought of
Cade, as handsome as a pagan prince, howling. He
caught her around the waist and drew her close. It
seemed so right to be with him again—she could almost feel her heart and soul settling back into place.
He was trembling as his mouth moved hungrily on
hers. His touch and the hardness of his thigh brush-

ing against hers sent shivers through her. Her arms lifted to his shoulders and she arched against him, telling him that she needed him, too.

They removed their clothes with an urgency that matched their need. Cade gazed at the tender pink tips of her breasts, then drew her against his chest, shivering at the touch of her exquisite curves. He ran his hand down the slim line of her back and over her firm, rounded backside. With a sudden breath he caught her and lifted her onto the bed.

Gabrielle trembled as he moved to her impatiently. Cade lowered his body over her slender form, his mouth covering her open mouth and their breathing becoming one. As warm skin melded against warm skin, his hand slid beneath her hips, lifting her to meet his thrust. A sweet heat built in her belly, and her breasts tingled against his hair-roughened chest as he pressed into her, impatient with need and desire. Gabrielle felt the flooding of passion and she surrendered herself, letting his fierce lovemaking course through her.

They lay breathless afterward, Cade supporting his weight on her body. He drew in a deep breath and kissed her forehead. "I love you, Gabrielle."

A glow on her face, she met his sapphire-blue eyes. "And I love you."

In the following weeks Gabrielle showed Cade all the things she had accomplished during his absence. They spent a great deal of time either alone together or with Laurel. Her face beaming with pride, Gabrielle took him through the schoolhouse and told him how much she liked the new teacher who had arrived during his absence. The days were precious to her for she knew that, sooner or later, Cade would be forced to leave again. They had talked about it, and she had finally accepted the fact that as long as the war lasted, Cade would have to leave periodically. She also acknowledged that it had nothing to do with his love for her.

One day the moment Gabrielle had been dreading finally arrived—John Freemont came riding up to the house. Before Cade stepped into his study to talk to him, Gabrielle put her hand on his arm and met his gaze squarely.

"I understand that you must do what you must do." If it meant another European trip, she wanted her husband to make his decision without pressure from her.

He searched her face and saw that she meant her words. He nodded and joined Freemont in the study. Freemont told him that an unexpected snag had developed in the relationship with the Mexicans. The negotiator they had sent down had run into a political quagmire. Freemont wanted Cade to see what he could do. He didn't know how long the negotiations would last. They could run from weeks to months.

When Tom Rawlings arrived at the ranch a couple of weeks after Cade's departure, Gabrielle was delighted. She had grown to like him, rude and uncouth though he could be. She had come to understand that beneath his abrasiveness was a man with an iron-clad rule of honor. He would go to any lengths for a friend, and she and Cade were his friends. She considered asking Tom to be godfather to Laurel Marie, and hadn't yet made up her mind. It was an important request, and Tom was a pretty rough character to be cast in the role of godfather.

Early the morning after Tom's arrival, they sat in the kitchen together. Tom had requested a private talk. He informed her that he had heard from Rudolf Adler. He was in the village of Paloma in Mexico, having traced Celeste and Ruben to the nearby hacienda of Senor Vincente Rodriguez, a wealthy Mexican who supplemented his vast income by sending his vaqueros across the border to pillage and steal. Tom explained that, although Rodriguez came from a genteel family, his name had become synonymous with ruthlessness and cruelty. His ranch was well fortified and would be difficult to overrun if that should ever be necessary. Tom read aloud from Adler's letter: "I don't know the exact nature of the relationship between the Americans and Rodriguez, but considering the Spaniard's reputation for violence, I hope it's casual.' "

Gabrielle looked at Tom. "What does he mean?"

"He hopes that Rodriguez will not feel compelled to protect them."

Gabrielle poured Tom another cup of coffee. "What should we do? Notify the authorities?"

Tom laughed. "If only it were that easy. No, we'll have to go after them. But we'll sit tight until Cade gets back. Then we'll go down there, check out the situation, and bring back Guillotte and your sister."

"Oh, Tom, I can't believe this madness will be over soon. I'm so relieved to know where she is and that she's safe. I know that Ruben has influenced her terribly. It makes me sad."

Tom sipped his coffee. "If I were you, I wouldn't waste my sympathy on her." He leaned back in his chair. "Where's Laurel Marie? Isn't she up yet?"

Gabrielle laughed. "I'll bring her down, Tom, if you won't curse in front of her. I don't want her first word to be a swearword."

Tom crossed his arms over his chest, looking self-satisfied. "There are worse things than cussing."

"I know. Oh, Tom, wait until you see her. She gets up on her hands and knees, and I swear she's trying to crawl."

"Well, go get her. She's the only female left who still smiles when she sees me."

Tom stayed for a couple more days, enjoying several hunting trips with Sam before he returned home. Strangely enough, Gabrielle felt uneasy in the days following his departure. Even Laurel seemed especially restless. Once, she would have slept through a commotion; now she startled easily into wakefulness. Helen told Gabrielle that Laurel only reflected her own touchiness, and nothing was wrong. For some reason, that didn't comfort her.

One day Gabrielle noticed a stack of letters on Cade's desk. She glanced at Maria. "Did you bring this mail from Follettville?"

Marie turned, a dustcloth in her hand. "Yes. Didn't Zeke tell you?" Seeing from Gabrielle's expression that he had not, she shook her head. "I suppose he just set them right there on the desk and forgot to say a word."

Gabrielle shuffled quickly through the letters, then stopped at one. The sender was James Maffitt, War Department, Richmond. Suddenly instead of the letter in her hand she saw Maffitt's swarthy face and the contemptuous curl of his mouth. She shivered, reliving the horror on the riverboat when she and Ruben had been caught. She squeezed her eyes shut in an effort to block out the picture. Why would Maffitt send Cade a letter? She bit down on her lower lip, knowing in her heart that correspondence from Maffitt could only bring bad news. Her heart thudding heavily, she opened the letter.

Congratulations on your very successful trip to Europe. Men of your dedication and service are a tribute to the South and to the ideals for which we fight.

Unfortunately, I am also writing with some bad news. The Committee has recently learned that the North has requested that we exchange Tyler St. Claire's niece, Gabrielle, for imprisoned Confederate Captain Alistair Piedmont. The request was made by Yankee General McDaniels, who was recently promoted from captain and is said by our inside sources to be anxious to gain the release of Miss St. Claire. I have tried my best to discourage the Committee from agreeing to the exchange, because although the request leaves no doubt about Gabrielle's guilt, she is Tyler's niece and is now your wife, as well as a new mother. However, the South has been trying to free Piedmont for some time, and the Committee is insisting on the exchange. Tyler is understandably upset.

> With all due respect,
> James Maffitt

Gabrielle reread the letter again and again. What did it mean? Would soldiers come for her? Would they one day, without warning, simply ride up and take her away?

She paced the room. "Oh, Cade, I wish you were here," she whispered. 'What should I do?" Shivering, she remembered how quickly the Yankees had ridden up before and torn apart the fabric of her life. What could be worse than being sent North, separated from Cade and Laurel Marie? She thought of the letter Adler had sent. A solution was so close at hand. It was only a matter of time before they had solid proof of Celeste's guilt and her own innocence. Why on earth did she have to face another crisis before then?

Her hand smoothed across the top of Cade's desk. She could no longer afford to wait for her husband.

The letter from Maffitt was dated two months ago, and at any time the soldiers might come for her. She sat in the desk chair, knowing suddenly exactly what she must do. She must go to Follettville and talk Tom into taking her to find Celeste. Now.

Immediately Gabrielle called in Sam, Helen, Zeke, and Maria and read the letter to them. They all worried about her taking the trip to Mexico, but agreed she faced a greater danger by simply staying at the ranch. Finally it was decided that Zeke would accompany her to Follettville to seek Tom's aid and advice.

Gabrielle and Zeke arrived at Tom's two days later, exhausted and hungry. While they ate, Gabrielle told Tom what had happened. "We can't wait for Cade to return," she told him. "We've got to do something now."

"I agree," he announced grimly. "We can't wait. But I'm going alone. It's a hard trip and you're too goddamned delicate to make it. So don't argue with me, Gabrielle. It's final."

"Damn you, Tom Rawlings!" she cried. "I can ride a horse. I can keep up with you. Why won't you let me go?"

He slammed his fist on the table. "Gabrielle, dammit, you know I can't let you go. Cade would kill me."

Gabrielle shook her head wildly. "You stupid, blustering fool! How long do you think it's going to take if the soldiers start looking for me? Everybody knows me. All they have to do is ask some questions. Someone will tell them I'm here."

"You don't know for sure they're coming."

"Dammit, Tom, do you know for sure they aren't?"

He stared up at her without speaking.

"And if they do, I will be conveniently waiting for them. Tom, use your head! It's more dangerous for me to be here than to travel with you in Mexico. If I'm sent North, I might never get back to Cade and my baby. Don't do that to me," she pleaded angrily.

Tom ran a hand through his hair as he paced the room, thinking and frowning at her. "Redheaded women," he muttered. "They ought to drown 'em at birth! All right, you can go, but you have to do exactly as I say. If something happens to you, Cade'll shoot me. Do you promise?"

Gabrielle nodded, weak with relief. "I swear," she vowed, knowing even as she said it that Mexico was likely to present hardships such as she had never known before.

Accompanied by one of Tom's men, they took a packet down to Brownsville, Gabrielle sleeping almost all the way. When she wasn't sleeping, she was eating. Tom figured it must be some female instinct for survival, for she would need all the rest and food she got. The rough terrain through Mexico would be incredibly hard, even for a seasoned rider. His only hope was that if Cade had finished his negotiations, they might run into him in Brownsville on his way back to the ranch. Montana could then decide what to do with Gabrielle. But the chance of meeting Cade was slim.

Gabrielle waited on the dock while their horses were unloaded, keeping a constant vigil, fearful that at any moment a soldier would clamp a hand on her shoulder. The only attention she received, however, was from admiring men whose interest had nothing to do with politics.

Tom was miserable, grouchy company. He made no secret of the fact that he didn't want her along. Knowing Cade would return home through Browns-

ville, Tom decided to leave Zeke at the hotel to wait
for him. He instructed the boy to show Cade the
letters from Maffitt and Adler and tell him what had
happened and where they were headed.

As Gabrielle, Tom, and Tom's muscular guard,
Manuel, splashed up the south bank of the Rio
Grande, Gabrielle gazed at the inhospitable land
ahead of them, then turned and looked back across
to Texas. With a shudder she nudged her horse
closer to the two men. "We're in Mexico," she announced unnecessarily.

Tom looked across at Manuel, then dropped his
glance to Gabrielle. "Yep."

Chapter 17

D ay after weary day passed as they plodded toward the village of Paloma to find Rudolf Adler. The sun burned down from a piercing blue sky, scorching an already arid land cut by ravines and cliffs and jagged rocks. Gabrielle saw all she wanted to see of coyotes, chaparral, prickly pear, and mesquite. She wore a wide-brimmed straw hat, but the reflecting sun burned her skin so badly that Tom finally smeared protective mud on her face. She didn't mind. Since the first day she had discarded the possibility of trying to keep clean and aimed for comfort instead. She applied a fresh mud paste eac time they happened upon a stream, ignoring Tom' teasing comments about what a comely wench she had become.

Never had she imagined such hardship. Her mouth felt too dry to swallow; her eyes teared from wind and sun. Hour after hour they moved deeper into Mexico, bent beneath the sun, the only sound that of the plodding steps of the weary horses. She didn't complain once. Each time she weakened and yearned for water and a bath, she vividly remembered what might lay in store for her back at the ranch. No, she could not go back until she cleared her name.

At night they lay beneath stars so bright that she thought she could reach out and touch them. Although the evening hours brought a respite from the heat, they did not bring Gabrielle peace of mind. She lay in her blankets, itchy from dust, tormented by thoughts of what might crawl into her blanket— snakes, scorpions, spiders, or those awful little lizards she had been noticing. Finally she forced her body to relax and closed eyes that were already heavy with exhaustion. Her thoughts drifted to Laurel Marie and the way a sudden smile could light her tiny baby face. That radiant image became a charm against Gabrielle's nagging, sleep-robbing fear.

After five days of constant travel, Gabrielle felt only a weary, numbed relief when they finally reached the village of Paloma. Reining up abreast of Manuel and Tom on a low rise, she gazed down at the scattered adobe huts that made up the sparsely inhabited town.

They walked their horses down Paloma's narrow main street. Noticing that the Mexicans glanced at her curiously, Gabrielle nudged her mare closer to Tom. "They must not see many white women," she whispered beneath her breath.

Tom's gaze narrowed to take in the caked mud on her face, and a grin stretched across his mouth. "They can't tell whether you're a white woman or not."

Gabrielle looked after the cotton-clad Mexicans who disappeared silently into an alley, then back at Tom. "They can, too," she protested uncertainly, absently brushing the crusted mud from her face. "They can tell by my red hair that I'm not one of them." She reined her mare up to the hitching post beside Tom's gelding.

Manuel swung off his horse and with a few brief

words in Spanish, disappeared into the dim interior
of a cantina. Short minutes later, he reappeared
through the batwing doors and pointed down a
hard-packed lane. "Senor Adler is staying down
there," he said, swinging into the saddle.

Gabrielle followed them down a street so dry that
puffs of dust rose from each step the horses took.
She glanced curiously at the structures alongside
her, thinking they hardly seemed habitable. None of
her uncle's slaves lived in such wretched squalor.

Manuel rode all the way to the end of the street
and stopped in front of the last tumbledown shack.
"Looks calm enough," Tom muttered as he reined
up alongside. He glanced up and down the street
before dismounting and tying his black horse to the
railing. "After such a damned hard ride, it's not very
welcoming, is it?" he said to Gabrielle as he reached
up and lifted her off the horse.

She shook her head, too preoccupied to reply, and
followed him to a broken-down porch. Tom's brief
knock brought the barrel of a gun poking through a
hole in the window shutter. Rapid Spanish issued
from inside, and Manuel answered in Spanish, explaining who they were. A moment later the lou-
vered door, flimsy and squeaking on rusty hinges,
swung open. With a quaking heart, Gabrielle trailed
close behind Tom and Manuel as they strode inside.

All the shutters had been drawn and bolted, but
sunlight slanted through the cracks, slashing light
across the shabby interior and across at Rudolf Adler. Tall, gaunt, pale, and balding, he was uncom-
monly plain.

Adler glanced at them with alert eyes, then walked
over to the bed and began to stuff his few belong-
ings into a worn leather satchel. "I've been found
out," he said flatly.

The buzzing of a fly punctuated the silence that

followed. Tom walked around the end of the sagging cot. "What do you mean?"

"They know I'm here looking for Celeste and Ruben, that's what I mean. I also found out that Guillotte has gone into a partnership with that bastard Rodriguez. He's a powerful force in this part of the country, with enough hired guns to set up his own army. That means we can't just walk in, take Celeste and Ruben, and ride back to Texas. They have protection now."

Adler's gaze swept the room for items he might have missed. He stuffed a couple of dog-eared books, a near-empty bottle of liquor, and his shaving supplies haphazardly into his bag. "Rodriguez and his men are going to drop on this village like a swarm of locusts before this afternoon's out." He buckled a gunbelt about his scrawny hips and tied it down at the thigh.

Tom frowned, his weight shifting to one leg. "What the hell happened?"

"It was the worst damned luck I ever had. I just went in for a drink at the cantina. I've been listening to the sun-baked bartender gossip for weeks." Adler shrugged into a threadbare black frock coat, dusty and sweat-stained. "A couple of days ago, to draw him out, I said I'd seen a blond woman riding with Rodriguez. He said he didn't know anything." Adler shook his head in disbelief. "Well, today, I was sipping tequila and that son-of-a-bitch bartender looked over my shoulder and said to me, 'Here's the man you need to talk to. He works for Rodriguez, and if there's a blond woman there, he'll have seen her.' Well, I turned around and looked into the face of Nathan Prophet. I knew him from Tennessee. Bad blood and a hired gun. You couldn't piss on a cottonmouth and arouse more venom than is in Nathan Prophet! He looked me straight in the eye and, without blinking, said real slow-like, 'I don't think I can help Mr. Adler.' He downed the liquor that the bartender had set in front of him, dropped his money on the bar, and walked out the door. He knew me, all right.''

Adler tossed his saddlebags over his shoulder, then hefted his satchel. ''I advise you to come with me. As soon as Prophet lets 'em know, they'll be all over this village. If you're here, you're going to be in trouble.''

They left immediately, riding northeast. Manuel, who knew the country better than Tom or Adler, led the way, his destination a maze of canyons where they could not be tracked.

They rode their mounts hard. Gabrielle hated to push the animals past their endurance, but she didn't dare ask to slow down. Tom's face was set in the most grim lines, and she knew they were in extreme danger.

Suddenly Adler's long arm swooped out, his coat-tails flapping behind him, his finger pointed toward their flank. Gabrielle glanced over her shoulder and saw black dots angling in from the left. Swinging her head, she saw more cutting across the mesa on her right. Riders! she realized, her stomach lurching.

Tom pointed toward the rocky outcroppings ahead. Gabrielle nodded. She leaned low over her horse, feeling the animal stretch out beneath her, giving its last bit of strength without question. Through wind-blurred eyes, she realized that the pursuing riders were steadily gaining on them.

Tom yelled at Manuel. The Mexican nodded, but the wind whipped his words away. She heard a distant popping. Gunfire! Tom pivoted in the saddle, returning the fire. She leaned closer to the horse, expecting to feel a bullet slam into her back at any minute.

Dust flew from the lead horses, and the thunder of hooves pounded in her eardrums. Ahead, Adler's horse began to lose pace. Gabrielle watched the scarecrow of a man lurch forward over his horse's neck and wondered wildly why he would risk falling. Then he slumped sideways in a peculiar, unnatural manner. Dear God, he'd been shot! He dropped to the ground and her horse passed within feet of him. Horrified, she saw Manuel streaking toward the red rocks rising ahead.

Tom's horse edged nearer hers until they were neck and neck. Tom lifted his revolver to fire behind him, but suddenly the gun seemed to leap from his fingers. A terrible moment later Gabrielle realized a bullet had hit him in the back. Her horse staggered and she was jolted off balance. Grimly she hung on, then, without thinking, she tried to rein the animal around, her only thought that Tom needed help.

The riders were so close she could see the dim blur of their faces. A shot rang out and her horse stumbled again. She pulled desperately at the reins, trying to get the animal's head up, but the horse was going down. She kicked desperately, knowing she could be maimed if the horse fell on her. She landed hard, her body tumbling over and over. Lifting her head, she tried to suck air into her tortured lungs. Dust rose around her, impeding her vision and choking her throat. Numbed by the shock of her fall and her fear for Tom, she stumbled to her feet and headed toward where he'd fallen. Then she saw him, crumpled limply, lying in the dust like a broken puppet.

A horse and rider galloped up in front of her. A saddle flashed before her, black and ornately tooled with silver. Drawing a sobbing breath she tried to

circle around the other way, but another rider maneuvered close to her. With a muffled cry she
dodged left, only to be blocked again. Over and over
she was turned back to the center. Frantic moments
passed before she realized their cruel sport and
ceased her effort to escape. The horses formed a
swooping, blurring circle about her, like vultures
preparing to strike. Terrified, Gabrielle covered her
face with her hands, standing motionless, expecting
at any moment to be pounded to the ground.

Slowly the tumult of flying hooves stilled, until
only the creaking of saddle leather told her they were
still there.

"Hey, leetle one," a taunting voice called softly,
"you want to play? Pablo chase you good." A rider
wheeled forward. Gabrielle could feel the heat from
the horse against her skin. "Eez she pretty . . . or
ugly?"

The speaker caught her hands, jerking them from
her face. His black sombrero blocked the sun and
hid his features.

"She eez preety!" he called triumphantly to his
comrades. "We see what else there eez."

The Mexican leaned down, catching her blouse at
the neck and ripping off the top button. He tried to
reach inside her bodice, but she jerked away with
an anguished cry.

Another rider edged forward, his horse coming
between Gabrielle and the Mexican. "Leave her
alone," he commanded in an American voice that
projected unmistakable authority.

"She eez ours, no?" the first man objected loudly.
"We find her."

"No, she is not yours," the man with the blue-
black hair returned patiently. "We'll take her back
to Rodriguez. She's too good for the likes of you,
compadre."

"Of course. That eez why I want her." The other men laughed.

"Get that horse over there," the American ordered, pointing toward the black that Rawlings had been riding. "She can ride that one."

Gabrielle turned, her voice hoarse with pain and disbelief. "You can't leave my friend here."

Pitiless black eyes met hers. "He's dead."

Tears trailed through the dust on her cheeks as the Mexican brought the black horse to her and helped her to mount.

"Let's ride," the American prompted, nudging his horse toward her.

There were fifteen riders altogether, and they traveled south, heading toward the hacienda of Senor Rodriguez. Gabrielle tried to keep her horse alongside the American because the leers of the others made her skin crawl. Later that afternoon, the black stumbled, then came to a standstill, head drooping between spread forelegs. Gabrielle knew it had gone as far as it could go without rest.

The American lifted his gun from its holster. Gabrielle knew what he meant to do. "No . . ." she pleaded, sliding off the exhausted animal. "Please don't." Even as she stumbled toward him, he fired. Gabrielle closed her eyes, knowing Tom's beautiful black gelding was dead. Moments later, a steely arm encircled her waist and the American pulled her up in front of him. She didn't resist. It would do no good.

They rode steadily until the setting sun turned a dull orange-red and cast a burning glow across the land. At the rim of a canyon the Mexicans began to angle downward. Gabrielle saw a narrow ribbon of green at the bottom and realized it was a stream that flowed along the canyon floor. As they rode nearer, she saw it widened in the center to a valley with

trees and orchards and outlying structures that she
supposed belonged to the Mexicans. In the center
was a sprawling red-tiled Spanish hacienda, its color
soft pink in the setting sun. Surrounding the
grounds were thick adobe walls patrolled by rifle-
toting pistoleros with belts of cartridges crossed over
their chests.

Most of the riders turned in at the stables; only
she and the American headed toward the estate,
passing through a thick stone arch and riding up a
lane bordered by roses. A circular fountain lay directly ahead, the cascading water catching the light.

When they reached the front entrance, a young
boy flicked a shy glance at Gabrielle, then took the
horse. The American caught her arm and pulled her
down a flagstone path through an enclosed garden.
Even as they approached the recessed door, it swung
open. A small Mexican in immaculately white attire
greeted them with austere graciousness. Gabrielle
understood nothing of the two men's conversation
in rapid Spanish, but she did hear the name Rudolf
Adler mentioned once. A moment later, the butler
left. He returned in minutes, nodding, smiling, and
gesturing expansively to Gabrielle.

"He wants us to go with him," the American informed her, a sardonic grin twisting his wide mouth.
"Senor Rodriguez wants to meet you."

Gabrielle followed the man down a tiled hallway.
Her gaze swept the dark furniture and bright Indian
blankets. Brass and silver twinkled.

The Mexican opened an iron-bound oak door and
stepped aside for the American and Gabrielle to enter the darkened chamber. The first thing she noticed was a silver candelabra that blazed with tapers
on a long table.

"Gabrielle!" A female voice gasped softly.

A woman rose to her feet, a woman with shimmering blond hair and big blue eyes and the face of a saint. Celeste. Ruben Guillotte stood beside her, debonaire and handsome, his dark hair gleaming. Gabrielle's mouth twisted with contempt. At one time she had thought him such a romantic figure.

"The last time I saw you," she said slowly, "we were on board the *Jordan B. Mason*. I believed you, Celeste. I believed my torment would end when Ruben escaped from jail. But no word ever came from you."

A dark-haired man sitting at the head of the table stood. His hawklike features were handsome in a harsh way. A thin mustache slanted above his hard mouth, emphasizing a brutal imperiousness. Gabrielle knew he must be Vincente Rodriguez.

"She is your sister, yes?" he inquired.

Celeste nodded.

The Spaniard's dark brow lifted with pleasure, as if he had just tasted a fine red wine. "Ah, then *you* are the one who received the brand of traitor in your sister's stead." His mouth curled. "So, what brings you here, little sister? Revenge?"

Gabrielle was too overwrought, too saddened by Tom's death, to respond to his goading. "No. I came to find Celeste. I never dreamed that in the process people would die. Your vaqueros killed two men today. One, Tom Rawlings, was my friend."

Rodriguez shrugged. "I am sorry, querida, but I promised my friends that I would protect them."

"Protect them from *me?*" Tears brightened her eyes, but she refused to let them fall.

His black gaze glittered. "My men were sent to silence Adler. We were unaware of your presence." His gaze dropped over her bedraggled riding habit. "Why did you come?"

"I came to talk with Celeste. It's time she told the

truth. I want her to come back and tell someone in authority what really happened."

Senor Rodriguez smiled with genuine amusement. "Is that right?" The flicker of interest sparkled again before he glanced at Celeste. "Do you plan to do that?"

Celeste shrugged one pale bare shoulder, her slim fingers playing with the emeralds that encircled her throat. "I do not think so," she replied languidly. She looked at Gabrielle. "Wouldn't that put me in the same nasty situation you are in?"

Ruben lit a cheroot, then eyed Gabrielle. "You are still the most gullible creature. Simpleminded, in fact." He poured more wine. "Such an innocent. How fortunate for Celeste and me that you had such a romantic heart. You did everything you could to advance our forbidden courtship and, consequently, line my pockets."

"I am sorry," the Spaniard told Gabrielle with magnified gallantry. "I fear you have made your long trip for nothing." He sipped the wine, watching her reaction. "Your sister will not return, poor little girl. So what will you do?"

Although physically depleted, Gabrielle still felt the dull beat of rage. "Senor Rodriguez, I find your sarcasm annoying. You and I both realize I'm not in a position to do anything, so please don't toy with me."

Rodriguez straightened and a moment elapsed before he spoke. "I am aware that you married your captor." He glanced at Ruben. "A rather enterprising move, don't you think . . . for her to marry Senor Montana." His brows came together in a frown as he eyed Gabrielle. "I suspect he will come for you?"

"Yes."

"Then we will wait for him." He turned to the

Mexican standing in a shadowed recess. "Take her.
Have Elena and Rosa see to her needs."

"Sí, patron."

Gabrielle followed the barefoot girls to a candlelit
room where they bowed and left her alone. She
turned slowly, taking in the cozy sitting area to her
right and the canopied bed hung with lace. She
barely had time to notice her surroundings before a
tentative knock sounded on the door and it swung
open. The two brown-skinned girls reentered, carrying buckets of steaming water which they poured
into a copper tub. One spread a nightgown across
the bed, indicating that it was for Gabrielle.

She nodded, stripping out of her clothes and slipping gratefully into the warm water.

One of the women handed her a bar of soap. Gabrielle sniffed it and closed her eyes. Lavender.
Suddenly she heard the door open and glanced
over her shoulder. Senor Rodriguez stood in the
opening.

"Sir! You must go!" she protested, sinking further beneath the water. In her wildest thoughts she
had never expected him to intrude on her privacy.
He looked like a gentleman. The size of his estate
would command respect anywhere. She had
thoughtlessly expected the same old-fashioned courtesy that she would have received in a New Orleans
home.

Rodriguez jerked his hand, motioning for the two
girls to leave. With a frightened glance at Gabrielle,
they fled into the courtyard. Rodriguez shut the door
behind them.

Crossing her hands protectively over her breasts,
Gabrielle stared at him in horror. "What do you
want?"

"I'm not sure. Not yet." He walked closer. "Wash

your face. I can't see what you look like beneath that grime."

Gabrielle shrank further into the water, feeling like a rabbit confronting the snarling fangs of a wolf. "Stay back!" she warned.

His features expressionless, he placed his hand on her head and shoved her under the water, holding her there. Although Gabrielle fought, he released her of his own accord, handing her a towel as she came up sputtering. Gabrielle pressed her face into the fluffy softness, then glared at him, eyes wide.

His gaze moved assessingly over her, and after a moment he nodded. "Your features are finer than your sister's . . . and you have more spirit. Stand. I want to see how you are made."

Gabrielle's mouth dropped open. "No!"

He caught his fingers in her hair, intent on jerking her out of the water. Gabrielle's hands came up, seizing his wrists. "Please," she whispered. "Don't!"

His hawk's face came closer to hers. "Stand," he ordered softly.

She closed her eyes, knowing that she could not. Suddenly he gripped beneath her arms, and lifted her out of the tub. Her eyes flew open, locking on his face. His glance swept her body.

"*Magnifico*," he announced.

With the same suddenness he released her, and she dropped down into the water, her body trembling.

"You please me," he proclaimed.

"Senor Rodriguez, I am not a . . . commodity."

He returned her burning, indignant gaze with cool regard. "You are now." He walked over to the door. "You are familiar with mavericks? They belong to whomever manages to throw a rope around their necks." His black eyes bored into hers. "I will wait for Montana. When he is dead, I will make you mine." He stepped into the courtyard and closed the door behind him.

Despite her terror that Rodriguez would come back during the night, Gabrielle slept instantly when her head hit the pillow, the depth of her exhaustion bringing sound rest. When she opened her eyes morning light seeped into the room, and birds called outside the window. She blinked at the unfamiliar canopy, then, with a breathless gasp, sat bolt upright.

Celeste, sitting at a small table, put down her coffee cup.

Gabrielle stared at her. "How long have you been here?"

"Only a few minutes," she replied, smoothing delicately crocheted gloves over her fingers. Then abruptly her attitude hardened. "I cannot keep Rodriguez from you."

Gabrielle was taken aback by her bluntness. She had not expected her sister's help, certainly not after the events of the last year and a half, but to hear her say it seemed so callous. Gabrielle shook her head, feeling again that heart-wrenching disbelief that her sister, whom she had grown up with, loved, and admired, had turned into such a coldhearted woman, virtually a stranger to her. "Why did you do it, Celeste?"

"Why did I place the blame on you? Or why did I help Ruben?"

"All of it. Why did you do it?"

Celeste's beautiful face remained untroubled. "For Ruben."

"Do you know what you did to me?"

Celeste shrugged. "You're a pretty little cat, Gabrielle. You always land on your feet."

"How can you say that? I haven't landed on my feet. Terrible things have happened to me because of your lies!"

"You got everything as a child. All the love. You were a willful child but even so, Uncle Tyler loved you best."

Gabrielle was amazed by the depth of bitterness in her sister's words. She slid over to the side of the bed. "Celeste," she began carefully, threading her fingers tightly together, "I think he did favor me, but I didn't want him to. I was a child . . . I couldn't make it fair. I'm not to blame for whether he loved you or not."

Celeste shrugged. "Maybe not, but it made me dislike you in a way that I can't help. Oh, I used to try to be sisterly to you, and sometimes I managed. And then came the choice between you and Ruben. I didn't feel even a spasm of guilt when I decided. I knew I would do anything for him."

Celeste laughed sarcastically. "I couldn't believe it when I found out how the Committee had decided to punish you. You were exiled to Texas . . . to the ranch of Cade Montana. I thought how typical of your life. You went not to some rat-infested cell, but to the home of a man that eligible females would sell their souls for." She shook her head, a cynical smile touching her mouth. "Not only that, but he didn't use you and further destroy your already besmirched reputation. No, he risked ruin by marrying you." Her blue eyes clouded. "And then you came down here, trying to steal my happiness, you detestable little creature. And now, Rodriguez, the fool, wants you."

She stood up. "What is it about you, Gabrielle? Reba loved you. Uncle Tyler loved you. Your little maid, Hetty, loved you." Her mouth twisted. "I know Cade Montana loves you or he would never have married a woman who had been branded a spy." She looked directly at Gabrielle, her blue eyes piercing. "I always wondered why Ruben never wanted you." With a rustle of petticoats she walked over to the door, then turned back. "He never saw magic in you, like the others. He saw my hurt and despised you." She looked around the room. "I hope you enjoy your stay, but for my sake I hope it's brief."

Gabrielle jumped up, reaching out to delay Celeste's departure. "We're sisters!" she cried. "I don't believe you feel such hate for me!" Celeste opened the door and Gabrielle moved closer, her hands clasped together. "Please listen. You have to help me! The South plans to swap me to the North in a prisoner exchange. Celeste, why won't you tell the truth? What difference can it make to you in Mexico? I want to lead a normal life. I have a child, she's only a few months old, but I want her to have a normal life, too!"

Celeste stared at her for a moment. "There's a guard posted outside to make sure you remain in the cottage," she said.

Gabrielle watched the door close behind her, shaking so badly that she hugged her arms against her chest.

Chapter 18

Night had fallen over Brownsville by the time Cade's boat docked and he was able to get a carriage to his hotel.

"A young man has been waiting for you for several days," the hotel clerk said, scanning the lobby. He pointed through the potted palms toward an alcove near the entrance. "There he is."

Cade's brows came together in a frown when he recognized Zeke. He'd fallen asleep, his head lolling against the sofa cushion. Something must be wrong for Zeke to have come all the way to Brownsville.

Cade crossed the lobby, dropped his satchel on the sofa beside Zeke, and shook the boy's shoulder. Zeke opened his eyes instantly. "When did you get back?" he mumbled, sitting bolt upright with a guilty start.

"We docked about an hour ago. What are you doing here?"

"We got to talk . . . someplace private."

Cade felt a tightening in his chest. "Gabrielle—"

"She's all right . . . but there's trouble, Mr. Montana."

Cade pulled a leather chair closer and sat down across from Zeke. "This is private enough. Tell me."

Zeke fumbled in his pocket for the letters from

Rudolf Adler and James Maffitt. "Here, Mr. Montana. You better read these."

Quickly Cade scanned the words of Adler's letter. A muscle flexed along his jaw when he saw Vincente Rodriguez's name, for he knew it well. He also knew that getting Celeste and Ruben away from the Spaniard's protection would be difficult. Then he read Maffitt's letter and turned questioningly to Zeke.

Zeke took a deep breath and explained that Gabrielle had journeyed to Mexico with Tom and one of his men.

"What was she going to do once she got there?" Cade asked.

"I don't think she knew for sure. I know she feels she has to talk to her sister and convince her to tell the truth."

Cade shook his head. "Do you know what course of action Tom planned to take?"

"No, not exactly." Zeke frowned. "He said he wouldn't know till he got down there."

His thoughts racing, Cade paced over to the window to stare into the empty street. He lit a cheroot, listening to the sounds of a tinny piano drifting from the saloon a few doors down. He didn't think Tom would make a move alone. When he got to Paloma and talked to Adler, he would realize he was up against too many guns. Cade's strong dark brows came together in fierce concentration. Tom would size up the situation and wait for support.

The next move, Cade knew, belonged to him. He had to have men—good, battle-trained men—and Gus Cameron would be he first person he called on. Cameron was a Texas Ranger, and he knew professionals who worked both sides of the law. Cade flipped his cheroot into a brass cuspidor. "Come on,

Zeke," he said, picking up his satchel, "we have work to do."

Gus Cameron agreed to work for Cade. By the following night they had put together a fighting unit of ten men who agreed to travel into Mexico for a thousand dollars each—five hundred up front and five hundred when they returned with either Guillotte or Celeste, alive.

The group was a motley assortment of strong individuals, and at first Cade had misgivings about how well they would work together. They included a bounty hunter, a couple of Cameron's friends who were no longer with the Rangers, two hired guns, a gambler, a big Irishman, an out-of-work lawman, a blue-eyed half-breed, and a Mexican who could throw a knife with chilling and fatal accuracy and claimed he knew the country like the back of his hand. They were tough, silent men, some of whom Cade suspected were on the run from the law. Within two days after Cade's arrival in Brownsville, they were ready to ride.

They arrived near the village of Paloma on the morning of the third day after leaving Brownsville. Cade placed Gus Cameron in charge and left the men in a secluded valley on the outskirts of town. To avoid arousing suspicion, he rode into the village alone.

At first his questions were met with silence and shrugs. Then the bartender admitted he knew Senor Adler, but the man had left days before. Yes, two men and a woman had come to town, but they were gone, too; he didn't know where.

Cade stared down at the scratched surface of the bar, his face intent with thought. Why would they have left town without a word? Surely Tom wasn't contemplating an attack on the Spaniard. What had happened? He heard the batwing doors swing open and glanced over his shoulder to see a Mexican girl enter. Her gaze on him was speculative and purposeful. After a moment she approached him with a hip-swinging walk.

"You buy Francesca a drink?" she inquired softly, tossing her raven hair back from her face.

"I'll buy, chica," he answered, dropping his money on the bar. "But I'm afraid you'll have to drink alone."

He started to leave but her hand covered his and she regarded him with smoldering eyes. "Senor Montana," she intoned elegantly, stressing his name and allowing a slow smile to curve her mouth, "it would be most wise to stay."

Cade's glance sharpened on her face, watching as she drank her whiskey and shuddered delicately. His blue eyes looked for answers in her face. "You know something I need to know?" he demanded.

"Maybe." With a flirtatious swing of her skirts, she turned and walked away. "Come, gringo."

Cade followed her through a maze of dismal earth-colored huts and shanties. After picking their way down a steep embankment near the creek, they crossed a rickety wooden bridge and followed an overgrown path to a shack beneath a stand of cotton-woods.

Francesca grinned at Cade as she brushed through a clattering curtain of colored beads hanging across the entryway. Seeing his hand settle on the butt of his gun, she laughed softly. "A friend, not an enemy, waits for you."

Despite her assurance, Cade felt uneasy as he stepped into the shadowed interior. Before his eyes adjusted to the light, he smelled the scent of cinnamon and sweet spices. Then he saw Manuel, Tom's man, sitting across the table. With a sigh of relief, Cade reached across and shook his hand. "I thought all of you had disappeared. Where are Gabrielle and Tom?"

Francesca picked up a bottle of tequila from an open cabinet, bit down with strong teeth, and pulled out the cork. "Have a drink, senor," she said, plopping the bottle down on the table in front of an empty chair and gesturing for him to sit. "You will need it."

Cade gave her a sharp look, then sat down.

"It is a brutal story, Senor Montana," the Mexican said carefully, his face grim.

Cade's mouth thinned. "Tell it."

Manuel crossed his arms over his chest, his brown face without expression. "Vincente Rodriguez discovered why Adler was in Paloma. When the three of us rode into town he had sent the American mercenary Nathan Prophet and a dozen of his hired guns to kill him. We had to make a run for it. I escaped. They killed Senor Adler, shot Senor Rawlings in the back, and took your woman." He took a drink of the tequila. "She is being held at the hacienda. I am sorry, senor."

Cade closed his eyes, feeling as if someone had hit him in the chest with a sledgehammer. With a shuddering breath he got to his feet and walked to the door, his hand tightening on the frame until his knuckles turned white. Thoughts of what might happen to Gabrielle while in the control of an animal like Rodriguez twisted his stomach. For a moment he couldn't breathe, then he gritted his teeth, forcing the welter of debilitating images from his mind. He welcomed the cold, methodical rage that filled the empty space inside him. He would get Gabrielle back. And he would take Guillotte to Texas and get a confession, or he would kill the son-of-a-bitch with his bare hands.

Hearing a sound from the back room, Cade whipped his gun from its holster and whirled about. In astonishment he watched as Tom Rawlings staggered through the doorway. Automatically reholstering his gun, Cade stared at the bandage that crisscrossed Tom's chest. He could barely manage the minor exertion of standing.

Cade caught Tom by the shoulders and helped him into a chair. "God Almighty, Rawlings," he bit out, "I thought you were dead."

Tom leaned against the table for support. "Bastards shot me in the back, but they didn't . . . kill me."

Manuel had risen to his feet, "I brought him to my cousin, Francesca," he explained. "I knew he needed care, and I needed a place to hide him."

Tom lifted his head, stark pain in his eyes. "Gabrielle . . . they got her. He'll use her as . . . a hostage."

"I know. I'll get her back, Tom, don't worry. I've hired my own men. They're camped outside Paloma. You just heal up."

Tom's face had paled beneath his swarthy skin, his energy already depleted. "Rodriguez . . . is a killer."

Seeing that Tom was going to pass out, Cade caught him around the shoulders. Manuel hurried forward, and together the two men carried their unconscious friend into the back room and placed him gently on the narrow cot.

Francesca stared thoughtfully at her patient. "I do not believe Rawlings will die. He's a tough man." She looked up at Cade. "When he wake up, I make him think of me," she said, patting her ample chest. Her mouth twisted, "Not this Gabrielle he speak of."

Cade shook his head. "I have a feeling you're going to like this man a lot, Francesca. You two are cut from the same cloth." He started to leave, then turned back to her. "Have you ever been to the Rodriguez ranch?"

"*Si.*" She nodded. "Many times I go."

"Can you draw me a map?"

"Of course. I also know something else . . ."

That afternoon Cade reproduced Francesca's drawing of the Spaniard's hacienda by sketching it in the dirt for his men to see. "Our task is harder," he told them, "because Rodriguez has Gabrielle now, and he'll use her as a hostage. And he'll know I'm coming." He looked around the circle of tough, unshaven faces. "But they won't know when."

Kent Mosby, the gambler, looked up. "How much opposition are we facing?"

"Rodriguez has about forty armed men," Cade told him. "That means, to be successful against such numbers, we have to outwit and outfight them."

Mosby shrugged, undaunted.

"I've learned," Cade continued, "that the Spaniard has a big herd of horses that he plans to sell gathered in a narrow ravine. I figure we can use that herd to provide a distraction and split the strength of his forces. If we get those wild mustangs running and head them toward the border, Rodriguez is not going to think about protecting his ranch, he's going to concentrate on getting his horses back."

Gus Cameron laughed. "Hell, Rodriguez stole most of those animals. He'll just think some Texas rancher has come after what's his."

Cade nodded. "It'll take all of us to get 'em running." He looked up. "Zeke, you and John Voss will keep 'em headed north. Run the horses until they're ready to drop, then let 'em scatter and you two fade out of sight. The wranglers who come after you will have to round them up and drive them back to the hacienda. The horses will be exhausted, and it will take quite awhile."

He scanned the circle. "While Zeke and Voss are busy, the rest of us will drop away, circle, and meet back here." He pointed to a line drawn in the dirt that represented a dry creek bed. "We'll move down the creek until we get to the wall surrounding the hacienda. It's built like a fortress, so there's only one way inside—over." He pointed to where he expected to find men on watch. "There are approximately eight guards stationed at the perimeter. They'll have to be taken out of the action so they can't raise an alarm. You must move with absolute silence."

"What about the servants and other guests?"

"Tie and gag them and leave them. Celeste and Guillotte are the only ones I'm interested in, and they have to be brought out alive."

"What about your wife?" Cameron asked. "When we bust in, it'll probably scare the hell out of her."

"Gabrielle will be frightened. Get her out, even if you have to tie and gag her, too." He tipped his hat against the lowering sun, his expression grim. "She'll understand when she realizes what's going on."

The big Irishman, McGilly, shifted his weight, his hands resting on his gunbelt. "How long you reckon we got?"

"We'll spook the horses about midnight. It'll take us a couple of hours to get back into position. With luck, we can do what we have to do at the ranch and still ride out before dawn."

Mosby nodded in agreement. "We don't want to still be here when the wranglers start straggling in with the horses."

"Exactly," Cade answered. "We don't want to be trapped between the Spaniard's forces."

Just before midnight, as a cloud drifted across the moon, the riders topped a gentle incline and saw spread out below them the giant herd of horses. They had approached soundlessly, the hooves of their mounts having been wrapped in burlap.

Cade lifted his hand. When it dropped, the Texans kicked their horses into motion and crashed down the incline, firing guns and yelling at the top of their lungs. The horses, two or three hundred strong, started a slow drift. In minutes they became a torrent through the narrow valley. Cade knew the commotion would alert Rodgriguez's men, stationed nearby.

As they penetrated the herd, dust filled the air, reducing visibility to a few feet. In an unexpected shift of wind, Cade saw the rounds of silver adorning a sombrero as a rider emerged from the haze. The vaquero lifted his revolver at the same time that Cade fired. The motion of the running herd carried him forward at a breakneck speed, and Cade didn't see if the wrangler fell. Rifle fire sounded over the thunder of horses' hooves, then died away, and there was only the driving, pounding force of the herd in motion.

For a frantic time they rode, spurring the herd north, until finally Cade reined his mount to the edge of the running mass and broke free. Nudging his horse away from the choking dust, he circled back to the south. The wild horses were strong and rested, and the night was cool. Cade knew they would run for a long time.

It took him the best part of an hour to travel back to the spot where the men were to meet. He tethered the gelding out of sight and approached on foot through the willows and high brush. In the moonlight ahead, he saw the slim Mexican he had hired in Brownsville. Cade whistled softly and Luis Mejia lifted his hand in acknowledgment. Within the next few minutes, the rest of the men arrived. They admitted to having had some close calls, but there were no injuries.

Gus Cameron rode in last. "Sorry I'm late," he whispered. "I damned near ran right into that bunch of yahoos who were coming after the herd. It took me a while to skirt around them."

"How many were there, would you calculate?" Cade asked.

"I'd say there were fifteen or twenty men, riding hell for leather." Cameron lifted his heavy brows. "So far, the plan's working."

Cade's eyes swept the group. "Let's go."

They moved along the dry creek bed, their passage hidden by the willows along the bank. At the thick adobe walls, they went their separate ways.

Cade was first over the wall, dropping from the six-foot height and landing on gravel with a soft crunch. A sentry turned to look, light reflecting off the barrel of his gun. Cade tossed a handful of pebbles past the guard's platform, and when the man whirled at the sound Cade jumped onto the platform, his arm going around the man's throat and choking off his air. When he had ceased to struggle, Cade pulled him to the ground.

In fifteen minutes, having dispatched the guards, the Texans gathered again in the deep shadows of a grape arbor. Luis Mejia pointed toward the front of the house, identifying another guard. He motioned across his throat with his knife. Cade nodded. McGilly indicated that he had seen two more guards at the stables. Cameron went with him to help silence them.

Soon all three men were back. Cade studied their shadowed faces. "You know what to do," he whispered.

The men crossed the yard one at a time, melting into the darkness. Each hesitated in the doorway, then they were through, flowing silently and invincibly through the house.

An acute listener might have heard a sigh, a swish, a muffled breath, a closing door, a creak that could easily be a part of the night.

Cade opened the first door along the corridor. In the silvery light the shape of a woman showed on a bed beneath a canopy. Cameron and one of his Rangers slipped soundlessly into the room. One of them covered her mouth, the other tied and gagged her, moving so quickly and efficiently that the woman was bound before she came fully awake. Cade saw the shimmer of blond hair. It was Celeste.

"Take her outside," he whispered.

Cameron nodded.

Cade proceeded down the corridor, Luis Mejia falling into step beside him. At the next bedroom, both came to a stop. Hesitating, Cade turned the knob, then let the door swing open. A man lay sprawled on the bed. He was too small to be either Guillotte or Rodriguez. Moving together, Cade and Mejia bound and gagged the frightened man. Whispering in Spanish, Luis told him he would be killed if he made a sound. *"Comprende?"* he whispered, his mouth close to the man's ear.

The Spaniard nodded.

The two men slipped back into the dark hallway. Ahead, the corridor split. Cade motioned for Luis to take the left hallway; he took the right. The odds were getting higher that Gabrielle, Guillotte, or Rodriguez would be inside the next room. Standing slightly to the side, Cade pushed open the door.

Nothing happened. Lifting his gun, he peered inside. The rumpled bed was empty. The window had been flung wide open, and the lace curtains curled gently in the breeze.

Pulling the hammer back on his gun, Cade edged into the room. Just as he cleared the door frame, he heard a man's breath as he gathered himself for a lunge. Reacting instinctively, Cade dropped sideways just as a wickedly long knife blade whispered past his shoulder. The weight of the man's body sent him careening against the armoire. His hand hit painfully against a sharp edge, and the revolver was knocked from his grip as the two men crashed to the floor. Cade rolled and sprang to his feet with the lithe agility of a cat poised for attack. His opponent came up more slowly, knife in hand. In the moon-dappled darkness the two men circled.

"Cade Montana," the voice smirked. "Ruben Guillotte at your service." Ruben laughed softly and moved the knife as if it were a prop in a sensuous dance. "You came for Gabrielle?"

Cade circled to the left. "You knew I would."

Guillotte gave an ugly bark of laughter. "I'm going to kill you, Montana." His body readied to strike, Guillotte moved swiftly, twisting the knife in front of him. "Don't worry about Gabrielle. Vincente wants her." He swung the knife in an arc. "His eyes eat her up. He's watched her every move like a hungry cat with a mouse."

Guillotte sprang forward. Cade pivoted, and the deflected knife slashed through empty air. The men came together, muscle straining against muscle as Cade caught Ruben's wrist and struggled to keep it from chopping downward toward his heart. Teeth clenched, Cade twisted Ruben's arm until he gasped with pain. Then, with a savage blow against the armoire, Cade knocked the knife from Ruben's hand.

The gleaming weapon lay on the floor, the two men motionless above it. "I don't want to kill you, Ruben," Cade rasped, breathless from exertion. "I need you alive. You have to testify."

Ruben dived for the knife, but Cade retrieved it first. Ruben rushed him with a muttered oath, and the two men sprawled across the hardwood floor. The fierce battle continued, then suddenly, Cade drove the knife home.

Cade shoved Ruben's heavy body away and rose to his feet just as Mejia appeared in the doorway.

"You okay, senor?"

"Yeah." Cade picked up his revolver and slipped it into his holster.

"Is that Guillotte?"

"Yeah, that's him." Cade bent over the fallen man, touching his throat and feeling a barely discernible pulse. "I need him alive. See if you can stop the bleeding and patch him up."

"*Si*, senor."

"Have they found Gabrielle yet?"

"Not yet," Luis answered. "She must be on the other side of the house."

Cade nodded, then looked up as the sound of gunfire reverberated from deep in the house. A bell clanged. A second later the tolling stopped instantly, as if a giant hand had wrapped about it. Cade raced through the darkened interior. In the kitchen he found Ken Mosby and several other men right behind him. "You find Gabrielle in that section?"

"No, sir," Mosby replied. "Just Mexicans. Did you find the others?"

Cade nodded. "Celeste and Ruben." He looked around the circle of men. "My wife and Rodriguez are the only ones unaccounted for."

As if in reply, a voice rose from outside, behind

the house. "Senor Montana, are you there?" Dread held the men motionless. The voice called again. "Senor Montana, please be careful. I have your woman."

The eerie light of a fire began to flicker against the windowpanes. Cade ran across the stone floor of the kitchen and swung open the door. At first all he saw was a mound of hay blazing a strange orange light. The figure behind it materialized slowly, and the sight chilled his blood. The Spaniard was holding Gabrielle, gun glittering against the straining line of her throat. His other arm was wrapped around her slim waist, his skin dark against the white of her cotton gown. Gabrielle shook her head at something Rodriguez hissed in her ear.

Cade's face blanched. Intense pain stole his breath. "Jesus." He closed his eyes and dropped his head against the door frame.

"That son-of-a-bitch," Mosby growled from somewhere behind him.

Cade turned to Cameron. "Spread out the men and look for some advantage."

Cameron nodded, and the Texans started drifting back through the silent house.

In the glowing light Cade's face grew as ruthless and determined as the Spaniard's. "Let's compromise, Rodriguez. Release Gabrielle, and we'll ride away. The hostilities do not concern you and me."

Rodriguez laughed, his fingers spreading over Gabrielle's stomach, his thumb coming between her breasts. Her soft indrawn gasp sounded clearly in the still night. "What are you talking about, Senor Montana? No hostilities? I have killed some of your men, you have killed some of mine. And," he added tauntingly, "you have run off my horses."

"You'll get your horses back."

"I will not compromise," Rodriguez rasped, his

voice turning brutal. "I have your woman, and I know you won't make a move against me for fear of killing her. All the advantages are mine. All I have to do is wait until my men ride back in. I might even enjoy myself with your woman while I do so."

Cade pulled himself out of sight, his teeth clenched in rage and helplessness. The Spaniard held all the cards. As long as he knew help was coming, he could keep Gabrielle hostage and not have a moment's worry. Cade knew all he could do was run a bluff and hope it would work. He lifted his voice. "But your men won't be coming back. I've arranged a small surprise for them—Texas Rangers laying in wait about ten miles north of here. When your men are trying to round up those mustangs, the Rangers will pick them off one by one."

Rodriguez laughed. "You're bluffing, Montana. The Rangers won't cross the Rio Grande."

"Are you sure?" Cade moved so that he could see Rodriguez. "You've been a plague to them for years with your raids across the border. They're anxious to have your hide and you know it. For a little incentive, they are willing to forget international rules."

The Spaniard started dragging Gabrielle back toward the cottage. "I believe you're bluffing, gringo." The straw that had flamed high and bright now rolled in a flutter of sparks along the ground and the night once again turned dark. "I will wait for my men to come back, and I will kill your woman if you make a single move against me."

Rodriguez swore as he pulled Gabrielle into the cottage that had been her prison since she arrived. Flinging her on the bed, he grabbed her hands and tied her to one of the canopied bedposts. Lifting his gun, he walked over to the window and peered out. "So what is the truth here, eh?" He spoke softly, as if Cade were actually listening. "Are there Rangers waiting for my men, or are you bluffing? The Rangers want me, that is true, senor. And they have crossed the border more than once. And yes, I think they might have come after me. So what do I do to outsmart you, Montana?"

Gabrielle could see his dark form moving back and forth as he paced. "Senor Rodriguez," she pleaded softly, "please let me go. There doesn't have to be more bloodshed."

Rodriguez snorted with contempt. "Women are weak. You take the soft way," he scoffed. "Scratch my skin, scratch Montana's skin, and underneath you find the instincts of a predator. We have become enemies." He sucked in a deep breath, "Hate is alive between us, and the unspoken challenge has been issued. Like the magnificent bulls of the arena, we shall fight until one is dead."

Gabrielle shivered, finding his glorification of death barbaric and his obsession with Cade terrifying. Rodriguez had come to the cottage many times over the last few days, his conversation frequently colored with images of death, blood, ritual . . . and a twisted sense of honor. It had made her skin crawl to listen to him. He had explained to her that she would be his mistress, that he would treat her leniently as long she pleased him. Luckily his warped ethics forbade him from touching her as long as Cade still lived. The Church, he said, forbade him from taking another man's wife.

Rodriguez laughed suddenly, and Gabrielle flinched as he sat beside her and placed the cold steel of his revolver against the soft skin at the back of her neck. He moved the barrel up under her chin and along her cheek.

"I know what I'm going to do," he whispered, leaning forward and kissing the exposed skin at her shoulder. Gabrielle shuddered at the brush of his mustache. "Why should I wait to find out if Montana is telling the truth? I have been awake a day and a night and, as I grow more tired, I will grow more careless." His voice lowered as if he were speaking to a lover. "At daybreak we shall leave, querida. I will request two horses." His hand drifted over her shoulder and down the slim length of her arm. "I know every hideout in this country. They will never find us." He stood up, his voice turning brisk. "Now get dressed."

The wait for daylight seemed interminable to Cade. He had considered all the possibilities and as long as Rodriguez held Gabrielle hostage, there was nothing he and his men could do. The adobe cottage had shuttered windows, bolted from the inside. The one door opened onto a tiny enclosed patio that allowed no room for a direct assault. Besides, any move they made would threaten Gabrielle's life.

Just before dawn Rodriguez called out again. "Senor Montana, are you there?"

Cade walked to the door. "I'm here."

"I want you to saddle two horses at daybreak and have Guillotte bring them to the front of the cottage. Do you understand?"

"Guillotte has been wounded," Cade informed him. "He can't do it."

The silence stretched as Rodriguez digested this information. "That's most unfortunate, senor," he called, "since you need him to testify. But send his woman. Come daylight, send Celeste with the horses. Remember, I have Gabrielle." He laughed softly. "She is most pleasurable, your wife."

The Spaniard's silky, taunting voice made Cade's insides twist with revulsion. He stepped into the doorway. "If you've touched her—"

Kent Mosby caught his shoulder and dragged him

back. "He wants you to take chances. That's why he's goading you."

"No, no, senor, she is . . . fine," Rodriguez answered. "After all, your lovely wife guarantees my safety."

McGilly swore. "I wish I could get my hands on that sleazy bastard. This job isn't just a job anymore. It's gotten personal with me. I hate that son-of-a-bitch."

The sun was just coming up, casting soft light over the compound, when Rodriguez opened the cottage door. Gabrielle stood in front of him, hands tied. Using her as a shield, he half carried, half pushed her out the door. Once in the open, he placed the barrel of his gun to her temple. "Montana," he called, "you got the horses saddled?"

"We have."

"That's good. Now listen to my instructions carefully. First I want you and your men to come out and line up. Bring your weapons."

Gabrielle watched as tough-looking men she had never seen before filed slowly into the light and formed a line in front of the stable. Cade was the last to appear, and at the sight of him her knees weakened. She knew Rodriguez was perfectly able and willing to kill him.

"Now," the Spaniard growled, "I know there are other men. I would estimate three. Have them come out, Montana."

Cade's expression was flinty hard as he hesitated, then motioned. Three more men ambled across the open space to stand beside their compadres.

Rodriguez nodded. "That's good. Now, one by one, I want you to file over and throw your weapons into the well." When the men didn't instantly react, he drew the hammer back on the gun.

Gabrielle closed her eyes at the deadly click. A breathless eon later, she felt Rodriguez relax slightly, and when she looked again, the men were following his orders. Gabrielle knew that without their guns Cade and his men faced an even more perilous situation.

When they were all back in place, Rodriguez nodded with satisfaction. "Have the horses brought out."

An instant later Celeste appeared, leading the horses forward. Her shimmering hair hung straight down her back, and Gabrielle thought she looked as she had when she was a young girl. She walked slowly and deliberately, her wide blue eyes riveted on the Spaniard's face.

When she was within reach, Rodriguez grabbed the reins from her hands. "Now go back," he ordered.

Tears appeared in Celeste's eyes. "Vincente, let me go with you," she whispered desperately. "If you don't, they'll take me back to Texas. Ruben doesn't stand a chance if something happens to me. I must stay free." In supplication, she reached for his hand.

Rodriguez jerked back, the sudden action knocking Gabrielle to her knees. "Get the hell away from me," he hissed.

"Help me, please," Celeste cried. "Take me with you. You said that if we put the money into your ranch, you would help us!"

Rodriguez released Gabrielle for an instant and knocked Celeste to the ground with a backhanded blow. In a fury he aimed the gun at her head. "You slut! Don't jeopardize my escape with your sniveling!"

As if in slow motion his arm leveled out, the revolver beginning its lethal tilt. The knowledge of approaching death flared in Celeste's blue eyes.

"No!" With an anguished cry, Gabrielle flung herself at Rodriguez. The gun discharged just as his hand struck her head and she fell to the ground with a breath-robbing jolt. She saw only a blur as Cade tackled Rodriguez, knocking him down. The gun flew from the Spaniard's hand and skidded across the hard-packed earth. Both men dived for it, tumbling over and over as they struggled for possession. McGilly ran forward to help, the other men following, crowding around the combatants. The gun fired again.

For one brief eternity they all stood frozen in the early morning light . . . and then slowly, the men separated. Gabrielle took a deep breath, too terrified to pray. Then she saw Cade standing.

With a cry she ran forward, throwing herself into his arms. He held her tightly, his face buried in her hair, a prayer on his lips. "Are you all right, sweetheart?"

He saw her nod, saw the scattering of freckles across the bridge of her nose, the intensity in her emerald eyes. He laughed huskily. "Dear God, Gabrielle, I love you," he whispered, claiming her mouth with a fierce kiss. His teeth flashed white against his skin. "But I have the rest of my life to tell you that when we get back in Texas. Those bushwhackers will be riding back in at any moment."

"But what about the Rangers you said would intercept them?"

He grinned. "Rodriguez was right. I was bluffing." His concerned gaze dropped over her. "Can you make the ride?"

"Oh, yes!" Gabrielle laughed, standing on tiptoe and kissing his mouth. "Nothing can stop me." She turned and, at the sight of her sister, went suddenly still. Celeste was gazing down at Rodriguez. Gabrielle put her hand on Cade's arm, and her eyes met his. "I have to talk to her, Cade."

"There's not much time," he warned.

She nodded, noticing that the men had already started leading the horses from the stable. She kissed his cheek, then walked thoughtfully to Celeste. Rodriguez lay on the ground, a bloodstain on the left side of his chest, his face almost youthful looking in death.

Celeste seemed to sense her sister's approach. "He was going to kill me," she said slowly, disbelievingly. "Just because I might slow him down." She shuddered, then turned to Gabrielle. "You risked your life to save me. You only did it because, with Ruben near death, you need me to testify, don't you?"

Weary sadness filled Gabrielle. "Celeste," she said gently, "I didn't think of anything when I helped you. I only knew that I couldn't let him kill you. You're my sister." That was all the explanation she could give. She was quiet a moment. "How's Ruben?"

Tears filled Celeste's eyes. "He's lost a lot of blood. He'll die if your husband forces him to make the journey."

Gabrielle nodded. "Celeste, I've only minutes to talk to you, so please listen carefully. I've no desire to see you taken back to Texas to face what I've faced, and I believe I have a solution. If you'll write a letter to the Committee, telling them that you and Ruben stole the documents, and explaining how and why you implicated me, I'll ask Cade to leave you here with Ruben. All I want is to be free of a shame I don't deserve."

Celeste didn't move. When she finally turned to

Gabrielle, her eyes were wary. "Why would you do that? What if the Committee refuses to believe what I write in my letter?"

Gabrielle's face softened. "I'll do it because you're my sister." She shrugged, knowing Celeste still didn't understand. "And I think the Committee will accept a letter as proof." She turned, her hand sweeping the compound. "We have so many witnesses who've seen you with Ruben. That should be enough."

Celeste crossed her arms over her chest, her expression thoughtful. She didn't say anything for a long time, and then all at once the wariness was gone from her face. "Not only will I write a letter, but I'll tell you the account numbers of both mine and Ruben's secret bank accounts in Boston."

Gabrielle's emerald eyes clouded. "Why did you do it?"

Celeste brushed silky strands of blond hair over her shoulder. "For Ruben. He's everything to me. Without his smile, I feel no sunshine. I didn't want you to get hurt. Ruben told me you would be cleared sooner or later, and that we would be together forever."

Gabrielle's voice shook. "I have gone through so much."

"I know it's not much consolation," Celeste said, her tone restrained, "but I'm sorry."

Gabrielle nodded sadly.

The farewells were hasty, and within a short time the riders from Texas were on their way home.

Luis Mejia led the way. Knowing they had only a small head start on the Spaniard's hired guns, the Texans kept to the low-lying areas where they were less likely to be spotted against the sky. Just below a rocky ridge a few miles from the hacienda, Manuel split from the others. He and Cade had already agreed that he would ride to Paloma to warn Francesca of what had happened and help her care for Tom until he was well enough to be brought back across the border.

All that morning the Texans pushed their horses hard, then in the afternoon they slowed to a walk. The sun burned relentlessly down on them. Cade had been riding most of the day as scout, and Gabrielle watched as he returned to the main group, angling down from a low rise. He crossed a sandy-bottomed gull and brought his gelding up beside her horse. "How are you doing?"

Just looking at his lean, handsome face made her heart sing. "I'm wonderful." She touched his hand, her eyes sparkling. "Just wonderful." Then her expression turned somber. "Will they come after us . . . even with Rodriguez already dead?"

"I don't know. But we can't take a chance. We're short on weapons." His mouth twisted with bitterness. "Too bad we couldn't have killed that son-of-a-bitch before he made us throw our guns in the well. Kent Mosby found a rifle in the house and three pistols, but that's not enough if we're caught in a gun battle."

"But why would they come?" Gabrielle persisted. "Rodriguez is dead."

"Guillotte may send them."

"He's unconscious."

"We'll see." Cade shrugged. "I think they'll come. They're like a pack of wolves—they smell blood. We have no alternative. We have to outdistance them."

Gabrielle shuddered. Cade twisted in the saddle, squinting against the sun as he scanned the hills for signs of pursuit. Nothing moved except a hawk circling lazily in the cloudless sky.

Later that day, however, it became clear that they were being followed. The pursuers were a long way off, but dark specks appeared occasionally against the horizon. Cade thought there were twenty riders.

They rode throughout that afternoon, resting only briefly for the horses. Day turned into night, stars filled the sky, and a chill crept through to their bones. Still they kept moving. Small night creatures scurried out of their way, and an occasional coyote howled at the moon.

At daylight the exhausted riders stopped along the banks of a shallow, sluggishly moving stream. The men slid from their mounts, lay on their bellies, and submerged their dusty faces in the water. Gabrielle knelt and splashed water on her face and arms, then led her horse into the stream and poured water over its back and head. Glancing at the empty horizon, Cade suggested the men walk for a while. The horses needed rest.

The Rio Grande couldn't be far ahead. Gabrielle and the men had fanned out on the flat ground, walking abreast. Her feet hurt and her mouth was so dry she couldn't swallow. To occupy her mind, she concentrated on her life on the other side of the river. Next week she would be giving Laurel Marie her morning bath, pressing her cheek against the dewy dampness of her daughter's. She would pick roses and arrange them in every room of the house. She would sit with Helen in the kitchen early in the morning and plan the day's menu. She would ask the teacher how the children were doing, who was being good, who was skipping school. How wonderful her life was.

Gabrielle glanced at Cade. Most of all, she wanted to go back to the stream where they had once made love. She wanted to walk across the log that spanned it, she wanted to slip and fall in. She wanted to play in the creek like a child . . . and then she wanted to make love to Cade on the grassy bank.

Suddenly she heard a shout and saw McGilly swing into the saddle. "They're making their move," he yelled. "Let's ride."

"Mount up," Cade ordered, even as he hefted Gabrielle into the saddle. He looked deep into her eyes. "It's less than a half mile to the river. You can make it, Gabrielle."

Her heart twisted with sudden fear. "Cade," she whispered, "what are you going to do?"

He turned to Mosby. "Make sure you get her across the river!"

Kent grabbed the reins from her hands, forcing her to clasp the saddle horn. She could barely keep her balance, but she managed to glance quickly over her shoulder. Cade and McGilly took refuge behind a rocky escarpment just as the Mexicans raced with bloodcurdling yells across the flat, brush-covered land. Burning tears began to roll down her cheeks as she realized what Cade meant to do. He would risk his life to divert the Mexicans while she made her escape. Her cries to Mosby were whipped from her mouth by the wind as they raced toward the Rio Grande. The sun glared on the water, and tears blinded her eyes. Then, in disbelief, she saw a new group of riders from the American side of the river splashing into the water.

Mosby laughed. "Texas Rangers!" He gave a chilling Rebel yell and saluted one of the men riding past. "Give them bastards what they deserve!" he shouted.

The tired horses pounded headlong into the wa-ter, then slowed as the river rose to their chests. They waded up on the far bank, and Gabrielle called out for Mosby to stop. When he didn't, she slid off her horse and collapsed to her knees on the wet sand. Yells and gunfire sounded from the other side of the river. For agonizingly long moments she could see nothing. Then Cade and McGilly were riding toward her, like apparitions in the shimmering heat-waves.

A sob rose to her throat. "Cade! Oh, God, thank you."

She ran forward, wading into the water, her drenched skirt slowing her progress. "Cade! Oh, dear God, you're safe!" Tears streamed down her cheeks as he slid off in midstream and caught her against him. He laughed and kissed her face. "We made it, Gabrielle. We made it!"

Epilogue

G abrielle felt the warm sun slanting through the leaves as she turned to Cade. Her horse seemed to be favoring its right front leg, and Cade was checking to see why.

"It's just a stone," he said, picking up a twig to dislodge it.

"That's good," Gabrielle returned absently, feeling almost sleepy with contentment. So much had happened in the few months since they had returned from Mexico. Best of all, they had received a document from the War Department clearing her of all suspicion of spying and expressing regret that she had suffered unjustly. They had assured Cade that all records would be set straight.

Preoccupied, Gabrielle walked toward the gently flowing stream, her thoughts on the changes that had recently occurred. McGilly, John Voss, and Luis Mejia had all hired on at the ranch. Tom Rawlings had mended enough to return to Follettville. When she and Cade had met him at the boat they hadn't been particularly surprised to see who helped him down the gangplank—Francesca. Just as Cade had prophesied, they made an incredibly loving, quarrelsome pair. Gabrielle had even asked Tom to be Laurel's godfather, and had been touched when he ac-

cepted with teary eyes. Tom was just a gruff old bear
with a soft heart, she decided with a tender smile.

Laurel Marie had captured everybody's heart. The
men spent hours whittling toys for her instead of
playing poker in the bunkhouse. The little minx had
a carving of just about every creature imaginable.
And, of course, Cade indulged her. Gabrielle often
watched her beautiful daughter pout and charm to
get her way and, when that didn't work, she didn't
hesitate to throw a good old-fashioned tantrum. The
silky-haired little angel was just now trying to walk;
in another month she'd be getting into mischief on
both feet.

Gabrielle turned to her husband as he patted the
horse on the rump and walked a short distance
away, arms akimbo, gazing like a king across the
sweeping acres of his land. "This is going to be the
finest ranch in Texas," he said proudly.

Gabrielle grinned, awed by her husband's virility
and masculine beauty. Suddenly she wanted to
make love to him, here, now. A leaf swirled in the
creek, round and round, caught in an eddy.

"There's a lot of work to do," Cade mused aloud,
tipping the brim of his hat against the sun's glare.
"The first thing is to build some dams along these
streams . . ." His words trailed off at the sight of
Gabrielle unlacing her corselet and struggling to pull
it over her head. Her firm round breasts jiggled provocatively with her efforts. Her dress already lay
discarded on the bank.

Gabrielle laughed softly. Naked from the waist up,
she ran her hands slowly along the side of her
breasts and down to her waist.

"What are you doing?" he asked, his mouth dry.

"I'm taking off my clothes," she answered, arching a delicate brow.

Cade swallowed. "I can see that." She lifted her

petticoats and walked across the fallen log. On the other side, she turned and walked back to the center. "See anything that interests you, Cade Montana?"

He grinned. "I sure do. Come here, you."

"No, no. It's not that easy." Her slow, wicked smile showed pearly teeth. "Don't you remember? You have to come and get me."

Cade started pulling off his boots, and a second later unbuckled his gunbelt and let it drop to the bank. His blue eyes glinting like sapphires, he moved toward her. "It'll be my pleasure, ma'am."